Dare to Fall

Tamara Boothby

Contents

Chapter 1

"I have a perfectly good explanation for all of this," I gestured to the boy now lying on the floor.

The hallways were crowded with students of all grades, staring at either awe or fear at my done deed. The principal however, did not look at all pleased.

"My office. Now." He said stiffly.

I groaned internally before I followed his tail, but before he could walk any further, he pointed at the helpless body lying on the floor. "Oh for heaven's sake. Somebody help that boy up. I need to speak to the both of you."

The boy's friends stepped out of the crowd to his aid until I stopped them by shoving my palm to their noses (while the principal wasn't looking, of course.)

Their faces looked like they pissed in their pants when I gave them the sweetest smile I could muster. "I'll do it. I'll help him up. After all, it's my fault he's this way now, right?"

Then after releasing a sarcastic, girly giggle, I grabbed the boy's arm and with a swift kick to his stomach, I got him to stand up. I placed his arm over my shoulder for support and then carried his useless body towards the principal's office.

He whimpered like the coward that he was. I could hear whispers, silent laughter and accusing chatters as I passed by with the staggering ugly right beside me.

Noobs.

When we arrived at the office, I carefully lay the poor boy down the chair (read: carelessly threw the jerk down) and sat right beside him. Before I turned to look at our principal, I studied the boy.

His face was colorful - there were bluish-purple, red, pink, and a purple that was close to becoming black. He even stiffened when he noticed I was observing him.

"Oh my," I put a hand over my mouth. "Who could have done this to you? You look terrible!"

He looked at me a bit irritated, a bit scared. I smiled again. "Oh right. That was me. Sorry. But I gotta admit, I like that shirt. It matches your black eye." I winked at him.

"Ms. Jadsen would you please stop tormenting him? And explain yourself. What did you do this time?" Principal Steele sighed in exasperation upon rubbing his temples.

I crossed my legs and folded my arms like I owned the place. Irritation was slowly creeping in my system. "Why does everybody assume it's all my fault?"

He stared at me and then at the boy. I didn't even catch this boy's name. I groaned. "Okay. So I beat him up. But I'm the victim here!"

The person behind the desk chuckled humorlessly. "Do share."

I furrowed my brows as raked my brain for a believable excuse. "I can't stand him. His mere existence irritates me."

"Mr. Steele, she just punched me in the eye out of nowhere! Then she beat me up - I don't even know her! She should be sent to jail for this! This is harassment!" The boy spoke up but his voice cracked in the middle of his sentence when I glared at him.

"Oh you want to talk about harassment? You? And you don't know me? Please! You've been stalking me since last month. I was going to keep quiet until you - "

I stopped when I realized I was already shouting. I took a breath to calm myself down before I continued. Principal Steele was listening to my side of the story patiently while the boy kept his mouth shut, knowing I'd beat him up again if he said something to anger me.

I didn't have the best temper in the world. Boo-hoo.

I looked at the principal seriously. "He hurt my friend. There were bruises on her wrists, proof of her resistance. She already told him she had a boyfriend, but he still kept on pestering her."

"Liar!" He said, his voice cracking mid-syllable. "You don't actually believe any word she's saying, right?! She's Mira Jadsen, the girl who beats anybody up without reason!"

He practically gave himself away already when he said my whole name. He just said he didn't know me.

"Nothing's ever without reason, you little prick," I said each word slowly and menacingly. He was popping my nerves one after another.

He was dead-set on insisting his non-existent innocence, ignoring my threatening looks now. "Mr. Steele she's lying! You gotta help me out!"

And yet he said nothing to prove his innocence. I rolled my eyes and looked at our principal. He'll be the judge of that.

Principal Steele looked like he already made up his mind though.

"We'll see who's lying and who's telling the truth. Everything happened in the hallways so it was caught in the security cameras. Until further investigation, I'm letting you two off the hook. I'll call on you two again when I see the video, then your punishments will be decided."

We were both silent.

"Mr. Ink you may go now."

I gave him a last glare before he uneasily stood up and staggered quickly towards the door. Such a wimp. When he was out of earshot, dear principal spoke with me.

"Mira," he said softly, careful not to hit a nerve. He was always different when we were alone.

"I'm sorry uncle," I mumbled. Yes, our Principal was my dad's cousin, therefore my uncle. And he always had a soft spot for me, but I urged him to keep our relationship a secret.

I didn't have the best reputation at school, and I don't want anyone thinking I always got away with it because I was related to the Principal.

"It's okay Mira," he said with a warm smile. "You always do this when your friends are involved, that's admirable. But I think you should stop beating up boys. You don't want to make dangerous enemies now do you? I can't protect you all the time when that happens."

I looked at him like he was kidding, and he got what I meant by that look alone. "I'm capable of protecting myself, uncle. And besides, nobody will dare make enemies with me. Plus, I'm likable."

He didn't look affected with my first half of the sentence but when I mentioned the word likable, he snorted. "Likable. Hah. Where."

Before I could retort, he stopped me and told me to go back to class. I whined like the mature 17 year-old I was. I thought I could ditch Biology if I stayed a little longer in here. Being the Principal's niece wasn't all that great after all.

"Mira!" My two bestfriends came running as soon as I stepped out of the office. I smiled and felt my insides warm up when they approached me.

"Are you in any trouble?" Nichole held my hands and squeezed them. "I'm so sorry I got you involved! I should go there and tell the principal my side of the story too."

I glanced down at our hands and I frowned when I saw the light bruises still on her wrists. She got bruises easily, this girl.

"It's okay Nichole," I laughed reassuringly. "The principal knows I'm innocent. The security cameras are my witnesses." I pinched her cheek and ruffled her hair. "You worry too much."

"You're like her boyfriend or something. I thought I owned that title." My other best friend, Leo mumbled.

I let go of Nichole and punched his shoulder roughly. He took it well with the hard muscles he had. "Some boyfriend you are. Where were you at that time?"

He looked at Nichole and then at me guiltily. "Sorry, coach called for me. I didn't know what happened until Brandon told me. I'm sorry."

Brandon. The mere mention of his name caused my eye to twitch. I haven't met him personally yet. Leo occasionally mentioned him and I'd see him in the hallways from time to time, but we never really spoke.

Just sort of... Glared at each other every time we passed by each other's paths. I just get a bad vibe from him, and I'm sure he feels the same, hence the glaring.

I patted Leo's shoulder, the one where I punched, and smiled at him. "It's not your fault, I was just kidding. You know I'd do anything for you guys."

Nichole let out a wail or a groan, I don't know. Leo scratched his head. "This! This is what I'm worried about. Mira, you're... You're manlier than me!"

My eyes narrowed into slits immediately. His eyes widened when he realized what he just said. He took it back quickly.

"No! You know that's not what I meant! I meant it in a good way! What I meant was, you're too nice! And people get the wrong idea from what you do. I think it's unfair. And I think we owe you a big favor."

A smirk curled up my lips, attempting to change the subject. I was uncomfortable with people kinda-sorta-maybe praising me. I'm not great. "You just admitted you're gay. I have bigger balls than you."

Nichole giggled while Leo frowned. He shoved my inappropriate innuendo off and continued what he was saying.

"Mira, what I'm telling you is, let us return the favor. I know it's not much and it won't make up for everything, but at least let me treat you dinner tonight. The three of will go together, just like old times."

"I'll chip in too," Nichole volunteered.

I stared at them wide-eyed. "You two? Treat me? It's so rare and historic. I'll take you on your offer!"

I was so excited! Food!

"I'll probably bring Brandon along too. He's helped me a lot of times, and I'll introduce you two properly this time," Leo said with a grin.

My smile dropped. Oh no he did not.

"I'll text you guys the details later. Look forward to it!" His cheeky grin couldn't go wider than that.

And look forward to it?

Yipee-dee-doo-haa.

Chapter 2

Nichole was all dolled up. She wore a yellow blouse and a white flowy skirt that trailed just above her knees. Her hair was pulled up into a neat ponytail and the end was curled into perfection.

She looked so excited as she patted her face with some light make-up and I was a bit envious at how lovely she looked.

"Do I look okay?" She asked as she twirled around, her skirt flaring ever so slightly when she did.

I smiled. "Do you have to ask? You're beautiful. Leo's gonna flip."

She laughed quietly as she observed my choice of clothing. I wasn't at all conscious but I wasn't at all confident as well.

I wore a gray V-neck shirt, a pair of dark jeans and my beloved pair of sneakers. I let my hair fall down into big waves behind my back. Soft bangs framed my face making me look more feminine. My clothes weren't that fashionable but I'll manage to carry it in a way to make it look a bit more attractive.

I stopped in my thoughts.

Who was I trying to impress anyway? I was just going out to dinner with my two best friends. And a guy I hardly knew.

"You're gorgeous Mira," Nichole poked my rib. "I'd kill for a body like that."

"Ha-ha," I laughed sarcastically. "Are you done?"

"Just a sec," she mumbled. She took out a small bottle of perfume from her purse and sprayed it all over her neck down to her clothes.

When she saw that I was looking at her weirdly, she took another bottle of perfume and surprised me by spraying it on me.

"Ugh! No! Yuck!" I whined as I swatted the bottle away. She kept laughing as I sniffed myself and made a sour expression. "Nichole! You know I hate perfume!"

"Oh c'mon Mira!" She returned her things to her drawer. "Brandon will be there. You need to make a good impression! Who knows, he'll - "

"No," was my immediate answer. "Nothing's gonna happen between us. I'm just going because of you guys and because of the free food. I'll probably ignore him for the rest of the evening."

She was already used to my stubbornness so she didn't have much of a reaction. Instead, she tilted her chin up with her finger and smiled. A very suspicious smile.

"He's kinda hard to ignore though. And since it's you, he might make a move as soon as you two are introduced."

I laughed internally. She doesn't know about the silent glares we've been exchanging for the past few months.

"Can we go now?" I asked, rubbing my shirt with my hands, an attempt to rub off the smell of perfume as well.

It was a futile attempt.

"Let's go," she cheerfully linked her arm with mine.

"You're late," Nichole had a stern expression on her face as Leo stood in front of our table.

"No, you're just too early," he tried to joke but the humor died quickly because Nichole glared at him. "I'm sorry! It's because Brandon was taking too long in the shower!"

I snorted despite Nichole nudging my arm. "Is he a girl," I mumbled, mostly to myself. I don't know why I found it so funny.

"Well where is he?" She asked, her mood softening. She could never stay mad long enough when it comes to Leo. Not even if she tried.

Leo gave her a shy, boyish smile, or a guilty one. I could sense Nichole scowling already. "H-He's coming."

I hid a smirk. My best friend is so whipped. I've known Leo since we were 12 and he's never acted like this to his past girlfriends.

Now that I think about it, I brought this two together. They owe me big time.

Leo finally sat down at the opposite side of the table and ordered our food. We were at a small restaurant a few blocks away from school, but I heard the food here was great.

The three of us talked for a while until our food arrived. Well that was quick. We dug in immediately, laughing at ourselves in between chews. We looked like we haven't eaten in days.

Hm, did the waiter get our orders wrong? I could've sworn I ordered the super spicy burrito. This wasn't spicy at all.

In the middle of my burrito, Leo's eyes lit up and he held his hand up, waving at someone behind us. I cussed internally. I forgot we had another guest.

"Brandon!" Nichole exclaimed as he jogged to our table. Before he could greet them back, our eyes met for a second. Instead of a glare this time, he looked surprised. He probably didn't know I was coming along. Sucks for him.

"Sorry I'm late," he smiled as he slid to the seat next to Leo and in front if me. Great just great.

"What took you so long?" Nichole was the first one to ask.

"I had to take an extra minute in the shower. Gotta smell good for our friendly little date," he winked.

Honestly, I wasn't expecting him to be like this. I always thought he was quiet and just randomly glared at strangers. Maybe my perception of him was wrong all along.

"Extra minute?" Leo scoffed. "More like an extra hour."

He was about to take a bite from his French fry when Brandon grabbed his wrist and ate it. Oh. Ew.

"Dude!" Leo whined.

"Don't be shy now Leonard," he teased. Nichole was giggling at them while I stared at them weirdly. "We do this all the time when we're alone."

And then he winked again. Leo almost blew chunks. He hit him hard on the arm, his friend just laughed playfully. "Gross!"

I quietly studied his features. He was actually cute up close. His hair was a light shade of brown, styled neatly but fashionably unlike Leo's messy-do, his skin had a fair complexion - not too dark, not too light, his eyes were crystal blue and how do I put it? It was shiny or something. This is the second time I can say that a guy's eyes are pretty. The first is Jensen Ackles of course.

And his jaw-line. It looked so strong despite his features. I don't know why I'm so attracted to jaw-lines. His choice of clothing were nice as well. A simple black shirt, a pair of jeans and a pair of white sneakers. I think he managed to pull that look off better than I did.

Brandon continued teasing Leo as Leo complained non-stop. It was hilarious to see how Leo was taking it so seriously.

I didn't hold back my laughter. Leo was overreacting. Maybe it was because of Nichole's presence.

"Aaw," I cooed, earning their attention. "Little Leo already lost his manliness against me. Now he's gaining femininity."

Nichole burst into a fit of giggles after giving me a high-five. Leo didn't look happy being the center of our jokes.

He slung his arm around Brandon's neck mischievously and pulled him down, his opponent began to struggle. "Mira," he called, holding his victim still. "This is Brandon Pierce. Brandon, this is Mira Jadsen. Now be friends."

Brandon broke from his grip as soon as Leo finished introducing us in a rather playful fashion. He glanced at me. I waited. What was he gonna do?

Nothing. That's what he did. Did he really see me? He turned back to Leo and pinched his cheek. "Yeah I already know her."

Leo swatted his hand off his face. "Dude stop acting all over me!"

I didn't get him at all. Did he hate me or did he simply not care? I shrugged my thoughts off. Why should I care anyway?

Ignore him.

I noticed that Nichole was quiet and when I glanced at her direction, she was texting under the table. I was about to ask her what it was since she looked a bit irritated, but she beat me to it.

"My sister's outside." She groaned. "Wait a bit you guys, I just need to get something from her," she quickly stood up from her seat and grabbed her purse. Leo stood up as well and went outside with her. Why did he have to be such the gentleman?

And why did they leave us alone? Why.

I watched them both leave the restaurant. Cry.

This is going to be so damn awkward.

It was silent for a few seconds. We were occasionally stealing glances from one another, wondering if one should start up a conversation or something. I avoided all eye-contact because it was getting weird.

He decided to eat his burrito. I took my phone out and pretended to text, to distract myself and not look like an awkward turtle.

I was too occupied pretending to be occupied when I heard my companion mumble something incoherent.

I glanced at him and my brows rose when he was looking at me wide-eyed, his mouth tightly shut. He swallowed before sticking his tongue out. "Shit! It's hot!"

"Hot? That's my burrito then!" I realized.

He glanced at the glasses on the table. They were all empty. Until his eyes landed on my beloved milkshake.

"Oh no you don't!" I growled, grabbing my milkshake and holding it possessively.

"Just a sip!" He begged. A small bead of sweat trickled down his face as he pleaded with his eyes.

I was cruel and heartless, I know. But I'm not sacrificing my milkshake. Especially since Leo and Nichole paid for it, which was historic in itself. "No."

He stood up and sat on Nichole's seat right beside me. His hands were aiming for my drink but I held it away from him as far as I could.

I was already uncomfortable with our position. He was leaning a bit too close for my liking and I had no means of covering my front because my hands were too busy guarding my milkshake above my head.

"Hurry up it's burning!" He cried out, still trying to reach my glass.

"Then go ask for some water from the waiters!" I argued.

He stuck his tongue out again and released a strangled sigh. Was it really that spicy?

To my surprise, he stood up and grabbed a hold of my milkshake. I yelped as he began pulling it away from my hands.

"Let it go!"

"Can't hold it back anymore?!" I even managed to pull off a sarcastic joke.

It was a tug of war now, my drink was the trophy. It was slightly spilling because of all the pulling from opposite directions. I wanted to cry from the sight of my glorious drink getting wasted bit by bit.

If it were Nichole, I'd give her my drink easily, but to this guy? There's no way I'm letting his mouth touch my drink and expect me to drink it again. It's an indirect exchange of saliva.

I yanked the drink harder, at the same time, his hand slipped and the entire glass spilled all over my jaw down to my neck and shirt. I cringed from the cold. I was about to cuss at him but what I didn't anticipate was what he did next.

He grabbed me and pressed his lips on my neck. He hurriedly sucked the remains of the milkshake from my nape down to my collarbone.

I froze up.

I had no reaction at first because I was too shocked to process everything, but the warm sensation on my tingling skin snapped me out of my senses.

When I looked down, his hand was on my left boob. Did he even realize that?! My vision turned black. And then I lost it.

I pushed him away as hard as I could, and glared at him with all my might. He wiped his mouth before taking the half empty glass on my lap and chugged down the remaining contents.

"You! Shameless! Pervert!" I screeched, covering myself out of instinct. I held the burning sensation on the nape of my neck and when I realized what it was, I grew even more furious. "I'm going to fucking kill you!"

"Uh..." A voice behind us startled me. It was Nichole and Leo, staring at us wide-eyed. I was half-relieved because they were back and half-humiliated because of what they probably just witnessed and because of the sticky milkshake all over my shirt and skin.

"Nichole!" My voice almost broke into a cry. Almost. Leo took the jacket hanging on their seat and covered me up. Nichole helped me up and hurriedly assisted me towards the exit.

"I'll take her back to the apartment," she told Leo and gave Brandon a wild glare. I didn't dare look at him.

Just who the hell did he think he was?!

Chapter 3

School again. Ugh.

I used my hair to cover up the certain marks around my neck down to my collarbone. I was suddenly thankful I hadn't cut it short yet.

At school everything was a normal day for everybody. Well, in my case, I looked like I was having a normal day too, except my brain was driving me nuts with my rather motivated killing intent.

I casually walked across the hallways, scanning the crowd if there were any signs of a certain douchebag. None. Was he hiding?

"Mira!" Leo and Nichole both jogged towards me.

"What?" I asked, a bit distracted. I walked to my locker as the two of them followed me from behind.

Leo stood in front of me, blocking me from my locker, eyes pleading with guilt. "I'm so sorry about last night. I didn't expect Brandon to do that. He just really can't stand spicy food and - "

"Where is he?" I asked, my tone probably sounded villainous because Nichole winced. "If he wants to apologize then he'd better tell me himself. Don't apologize for him."

He was about to say something else but stopped himself when he realized I was right. Slowly, he got out of my way and let me stuff my things in my locker. After I was through I slammed it shut and walked away. They were still following me.

"It's partly my fault for leaving you two, so I'm sorry too," Nichole said. I stopped in my tracks and faced my best friends, giving them a reassuring smile. These two worry too much. And that's why I love them to death.

"None of this is your fault. Okay? It's Brandon's. Now I need to find him and offer him my gratitude for doing that to me last night." I ruffled their hairs. Nichole didn't complain like she usually would. Leo nodded his head.

"Are you gonna beat him up? You can, if you think he deserves it."

A very nice and tempting suggestion. But no. "I'm just gonna talk to him. Even if I can't stand his ugly face and intolerable voice."

"Who's the ugly face?" My head quickly snapped behind my shoulder when I was sure who it was.

Brandon.

He even had the guts to stand so close behind me.

I turned around and faced him directly, hiding my clenched fists inside my pockets. Don't. Punch. Him.

He tilted his head a bit, never leaving my eyes for a second, and then he grinned at me.

"Is my voice that hot that you'd deem it intolerable?" He folded his arms as his eyes studied me curiously.

I couldn't hold back my glare. Instead of pounding him like the uncivilized gorilla I was, I decided to act civilized and just looked at him with expecting eyes. Who knows, this might do me good.

"Let's talk." He finally said, seriously.

"Fine by me." I replied. He tilted his head to a certain direction and I nodded stiffly. He went ahead as I smiled at my best friends again, reassuring them that I was gonna be alright, and it was Brandon they should be worried about.

And pray he'll live until last period.

"Okay douche, talk." I said as soon as we settled in the back part of the school. I didn't even know there was another parking lot here. A lot people probably didn't know, because there were in fact no cars parked in the area.

"I'm not gonna apologize," he said with finality. I stood there wide-eyed at his sudden proclamation. What the hell? "It was your fault for being greedy. You should've given me your milkshake."

I opened my mouth to yell at him but stopped myself. Be cool. You only just met the guy. Oh wait. I don't care. "Are you kidding me right now?"

"I like to kid around but this is not one of those moments," he grinned.

He was most definitely taking everything as a joke. I must refrain myself from killing him. Control yourself, Mira.

"Listen here, dick," I said through gritted teeth. "I want you to apologize right here, right now. Then, we can pretend all these never happened and we can go back to glaring at each other everyday."

"You thought I was glaring at you?" He laughed. "I wasn't. That's just how I normally look at pretty people."

"Spare me your compliments," I rolled my eyes. I hated it when guys do that. It was so fake. "What you did was unreasonable. Look at what you did!"

I shoved my hair behind my back and showed him the now purple marks on my neck. "And this was all because of a spicy burrito! And a milkshake!"

He made an unexplainable face when he saw his art on my skin. He didn't even look like he was regretting it. "It's pretty nice if I say so myself."

"Nice?" I almost gagged. "You call these bruises nice?"

He glanced at me weirdly. "It's just a bunch of hickeys. So what. It's not like you've never had one before."

I bit my lip. I've never had one before. But he didn't know that. He didn't need to know that.

"That's not what bothers me," I said, covering the sides of my neck with my hair again. "Just the fact that they were from you."

He groaned. "You're making such a big deal out of this."

I can't even explain how much I hate him right now. He's a rude, insensitive jerk. Was it that hard to see that I was a delicate girl?

Pft. Delicate. I make myself laugh sometimes.

"You groped me," I pointed out, much to his surprise.

His eyes widened before he looked at his hand, as if he didn't believe it himself. "I... what? When?"

Don't tell me he thought he was grabbing my shoulder when he forcefully kept me still last night.

I shook my head. "You're such an idiot."

I knew this conversation was pointless so I decided to leave. Why did he even bring me here to talk if it wasn't to apologize? Such a waste of time.

I was already a few meters away from him when he snapped out of his senses. He caught up to me and blocked my way. What is it with guys blocking my way?

"I didn't notice I was holding your uh..." He awkwardly pointed at my chest. My eyes narrowed at him, feeling a bit offended.

"My boob?" I clarified without embarrassment. I was too mad. And it was more embarrassing for his part anyway, judging from his expression. "You didn't notice you were holding my boob the whole time you sucked my neck? Oh very believable Brandon. You just made the best excuse in the world."

His ears turned red but his face remained calm. "Way to put it that way. You make me sound like a total perv."

"You are a perv."

"No I'm not," he argued, a bit childishly. "It's just... Spicy food. And the only thing that can cool my tongue was on you. So... I had no choice."

I nodded my head slowly, not at all convinced at what he was trying to say. It was a bit hard to glare at him properly because he was a head taller than me. "And when you groped me? What's your excuse for that?"

"I didn't notice!" He said, almost desperately. Why was he more bothered with that than all the hickeys he gave me? I can't understand him at all. "Uhh. Can't you just let this one slide?"

Let it slide? Was something wrong with him?

Obviously my answer was no, but then an idea struck me, and then I smiled. He looked relieved, thinking he was off the hook because of my smile. He did not know about the fearsome intentions behind my sinister smile. Bless him for his ignorance.

"Alright." I said.

He was probably about to make another smart statement when I interrupted. Probably with the most surprising interruption he can ever think of.

I gave him a kick infused with all my feelings of hatred for bastards like him - my dignity as a girl which he so much ignored - and my pride as a fighter, which he probably didn't know that much about.

A kick to his crotch. My special technique, Mira Kick!

His eyes rolled up to his head before he got down on his knees, holding his precious as he held back a whine. His groans were concealed by keeping his mouth shut but anyone could tell he was writhing in agony.

"Now we're even," I said. I was about to leave, satisfied, when another idea hit me. I went back to the fallen idiot. "You're lucky I'm kind-hearted."

It sounded more sarcastic than I had intended though.

I did to him what I did to my last victim. I pulled his arm up and kicked his stomach so he'd stand up, quite barely if I may add, and then placed his arm around my shoulder for support. Then I carried him back to our friends.

See? I'm so nice I'd even carry my victims myself. Such a girl I am.

Chapter 4

"Please tell me you have a good reason this time," Principal Steele rubbed his temples as he gave Brandon an ice pack to put to his crotch.

I shrugged my shoulders. "I just found him lying on the parking lot like a piece of trash so I decided to be a good citizen and picked him up. Aren't you proud of me?"

My uncle didn't believe me. Brandon was wincing as he kept the ice pack still on his crotch.

"You're still under probation for beating Samuel Ink yesterday. And now this?"

"His name was Samuel? Doesn't suit him very well," I wrinkled my nose. Brandon spoke up.

"So you really did beat that kid up? I thought it was just a rumor."

I looked at him with a playful glint in my eye. "Better choose what rumors to believe buddy. Maybe that'll save your ass next time."

Not specifically his ass though.

"Would you please take this seriously!" Principal Steele groaned. "If it's just a little game between you two then I'm letting you go. I have work to do."

"It was just a game. Right Brandon?" I glanced at him, semi-glaring at him to agree. He glared back at me, but after realizing that agreeing with me was the better option, he nodded his head quickly.

"Yup. Just a game."

Our principal looked at us seriously before letting us go. When we left the office, I pushed him away to keep distance. He painfully hopped a few times before regaining his balance. And then he glared at me again.

"Damn sadist," he mumbled. I scoffed.

"Fucking masochist."

I began walking away from him, deciding that if I stay with him for another minute, I'll explode.

Brandon was determined to annoy the hell out of me, so he followed me. There were a few seconds of silence until he broke it by starting a casual conversation.

"I never thought Principal Steele was so forgiving."

I snorted. Yeah, forgiving. He only let me off the hook because I was his niece and he knew I had a good reason for this.

I looked at the ice pack being pressed on his crotch and offered him a sickly sweet smile. Torment him. "Need some help there sweetheart?"

He chuckled weakly in reply. "In another time babe, without the ice."

I rolled my eyes. How many eye-rolls does it take to make him go away? And he could still come up with a good comeback in that condition.

I walked ahead to look for Nichole as Brandon limped behind me. Wherever Nichole was, surely Leo would be there too. They were stuck to each other like glue.

I found them waiting near my locker. I waved at them, excited to show them what I did to the shithead. "Guys!"

"Mira!" Nichole ran to me immediately. Leo looked a bit amused when he saw his best friend staggering behind me.

"What'd she do to you?" He asked. Brandon chuckled again, looking more amused than pained.

"She kicked me right on the forbidden zone."

"Serves you right," Nichole spat, and then turned back to me. "I heard you got sent to the Principal's office again?"

"Not really," I replied. "I went there at will to get some ice for him. The clinic was closed."

"You should've just left him on the ground. You're too nice," she said. I laughed.

Nichole and Leo knew I was related to the Principal. Brandon on the other hand, had no idea. "You're close with Principal Steele?"

I smiled at him. "Yeah. Because of my occasional visits alongside almost-motionless-bodies, I guess you could say that."

Instead of fear, he looked rather impressed. That was not the kind of look I was hoping for.

"Let's grab some lunch," Nichole said, linking her arm with mine again. We headed to the cafeteria with the whole milkshake-thing and kick-to-the-balls thing temporarily put aside for the sake of food.

Leo helped his injured friend walk and followed us from behind. I'm surprised he could still walk.

It was a week since the incident. Brandon started hanging out with us. I wasn't mad at him about the whole milkshake thing anymore, but I developed a new kind of hatred for him because of his constant pestering every damn day.

But at least, it was tolerable. My patience is amazing.

My uncle, after scanning the security cameras, concluded that I was telling the truth and that Samuel Ink was the one at fault. But I wasn't off the hook that easy. I was given two weeks detention for beating that guy up.

If only you could punch people without consequences. I sigh.

I was on my way to my last day of detention for the week when Brandon graced me with his presence. I gave him a weird look when he kept smiling at me, not saying anything.

"What do you want?" I politely (read: rudely) asked as I continued to walk towards my destination. His smile widened as he followed alongside me.

"Nothing," he said. "Just memorizing your beautiful face so I can see you when I close my eyes. We won't see each other for a few hours. I'll miss you."

"That's adorable," I said, sarcasm so obvious from my tone. And then I narrowed my eyes at him. "You really know how to sweet-talk. Makes up for your lame weakness to spices."

He grinned proudly, as if I had just complimented him. Damn it I intended to sound offending. "Just to pretty girls like you."

"Why thank you," I went along with it. Why am I dancing to the tune of this idiot? "Aside from this pretty face, I have a rocking body to match."

His brows rose, his eyes sparkling with playfulness. He nodded his head in approval. "I know. It felt like a C."

I was confused for a moment until he showed me his opened palm and bent his fingers a bit, so it looked like he was holding a ball or something. I scoffed.

"Seriously, Brandon?" I mused. "You said you didn't remember."

He gave m an innocent wink. "My memories were a bit hazy at that time. Now all the most priceless details are coming back to me."

Liar. I knew he was just making it up but I couldn't believe how he got my cup size right. Oh wait. He's a guy. He has eyes for a reason.

I shoved him away when I reached the detention room. He probably wanted to follow me even inside but I gave him a warning glare.

"Go away."

"It's okay I'll wait," he flashed me another smile.

I couldn't help but laugh a bit. "Sure. You'll wait for three hours. Whatever Brandon."

Without even giving him the chance to reply, I shut the door close and went to my seat in the half-empty classroom. The teacher in-charge was snoring his head off on his desk.

Ugh.

I got out of the room as soon it was over, and I had to restrain myself from shouting out my freedom.

It was Friday. I'm free!

I looked around the hallways and smiled, relieved. I knew he wouldn't wait. Peace was at my side today.

"Looking for me?" A hand crawled to my shoulder as I felt a warm breath near my ear. I squeaked from the sudden contact and shot him a menacing glare. He chuckled in response. "Took you long enough."

I opened my mouth to say something, but I had nothing to say, so I shut it. He really did wait. It was just an illusion of peace. I was going to live the rest of my school life in chaos because of this jerk.

Brandon stretched his arms and legs a bit, then rotated his shoulders as if he was doing an exercise or something. I gave him a look.

"Where were you hiding?"

He shrugged his shoulders nonchalantly. "Beside the door. On the floor."

Oh.

I tried imagining it and a tinge of guilt disturbed my senses. Won't that strain his muscles or something?

"Did you wait long?"

He smiled again. Damn it why does he keep smiling? Is this a new tactic? I would never have guessed this was the boy who used to shoot daggers at me all the time.

"I had your image in my mind the whole time, so time was out of the picture," a cheeky grin then appeared on his attractive features.

I groaned loudly before punching his shoulder. It was a ridiculous pick-up line but I still found myself laughing.

"There they are!" Leo said when Brandon and I entered the cafe where we usually hung out. Before, it was just the three of us, but starting last week, douchebag Brandon started tagging along.

"What's up you guys?" I happily sat on my usual seat beside Nichole. I was feeling rather giddy because it was Friday, and I can sleep until noon tomorrow.

Best. Feeling. Ever.

Leo took a sip from his and Nichole's drink - they were sharing - before making googly eyes at me and Brandon, who was sitting right beside him.

I knew that look. And that look never meant good. To me, at least.

"I knew you guys would get along soon."

I snorted the same time Brandon did. Get along my ass. It's been just a week since I met him, and he's driving me insane.

I looked at him and noticed that he was looking at me already. I rose a brow and then he winked at me. I narrowed my eyes.

"He's a flirt," I pointed out to my two best friends. They saw the whole thing so I had proof.

"That's because you're flirtable." He smirked.

"That's not even a word."

"It is now," he folded his arms as if he just won an argument. "I just put it in my dictionary. And you're the etymology of it."

I mockingly made a coo. "That's so sweet Brandon. Keep that up and I might fall for you."

Leo howled at my comeback and Nichole was just quietly smiling at me. Oh no. Did I say something wrong? Don't tell me they took it seriously?

"Are you saying you like me?" He put his arm on the table, leaning in closer to me, a smug look on his face.

I can't stand that look. It was as if he was looking down on me.

Being the girl who won't lose to anyone at anything, I did the same, only I leaned a bit closer so our faces were inches apart. I could hear Nichole squealing in delight.

"You want me to?" I said as low as I could. I was seconds away from bursting into laughter, but I held it in so I can beat the bastard. I probably looked ridiculous right now.

Brandon's lips curled up, his eyes studying my face and settled a little longer on my lips. I wasn't sure, but I had to stifle a gulp.

"Even if I don't want you to, you will," he lowered his voice into something husky, probably to match mine.

When his statement sunk in my brain, I tilted my head a bit, leaning closer and closer to him, as if I'd kiss him. He looked like he was expecting one too, but as soon as I felt his breath on my face, I backed away and sat down on my seat with my back pressed against the hard chair.

Nichole and I giggled at his suddenly confused and slightly disappointed pout, but he quickly concealed it with his usual grin.

I folded my arms against my chest, which was probably a bad idea because his eyes widened at the sight of it, so I put my arms down again.

"Like you? Hah. How sure are you? " I gave him my best smirk, giving him the message that he was not the only one who knew how to play this game.

I was getting myself in trouble.

"You'll like me, that's just how it always ends," he said, the smug look on his face was beaming with confidence.

"And if you'll like me first?" I challenged, feeling confident myself.

"Unlikely," he chuckled. "But do try."

"Oh I don't have to," I bit back a smile. We sounded like kids, but I loved the humor of it, so I pushed further. "Prepare yourself Brandon Pierce. You messed with me, now accept the consequences."

He looked excited. And that look dangerously excited me as well. "Mira Jadsen, you just declared an all-out war against me. It is so on."

We were exchanging challenging smirks and smug looks, between the two of us, nobody seemed to want to back down. Especially me.

Leo laughed before ruffling Brandon's hair. He had the look of amusement all over his face. "Would you two just go out already? The sexual tension is so. Ugh."

I rolled my eyes laughing and threw a fry at him. Brandon smiled at me, but I knew that smile meant something else.

Oh it was so on.

Chapter 5

"Rule number one, no buying or paying for anything for the other party. That's considered bribing," he stated as I wrote down what he said on the little notebook I barely used for class.

"Rule number two," I continued. "No physical contact."

"What?" He complained. "Then how am I going to seduce you?"

I chuckled cruelly before placing my pen down on the table. Seems like this was going to be a long argument. "Seduce me how, actually? By touching? Brandon, I'll rip your hand off."

"Then," he mumbled. "If that rule is agreed on, I can't touch you and you can't hit me?"

I nodded my head, and then I stopped. We both thought about it. I don't think that rule will last since I can't take not hitting him, and he probably can't keep his hands to himself.

"Alright we'll just write the specifics," I mumbled, taking my pen again.

"You guys are taking this way too seriously," Leo said as he continued munching on his chicken sandwich.

It was Monday and we were currently having lunch at the cafeteria. And as soon as Brandon and I saw each other again, we sat down and talked business immediately. Nichole and Leo quietly sat down next to us.

I ignored Leo as I thought about what to write next. Specifics, specifics.

"Holding hands and hugging is fine," I said.

"Hugging as in, in any area, or are there any restricted areas I can't touch?" He asked. Leo chuckled, knowing exactly what he meant.

I didn't quite get it, but I knew it was something stupid. Nichole snorted at my stoic reaction.

"You'll know what not to touch if you don't want to lose your fingers one after another." I said seriously.

He smirked as I wrote it down. Before we could make another rule, Nichole raised her hand.

"Yeah?" Brandon asked. Nichole smiled a bit suspiciously.

"Kissing is allowed," she suggested.

Brandon nodded in agreement quickly, but I was dead-set on disapproving. "Hell no. I'm not exchanging spit with him. Direct or not."

He pouted. I had to convince myself that it wasn't adorable. "You make everything about me sound so unappealing."

"That's because everything about you is unappealing."

"We'll see about that," he mumbled. "I want kissing to be allowed. I'll make you change your mind."

I hated how confident he sounded.

"I said no."

"Don't tell me you're afraid?" He smirked. "You know you liked it when I kissed your neck."

I was trembling in anger but I held it in yet again. The one who loses his temper first loses all.

I looked at him, grinning slyly. "If that's what you'd call a kiss. Pft." He was about to to say something, but I quickly continued. "Fine. We'll allow kissing. But there's a time limit."

"Thirty minutes!" Leo slammed his hand on the table, chunks of his sandwich showered upon Nichole's hair. She hit him.

"Twenty minutes?" Brandon suggested. I shook my head.

"Five," I challenged.

"Fifteen," he said.

"Ten."

"Ten minutes it is," he said satisfied as he pressed his back against the chair. Did he just trick me?

I wrote down the third rule. "Rule number three. Kissing is allowed but only for a maximum of ten minutes per day."

"You'll be begging for more. Nobody can resist these kissable lips."

I snorted a bit too loud and ended up laughing like a madwoman. It was hilarious and at the same time irritating at how confident he was. "Screw you and your ego Brandon."

"Screwing, huh?" He leaned against the table again. "That allowed?"

"You can dream of it," I replied. I wanted to applaud myself for sounding so cool. "Rule number four, no pet names."

"What!" He complained again. I sighed in exasperation.

"What now?"

"I can't call you any endearments? That's like, so plain."

"Are you a girl?" I huffed. "Names like baby, sweety, boo, bae, honey and shit. I don't like it!"

He whined, turning to Leo for support. Our best friend just shrugged his shoulders. "C'mon Mira stop being such a granny. Let him call you those things. It's just a game right?"

My eye twitched. Granny?

I looked at Brandon intensely before sighing again. "Fine. But only ones I approve of. Now give me what you're planning to call me so I can write it down."

A triumphant grin crossed his face when I said that. "Potato."

My jaw dropped.

"Potato?" I almost broke my pen. Is he making fun of me? "Why a fucking potato?!"

"Because potatoes are delicious." He replied easily. "Potato wedges, potato chips, potato fries, mashed potatoes. Awesome."

Why do I even bother with this idiot.

"Fine," I gave up. "Potato it is then." I was about to write it down when I noticed he was looking at me with the accursed puppy-eyes. "What?"

"What are you going to call me?" He looked like an excited kid in a toy store. Seriously? He wanted me to call him something stupid too? Why the fuck did I agree to this stupid game.

I raked my brain for some possible options. Cheese? Chip? Chicken? No, I'm just naming food.

Shithead? Douchebag? Dickwad? No, those weren't even endearments.

What the hell am I going to call him?

I give up.

"Uuhh..." I mumbled. Why is this so damn hard?! "Can't I just call you what you call me?"

"You want us to call each other potato?" He asked, sounding amused. I had to refrain myself from strangling him.

"Yeah."

"Okay," he said, pleased. "I'll be in your care from now on, potato."

Cry.

After I wrote all those things down, he gave the last rule, probably because it was almost time for our next class. "Rule number five, if any of the rules mentioned are violated, the punishment will be decided by our most trusted best friends, Nichole Shirley and Leonard Bennett."

We all agreed.

I gave Brandon a copy of those rules and we both signed on each of the copies. After that we shook hands.

The game starts now.

"Babe," he wrapped an arm around my shoulder as we passed through the crowded hallways. "Baby potato."

A few heads turned to stare at us, but Brandon didn't seem to care. I gave him a quiet smile. "What is it, soon-to-be mashed potato?"

He smiled as he tightened his grip around my shoulder and pulled me closer to his side. "Wanna go on a date?"

I giggled sarcastically before I changed my current position and turned around so I could look at his face. His hands fell down to my waist as he waited for me to speak. "As much as I want to, my potato darling, I can't. I have detention for four more days."

His face didn't fall like I expected. Instead, he looked determined. See, this is the thing about idiots. They demand to be unpredictable.

"I'll wait."

That scared me. Maybe because I knew he really will.

"Don't," I said. I don't really want him to wait three hours for me again while sitting on the floor. "I'll just make it up to you next time."

"I'll wait," he said, firmly.

I sighed. "Brandon."

"Mira." He matched my tone. "I said I'll wait. I want to."

I watched him closely and noticed he was serious. What. Brandon, serious?

"Fallen for me yet?" He smirked. I scoffed before swatting his hands off my waist.

I knew it.

"Alright. Fine, wait there," I said, smiling sweetly at him. I'll make him like me first. There's no way I'm losing this game. "Then we'll go on a date. Deal?"

He smiled in return. "Deal. See you in three hours sweet potato."

He sat on the floor beside the door of the detention room like a good kid as I entered the room of boredom. Was it wrong that I was getting unusually excited about the date?

Why were we even playing this game? And what happens after one of us ends up really liking the other? What then?

I don't want to know. I don't need to know. After this, everything will be back to normal, before the milkshake thing ever happened. And Brandon and I won't talk to each other again. Simple as that.

I shouldn't be bothered.

Brandon took me to the mall to watch a movie. To watch a horror film.

I smiled to myself. He thought he could see my weakness with horror films? Sucks for him then, because I love horror films, especially the gory ones.

I didn't tell him that though. I want to see what he'd do during the movie. If he'd secretly hold my hand or casually put an arm around my shoulder like those cliche stories I've read about.

We shall see who has the bigger balls between the two of us.

Of course, as stated in rule number one, we paid for our tickets and snacks separately. After we got out of the long line, we went inside the theater immediately, picking the best seats for viewing the movie.

The movie hadn't started yet, so I decided to glance around the place. My eyes narrowed when I saw nothing but couples everywhere. Seriously though.

The lights turned dim, and then the movie started.

It begins.

"Stupid bitch don't open the fucking door!" I mumbled to myself. We were in the middle of the movie now. The part where the stupid girl opens the door with the killer behind it. Typical horror.

"Scared?" Brandon whispered quietly into my ear. I smirked. Did he really think I was more scared than annoyed at the dumb main character?

"Oh very," I said.

"Don't worry," he held my hand, squeezing it gently before planting a small kiss. "You can just throw yourself at me if you get scared enough."

Even in the dark I could feel the smug look growing on his face. It was, yes you know it, annoying. But at the same time challenging.

"Right back at you, you rotten potato," I pressed my lips against his ear, causing him to take a sharp intake of breath. Bet he didn't expect that now did he.

The sound effects of the movie were surprising us every minute. Every minute we'd jump in our seats and utter a shocked yelp or two, but our hands were still entangled. Which for me was scarier than the movie.

He won't let go.

I glanced at him secretly. He was so focused on the screen.

"I have to go to the bathroom for a bit," I told him before standing up. I tried to withdraw my hand but he just tightened his grip all the more. I stared at him.

"Don't go Mira," he said.

"Brandon..." I looked deep into his serious eyes. It was such an intimate moment, the darkness was slightly disappearing because of the different lights the screen produced, and those lights reflected on his eyes.

Yes, such an intimate moment.

And then I laughed.

"You're scared."

He gave me a quick glare before his eyes went back to the screen. He'd rather look at the horror film than my victorious grin. Wimp.

"No I'm not," he replied childishly.

I sat back down and caressed his hair, cooing teasingly at his ear. "Don't worry about it my frightened little potato," I whispered. "You can just throw yourself at me if you get scared enough."

"You're wrong, sadistic potato," he mumbled, turning his head. Our noses bumped into each other and I felt our hot breaths mixing. "I'm not scared."

I slowly watched what was happening in the movie from the corner of my eye. I didn't know why I didn't back away. The movie was getting to the good part I suppose, because people were hanging on to their seats, and the sound effects were so quiet - it was heart-pounding.

After that silence, the expected surprise came, and the killer appeared. The sounds were so loud it was enough to give me a mini heart-attack. I was about to scream but unexpectedly... Brandon beat me to it.

His scream was cut short when he held a hand to his mouth. The rest of the audience were still screaming. I was too busy laughing to scream along with them.

"Po..." I tried to breath along my laughter. "Potato..." I couldn't help it. It was so fucking hilarious.

"S-Shut up. The sounds surprised me," he was trying to avoid my face but that just made me laugh out more.

"Loser potato..." I choked out in between laughs. "Scaredy potato."

"Shut up potato." He mumbled softly.

The rest of the movie was history. I didn't know what happened after that scene. All I know is that I was laughing my ass off at a certain frightened potato.

CHAPTER 6

Leo released a high-pitched sound close enough to match a female walrus in heat. Of course, I just made that up, because the description sounds fitting.

I don't know how a female walrus in heat sounds.

And I don't want to.

Anyway, Leo was laughing his ass off as I told him how my date with Brandon ended up last night. I guess it was indeed funny in a sense, but he was laughing just a bit too much.

And he wasn't even there.

Nichole rolled her eyes at her exaggerating boyfriend as she gave me an amused smile.

"I mean, c'mon!" Leo choked out, his chuckles getting the best of him. "What a loser! Screaming at some horror movie."

I gave him a look and was about to ridicule him but Nichole beat me to it. "At least he only screams. You on the other hand, almost pissed in your pants when we were watching Insidious 2 the other night."

Leo's laughter stopped abruptly. I could see the small glare he was giving our best friend, but I was determined to make it worse.

"Aha," I smirked. "Just as I thought. You're just a chick with a dick. Just like Brandon."

"And you're a dick in a chick." He quickly replied. He probably thought he sounded smart until we stopped and stared at him. Leo thought about what he just said for a moment and then rephrased his sentence hurriedly. "I mean, you're a dick disguised as a chick."

Pft. What an idiot.

"That's gross you two," Nichole wrinkled her nose, but she was concealing her laughter.

The bell cut our pleasant conversation short and we were forced to say good bye and go straight to class. Unfortunately for me, I had no classes with neither Leo nor Nichole. And fortunately for them, they had the same classes together.

Stupid lucky couple. They always come and go as a package deal or some sort.

After we parted ways, I advanced to my next class. And as excited as I was to pay attention to our new history lesson about a dead guy who used to wear a curly white wig and a pair of tights (not to mention the tacky pumpkin shorts), I just couldn't help but wonder: where was my stupid potato? And what was he doing right now?

I was just curious. No special reason.

I entered my classroom and as soon as my butt touched the seat, our teacher began the lesson. Oh goody.

"Let's go on another date, gossip potato," Brandon said a little bitterly as we made our way to his car. Nichole wanted to buy a new pair of shoes so I was compelled to go with her. And of course,

Leo got dragged along, and as usual, Brandon was our ride to the mall.

Leo was still snickering behind us, making fun of Brandon. "He just wants you to forget about your first date."

He shot Leo a glare before I cooed at him and pinched his cheek like he was a ten year old. "Don't mind him, loser potato."

He irritatedly took my hand off his cheek and stomped to the driver's seat. I couldn't stop my giggles. He was mad because I told Leo and Nichole about our date and how he screamed like a girl.

It really wasn't that big of a deal. Wonder why those two took it so seriously.

When we got to the mall, Nichole pulled me towards the women's shoes department immediately. Leo and Brandon just quietly followed us from behind.

It took us at least two hours until she finally found the pair she wanted. And it was the first pair she chose too.

I'm a girl and I still don't get it. I buy clothes and stuff too but when I look for something, it's not that time-consuming. I see something I like, fits me perfectly and if it's affordable, I buy it.

Nichole was a different case though.

"Why don't you go buy yourself some clothes too." She offered when she noticed the bored look on my face. "I'm gonna buy Leo a new shirt to go with mine. It'll take time, you know it."

I was about to protest until Brandon put his hand on my head and patted it. Not in an affectionate way, if anyone's curious.

"Ooh couple-items," he sounded like he just got another bright idea. I narrowed my eyes at him suspiciously but he just grinned deviously. "We'll look for things like that too. Right potato sweety?"

I gave him my best fake smile. Don't back down Mira. You can take him. "Of course my potato darling. But don't forget rule number one."

"Who could forget rule number one," he chuckled as his hand fell to my shoulder. He was side-hugging me. "We pay separately as usual."

He gave me another grin before we both turned to our best friends. "Text us where you are when you're done."

"Okay!" Nichole chirped happily.

If this guy was playing another game, then he better expect to lose.

"How about this one?" He pointed at the two shirts in front of us. I studied it a bit and shook my head.

"No. Too common."

It was a couple shirt. It was red and one shirt read 'he's mine' with an arrow pointing to the left while the other shirt read 'I'm hers' with an arrow pointing to the right.

Brandon quietly agreed with me and we proceeded to find a more suitable couple-item for us.

I don't understand why we need to get one since we're not a real couple anyway, and we were just playing a stupid game.

But I still went with it. Why.

Something caught my eye but as I was about to show it to him, he quickly took my hand pulled me to the opposite direction.

"What - "

"This." He smirked as he stretched the fabric to my face. I gaped at him. "This is perfect."

It was...

Oh my God I can't even say it. It's so embarrassing!

Pause for dramatic effect.

Okay. Here it goes.

It was a potato-patterned shirt set. A shirt and pair of boxers for the guy and a cropped shirt with matching shorts for the girl. It was a pyjama couple set.

I can't believe it even existed.

I grabbed the tiny pair of shorts Brandon was holding to my face and put it back on the hanger. He gave me a playful questioning look.

"Why buy it when nobody'll see it?" I said, trying to make a point.

"It's not for anybody to see," he took it again and gave the female set to me. "It's for our eyes only."

I shoved it back to where it belonged. "When and where are we going to wear this, exactly?"

"When we have a sleepover, duh." He took it again and gave it back to me as he took the male set. "Unless of course, you have other ideas?"

He smirked as I raised a brow. "A sleepover, really? With just the two of us?"

"Yup," he wagged his brows suggestively. "Doesn't the idea sound exciting?"

I was about to punch him for even bothering with the idea when I remembered: we were just playing a game. There was absolutely no harm in this.

I changed my attitude and smiled at him, holding my set firmly against my chest. I think I'll have a little fun with this.

"Okay," I said, linking my arm with his. I looked up to his smug expression and grinned innocently. "Let's try these things out then."

He returned my grin. "Wanna share the same dressing room? It'll be more convenient for everybody."

The corner of my lip curled up. I was open to the suggestion. I was ready for the challenge. "Let's."

We were currently inside the dressing room, and luckily it was big enough to fit the two of us and left enough space for us to move around.

There were two full mirrors on the two walls in the room, and the light was great. Not to mention the many hooks on the vacant wall. It was so convenient.

The small space between the two of us kind of made me panic there for a bit, but after seeing his smirking face, the panic slowly dissolved into determination.

We'll see Brandon. We'll see who flinches first.

"Okay. Undress," I gestured to him as I hung my bag on one of the hooks. His eyes widened when I said that.

Oops. A little too misleading, wasn't it?

"Slow down my feisty little potato," he chuckled. "Although I do like that part about you too."

I laughed. "You're yet to like the whole of me then. Now hurry. Undress."

If I'm not mistaken, I think I saw a hint of panic cross his face. Oh. Was this scaredy potato just bluffing when he suggested we fit the couple set together?

"Why just me?" He said. "You should too."

"What," I challenged. "Not confident with our body now are we?"

He looked offended and I just wanted to laugh. Why oh why did I find this so funny? Or maybe I was just getting excited.

He quickly took his shirt off, revealing his perfectly toned muscles. I forgot he was an athlete, I forgot what sport. He may not have the ideal six-pack, but it was all good. It was all damn good.

I tried to act like I was used to seeing men's bodies and was silently hoping my cheeks wouldn't give me away.

I nodded my head as if I was approving. When I looked up at him, he was grinning. I bit my lip unconsciously.

I'm digging my own grave I knew. Sue me.

"Now let's try this thing on," I quickly took the potato-patterned shirt and wore it over his head, which was a bit of a challenge in itself since he was taller than me.

It was a perfect fit. I tried to wake up the inner seductress in me so I can make this whole process quicker and win the game, but it was a risk.

How stupid will I look, oh God.

Well. Might as well try anyway.

I pretended to pat the the shirt on him while in fact I was feeling his abs underneath the cloth. My hand was slightly trembling.

What the hell what the hell what the hell am I doing.

"Fits perfectly," I silently wished my voice didn't stutter.

"Yeah..." His voice sounded strangled. When I looked at our reflections in the mirror, I almost - almost - flinched. Why was he looking at me with that dangerous expression?

I'm not scared. I can be... Scarier.

"Now for the boxers," I avoided his gaze and looked down. My hands were on the button of his jeans before I knew it, and I mentally hit myself. Was I getting a little too into this? "I'll help you take your pants off."

"No!" He was quick to react. I withdrew my hands immediately. His ears were getting red and I just knew he was getting flustered. I was relieved to know I wasn't the only one. "I'll - I'll do it. Thanks."

He did it pretty quick. As soon as he took off his pants, he slid the matching potato-boxers up his legs up to his waist. After he wore the whole set, he grinned at his reflection a little childishly, making a few ridiculous poses at that.

"I rock this potato-pyjama-set."

"You sure do," I laughed, taking my phone out to take a picture - no - a lot of pictures. This was just too great an opportunity to pass.

Brandon was no kill-joy either. He practically made every stupid pose known to man. It was such an epic attempt, imitating Victoria's Secret angel's poses and facial expressions.

It was so disgusting it was hilarious.

When our fill of pictures and laughter were satisfied, he smirked at me.

"Now it's your turn." He said as he took the female set off the hanger. "Now, undress."

Was I laughing just a while ago? Suddenly I don't know what's so funny anymore.

I tried to keep my breathing steady. I started this. He's just copying what I did to him. I can't be flustered. Otherwise, I'd lose.

"C'mon Mira, potato baby," he teased, wiggling the shirt in front of my face. When I was unresponsive for a few seconds, he grinned triumphantly. "Not confident with our body now are we?"

Damn him to hell for using my own words against me. Damn me too for using it without thinking.

I straightened my back and gave him my best game smirk.

Screw it.

Chapter 7

I turned around, away from Brandon's face but it was a futile attempt to even hide because of the damn mirrors. So even if he was behind me, he could still see what was going on in front.

"I'm waiting," he sang as he folded his arms. He looked ridiculous because of the potato-patterned pyjama set, but I couldn't laugh. Not in this situation I'm in.

I put on my best game face and smirked at his reflection in the mirror. Here goes nothing then.

Good bye sane me. Hello crazy bitch.

I peeled my shirt off, carefully and slowly, enough for Brandon to get impatient. My heart was beating faster every second, knowing how stupid I am for doing this and not stopping when I have every chance to.

When I was finally standing there in my bra - I'm glad I wore the presentable one today - I turned around forced-confidently and put my hands on my waist, grinning at his expression.

He swallowed hard before attempting to act cool, just like what I did earlier. His eyes travelled up and down to places I don't even want to mention. A smug grin crossed his face before he nodded his head in approval.

"I was right," his eyes settled on my chest a little longer, making me want to cover up and smack him. "It was a C."

"Yeah," I said coolly, resisting the urge to kill him. I'm just so stupid, so stupid.

Did I just fucking strip in front of him?!

I put the damned cropped shirt on. It was hanging a bit loosely just above my stomach. I checked myself in every angle, it fit just okay.

And now for the shorts.

I decided to be recklessly brave and stupid again. I wanted to do something Brandon couldn't.

I looked at him slyly before gesturing to my pants. "Help me take this off."

"S-Seriously?" He stuttered. I smiled while nodding my head.

Again, he swallowed hard and looked like he couldn't believe what he was hearing. I gave him an encouraging smirk and that did the trick.

His hands immediately grabbed a hold of my jeans. I held my breath from the sudden contact, even though I was expecting it.

He bent down a bit, his eyes slightly squinting in full concentration. He looked like he was diffusing a bomb with that expression.

I somehow managed to attain superhuman powers at that short moment, because I became too aware of the situation, and my senses intensified tenfold.

In my head, everything was mute, but I could hear my breathing - his breathing mixed, the blood rushing to my ears, my heart going wild inside my cage and my damn skin - it tingled every time his fingers brushed a part of my exposed stomach, even if it was just a little bit.

When did I get so sensitive?

I know. I have to change my body soap.

And what was taking him so long? I risked a glance to see how he was doing. His expression was still the same. At first, he couldn't undo the button since it was a bit tight, so he pushed his thumb a bit harder on the button.

My legs felt like they've been shot by a lethal doze of anesthesia.

Slowly, whether it was to torture me or because he was just plain nervous himself, he undid the button. After that, he pulled the zipper of my jeans down.

Oh my God I think I'm gonna fart.

Nah I'm kidding.

As he was about to slide the cloth down my legs, I panicked. This has got to stop before I faint. I stopped him by holding his hands, earning a surprised look from him.

"Thanks, I'll take it from here."

He nodded stiffly before standing quietly in the corner of the room, which was actually just a few inches away.

Mothertrucker this is so awkward. Why did I do that?

I took a deep breath and consciously slid my jeans off. He was observing my every move and I was about to pass out.

Stop looking. Stop it.

Wait.

No Mira, let him look. You're winning.

After sliding the jeans off my legs (and stripping a huge part of my dignity), I sighed in relief when I realized I wasn't just standing in my underwear. Lucky I wore a pair of cycling shorts for our gym class earlier.

I put on the matching shorts and when I was through, I laughed at both our reflections, silently hoping to lighten the tense atmosphere. We looked so stupid!

He grinned while taking his phone out too. Oh no. "Say potato!"

I was a sport. I mimicked his poses from earlier and made a complete fool out of myself. It was fun though, that I had to admit.

"Now let's take a selfie to commemorate the day we made complete idiots of ourselves," I said as I took my own phone out.

I switched it to front cam and you know what comes after.

"So what'd you guys buy?" Nichole asked, sounding excited. We were on our way home now, Brandon and Leo were gonna drop us off our apartment.

I shrugged my shoulders and grinned slyly at Brandon. I was in the front seat while the two were in the back. "It's a secret."

He smiled playfully at my reply, knowing what I meant. We agreed not to tell or show anybody those embarrassing pyjamas. I don't understand why we even bought them in the first place.

"Ugh. Please don't tell me you guys bought something dirty?" Leo made barfing sounds and I resisted the urge to hit him. He was lucky he was sitting in the back.

"It's purely innocent, if you must know," I said.

"Yeah," Brandon agreed, eyes still on the road. "And it's purely for our eyes only."

I wanted to laugh but held it in for the sake of misleading our friends. It was amusing. In a way.

Leo gagged. "There it is! Stop that! Hearing you two say that is one thing. But imagining... Ew!"

"What the hell is going on in your head?" Nichole asked, incredulously.

"My two best friends screwing around." He said. "Gross. Just. Ugh." Leo pretended to wipe some sweat from his forehead. I rolled my eyes.

"Dude that's sick," Brandon said, his face wrinkling in disgust. "Stop picturing me naked."

"Me too," I came to his defense. "I don't go around imagining you and Nichole doing the nasty."

As soon as I said that, everybody shut up immediately.

Well. This was awkward.

Brandon cleared his throat not a moment later. "So, you girls are roommates?"

I'm so glad he changed the topic. It was such a weird conversation. I'm gonna erase it from my mind right now. "Yeah. We live in the apartment Nichole's aunt owns."

"Must be very convenient, since it's so close to school."

"Yeah," I nodded my head. "What about you guys? I thought you were roommates too?"

"We are," Leo replied for him. "Our apartment is just in front of yours actually. Wait, you didn't know that? Some best friend you are."

He pretended to sulk and I just laughed at him. "Stop making that face. You're so ugly."

"Yeah well, Nichole doesn't think so. Right babe?"

Nichole sent me a smirk before whipping her hair to her back. "Nope. You're fugly."

Brandon and I burst out laughing. That's right bitch. It's sisters before misters. After that good laugh and Nichole cheering Leo up because he actually took that seriously (talk about sensitive), we arrived at our apartment.

Nichole gave Leo a sweet kiss on the lips before she went out. I was about to go out as well until Brandon held my arm, preventing me from even opening the door.

I sent him a questioning look, but he gave me expecting eyes in reply.

"Where's my kiss?"

I unconsciously took a sharp breath. My heart decided to give my rib cage a single, huge punch. What was happening to me lately?

"Excuse me?" I chuckled in disbelief, concealing my self-confused state. "Why should I kiss you?"

"Because you like me?" He cockily suggested. My breathing went back to normal as I pouted playfully and laughed.

"Wrong answer. But today was fun, so I guess I'll give you a smack."

He looked excited as he got in a more comfortable position in his seat. He leaned in a bit and closed his eyes.

Poor thing.

I did what I promised, and smacked him with three powerful fingers, right on the forehead. His eyes shot open, probably from surprise. He looked at me, his forehead slightly glowing pink from the impact.

"Have a good night pink potato," I smirked, and then shut the car door close. I could hear Leo laughing his guts out even from outside the car. Nichole was giggling by my side as we made our way up to our floor.

Served him right for making me act like this.

"Baby," his voice sounded different in the phone - a bit muffled, deeper. I was guessing he was currently lying down. "Potato baby."

I'm still wondering how I managed to get used to that dumb pet name. And why I'm smiling to myself now that no one's watching.

"What do you want potato?" I mumbled myself. I was about to fall asleep when this dolt called and disturbed my peaceful night.

He laughed slowly. The sound of his laughter was nice, so I pressed my phone a bit harder on my ear. "Nothing. Just wanted to hear your voice."

I don't know how to describe this correctly, but I felt like a dozen huge bubbles collected inside my chest and caused my breathing to quicken.

Ridiculous, I know. I must be tired already.

Hearing nothing but my breathing as my response, he continued. "I had a really great time today. Thank you, really. Good night Mira."

He hung up before I could even give a smart reply. He knew me too well.

I clenched my phone in my hand and sighed deeply. I'm forcing myself not to smile like an idiot right now. Why. Why do I feel so happy after one phone call?

I know he's just doing it for the sake of the game. But still. It's weird.

He's weird.

The game itself is weird.

That's right, after this stupid game everything will be back to normal, so I'll just keep going. Brandon is dangerous for my health. I have to finish this game quickly. That should be the right thing to do.

Right?

Chapter 8

"Just you and me today potato grumpy," Brandon said against my ear upon closing the distance between us. I shoved him away.

"Go away, touchy potato."

I wasn't in the mood today. Somehow, I felt uncomfortable and I wanted to punch something. I don't know.

He sent me a small grin. "Why're you grumpy? Stop frowning."

"I'm not frowning."

"Yeah you are."

"No, I'm not."

"Yes, you are."

I looked at him and groaned heavily. He wasn't going to stoop down anytime soon with this pointless argument, so I just shut up and glared at him.

I walked away, away from him because I really wasn't in the mood. And I felt like crying all of a sudden. I felt so unlucky. Unloved.

Oh my God what was that?

Why was I suddenly getting emotional right now? So gay dude.

"Is it because Nichole and Leo are skipping and left you behind?" He asked, his tone softer this time. His expression looked hopeful, and I was actually compelled to give him my attention. Damn it.

"Not really," I shook my head at him. I even forgot those two were skipping today. It was their first year anniversary after all. "I just feel down. That's all."

"Hungry?"

I shook my head again. Even I found it strange that I was unusually quiet today. What was going on with me lately?

"Well," Brandon scratched the back of his head, seeming like he didn't know what else to say or do. He patted my head softly and offered me a genuine smile, not his usual mischievous grins, but a real smile. "I hope you get better. See you at lunch?"

I smiled back and nodded my head. He was too good at faking to be sweet.

It was scary.

Ten minutes before lunch, and I felt my insides getting squeezed, wrung, tortured. As if there was a battle being fought in my uterus. And I was feeling rather uncomfortable down there.

Shit. Was it that time of the month?

"Want anything else?" Brandon set a tray down in front of me. I looked at him, confused.

"Why are you so nice to me today?" I pushed the tray away from me and to his side of the table. We were at the cafeteria now. Lunch break started over an hour ago and I still couldn't work up the appetite.

Surprising, I know.

He pushed the tray back to me. "You don't look well. Eat something."

"No," I pushed the tray away from me again. "It's fine. You eat this, you bought this right? You'd be violating rule number one if you treat me lunch."

He didn't look pleased at all. He took the chocolate drink beside the unappealing cafeteria food, stabbed the straw in it and gave it to me. "I don't care. Leo and Nichole aren't here anyway. At least drink this."

I shook my head. "I don't get you at all. You're so weird."

"Drink it?" He offered with an adorable smile, ignoring my previous comment. After staring at him for a while, I groaned loudly and took the drink from his hand.

Don't get me wrong. It wasn't because he looked adorable. It was because I knew he'd insist I drink it until I do.

Sigh.

Yeah Mira, keep telling yourself that.

A satisfied grin was on his face when I put the straw in my lips and sipped chocolate drink. It only took about three long sips and the cardboard box was empty.

"So you were hungry." He raised a brow when I clenched the empty box and set it aside.

"No," I replied. "Just thirsty. And I loved that drink so that's why."

He didn't look convinced but he smiled anyway. For the next five minutes, he decided to eat the lunch he bought for me so it wouldn't be a waste. I found myself drifting away in my thoughts. Memories about last night.

He called me. He said good night. His voice was wonderful.

I shook my head quietly.

It's just a game. It's just a good tactic. It's not real.

I felt an annoying discomfort between my legs as I was in the middle of my thoughts, and I was unsure whether it really was that time of the month or not. Not waiting to find out, I stood up.

"I'm going to the bathroom," I announced. Brandon nodded as I began to walk away.

But not until he called me back.

"I'll be quick," I said. He awkwardly motioned his finger clockwise, maybe gesturing me to turn around, and he was trying his best to avert his gaze. I cocked my head to the side. "What?"

"You have um..." His face coloured into the lightest shade of pink. "Uh... A red stain on your pants."

It didn't take a genius to get what he meant. My eyes widened, realizing what it was as my hand shot down to cover my behind. Shit!

I sat back down and internally debated whether to rush to the bathroom now or wait until everyone else leaves.

Cry. Why did I leave my bag in my locker? Now what do I use to cover up?

"Um..." Brandon suddenly reminded me of his presence. "I'll cover you."

I gave him another weird look. "You're so nice today. I can't help thinking you have an ulterior motive."

He rolled his eyes before standing up and grabbing my hand. "C'mon, I'll take you to the bathroom."

"Now you're just creeping me out." I said. He pulled me up abruptly, almost causing me to lose balance. He caught my shoulders behind me and commanded me to march forward.

"This is ridiculous!" I complained, but walked forward anyway. We looked so unnatural by the way we were walking so close to each other. And for me, it looked pretty obvious that he was hiding the stain on my butt.

We earned a few stares of course, that was inevitable. And it bothered me. But what bothered me most was what Brandon was doing.

"You'll get blood on yourself if you come any closer," I said, to make him feel disgusted and back off. But no, it just made him firm his hold my shoulders.

I grunted, feeling annoyed and embarrassed. Well, annoyed because I was embarrassed. I never thought he'd do something like this for me.

I decided to just let him do what he wants. It was for my own benefit anyway. Why do I always give in in the end when it comes to him? I can't accept it.

When I remembered I had no spare tampon in my bag and all the tampon and tissue-pack vending machines were busted, I mentally smacked myself.

Great.

I would've went to the clinic or asked some of my friends if they had a spare, but I was too uncomfortable to waste anymore time. So I told Brandon to take me back to my apartment.

"Sorry," I mumbled as I got in his car. I placed a piece of paper under my butt in case, you know, it gets messy.

"You can't help it," he said reassuringly. It did not reassure me at all. Now I'm indebted to him. "My mom experienced that before, and we were at the mall that time too. So I get it, don't worry."

Did he mean to say he covered for his mom too? Is this guy a real gentleman or is this just a facade?

Ugh I can't think straight anymore, the cramps are killing me.

When we arrived at our apartment, I made a run for the bathroom - I never knew I could run so fast in my life. I shut the door close, leaving behind an idle and confused Brandon.

I forgot something a bit crucial since I was in such a hurry, and I was already sitting on the toilet, so I texted him.

| Grab me a tampon from my room please? |

I know, shameful of me. But I just couldn't go out now that I'm here. I can, but I don't want to. Girls will understand this.

My phone vibrated, I read his reply.

| Where? |

I had to admit, I wasn't expecting him to be so agreeable.

| Second drawer inside my closet. My room is the one on the right side. |

| Got it. |

After a few minutes, I heard a knock on the door. I opened it slightly so only his hand fit through it. He blindly handed me the pack of tampons and I took it quickly.

"Thanks so much Brandon," I breathed, feeling a bit awkward. I feel so dirty. I hope he doesn't find me disgusting or anything.

I'm still a girl. Of course I'm conscious about these things.

After I was through with my business and washed that stain off my pants, I went out. He was waiting near our television, looking distracted with the phone in his hand. Was he texting somebody? I wonder who?

Stop it. Don't get too curious.

"Hey," I announced my presence. He gave me a brief nod, probably feeling a bit awkward with the situation. "Sorry."

"It's alright, really," he chuckled. "My mom stayed in the bathroom for hours when she got her period. She kept yelling at me for no reason too."

I looked at him. "Are you close with your mom?"

He shrugged his shoulders. "You can say that. She's not my real mom though."

What..?

I was about to press further when he spun on his heels and headed to the door. "Let's go. We can still make it to next period."

"Oh, okay," I followed him. I'll ask him about that issue in another time then.

As he was about to open the door, I stood up on my toes and gave him a quick peck on the cheek. He stiffened and I swore his neck almost snapped when he turned to stare at me wide-eyed.

I smiled shyly at him. Shit. Shyly. Me? I'm turning gay. "That's... Thanks..."

A foolish grin spread on his face, but he didn't say anything. He looked distractedly happy when he finally opened the door. I was just quiet beside him.

What met us behind the other side of the door was definitely what broke my silence. The woman stood there smiling warmly at me, but her smile dropped when she saw my companion.

"Mom?" I croaked.

"Who's this?" She eyed Brandon critically before transferring her intense stare at me. "I thought you were living with Nichole. Did you lie to me?"

"No!" I cried out, almost too defensively. But it was the truth. Mom looked at me unconvinced. "I really am living with Nichole. Um... This is Brandon, Leo's best friend. He just dropped me off. I kinda had a little accident at school."

"Accident?" Her gaze softened into worry. I was suddenly relieved she didn't look mad anymore. But now, I had more explaining to do. "What accident? Are you okay?"

Sigh.

Now for the explanation.

"She was such a tomboy, this kid," mom chuckled. She and Brandon were currently discussing my not-so-cute childhood in my kitchen. I, the topic of the discussion, was standing behind the counter, making my guests a few sandwiches. I wasn't really invited to the discussion.

Not nice, mom.

"She'd beat up kids who made fun of her teeth. She had such crooked teeth before - "

"He's not interested in my lame childhood story so stop talking mom," I said, placing the sandwiches on the table. She smiled sweetly before taking one of the sandwiches I made.

Brandon on the other hand, looked amused. Very amused. "I don't mind. Kid Mira sounds awesome."

He sent me a wink and I scoffed. Mom caught us and she squealed.

The woman squealed.

Squealed.

Did anybody spot what's wrong with this sentence?

Let me give you a hint: she squealed.

"So are you two like, going out now?" She asked, sounding like she was our age. I was about to correct her when Brandon held my waist and pulled me to his side. What -

"Not yet," he smiled at my mom. "But soon. Probably. If she admits she likes me."

I pushed myself away from his grasp and gave him a warning glare. He mustn't tell my mom about the stupid game. Or else he'll have to live with the possibility of being unable to father children in the future.

"Oh Mira!" Mom looked at me expectantly. "Just say you like him already! He's such a nice boy."

She held Brandon's hands and gave him a pitiful look, her lips pouting slightly. "I'm sorry you have to put up with this prude of a daughter of mine."

"Not at all Mrs. Jadsen," he grinned. "I enjoy her company no matter what she does. I'd like to stay by her side until she admits she likes me."

My mom cooed, pleased. "Just call me Paige, Brandon. And Mira, stop playing hard to get would you? You'll end up losing this great guy!"

"Don't be fooled mom," I warned. "He's a wolf in sheep's clothing."

"This gentleman?" Mom scoffed. Yeah right, like she knew him like I did. She just met him! Now they were in first name basis!

"Whatever," I took the empty plates from the table and placed them in the sink. They ate the whole thing already. "I'm not gonna admit anything until he admits he likes me first."

Brandon and I exchanged grins. My mom was oblivious to what was really going on. She seemed as if she was about to say something until her eyes landed on our clock. A look of panic crossed her face as she abruptly stood up.

"Work! I forgot!" She gave me a quick kiss in the cheek and hugged Brandon before rushing to the door. "I was just supposed to leave the salad while you were at school, but I forgot! I'm not even going to ask why you're not in school." She gave Brandon a knowing smile. Ugh. "See you tomorrow honey! Nice meeting you Brandon!"

"You too Paige!" He called out before mom slammed the door close behind her.

As soon as she left, only silence enveloped the room. I still can't believe she was here. That woman was fast as well - guess now I know where I got my speed from.

I began washing the dishes, ignoring the guy who just tricked my mother into thinking he was some sweetheart. Psh.

"About what you and your mom said," he started. I didn't spare him a glance and just continued doing the dishes. "About me being a wolf in sheep's clothing and being a gentleman."

Yeah, I could care less.

A hand snaked around my shoulder and I squeaked when he pressed his lips on my ear. Why does he keep doing that! "I'm just going to clarify some things."

I didn't dare move my head, because if I did, I knew he'd kiss me for sure. And I wasn't prepared for that yet. I felt his lips curl up into a sly smile, making me tingle all over. "Remember. A gentleman is just a patient wolf."

Chapter 9

"A gentleman is just a patient wolf."

A patient wolf? That weird potato? Him? A patient wolf my ass.

A day passed since my bloody situation, but I still couldn't get what he said out of my head. What did he mean? Was he implying something?

Or was he just stating a quote from some site? Because I swear I read that in 9gag before.

Recalling what happened yesterday after he delivered that sentence, I sighed. We skipped the afternoon classes yesterday because mom came and after that we were too lazy to attend anymore, so Brandon just went back to their apartment as I slept.

Wait. Maybe I was just over-thinking again because I was on my period?

I smiled to myself. That explained everything perfectly. I wonder why I feel so relieved all of a sudden.

Leo and Nichole were finally back, but we barely had time to see each other because of our classes, much less talk. But somehow,

Brandon still managed to find me. Where the hell did he get my schedule? He seemed to know where I was at all times.

"Stalker," I mumbled as he made his way towards me, wearing that usual wide grin on his face. He heard me loud and clear, as well as a few students because they began staring. What.

"Now," he said, teasingly. "Is that what you should be saying to your human-cover-for-blood-stains?"

I threw him a dirty look but shrugged it off immediately. He didn't sound this confident yesterday. And I was indebted to him. Damn it.

"I'll claim my reward," he put both his hands on my shoulders, stopping me from walking away. I was expecting he'd ask for something dumb but he instead, he claimed his reward himself.

He kissed the corner of my mouth, brushing my lower lip just a little bit. If my sharp intake of breath didn't distract me, I would've slapped him upside the head already. "Thank you."

"Hey!" I complained, still looking at him in complete bewilderment. I hope my cheeks didn't betray me now. Shit why do I feel faint. "You - "

"Not so loud now. People are watching." A victorious grin crossed his face. I looked around and saw that it was true. I scoffed. People were so nosy.

I looked back at him, my stare intensifying. I hate this. Now he's got the upper hand. I hate this so much.

But I somehow liked the feeling of it, that kiss - no. Stop thinking. Yeah, you're over-thinking again because you're on your period.

Dramatic sigh.

Why do I always try to convince myself inside my head.

It's just... Sad.

"Let's go out again. Let's date," I told him. This can't continue. I have to turn the tables. He sent me a questioning look, probably wondering why I was the first to invite him this time. He agreed quickly yet unsurely.

"Your detention's over now right?"

"Right," I replied. I didn't attend yesterday but whatever. The teacher in-charge didn't seem to care as well.

Brandon's lip curled up into a smirk. Oh he was into this as well. He probably knew what I was thinking. Good.

"We'll meet in my car after class," he said before I headed off to my next class, which he probably knew where and until when. He nodded and sent me away with a quiet smile.

I'm gonna wrap him around my little finger.

Downtown, the place was crowded, noisy, and the worst nightmare for someone with claustrophobia.

I decided to set our date here since everything was cheap and I hadn't been here since my dad brought me years ago.

A sad memory attempted to block my thoughts, but Brandon interrupted just in time for me to snap out of it.

He held my hand so we wouldn't get separated. We walked around the streets and made a few stops at some stalls that seemed interesting.

"Hey look at this," I pointed at the large sign posted outside a small restaurant. "Burger-eating contest. Winner gets free mug and shirt."

Brandon snorted, obviously making fun of the prizes. It didn't sound all that appealing, and the sign wasn't so attractive. "Waste of time."

"I'm with you," I linked my arm with his and hugged it lightly, pressing my cheek against his arm. "You said time was out of the question when you're thinking of me. Well, I'm here in the flesh. Let's do it."

He seemed reluctant, but after I kept tugging his sleeve and made ridiculous pouty lips at him, he groaned, sighed and gave in.

Easy.

"I'm warning you though," Brandon said as we entered the small restaurant. It was half-crowded already. A lot of people actually joined. I don't know if it's because of the prizes or they just came for the food. "When it comes to food, my stomach is steel."

I held back a snort. "Be gentle with me now, potato."

He chuckled as he wrote our names down on the list of contestants. Judging by appearances, the people we had to beat were either obese or super skinny. Some looked normal, some looked plain weird.

Oh well. They don't matter. As long as I beat Brandon.

And I had a trump card up in my sleeve. I laughed to myself. My win is already decided.

"Fuck... This... Mmrph..." Brandon mumbled before he gagged. His face was pink or green, I'm not sure, but it was hella funny.

I took the keys from his pocket and decided to drive him back to his apartment since he wasn't in any condition to drive. I felt sorry - kinda - but it was unnoticeable because I was smiling up to my ears.

As soon as I started the engine, he threw his head back in the front seat and held his mouth. "Be careful... With my... Baby..."

I rolled my eyes. Not the first guy I've met who calls his car 'baby'.

"Cheater..." He said, more like breathed. He looked close to puking. I don't care if he blew chunks on the car, just not on me. "You knew there'd be jalapeños on the last batch of burgers... Else I wouldn't have... Lost..."

I hid my smirk and looked at him innocently. "I didn't know. It was the last round, and we were in a tie. That had to be the icebreaker. How could I have known?"

Nah, I knew. It was written in really small letters under the sign posted outside the restaurant. But he didn't need to know that.

I'm still surprised we managed to beat our opponents. It was pretty cool. The burgers tasted amazing, but I don't think I can touch another burger within a month.

He released an incoherent cuss before I started to drive.

Now I'm satisfied.

"You done?" I gently tapped the door of his bathroom. He ran to the toilet as soon as we got to his apartment. I could see myself in his situation because it happened to me not long ago - specifically yesterday.

Except, I was rushing because of my period. Him, because he was gonna throw up.

I could hear him groaning from outside. "Fuck spices!"

Way to blame the spice. Why couldn't he just admit that he lost because he couldn't take the amount of burgers?

I, on the other hand, wasn't so surprised at how I managed to eat twenty-one whole burgers in just half an hour. This wasn't the first food-eating contest I participated in, and the monster in my stomach worked double-time when I was in my period. So, good for me.

"What happened to your stomach of steel?" I chuckled, knowing I've already won this match.

This feeling of superiority is so awesome.

The door opened, and I was met with a groggy-looking potato. His face was wet so I assumed he splashed some cold water on his skin. The way the drops of water trickled down his jaw made me stifle a gulp.

God, his jaw was just so hot. I wanted to bite it.

No. Cut it out. Shut up. Focus, you hormonal idiot.

He didn't seem to notice me gawking at him, which was obviously a good thing for my part. He grabbed a towel lying around somewhere and proceeded to his room. And of course, I followed his tail.

His room wasn't as messy as I've expected, but there were small piles of clothes in random corners.

"I wasn't expecting any guests. Sorry for the mess. And half this junk are Leo's, so don't take it all out on me." Brandon grabbed a fistful of clothes and threw them to a nearby laundry basket. Ah. So a laundry basket actually existed here.

He lied down on his bed and groaned again. No, the more accurate way to put it was he collapsed on the bed and whined like the mature seventeen year old that he was.

"I feel sick."

I scooted over the bed so I was right beside him. The thought of being alone with him in this place didn't bother me at all. In fact, I was feeling rather comfortable and secure. Maybe it was because I trusted him?

Or maybe it was because he was powerless at the moment.

"Does your stomach still hurt? Do you want medicine?" I asked, sincerely.

He shook his head slowly. His eyes were already closed. "I'm not actually sick sick. I threw up most of the burgers so I'm feeling better actually. It's just... The spice triggered something in me and I'm just weak against it."

I held his forehead and concluded that he didn't have a fever or anything. But he really did look tired.

He really did hate spices.

He didn't seem comfortable in his clothes since he was shifting from one position to another, wrinkling his forehead in an attempt to find a good post.

I felt kind of bad. And out of instinct, I offered to help him change his clothes, which he rejected quickly. I sighed. Why was he being shy now?

"I'll change later. Now I just wanna take a nap. You can go home now, thanks for dropping me off. Sorry I can't drive you back," he mumbled, burying his face on his fluffy pillows.

I forcefully peeled his head off the pillows. Clearly he doesn't know me that well. "No. I'm helping you change before I leave."

A part of me wanted to do it because I really did want to help him, but another part of me wanted to do it to use it as leverage and make fun of him in the future. I might even take a few stolen pictures of him while I'm at it.

He looked reluctant and a bit embarrassed at the mere suggestion of me changing his clothes as if he were a kid, but agreed anyway since he knew I wouldn't leave until I do.

"Good potato," I cooed teasingly as I walked to his closet and took a shirt. I didn't bother looking for shorts or boxers anymore because I assumed he was already wearing one under those jeans.

When I returned to his side on the bed, I noticed he was eyeing my every move cautiously. Not that I felt conscious.

"Can you sit up?" I asked. He weakly shook his head.

"Tired."

Useless. Weakling.

Without another word, I proceeded on tugging his shirt up his head while he was lying down, and it was quite a challenge since I was doing it beside him, in a rather awkward angle.

Patience was never one of my best traits. I got frustrated immediately and decided to just sit on him.

No. Do not think of anything. This is purely out of the kindness of my heart and the desire to change his t-shirt so he'd feel comfortable when he sleeps.

Trust me, that wasn't sarcasm right there.

He didn't even look surprised anymore. But his eyes narrowed, and he barely made any movement. He was like a lifeless body who can breathe and had open eyes.

I may have looked like I was straddling him, but trust me again, I had no ulterior motives. Aside from taking ugly pictures of him for future blackmail purposes of course.

I say things like this in my mind but in reality I was actually searching for where the hell my breath went - and wondering why the hell I decided to do this - and I want to kick myself in the balls even though I don't have an actual pair.

I didn't say anything, because I was afraid my voice would betray me, so I just did what I said I'd do. I peeled off his shirt in that compromising position.

He was so damn heavy, and he wasn't helping at all. He just continued staring at me quietly as I struggled to pull the shirt up. I bet he was making fun of me in his head. Bitch.

When I finally managed to pull the shirt off his head, I mentally gave myself a high-five for the achievement, and a mental slap because my eyes got glued to his wonderfully sculpted upper body.

Well, shit.

"Don't stare at it so much. I'll melt," he mumbled. I jumped a bit when he said that. I thought he didn't have the strength to even talk anymore. And maybe I stupidly assumed that he was sleeping with his eyes open.

I rolled my eyes at his weak smirk. He was already tired, yet he's still joking around. Well, that was probably a good thing, to decrease the tension and all.

And woo. Was it getting hot in here? My legs are burning against his legs, even though the material of our jeans served as obstacles for our skins to meet.

Like I said. He is definitely not good for my health. Yet I'm the one doing this right now. I don't even know if I'm plain reckless or just stupid. Maybe both.

"Unbutton my jeans please," he said slowly, his eyes closed now. Was he dreaming? "I can't breathe well."

I gulped. Was he being serious right now? Back when we were trying out those potato pyjama sets, he didn't sound this demanding at all. Where did the wimpy potato go?

I saw him holding back a smug grin, and immediately my eye twitched. He was doing this on purpose. He thinks I can't do it. He expects me to be flustered.

Well guess what jerk, I'm not. And the flow of this game is going to be in my favor until the end.

"Fine," I said, but my voice came out as a hoarse whisper. I couldn't focus on his jeans because my eyes were too fixated on his damn chest and toned stomach.

When I finally mustered up the courage and will power to do so, to win this match, I unbuttoned his jeans quickly. It was done in a second. His pants were not even that tight! Why did he complain about not being able to breathe?

I put a hand on his chest, I couldn't help it. It was more like an unconscious reaction. I was caught off guard when I felt his rapid heartbeats against my palm. Was he... Was he getting nervous?

I smiled to myself.

Now I have the advantage. I grinned smugly at him when he opened his eyes. He looked really sleepy just a minute ago, now he's awake. "Aw. Your heart's racing."

He was probably about to make another smart comment in his defense when we heard a loud thud on his door.

It didn't take a second for it to completely burst open, revealing a beaming Leo with an excited looking Nichole under his arm.

"Bran - "

Leo's mouth hung open when he saw me on top of a shirtless Brandon. Oh, and did I mention his jeans were unbuttoned too?

Yay timing.

"What the actual fuck?!" He fumbled in his words before he finally let out a clear reaction. He covered his eyes and turned around. "My worst nightmare! This scene! Oh hell no!"

"Mira!" Nichole squealed, looking very much excited.

I casually jumped out of the bed because I didn't want them to witness me panic, though in my head I was freaking out. Why were they here?!

I threw them a cool smile while waving my hand a bit. Do not let them see through this bluff. "Hi guys. So, what's with the sudden visit?"

Chapter 10

"Uh-huh. Mm." Leo mumbled while nodding his head. His hands were folded against his chest; his legs crossed while sitting on the edge of Brandon's bed.

It took quite some time to explain to my best friends what actually happened. Leo was the hardest to convince.

"You were sitting on him Mira. Sitting on him. Do you understand what you just did?" Leo scolded. I sighed heavily. "You're lucky Brandon didn't attack you. You know how much of a manslut he is."

I snorted a bit too loudly before I burst into a fit of chuckles. Nichole followed after me. Leo was being serious, but what he said was just hilarious.

"Hi, I'm awake." Brandon mumbled. He was still lying on his bed, his tone dripping with annoyance. Thankfully he was wearing a shirt now, Leo helped him take off his jeans earlier.

I secretly took a photo of that precious scene. I will never live this one down.

Leo shot him a look. "Stop feigning sickness. You planned this, didn't you?"

I snorted. Leo was acting like my dad right now. Better than my dad actually, because my dad was a lying bastard.

"I'm not!" Brandon whined, sitting up - barely. "I'm really sick!"

"Sure you are," Leo said, not at all convinced.

"Whatever man. I told you I'm sick. We joined a burger-eating contest earlier, and the last round had jalapeños on them." He shuddered from the memory, the color on his face drained.

Leo looked at me and silently asked for my confirmation; I nodded. The judgemental look on his face slowly softened into a concerned one. He sighed before running his hand over his face. He was such a drama queen sometimes."You okay?"

Brandon groaned quietly. "I threw up most of what I ate. And the burning sensation on my tongue is gone too. I just wanna take a nap."

Leo shook his head like he understood why. I didn't get it. All this, after just a few spicy burgers? Why was his body reacting like this? It makes no sense at all.

"Well, get some rest now. We'll be outside," Nichole said as she made her way out the door, pulling my arm so we'd go together. I glanced over my shoulder and saw Leo quietly talking with Brandon.

I'm so curious. So curious.

I sat comfortably on Leo's sofa. His room was a lot like Brandon's, only messier. I had a hard time finding the sofa since it was concealed by a pile of clothes and some unidentified objects.

We've been hanging out here for two or three hours already. I'm dying of boredom.

Nichole cleaned up parts of the mess; Leo didn't seem to care. I glared at him, hoping he'd notice. Why the hell does he keep his room messy if Nichole occasionally comes to visit?

"I don't get it," Nichole broke the silence among us. "Why's Brandon so weak against spices? I get that he isn't fond of them. But isn't he just exaggerating to get Mira's attention?"

My brows rose immediately. "How'd you come up with that conclusion?"

Nichole shot me a look, as if she knew I was playing innocent. I wasn't. I didn't understand at all so she shrugged it off and waved an airy hand. "It's so obvious that he likes you."

My mind was convincing the whole of me that that wasn't true, but my heart was a badass rebel. It punched my cage a bit too hard that the impact affected my throat and caused me to swallow hard.

I love it when I talk nonsensical science in my head.

"Nichole," I said calmly, ignoring the weird sensation I'm currently feeling. "We made a deal, remember? Whoever likes the other first, loses. If he already liked me then he would've lost and stopped already."

I repeated that inside my head and nodded, agreeing with myself. That was a fact.

Nichole groaned loudly as she threw Leo's stuff in a basket under the table. Leo let out a short, high-pitched cry when he saw how his girlfriend forcefully pressed her hand against all his things inside the basket, stuffing it all in an unorganized fashion to save space.

I assume he had something precious in there and she probably murdered it already, but he didn't have the heart to tell that to her.

"I never knew you were this dense. God," she sighed in exasperation.

I released a heavy breath. I hated it when I'm being criticized, especially if the one doing it is my best friend. But I didn't talk back. She might be right. I'm in the middle of confusion myself.

Maybe what she said was true. Maybe Brandon really did like me. Maybe he just used this game as an excuse to get close to me. Maybe. Maybe.

Maybe I'm out of my mind for considering those possibilities.

Maybe I'll get hurt in the end.

"About his condition," Leo intervened, probably sensing where our conversation was going. Good Leo. "You know those things associated with trauma?"

We didn't know where he was going with this but we gestured for him to continue.

Leo nonchalantly grabbed his basket of stuff under his desk and checked if his things were still intact after its unintentional assassination by Nichole. "Something happened to him when he was a kid that involved chili, so every time he eats anything spicy, he gets weak or something."

I was slowly sinking in that new piece information in my brain.

Trauma?

"What happened to him when he was a kid?" Nichole asked.

Leo shrugged his shoulders. "I don't know. He never told me about that, and he looked uncomfortable with the subject so I stopped asking about that a long time ago."

Nichole and I quietly nodded our heads. I didn't know what to think. His weird condition. Was it serious? Was it even considered a condition? I don't know.

As I thought. He really is weird.

"Oh yeah," Leo exclaimed, looking like he just remembered something. He rummaged his bag for something then held out a DVD in front of us. "We were about to show this to Brandon earlier before we walked into your guys fun."

I sent him a hard glare but he just swatted it off. Bitch.

"I want to watch this new horror movie with him and make fun of him when he cries at all the gory scenes." He proudly announced.

I didn't resist an eye roll. Leo was such a kid. Nichole scoffed right beside him. "Like you're any braver."

He put an arm around her shoulder and smiled wryly at her. "Baby, I'll show you how much I've changed after watching Insidious with you." And then he leaned closer to her face. She didn't look affected in the slightest. In fact, she looked annoyed. Hah. "You'll be the one clinging to me this time."

"Right." She said, uninterested. She took Leo's hand off her shoulder and stared at me, motioning her head to the door. "Since we're all here, let's watch it together. Mira, go get Brandon."

What? No no no.

"But he's still resting!" Leo complained before I got to say no. Go tell her Leo!

"It's been three hours. He's rested enough. Now go get the manslut."

Leo and I exchanged close-to-crying-faces. Me, because I was too awkward to see him again because of what happened earlier and of what Nichole made me think of him, and Leo, because of his concern for Brandon, maybe.

Nichole was a sweet girl. But she can be pretty demanding at times. And since she's our best friend, we can't say no to her. The same goes for her towards us.

I grudgingly got up from my seat and went to get him. The sooner I get this task done, the better for my health.

"Are you sure you don't want to sit this one out?" Leo said, sounding partly concerned, partly smug. "Want me to give you a handicap?"

Brandon raised his brow at his stupid roommate. "Is that an insult?" He was better now, thankfully, but I couldn't tear my eyes off his bed-hair. It was tousled softly and generous dark-brown strands flowed down to his forehead, framing it gorgeously.

My potato was offensively attractive right now.

He didn't seem to notice me enjoying the wonderful view he was providing me with, and continued measuring dicks with Leo. "I'm game bro. But if you scream before any of us, you owe me lunch for a week."

Leo opened his mouth to retort but after subtly thinking about it, he agreed. Not a good move Leo. "Fine. But if you scream first, I own your car for a week."

It was a great loss for both parties, but since both parties were airheads, they came into agreement. Nichole and I exchanged sighs.

I tugged Brandon's sleeve and felt my breath get caught in my throat when he looked at me. What was wrong with me lately? My period is messing with my head. "Are you sure you're okay now?"

He sent me a warm smile, his eyes narrowed softly. Ohh man. His eyes were so pretty. "Yeah."

Nichole jumped at my side and hugged my arm. She looked so excited. "The movie's called Ouija. I saw the trailer. I can't wait to see it!"

"Is it that good?" I replied with the same enthusiasm. Nichole and I shared the same love for horror movies, which was a major disadvantage for the boys we were with right now.

We were given strange looks. We were used to that now so it didn't bother us anymore. It should be us giving them the weird looks because we had bigger balls than them.

Leo had a smug grin on his face when he led us to their living room where their flat screen was. I turned off some of the lights to set the mood and Nichole went to get some snacks.

"Dude, I can't wait to hear you cry and scream. You'll be begging me to turn the lights on." Leo smirked.

My expression mirrored Brandon's; a look of disgust. Why is my best friend such an idiot? He quickly recovered. His previous expression was replaced with a smirk. "Dude, I never knew you wanted me this bad."

Oh man.

Cue in maniacal laugh here.

"See, I told you he was gay," I whispered loud enough for them to hear. Nichole, who was making herself comfortable on the couch, laughed and set the snacks on the coffee table.

Leo, slow as he'll ever be, realized what he just said and complained. "No! You know that's not what I - ugh! Never mind. Let's just watch the movie."

Aw, our little Leo gave up just like that? I was expecting he'd put up more fight, but oh well. Maybe he's still mentally preparing himself for the movie.

He and Nichole sat on the couch while I settled on the floor. I didn't want to disturb whatever it was they'll do during the movie. Last time I went with them to the movies, they snuggled and flirted the wholoe time. And they started playfully biting each other's fingers too.

I had fun with my popcorn, though. My popcorn loved me.

Anyway, I didn't want to experience that again. As much as I love my best friends, it was still weird seeing them doing those things. It was like watching your siblings flirting. Oh. Ew. Forget I said that.

Please tell me I didn't just ruin their image.

Brandon probably felt the same, so he decided to sit beside me on the floor. Too close beside me.

He silently snorted before he stared at me, engaging himself in a quiet conversation with me about our best friend's stupidity. Leo was stupid. But we love him.

It was slightly dim, and I don't get why that weird sensation I felt from earlier enhanced dramatically. Dim, but I could see him clearly.

That look on his face. That playful grin. That damn mouth.

The conclusion was simple.

Brandon = Dangerous.

"Stop flirting with my best friend you asshole," Leo said but bitterly. I held back a blush. Shit. I blush? He was just looking at me. How can Leo confuse that with flirting? "Play the movie already."

Brandon gave me a last smile before he glared at Leo but did as told anyway. The movie started, but I couldn't concentrate. He sat too close for my liking and I could feel his body heat radiating from his skin. I was too conscious.

Snap out of it Mira.

Okay, so at horror movies, usually the girl clings to the guy out of utter fear then the guy releases all his cool moves to get himself points, so he does everything he can to comfort the girl, right? What do guys usually do? I'll tell you the stereotypical facts.

Cliche #1 - He'll hold your hand.

In our case, it was Brandon and Leo who ended up holding hands. We were at the part where the kid with stitches on her mouth showed up. I criticized the lack of creativity with the make-up while Nichole complained why there weren't enough exciting soundtracks to fit the scene.

Of course, the boys had to play it cool, so they nonchalantly let go of each other's hands. I don't get it though. I was right beside Brandon, and Leo was beside Nichole. Why they chose each other instead of us was a question neither of us could answer.

Cliche #2 - He'll embrace you; make you feel safe.

Nichole probably wanted to snuggle with Leo like they usually did, but he just kept jumping at all the surprising scenes. Nichole gave up and sat down with me on the floor, deciding that I was more fun a companion than Leo in watching this kind of movie.

Brandon saw his chance and climbed up the sofa, sitting right next to Leo. Another surprising scene flashed from the TV screen, and unconsciously, the two boys were wrapped up in each other's arms. Adorable little ugly pansies.

Cliche #3 - He'll tell you 'don't be afraid'.

"This is just a movie," Leo chanted, thinking we couldn't hear. "This is just a movie. It's not real."

Well, they were pretty much in the middle of convincing their selves not to be afraid.

"It can happen in real life," I reminded. I mean, I've read about this things. Spirit boards, which was what the movie was all about, aren't to be played with. Leo was silent for a bit. Brandon made up his own chant in his best friend's silence.

"It's just make-up, effects and really good actors. It's just make-up, effects - shit." Nichole and I tried hard not to laugh. This was ridiculous. How could they be so afraid of this movie? It wasn't even that scary.

I released my legs from my cross position and hugged my knees to my chest, burying my chin on my knees on the process. My eyes were glued to the screen. We were finally at the climax.

"We're not playing that board game, but we're watching them doing it on-screen, so doesn't that mean the same thing? Will we get cursed too?" I heard Leo ask Brandon. He wasn't even being sarcastic. He was serious. "What if this movie's like that one film where an Asian chick with really long hair climbs out of the screen? Fuck, why did I even choose this movie?"

I concealed a snort. I can't take this anymore.

Remembering their deal, I thought of a great idea. Both of them got scared, yes, but none of them yelled just yet. I will not be satisfied with my night if none of them screams. So I told Nichole what I had in mind.

I said it low enough so they wouldn't hear. My best friend laughed and agreed quickly. We had one mind when it comes to things like this.

When the movie was nearing it's end, Nichole and I quietly crawled on the floor behind the chair. The boys were so deeply engrossed in the movie that they didn't notice us at all.

We slowly stood up, leaning close enough to each boy's ear so they could hear us clearly, but far enough so they won't know what's coming.

The last part came where the girl looked through the glass. Nichole and I took this as our cue and whispered with hoarse and scary-like voices to the boys - "Hi friend."

It was like the tagline of the whole movie. As soon as we delivered the sentence, both boys jumped from the couch and released high-pitched screams with all their might.

Before they noticed who had done it, they both ran to Leo's room and slammed it close. Nichole and I roared in laughter, our eyes pooling with tears.

I can't believe those boys were such wimps. It took them at least ten minutes before they realized who had done it. I assume they thought we were caught by the ghosts, not that we were the so-called ghosts ourselves.

They were mad, yeah, but it was worth it. And they didn't say a single thing about the bet. They both screamed at the same time.

Two grown men afraid of horror films. This was precious. Precious blackmail.

Brandon couldn't even look at me. He was probably embarrassed with what they had just done. They just completely proved their unmanliness to us tonight.

And I'm sure tomorrow, they're either gonna do their best to make up for it, or they're going to plot revenge against us.

Either way though, they'll lose.

I smiled quietly to myself. I can't wait to see what my unmanly potato will do.

Chapter 11

Nichole and I drove to school using Brandon's car today. I was the one driving and Nichole was riding shotgun.

How did we get his car? Simple.

Since both of them lost the bet last night, Nichole and I took custody of their rewards. I got Brandon's car, and Nichole got free lunch for a week from Leo.

"This is why we're awesome," I said as I drove our way to school. The boys were sitting at the back, quiet as ever. I don't know if they were sulking or praying for their lives. I was a good driver.

In my own way.

"They can never say no to us," Nichole smugly added. I laughed. It was true. When we insisted that we deserved the rewards since they both screamed at the same time - thus a tie - they strongly disagreed. But when I showed them the picture I secretly took when Leo was changing Brandon's jeans, they gave in.

I knew this precious picture would come in handy.

When we arrived at school, Brandon opened his hand at me, probably asking for the keys. I smiled sweetly at him before shoving it in my pockets. "This is mine for a week. I'll return it then."

His face paled. Leo and Nichole already went ahead - Leo was still on the process of convincing his girlfriend that he'd pay for just half the price of the lunch, not the whole thing. He was such a cheap bastard as always.

As we made our way to our lockers, we bumped into a certain person. And when I say bumped, I meant I headbutted the other person with maximum force.

I can proudly say my head was harder than his chest.

And guess who it was?

I was still rubbing my forehead (it didn't hurt. I just did it for effect) when I noticed who the person standing in front of me was. He had a blank expression on his face. Speechless, I think. I gave him my best grin upon waving my hand.

"Samuel! I see your injuries are healed now," I noted. The black eye I gave him weeks ago already faded away, and his face was good as normal.

Brandon stepped forward, studying the boy. Realization hit him and then he gave him a friendly pat on the shoulder. "You're Samuel Ink, one of her many poor victims. I sympathize with you."

I stepped on his foot with my heel, causing him to wince and utter a short yelp, before I glanced at Samuel, expecting at least a reply from him.

I may sound ridiculous but I don't hold grudges. I want to make peace with my victims after every (one-sided) fight.

"Yeah, I'm alright now," he said. I almost sighed in relief when I noticed his tone had no hint of sarcasm, hatred or fear. It was normal. As if I didn't just beat him up before.

"Good." I said, taking his hand and shaking it. "We'll be friends now right? But if you bother Nichole again - "

"It was a misunderstanding," he interrupted. I blinked at him. He slowly took his hand back and slid it inside the pocket of his jacket. He looked down as he continued. "I didn't mean to hurt her. It's all just a misunderstanding. I'm sorry."

I raised a brow. Now I was curious.

"Then what really happened?"

It took him half a minute to reply. And his reply was a sigh. Well, way to arouse our suspicion.

He shook his head before he stared at me for a few seconds. I just noticed how green his eyes were. They were like emeralds. "Sorry. See ya."

And then he left us hanging, just like that. He disappeared into the crowd of students and Brandon and I just stared at each other.

"He's..." He said unsurely. "Nicer than I thought."

"Yeah..." I replied, quite unsurely myself. What's his deal? Why'd he look so uncomfortable talking to me?

On second thought, don't answer that.

The bell rang and it was time to go to my first period class. Brandon had a different class, so this was where we part ways.

"Take care of my baby's pacifier," he said. It took me a moment to get what he meant.

He meant the damn keys to his car.

I rolled my eyes. "Whatever. See you at lunch."

Seriously. Guys and their cars. And car keys. Seriously. Dude.

Afternoon classes were cancelled because of a faculty meeting. For us students, it was a matter to be celebrated with.

But this time, I decided to go home. Leo and Nichole were going out anyway, and I'm sure they wanted to be alone.

On my way to Brandon's car (my car, for the time being), I saw Samuel walking my way. He didn't notice me yet, and I wanted to talk to him about earlier before he tries to escape again.

As soon as he was about a few feet away from where I was standing, I walked up to him and blocked his path. When his eyes lit up with recognition, he halted in his steps and attempted to nonchalantly walk the other way, but I grabbed his shirt.

"Hey," I said, slowly pulling him so he'd give me his attention. He was looking at everywhere but me. Was he afraid of me after all? "I need to talk to you."

His eyes finally met mine. I didn't know how to read his expression. It was either fear, awe, disbelief or amazement - I don't know.

He didn't hold his gaze any longer. I think he was looking at my nose, not my eyes. And he looked so uncomfortable.

I let go of his shirt and crossed my arms against my chest. "This'll be quick I promise. You can go after you tell me what I want to know."

He quietly nodded, still focusing his attention on my nose. Okay, so I was getting uncomfortable too. What if he was looking for blackheads and stuff?

I cleared my throat and decided to just get this over with. We were blocking the hallways just standing there. "What did you mean when you said it was just a misunderstanding? What did I misunderstand?"

He lowered his head. His hand shot up to the back of his head and he began scratching it in a rather impatient matter. Typical behavior when someone gets irritated.

"Trust me," he said, finally. The seriousness in his tone made me take a step back. Whoa. "You don't need to know. It doesn't matter."

I stepped forward again, openly showing him I wasn't intimidated, even if I was for a bit. "If it concerns my best friend, of course it matters. What you did to her a few weeks ago - if you say that was just a misunderstanding, then please, enlighten me."

He held his gaze longer this time, a hard yet dull gaze. "The reason isn't important. Just tell her I'm sorry for her wrists."

"No," I pressed. I hated it when people apologize indirectly. It was so insincere. "You want to say sorry, tell it to her, not to me."

"Fine." He deadpanned. Something in his expression told me that he really did want to apologize to Nichole, which relieved me a bit, but I was still suspicious.

That probably marked the end of our conversation. I didn't press any further. It was between her and Nichole now.

He retreated as soon as he noticed Brandon approaching. I didn't stop him this time. My gaze followed him until he disappeared into the crowd of students.

"What's up?" Brandon asked, glancing at Samuel's back before looking at me. I shrugged my shoulders.

"Nothing. Hey, I'm going home now. I'm taking your car. Have fun walking back to your apartment!"

Before I could sprint towards the parking lot, he grabbed me by the elbow. "Stop."

"What?" I whined. He raised his brows at me before his lips curled up into a grin.

"Let's hang out at your place."

I coughed voluntarily at the suggestion. "But why? I have nothing there to entertain you."

"You're there." He smiled. I scoffed.

"Wanna watch another movie?" I gave him a challenging yet teasing smirk. His smile vanished from his face.

He pinched my cheek roughly, causing me to squirm and release an unlady-like yell. After I yanked his fingers away from my swollen cheek, I glared at him.

"We'll figure out what to do when we get there. Now c'mon." Without warning, he grabbed me by the waist and dragged me to his car. "You're driving, as you wish."

Damn it potato.

Brandon was making himself comfortable in my bed. Not the way you're probably hoping though. He had already claimed ownership of most of my pillows, including my blanket and stuffed animals.

I was sitting on the other side of the bed, well, awkwardly. It was a bit chilly today and our heater was broken. And Brandon had my blanket.

He sensed my intense stare, burning he back of his head despite the coolness of the room. He glanced at me and smiled innocently. "Wanna snuggle?"

My face lit up with sarcastic amusement. "Taking advantage of the situation, now aren't we?"

He smirked. "C'mon Mira, it's cozy. You know you want to do it."

I didn't allow the heat to travel up my cheeks. I mean, I'm not sure. I tried. Maybe it worked though.

Without another word, I kicked my shoes off and went under the blanket with Brandon right beside me. He shifted closer to my side and wrapped his arm around my shoulder.

It felt so warm and comfortable.

"See?" He said slowly. I could feel his breath fan my forehead as he spoke. "I told you it was cozy."

I playfully smacked his chest.

He hugged me.

"Too close," I mumbled. "Stop violating the rules."

His chest vibrated when he laughed, and it felt so foreign, but nice. "Violating the rules, or violating you?"

I smacked him again, and he hugged me tighter.

"If someone's doing the violating, it's going to be me." I said. Why the heck did I just say something so wrong?

My competitive nature always gets me in trouble.

He looked amused by my reply. "I knew you'd say that. That's just so like you."

He meant it in a good way, perhaps. An idea struck my mind, and I was determined to do it to get things in my favor once again.

I looked up at him and saw that he was already staring at me. Gulp. No, no, don't get distracted. I sent him my most mischievous smile ever and attacked his neck.

Yup, you heard me damn right. I attacked his neck.

I trailed butterfly kisses on his nape up to his jaw, then down again. His sharp intake of breath gave me the sign that I was doing something right.

"Stop that," he breathed, but his tone told me he didn't mean it.

I remembered what he did to me when we first met. And I decided to do the exact same thing to him.

I found a specific spot on his neck that I liked, so I settled there and pressed my lips harder against his skin. He smelled nice.

Judging by his expression, I was clearly winning. Ha!

His hand shot up to my head and weakly pushed me away. It didn't work. He didn't want me to stop. And I didn't want to stop either.

My hand travelled up to his warm chest and I pressed my leg on his thigh. I felt him shiver under the blanket we were both in and I was very pleased.

He was so weak against this.

I stopped what I was doing and proudly looked at the mark I just left on the side of his neck. But I wasn't done yet. I continued trailing kisses on his jaw. I always wanted to kiss this strong jaw of his. He was breathing heavily, and since my hand was on his chest, I felt how fast his heart beat inside it.

I just realized my heart was doing the same thing.

"Stop. Mira, stop," he said. I didn't. "Mira, if you don't cut that out I'll - "

I cut his sentence short when I took my head off his neck and pecked his lips. He was petrified on the spot.

When did I become so bold?

To seal off my win, I gave him a smug grin as I brushed my thumb across the mark I made on his neck. "See? Told you I'd be the one doing the violating."

That wasn't something to be proud of. At all. Scratch that. I just had the wrong choice of words.

The surprised look on his face quickly changed into something more serious, more dangerous. His eyes narrowed at my lips as his hands cupped both my cheeks.

I felt alarmed. Was he going to kiss me?

Now that I think of it, I initiated my first kiss with him. Now he looks mad. Oh shit.

Before I could pull away, he crushed his lips on mine, not giving me the slightest chance to retreat. I gasped when he brushed his fingers on the nape of my neck - I was cursed with having a ticklish spot there - when my lips parted for justba bit, he saw his chance and went deep.

Everything in my mind went blank. All I could think about was this.

Brandon was kissing me.

And I was kissing him back.

I didn't realize we were already pressed against each other until I felt our heartbeats in sync. My hands got buried on his soft, brown hair and unconsciously, I was pulling his face closer, in need of more contact.

I didn't know if I was doing something right since it was the first time I was doing this with someone, but it felt so natural. And this someone just happened to be Brandon.

He released his hand from my cheek and pulled the blanket up to cover us both.

The excitement that was boiling up in my system was unexplainable. And unreal.

He tilted his head to a certain angle to get better access and I shivered at how nice it felt. He tasted like mint. I was suddenly conscious of my own breath.

I bet I tasted like chocolate since I just ate a bar of Snickers on the way here.

I tried copying what he was doing so I wouldn't look like a lost idiot. I tilted my head to the opposite angle. Was I doing this right?

He sighed in between kisses so I guess I was doing it right. When he started sucking on my lower lip, I grabbed a fistful of his hair and stopped myself from releasing unnecessary noises.

His mouth had found its way down my neck. I panicked, knowing what he'll do. He breathed in my scent before trailing kisses on my tingling skin. I managed to pull him back up and kiss him again. Our lips were in sync.

I tried saying his name but since his mouth was pressed against mine, it came out as an incoherent mumble.

How long were we doing this? Why were we doing this? Mira!

I quickly withdrew from his lips. It felt so cold all of a sudden, but I needed to control myself. What the hell just happened?

I just made out with Brandon.

His expression mirrored mine. A mixture of surprise and realization. Don't even get me started at how our hairstyles were like now.

We were both out of breath, but we just kept staring at each other, wondering if that really happened.

"Ten minutes," I breathed. He looked confused for a second until I continued. "We can't kiss for more than ten minutes a day."

He opened his mouth as if he just remembered. And then a pout crossed his face as he looked back at me. "Was that ten minutes already?"

Nope. But I was afraid of what would happen if we continued so I stopped it.

I shrugged my shoulders, avoiding eye-contact. I feel so embarrassed. This is so awkward. We were still under the blanket as if we were playing hide and seek. Only, both of us were hiding.

He chuckled slowly before flicking my forehead.

"What was that for?!" I complained.

"You made me do something weird to you. That's your penalty."

I bit my lip to stop myself from talking back. He was right. I started this. I was so stupid. What had gotten in to me?

And why wasn't I regretting it one bit?

He held his neck for a while and looked at me quite smugly. "You left a mark didn't you?"

I tried my best to sound human. "Yeah. Payback for what you did last time."

His reaction was not what I was hoping for. "You can be so dense at times my potato babe."

I buried my flustered face on his chest. We were still lying close next to each other so it was alright. He began caressing my hair. It was so in warm here. I had no idea why I felt so comfortable, relaxed.

I know I lost. But why did I feel like I won?

Chapter 12

Leo and Nichole were creepy today.

More than creepy, actually. They matched the expressions of those confined in mental institutes - those wide open eyes seeming as if they just saw something new to play with, those even wider grins that'd beat a Cheshire cat's any day, and those maniacal laughs serial killers make before they slaughter their next victim.

Stop for a moment and imagine their faces, please. It's horrible. Horrible.

But the thing worse than the looks on their faces was the information they managed to get.

Hint: Brandon's neck.

It didn't take a genius to figure out what had happened to it. The mark on his skin was obviously not just an insect bite. And it was also clear who had done it.

"Miraa," Leo sang my name as Nichole teasingly combed my hair with her fingers. This was so scary. They were so scary.

I'm admitting it. So that's saying something.

"Yeah?" I stifled a gulp. Leo snickered before joining his girlfriend play with my hair.

"Brandon was glowing yesterday. What'd you guys do?" He already knew the answer to that. He just wanted to make fun of me. This brat.

"Wouldn't you like to know," I mumbled. Then I swatted their hands off my hair. Nichole giggled.

"Did you violate any rules now?"

I shook my head casually, trying my best to act natural. I hated it when people see me get flustered. "No. It didn't last for more than ten minutes."

"What didn't last, Mira?" Leo asked again, this time, his tone was in a sing-song voice and I held back to urge to slap him.

"The session." I simply said.

The stupid couple also known as my best friends gave each other knowing grins before they sent me looks of approval.

"Good job." They chorused, both giving me a thumbs up.

I honestly think I did a pretty bad job.

"Would you guys cut it out?" I told them, my words sounded like a long groan. "We were just messing around. You know it's because of the game. If it weren't for the game, I wouldn't have made any moves."

It was natural for me to say something like that, but when I did, I felt like I've been pricked in the chest. Weird body.

"Of course," Nichole said, not serious at all. She knew. She knew I was just saving face. She was my best friend, of course she knew.

Leo poked my cheek. "You know it's not about the game anymore. You like him, don't you?"

"What?" I can't believe he just said that. "No. Leo no. I'm serious in this game. You know me."

"Yeah, I do know you," he replied. "And I know Brandon too. I know you two like each other and you're just making the game an excuse. What I don't know is why you're even making an excuse."

I shook my head frantically. He was wrong. He was just so wrong. I didn't like Brandon. I was attracted to his looks, yeah, and he was kinda sweet at times, but that doesn't mean I liked him.

"You watch way too many dramas with Nichole," I said. "Leo, I don't like him, and he doesn't like me in that way. We're just playing."

I'm right. I should be right. Right?

Leo didn't look convinced. "Why waste so much time in this game if it'll lead nowhere?"

I was silent. How did a playful conversation turn so serious? Was this even serious? Or was I the only one thinking of it this way?

Nichole held Leo's arm, as if telling him to stop talking. My silence just proved how right he was. The game was just an excuse.

But an excuse for what? Call me the densest person in the world but I don't even know my own feelings. Do I like him? I don't think so. Maybe? A little bit? A little bit too much? But isn't that just impossible? No. I have to make sure before I call it quits.

But even if I did like him, I'd rather die than tell him. Not unless he tells me first.

My pride is queen.

I was just about to look for Brandon when I saw no other than Samuel Ink walking towards our table. He wasn't looking at me. Rather, his eyes were focused on Nichole.

Out of instinct, I stepped forward, semi-blocking Nichole from his view. I held her wrist protectively, and it seems like Leo had the same thoughts as me because he did the same.

"I'm not looking for trouble," Samuel spoke defensively, looking at Leo, and then at me. "I just want to apologize to her."

I know I shouldn't trust him after what he did, but somehow I believed his words. I must be going crazy. I glanced at Leo and he nodded.

"Let's talk. The three of us," Leo said, sounding more serious than the usual idiot I hung out with.

Samuel nodded stiffly as he followed them somewhere. Nichole sent me a meaningful glance, telling me they were gonna be right back, and it was okay so don't worry.

I smiled, feeling reassured. Leo was there. And Sam didn't seem like a really bad person. It's up to them now. I'm stepping out. It's none of my business anymore.

"Remind me again why I'm here," I asked as Brandon set the tray of snacks on his bed. I was currently sprawled on the floor, waiting for him to feed me.

He took a potato chip from the tray before he sat down beside me. He was about to take a bite from it, but when he saw my expression, he smirked and gave it to me. Fed it to me, to be more exact.

"Because," he explained, grabbing the tray from the bed and placing it in front of us so we could get better access to those heavenly potato chips. "Leo and Nichole are at your apartment. Talking. It makes sense that we stay here while they're there."

"But what are they talking about that they can't even share it with us? I'm so curious. And it's so suspicious." I pointed a finger at my open mouth. Brandon understood so he took another potato chip and fed me again.

I'm so spoiled.

"Maybe it's about their relationship?" He suggested. I gasped.

"Do you think they're breaking up?!"

He shook his head frantically. "No! That's not what I'm saying. Leo and Nichole break up? Impossible."

I sighed in relief after my exaggerated outburst. "Right."

I really want to know what Samuel told them. How did he apologize? Did he explain to them what he couldn't explain to me? More importantly, did they forgive him?

I know I said it's none of my business anymore but I'm just so curious.

Baah.

A few minutes passed, and we were just there quietly eating potato chips, staring at his ugly wall too.

Not that I was complaining about the potato chips. They were awesome.

"Wanna play a game?" Brandon suggested out of the blue. I nodded, thinking it was a good idea to pass time and boredom. "You know twenty questions?"

I nodded again. It's a simple game where he asks and I answer, then I ask and he answers. It sounds like a normal conversation, but the questions are usually not that friendly, you know, to spice things up.

Knowing Brandon, his questions will be unsurprisingly ridiculous.

"You start." I said. He shot me a wry smile. I knew that look. That look did not mean he was going to ask decent questions.

"Do you have any siblings?"

I looked at him weirdly. So he started with a normal question.

I still don't trust this guy.

"No, I'm an only child. Do you have any friends aside from Leo and us?"

This time, he gave me a weird look, as if he couldn't believe I even asked that

"Of course I do. I hang out with a lot of people, but you, Leo and Nichole are my best friends, so that's why I'm with you guys now."

Wow. Did he just call me his best friend? Why do I feel so happy all of a sudden?

"My turn," he said after I approved of his reply. "Have you ever liked a girl before?"

My mouth hung open. And then I smacked him on the shoulder. He was trying to control his chuckles. "Stupid question Brandon. Just because I'm manlier than you and Leo doesn't mean I'm actually a man. And the obvious answer to your question is no."

I was holding my glare at him, but since he was shaking in laughter, I couldn't help but stifle my own. Laughing was traitorously contagious.

"Shut up. Have you ever looked at Leo in a different way? Like, not in a bro kind of way. But in a 'oh my gosh he's so cute and I'm living with him, EEP!' kind of way?"

"Nope," he replied coolly. Damn it. He probably knew I was going to ask that so he was prepared. "How was your first kiss?"

I hid a blush. He didn't know he was my first kiss. I hope he doesn't ask. Please, please don't ask.

I sent him a confident smile. "Nice. Not very appropriate for a first kiss, but nice. What about you? How was your first kiss?"

He smiled as well. "Awesome. The girl initiated it though."

My eyes widened in surprise. Do girls always initiate the kiss with him? Because I did. Now I feel so stupid.

"When was your first kiss?" He asked.

Bam. Do I really need to answer that? Ugh. Can't I just lie? Why can't I lie?

I stalled by studying his room before I replied, looking at him in the eyes. At least he won't think I'm flustered if I look at him in the eyes. "Yesterday."

The grin on his face vanished as soon as I delivered my reply. Why was he so surprised? Why am I so honest?

"R-Really?"

"Yup." I said quickly. "My turn. Who was your first kiss?"

I don't get him. Why was he getting flustered? I was the one who was supposed to be flustered. Not that I wanted to be, but it's just weird. I'm practically just repeating his questions in a different fashion.

I looked at him expectantly. He was fiddling with the potato chip on his palm. Poor chip. Why was he so nervous? Now I was curious to know who his first kiss really was.

I know I won't be surprised if he said it was Leo.

"Umm," he mumbled weakly, stalling by studying his room as well. This is so fun. I am enjoying every second of this - watching him get flustered, I mean. "You."

"You?" I dumbly asked, still smirking. And then I realized what he just said. "Wait. You? Me? You mean me?"

"Yeah," he chuckled softly. "We were each other's first kiss. Isn't that just peachy?"

I was stunned. How was I supposed to reply to that?! This is... Is this embarrassing? I don't know. What am I feeling? My chest feels like it's going to explode.

"I... How many questions was that now?" I tried to dodge the topic. Oh my God. Really?

"Don't know. I wasn't counting," he smiled. Shit. Don't smile at me. "So, if I'm your first kiss, I was your first... Uh... Hickey? I mean, the first one to give you a hickey?"

I stiffly nodded. I look so lame right now.

Those were very inappropriate first kisses in my opinion.

"Oh," he mumbled. "No wonder you were so mad at that time. Well... Um... I'm sorry."

"Then I gave you your first hickey too?" I returned his question. This is kinda getting awkward. And is it just me, or is the room getting warmer?

I saw the red travel up his neck to his ears. He nodded. "Yeah."

"Okay, next question." I said.

Change the subject. Change the subject.

"How much do you like potatoes?"

My questions are so awesome.

He snorted. "As much as I like cheese."

"Cheese?" I gasped, temporarily forgetting about that awkward moment just now. Cheese. Mmm. Cheese. "Marry me."

He burst into a fit of chuckles. I don't know, but I liked the way he laughed. It was just so boyish, but his voice was deep and manly at the same time.

"I thought I'd be the one asking that question someday but of course, you had to beat me to it." And then he continued laughing.

I bit my lip. Did he even know what he just said? Did he know how I'd interpret what he just said? Did he know he was a stupid idiot for making me take this a bit too seriously?

Don't say things you don't mean, damn it.

I hate over thinking.

"Okay," he said, calming down from his laughter now. I don't get why he laughed so much. Was it that funny? Was it that much of a joke to him? "My turn. Are you a mommy's girl or a daddy's girl?"

I stopped in my thoughts. He looked at me patiently, waiting for my answer. He had no idea at all how that question stung an old wound in my chest.

Ah.

But since getting sentimental and crying and being gay is not my style, I just answered bluntly, like the usual.

"None. I love my mom. My dad's dead."

It took him a few seconds to make a reaction. A guilty one.

"Oh. Sorry, I didn't know."

I gave him a small smile before I rolled my eyes and clarified my previous statement. "My dad's not actually dead. But he's dead to me."

He looked confused for a moment. He just stared at me, probably debating whether to ask what I just meant or not. He chose not to.

The air got heavy and I despised that feeling, so I continued the game. It was my turn to ask. "What about you? Momma's boy or daddy's boy?"

His face lit up before he got to answer. I was guessing he was really fond of his family. Which reminds me of a question I've been meaning to ask him.

He formed a grin on his face and folded his arms against his chest. He looked so proud. "Both. I'm spoiled by my mom, and my dad's my best friend."

I couldn't help but smile warmly at his reply. "Such a good boy."

"Yeah," the glint in his eyes faded for a bit - just a little bit. It was barely noticeable, but I saw it. Er, saw something, if that makes any sense. "Even if they're not my real parents. I love them to death."

There. A huge bomb just blew up in my mind when he said that. My curiosity got ahead of my tact, so I asked.

"You're adopted?"

He nodded slowly, not taking his eyes off me, as if to see what my reaction would be. I didn't flinch or anything if that's what he was expecting. "Yeah. Did that make you like me less?"

My heart clenched and I unintentionally shot him a glare. How could he say that? "Adopted or not, you're still Brandon. That doesn't change anything. And it's not even a big deal. Were you worried about that?"

He laughed softly. Thank God it didn't sound forced. It came out naturally, as if he was relieved. So what if he was adopted? He's still a human being. "Kind of. I was bullied because of that before."

Bullied?

Just because he was adopted, it became a good enough reason to bully him? I unconsciously felt my fists clench and anger boil inside my chest. I don't understand why I feel mad for him.

He chuckled lightly. "I wanted to apologize to those kids who bullied me. But I never got the chance to."

I looked at him strangely, my mouth was slightly open. Did I hear him right? He wants to apologize to those bullies? He didn't mean the other way around?

"What do you mean?" I asked, raising a brow.

He shook his head and laughed. It wasn't his usual laugh. It sounded like a bitter release of frustration concealed in a laugh. I knew. Because I did that a lot in the past. Sometimes even now.

He stretched his arms behind his back. I knew he was just avoiding the question. I don't know anything about him at all.

I don't know why I feel sort of... rejected.

What. No! No. If there's someone doing the rejecting it's me.

Sigh.

My pride is such a bitchy queen.

"I don't know how many questions we're at now," Brandon said. "But I'll keep on asking. Okay?"

"Okay," I mumbled. I wasn't satisfied with the lack of details he was providing me with, but I guess he doesn't trust me enough to tell me. Or he's just uncomfortable with the subject. I don't know, but I'll drop it.

He sent me a mischievous grin, a look full of confidence. I think I know where this was going. I gave him a warning glare in reply.

"Did you like my kisses?" He asked.

I gaped at him. His grin widened when he saw my reaction. I felt my heart do a big flip and my breath hitched traitorously in my throat. Just when things were getting a bit personal, he just had to ask that.

This jerk wants me to get flustered again.

Of course, it wouldn't be Brandon if he didn't say something like that sooner or later. Okay Mira, do your thing.

I forced the corner of my lips to curl up, though I doubt it ended up looking like an irritated twitch or something, but whatever.

"Maybe."

He leaned in a bit, his grin growing wider, more playful. "Maybe, huh."

My gaze narrowed and got fixated on his neck. What have I gotten myself into?

"Did you like mine?"

I put on my most - uh - seductive smirk. I don't know. I probably look ridiculous. I hope he doesn't laugh. I need to practice this damn look in the mirror later.

I can see he perfected that look, much to my disadvantage. Damn it.

"I enjoyed it." He smiled, leaning closer.

Gulp.

Did I just gulp?

Is he gonna kiss me?

"Good," I replied, hoping my voice didn't croak. Why was he looking at me like that? When did he get so near?

"Twenty questions or not, I'll make this the last question," he said in more like a whisper. The intense look in his eyes caused the blood-pumping organ in my chest to flutter. Oh dear. "Do you want to kiss me again?"

I just stared at him blankly. Was this a test? A tease? A joke?

I steadied my breath and maintained the game face I'd been practicing on since I met this jerk of a potato.

He was staring at me. A long and expectant stare. No, it was more like a gaze. Or a wild look. Maybe my eyes were playing tricks on me too, because it seemed like his lips were zooming in. I mean, he was getting closer. I mean...

What? What was I saying again?

Well. Whether he was testing me or not, I don't think I even care if I pass or fail at the moment.

I guess there wasn't anything wrong with my vision because he really was so close right now. I felt his warm breath fan my face, his eyes studied my eyes, my nose, down to my lips.

I didn't realize his hands were already cupping my cheek, and my own hand had found its way to Brandon's chest.

I released a breath when his lips brushed just a little bit on mine, as if to let me savor the feeling or to tease me - torture me. Damn you to hell potato. "Yes."

Then he kissed me.

Chapter 13

Brandon was the dominant one during our kiss. I let him be, because I had no idea how to do it right. I still can't believe I was his first kiss. He seemed so natural at this. I'm just copying what he's doing.

He tasted like the potato chips we were eating just a while ago and no doubt I did too. And no, it's not as yucky as I described it to be.

It's potato flavored, c'mon.

I felt tingling sensations all over my body - ticklish yet satisfying. His hand went down to my neck, pulling me closer as if the tiny distance between us was still too much. His other hand began tucking my hair behind my ear. His touch was just...

I don't know how to describe it.

Cold? Since I shiver every time he does?

Hot? Since it kinda burns?

Ticklish? Because I get goosebumps?

I have no idea. All I know is I didn't want him to stop. As he pressed his lips harder on mine, I could feel how he was being careful. He wasn't forceful, he was doing it slowly and gently, and gave me just enough time to learn how to respond properly.

Brandon was an expert. Or something. I have no basis or comparison to say he was so good at kissing, but the feeling just made me feel drunk, dizzy, winded.

I felt him smile in between kisses. I smiled too, and I had no idea why. My eyes were closed and I didn't want to open them while this moment lasts.

We pulled away for a few seconds to catch our breaths and then dived back in as if our lives depended on it. His lips were warm and comfortable, his touch was tingling and reassuring.

I just realized I was trusting him more and more each day. I'm not sure why. I just feel safe with him. And comfortable. Should this be a good thing or a bad thing?

A consecutive number of beeps began from my phone. We ignored it for a few seconds, but after remembering what that was for, I held Brandon's face and reluctantly pulled away.

"Time," I showed him the timer on my phone. He laughed incredulously before scratching the back of his head in a boyish manner.

"You really timed it? Aw man."

I chuckled at his reaction before shoving my phone back in my pocket. I gave him a wry smile. "Why? Couldn't get enough?"

I was bluffing. It was me who couldn't get enough. But there's no way I'm telling him that.

He returned my smile. "Potato babe, it's the other way around. I warned you about my kissable lips. You know you can't resist."

"Dork," I snorted at the mention of his 'kissable lips.'

I stood up and dusted my pants. Before I got to his chair near his desk, he released a dramatic sigh. Dramatic enough for me to turn around and look at him weirdly.

He was pouting and folding his arms like an eight year-old. "I'm starting to dislike this ten-limit rule."

I hid a blush. No, no. I shouldn't be affected. He's just saying that because he enjoys kissing, not because it's with me. Or maybe he's just saying that to woo me.

I never run out of excuses. See? Even I know they're excuses.

Brandon and I watched reruns the rest of the day before I went back to my apartment. I went home as soon as Leo texted me saying he and Nichole were done talking and that he was going home and I should leave because he didn't want to walk in on Brandon and me doing something that'll burn his eyes again.

Such a drama queen.

"He's actually really nice," Nichole said as she brushed her hair in front of her mirror. I was standing right behind her, doing the same thing, only not as careful and I did it blindly since I didn't bother with a mirror. I was gonna sleep anyway, why was I even brushing my hair?

Oh yeah. It was an unconscious move since Nichole was brushing her hair like she did every night, and I coincidentally found a spare brush in her dresser drawer. You know the rest.

"He apologized and explained what really happened. I don't think he's lying. He looked really sincere. Now I feel bad that you beat him up because of that small misunderstanding."

I frowned. She was holding back the details. "What's his side of the story then?"

There was a small pause before she finally replied. Why was there a pause? "Well, he kinda did it for you."

My eyes widened. "For me? How so?"

She shrugged her shoulders, feigning innocence but I knew better. She was hiding something from me. That Samuel. Was I more involved than I thought?

I wasn't one to let go of something once my curiosity was triggered, so I pushed Nichole for some more details, but she just wouldn't budge.

"Why don't you ask him yourself?" She said, a bit frustrated at my persistence. I pouted.

"I did. He won't tell me." I said a bit bitterly when the memory of him trying to shrug me off fleeted in my mind. "I don't understand why you won't tell me. If you're hiding it then it must be something big. What is it?"

She put the brush down and checked her reflection one last tine before she stood up and looked at me. "I'm going to bed."

"Nichole!" I whined as she treaded towards her bedroom. I groaned and went to my own room. What were they hiding?

I'm a very curious person. I hate not knowing things, and if people like my best friends keep secrets from me, I'd feel really left out.

It sucks.

I lied down on my bed and released a frustrated sigh. I know this isn't a big deal, but I just feel like I was betrayed or something. I'm being ignored, disregarded, getting treated as a third wheel. The weight in my chest just got heavier.

Ugh.

Now I'm starting to sound like Leo with all this drama. Forget I said that.

Stop thinking about all this negative stuff. There must be a reason why Nichole won't tell me. I trust her. Yeah. Think of good things. Think of potatoes.

Potato.

Brandon's image suddenly appeared in my mind. It's not just an image though, it's a whole video clip. In my mind, he's talking about something quite enthusiastically and he's laughing, but I can't hear what it is. Why does his face look so bright? And what is that? Are those flowers popping out of his head?

What the fuck.

I abruptly sat up and ruffled my hair, trying to shake off whatever that was I just imagined. It was so creepy. I just daydreamed about Brandon.

No no no! That wasn't a daydream. It's night. So it was a nightmare. Yeah. That makes perfect sense. Very good Mira.

My phone began ringing while I was still convincing myself and I jumped from the shock. I think my heart almost escaped from my ribcage. Damn the person who was calling right now.

I grabbed my phone and before I answered it, his name flashed on my screen - Brandon.

Was I breathing? I was. Where was my breath? In my butt? Yeah I think I just farted it out.

What the hell just answer the call!

"What," I said flatly as soon as I accepted the call. I wasn't mad. That was just me trying to sound all chill despite being oxygen deprived.

Why am I panicking?! This isn't the first time he's called me.

His voice began on the other line and I had to conceal my heavy breathing. I should raise the volume, I can't hear his voice with all the noise my heart is producing. "I'm stalking you right now. Just wanted you to know."

I raised both my brows and then knitted them in confusion while still in the process of calming my poor heart. Was he outside of the apartment or something? "What?"

"On facebook."

Oh.

Why do I feel a bit disappointed all of a sudden? This week has been full of inner questions lately.

I heard him laugh softly. "Nice profile picture. My potato's really pretty."

I calmed down after a few seconds and I was back to my sane self. Phew.

"You got nothing better to do?" I asked, half-smiling. I didn't usually believe it when people complimented me, but hearing him say that even if it was meant as a joke or a sly tactic for me to like him, I was happy.

"You're the best thing I'd do." He quickly replied as if to defend himself. And then he cleared his throat and laughed again. "I mean, you know."

Yeah, I know. He was just bored and I was the best source of entertainment. Jerk.

Despite that, I played along. "Be careful not to look into my old photo albums. You might fall for me."

That was a bluff. DO NOT look into my old photo albums. I looked like a pubescent monkey, shit.

He laughed again. "Not gonna happen."

Ow.

Ow?

I shrugged a tugging feeling off again, knowing I'd just get more confused. I grabbed my laptop and quickly logged into my account. My jaw dropped in horror when I saw how many notifications I had.

Over a hundred, and still counting.

"Brandon!" I yelled at him. He was snickering on the other line. "Stop flooding me with likes and comments! My old photos will appear on all my friends' news feeds!"

Damn this guy! My embarrassing photos! My ugly pubescent monkey photos! Why couldn't he just like the current ones, where I evolved into something not monkey-like?!

"I shared my favorites - oh look. Forty likes already."

"What photo?!" I frantically went to his account. I screamed when it was the one where I was wearing a two-piece in the beach three summers ago. My fatty stomach!

I quickly deleted that photo before it'd get unnecessary popularity. I didn't realize I was already gritting my teeth as I pressed my ear harder on my phone against my shoulder, my hands deleting ugly photos in the speed of light. This is so embarrassing! He's seen my old photos! Why didn't I delete all those photos sooner?

Damn Brandon for making me so conscious all of a sudden!

"Cute potato curves. Naaww," he cooed over the phone. My temper just rose.

"BRANDON!"

The rest of the night went like that. Him liking and commenting on every photo he could find, and me deleting the horrible ones before I get the unnecessary fame I know I'll dread tomorrow. More than half the people I know at school are online too - they're bound to see my photos.

This guy certainly has a death wish. I'll make sure to remodel his face tomorrow, this brat.

While I was still deleting old photos and spouting nonstop profanities at Brandon, I noticed I had a new friend request.

I usually ignored it since it was from people I didn't know, but it was just one request this time, so I decided to check it.

When I clicked on it, I felt my whole body tense up.

Samuel Ink just sent you a friend request.

"C'mon it was just a joke!" Brandon whined as he followed me to my class. I ignored him. "Potato!"

Is he seriously going to do that right now? Because I might punch him before he says another word.

A friend of mine - meaning a face I know but a name I can't recall - called my attention and slapped my back in a bro kind of way.

"Adorable throwbacks Mira! I liked your pictures last night." He grinned before entering our class.

I shot his retreating back a glare as Brandon snickered beside me.

That was not funny.

"Why are you so pissed about it anyway? You were pretty cute in those photos." He said as a matter-of-fact.

I continued to erase his presence in my vision. Dimwit. Brat. Asshole.

I was about to enter my room but he blocked the door the door, preventing me from entering. I didn't even give him the pleasure of an eye-to-eye contact. I looked like I had grown a great interest on the floor since I was staring at it so curiously.

I saw one of his feet take a step closer to me and I unconsciously took a step back. I need to keep my guard up. "What do you want me to say, hm?"

Students from my class were forming a small group behind me, probably wondering what was going on, why an idiot was blocking the door and why I wasn't doing anything about it (read: beating him up for it.)

Brandon was persistent. "You were beautiful in those photos. And right now in the flesh, you're so beautiful it hurts!"

He pretended to wince and he covered his eyes with both hands, as if I was a sight so bright I'd blind him.

I can blind him just as good without any brightness if that's what he really wants.

The random people who heard that corny phrase applauded and howled, encouraging him to continue. Embarrassment just rose in my veins.

"Move," I spat.

"You're pretty when you're mad too." He smiled.

Another wave of applause for him.

I can't believe people don't find it weird how this nice boy got involved with someone like me. I'm afraid of what they'll think of me.

"Brandon. Get out of the way."

"Stop looking at me like that. It'll make me want to hug you." He tilted his head a bit and a lop-sided grin formed on his gorgeous face.

The small group behind me somehow evolved into a crowd.

I suppressed a large sigh. It was usually me gathering the crowds through my fist-fights, and I didn't care at all back then. But this case was different. Brandon was making fun of me. And I don't know how to fight back without hitting him just once.

"Move it, shitty potato," I tried to control myself. Maybe I can finish this without getting physical.

And if making a complete fool out of himself wasn't enough, he started singing with the most off-key tone a human being could possibly do.

"YOU LOOK SO PERFECT STANDING THERE - "

I didn't allow him damage my ears. He couldn't finish that single verse because I punched him right on the gut. He half-choked, half-coughed and then laughed.

My hand slipped. Swear.

When he barely recovered, he shot me another grin before chuckling in amusement. He's such a happy kid. Somehow seeing him in that pitiful state made me want to hug him.

What the hell NO. Scratch that. Hell, burn that. Forget I said that. Oh ew.

"Your love hurts, potato."

Our schoolmates were getting entertained at our little skit and not long after, Nichole and Leo pushed through the crowd and scolded us both. Yes, in front of everybody.

Disapproval was forming on her girlish features and I suppressed another sigh. It's still early in the morning. I don't have the energy for this yet.

"Oh my God Mira. You don't punch people who say sweet things to you!" Nichole shrieked, shaking my shoulders back and forth in an exaggerated manner.

At the same time, Leo sympathetically put a hand on Brandon's shoulder, "Dude, you don't say sweet things to people who'll punch you."

Ahh. My best friends are as supportive as usual I see.

I said nothing but rolled my eyes at them, showing how much of a good sport I am.

Brandon finally moved out of the way and let my classmates in. Each of them gave him a pat on the back or a thumbs-up as they entered. Seriously.

"Don't you guys have class too?" I asked. Translation: Get out of my sight, faggots.

Nichole was probably about to retort when something caught her eye and made her shut up. She quickly tugged Leo's shirt and gave Brandon and I a brief nod.

"See ya."

I turned my head to the direction for the cause of her retreat and found Samuel coming our way.

Huh. His sole appearance always causes interesting reactions.

He locked his eyes on mine as he treaded towards the door of our classroom, at the spot where Brandon and I were standing. I honestly didn't know what to do.

If I ask about what he, Leo and Nichole talked about a few days ago, would that seem too out of the blue? I really want to ask what Nichole meant when she said 'he did it for me.'

To do that, I have to start being friendly around him.

I hope this won't be awkward.

"Hey Sam!" I started, my voice cracking mid-sentence. Brandon noticed and snorted, making me punch him behind his shoulder.

My hand slipped again. Honest.

"Hey Mira, Brandon," he sent us a small smile. He sounded nice. Was this the beginning of a new friendship?

I mean, we're already friends in facebook, so that's a start. I think.

"What's up?" I casually asked, ignoring the dolt trying to conceal his laughter beside me. Was it that funny that I was being friendly to the guy I once beat up?

Sam adjusted the strap of his bag on his shoulder. "I'm going to class. Didn't the bell ring already?"

"It did?" I said. "Oh. I didn't hear. Well, you better get to your class then."

He laughed softly, as if I was joking. I laughed too, to go with the flow, but I had no idea why he even laughed.

I can't handle this 'being friendly' thing. It's too much for me, really.

"Mira, we're classmates in most of our subjects. Including this one. You really didn't know?"

My mouth opened and then closed, so I looked like an idiot. Why am I such an idiot? Brandon continued to snicker beside me.

"I'm so sorry!" I blurted out. "I don't pay attention in class, much less the people in it. Sorry!"

He slowly shook his head as if it wasn't a big deal, and his expression showed that he wasn't surprised. It just made me feel worse about myself. How horrible a person am I?

"It's okay. I sit behind you, by the way."

I felt like I was slapped with a chair. "I'm so sorry!"

I think my apology wasn't enough, that's why I unconsciously bowed and said sorry again. We were all surprised with my actions. I watch way too many Asian films.

Brandon laughed and bowed with me, enjoying every second of my humiliation. "Yes, yes. I must also express my deepest apologies for this woman's ignorance."

I glared at him. "Why would you apologize too?"

He grinned. "Because I'm your potato, and you're my potato. One potato's mistake is the other potato's mistake."

I wanted to retort but I had nothing to say against that. No, I'm too tired to say anything about that. I can never win an argument with an idiot.

"Anyway," I turned my head back to Sam. I don't know why I feel so sorry all of a sudden. And I really want to be friends with him, with reasons other than satisfying my curiosity. "Sorry again."

"I told you, it's fine," he smiled. "Ah. The teacher's coming. Let's go inside now?"

He's so nice. He's so gentle. Totally different when I first bumped fists with him. Is this what Nichole meant by a misunderstanding? Or maybe he's just tricking us?

I have so many questions and he has the answers. I need to talk to him about this matter soon. And I don't care if I'm taking this way too seriously. I hate it when nobody tells me anything, that's why I'm gonna find out myseld.

"Yeah let's go inside," I nodded when I saw our stout professor enter the faculty room to get more stuff to bore us with. I glanced at Brandon with a sharp glint in my eye. "Get lost."

He clutched his chest. "My heart's broken enough. But since it's you, I don't mind getting hurt forever."

Samuel chuckled at my annoyed expression.

"Leave," I commanded, swinging my arm to hit him again but he caught my wrist and pulled me closer to him.

I saw him peer over my shoulder, probably glanced if Sam was still watching, and then hugged me. I complained inaudibly since my mouth was buried on his chest. My heart was beating so fast.

When he finally let go, he pecked my cheek and ruffled my hair. "See you at lunch."

He looked at Sam again and gave him a nod of acknowledgement. After that, he left.

I just stared at his retreating back with confusion. He is so weird. Why was he so cheesy today?

"Are you two going out?" Sam snapped me out of my thoughts. Were we? Does pretending to go out count? It took me a few seconds to reply. I'm starting to think I caught a nasty case of Brandon's idiocy. I'm so screwed.

"I don't know."

Chapter 14

"I know the answer to that one," Sam said in a whisper. The whole class was so silent, even a drop of a pen could be heard. The teacher was roaming around the classroom, watching each of us closely.

"What is it?" I whispered back, not tearing my eyes off the teacher. It'd be annoying if we get caught.

"Rods and cones," he replied. I quickly scribbled it down before the teacher saw me leaning my back against my chair a bit too suspiciously. Sam sat behind me.

And yes, if nobody figured it out yet, we were currently taking a quiz. And I was cheating. Not proud of it, but I need to do it to pass Biology. I hate Biology.

A few more minutes later, the time was up, and we passed our papers. Before we left the room, I gratefully smiled at Sam, bumping fists with him on the process.

"Thanks so much. I forgot there was a quiz today."

He returned my smile. "Me too. I was just copying Luke's answers. It's him we should be thanking."

Luke was my classmate since grade school, and he was really smart. When I spotted him leaving the classroom, I waved my hand at him a bit too excitedly. "Luke! Thanks man!"

He looked surprised and confused, but waved back at me anyway. Sam chuckled at my actions. I sent him a questioning look.

"Actually, he wasn't aware that I was copying his answers." A playful grin spread across his face. I burst into a fit of laughter when I realized how stupid I just looked.

"Awesome," I said.

We grabbed our things and went off to our next class. I seriously don't know what happened. I think we kinda hit it off. Sam's actually really cool. I wonder why I didn't notice him before.

Now I feel really bad for hitting him before.

Lunch. My favorite subject in school. I was already at our usual table, eating. Man was I hungry.

Leo and Nichole were arguing about who should pay for their lunches today, and Brandon was silently eating beside me.

I sighed, with my mouth still full, and interrupted the lovers. "Why don't you guys just pay for your food separately?"

"No," Nichole firmly rejected my suggestion. "I always pay for our food. It's only fair that he should pay for mine today."

"What do you mean?" Leo complained. "I paid yesterday!"

"For the drinks, babe! The drinks that were practically free because it was a combo meal which I paid for!"

"Uuugh," I groaned. They always fight over the stupidest things. I ignored them as I continued to eat.

Brandon laughed. "Aren't couples really silly?"

It took me a few seconds to reply to that. I don't know. "Yeah."

As I slowly chewed my food, I caught Sam from the corner of my eye. He was with his friends, laughing their way to the table in front of us. He saw me too, and then we exchanged smiles.

I can't explain how light this feeling is. Being friendly is actually satisfying. I should really do this more often.

"You two seem okay," Nichole said. I glanced up and saw her sitting down, the irritation on her face slowly fading. Leo was already gone so I guess she managed to get him to buy their lunches for today.

"Yeah," I said. "He's really nice. I actually want to get closer to him."

When I said that, I meant it. Well, another reason why I said that was to make Brandon jealous. I secretly peeked at him to see how he'd react, but nothing.

He just continued eating as if he didn't hear anything. Maybe he didn't hear me?

"That's good," Nichole replied, obviously distracted. She was keeping an eye on Leo, who was currently talking to somebody, probably sweet-talking that person into paying for their lunches.

He was always cheap, that idiot. Ever since middle school. It makes me wonder how we even became best friends.

Back to my current situation, I lowered my head as I sipped on my juice.

"So he really is a nice guy after all, huh?" Brandon finally commented. I had to admit it surprised me. I thought he wasn't listening.

I laughed at myself internally. What the hell was I thinking, trying to make him jealous? What for? And why? I'm ridiculous. As if he'd get jealous.

Shut up, brain.

"He really is," I replied coolly. "He even let me cheat off him earlier at Biology."

"That's cool," he said.

Why do I feel so annoyed right now? More than annoyed, I feel strangely sad. No, no. Now I'm even more annoyed now that I know I'm sad. And now I feel sadder knowing I'm annoyed at myself for being sad. And now I'm annoyed at both.

My neurons must be exploding one after another since my mental ability has reduced to this state. Screw you, brain. Do your job properly.

I slapped my face unconsciously, earning surprised looks from my companions, including Sam and his buddies from the other table.

It was a few seconds before I felt my cheek sting. I looked at the palm of my hand and saw it slowly turn into a light shade of pink.

Ah, I've come to my senses now.

"Mira!" Nichole exclaimed. "Why'd you hit yourself?"

"Felt sleepy. Needed to wake up." I mumbled.

"Are you tired?" Brandon asked, mouth half-full.

"Not anymore," I said, not turning my head. Leo came with a tray filled with food on each hand. As he was about to sit down, he looked at me curiously.

"What's that pink hand-print on you face?"

"Blush-on." I replied sarcastically. Leo showed a hint of a cringe before setting Nichole's share of food on the table.

Brandon just quietly munched on his food, completely unaware of what ridiculous thoughts my mind harbored a few moments ago.

I hope he chokes on that chicken.

"I have to go somewhere before I go home." I announced as Brandon and I walked to the parking lot. He wouldn't let go of his phone and the whole time I was talking to him, his eyes were glued to the screen.

I'm annoyed.

"Yeah, where," he asked. Really? Was he even curious?

"None of your business. You can go on ahead." I replied, hoping he won't notice how insincere that sounded.

Please insist you'll drop me off like the usual.

But you know what he did? He just nodded and went in his car. "Okay. Take care."

What was with him today? Just earlier he was joking around like always and he even kissed me in front of Sam. Why was he acting so aloof right now? Did I do something to him?

Whatever. Fine. Let him be that way. I won't ask why he's like that. I don't care. Not at all.

I didn't take back what I said. It was so obvious his mind was somewhere else. Who was he texting? Was it a girl?

Ah. Stop this, Mira. Why should you care? It's not like he's your boyfriend.

I just quietly stared as his car left the parking lot. If his eyes are still glued to his phone while he's texting then I won't be held responsible for his death.

I decided to go to the mall after class, alone. I don't know why. It's not like I needed to buy something. I just wanted to walk around. Maybe eat a few snacks along the way but that's that. The less I spend, the better.

I just needed to get my mind off stupid people.

A few hours later, I walked on every corner of the mall. On every floor. Ten times. And I ended up buying a lot of stuff I probably won't need.

I'm so great.

I sighed exasperatedly, realizing I don't have enough money for transportation anymore. Guess I'll have to walk back to the apartment. It'll probably take half an hour at least.

I'm so excited. Note the sarcasm.

When I walked out of the mall, only then did I realize that it was already dark out. I checked my watch and was surprised myself. It was a quarter to nine in the evening ready.

What the heck, I murdered time walking around in space-out mode while buying useless stuff?

I didn't think twice and quickened my steps. Nichole's probably wondering where I am right now, if she's not flirting with Leo.

A thought slapped my face like a brick. Leo. I can use him. Cellphones were invented for reasons like this. I'll call him, make him pick me up and drive me back to my apartment.

Wow. Why didn't I think of this first? I'm such a genius sometimes, economically speaking.

I took my phone from my bag and called Leo. A few rings later, he picked up.

"Hello?"

"Leo!" I exclaimed, relieved to hear his voice. It usually took him forever to pick up my calls. "Help me."

"Why what's wrong?"

Before I could reply, a speeding car passed right in front of me, almost crushing my feet. The tires barely brushed the tips of my shoes. I screamed in terror and dropped my phone the same time the car beeped, signalling me to get out of the way. Well too late for that pal!

The best part? My phone broke. Not that it was that fragile, but it fell right in a puddle. The water got in the gadget and now it won't turn on.

Pause for dramatic effect.

"Aaaah damn this!" I yelled like a madwoman after attempting to revive my phone a few times.

I walked for a few minutes, attempting to find a public phone I could use but all of them were busted. I'm already far from the mall, it was already closing anyway. And it was getting late. Might as well walk home.

I was meant to walk. Fate did not want me to be lazy. But damn it fate, did you have to ruin my damn phone? You could've just, sent me a sign or something. Uuurgh.

You'll pay, fate. In cash.

I walked for about twenty minutes already, and then I realized something again. A very important thing I should've considered from the start.

I had no idea where I was going.

It was really dark and a few cars barely passed by the road, so I doubt I was in the right way. I know, shame on me, I know how to go to the mall from school, but I don't know how to go home from the mall.

There's a reason why I'm always with Leo and Nichole.

I had to admit, I was getting pretty scared. My senses tripled because of my paranoia, and I was suddenly conscious of every tiny thing and sound.

For potato's sake people, I quickly posed a fighting stance when a kitten passed by. Tell me I'm not paranoid.

I kicked myself in my head a few times, blaming myself why I watch too many horror films to figure out where I'm headed. Flickering lights from broken streetlights, isolated roads, whistling wind and me, the stupid girl in the movie, walking alone at night knowing I'll die.

I'll die?

NO NO NO!!!

I'm too young too die! I don't even have dreams to regret not chasing after yet! I'll die a miserable, ambition-less, pitiful death!

NO.

Negative thoughts must not consume me. I'm strong. I'm not like other girls. I'm not the stupid girl in the movie.

I'm the suave lead actor in the movie. The one with the awesome self-defense skills. The one who'll win. The one who with the sexy jaw-line and the hot six-pack.

I think there was something wrong with that last one.

Trust me, I wasn't being funny. This is how I normally think in situations like this.

Yeah, I'll probably die.

I heard a few rocks getting kicked behind me, and I cringed. Was that another cat? Please be another cat.

I slowly turned around, as not to be so obvious, and noticed a staggering figure just a few meters behind me.

I resisted the urge to scream zombie and run for my life.

It was probably just a random person with the same situation as me. I should empathize with him than be afraid of him. How rude of me. Sorry, staggering guy.

Wait. So why was he staggering?

Possibility: He got kicked in the ass by someone like me.

All the more reason to sympathize with him. Forget empathizing. Sympathize, empathize. I know the difference between the two, see? Find it in the dictionary. See how right I am. See?

I shook my head and quietly scolded myself. Why the hell can I still think about stupid stuff in this situation?! That's right, to distract myself.

I took a deep breath and continued to walk calmly, but I was too conscious of the guy behind me. It didn't help that I didn't know how to go home, and I had no means of communication.

Cry.

I heard footsteps walking closer just a few feet behind me. Oh shit oh shit oh shit.

I quickened my steps and noticed that the footsteps behind me followed my pace. And it didn't sound like it was only one person. I peeked slightly over my shoulder and gasped when I saw it was now two staggering corpses behind me.

Guys. Staggering guys. Not corpses. Damn those movies! I apologize to every girl I called stupid in the movie. Because right now, I'm walking in their shoes. And I'm gonna die in their shoes. No!

I felt a bony finger tap on my shoulder and that was it. I ran for dear life.

Adrenaline pumping, I sprinted forward, my legs moving so fast I felt like flying. The cold wind slapped my face and dried a few drops of tears that trickled down my eyelids, barely reaching my cheeks. My hair was continuously teasing my face, and the paper bags I was carrying with the useless stuff in it was about to rip since I was clutching it so hard.

The worst part of it all was that I had no idea where I was going. I didn't look back - I was too scared. Damn I wish I went home with Nichole! I wish I went home with Brandon!

DAMN YOU BRANDON!

Why didn't he pester me to tag along like the usual?! Why was he acting so weird earlier? Why am I thinking of him when I'm about to die?!

I'm so gonna haunt him first!

I decided to take a turn, hoping to lose the two guys behind me, who probably weren't even chasing me in the first place.

After a few more minutes, I felt my knees weaken, and I decided to stop and catch my breath. I looked around and felt like a huge weight sunk in my chest. Now where the hell am I?

I was out of breath. I wobbled my way to the nearest post to lean against and rest. I used too much energy. It was hopeless. That's when I heard a car approaching.

Two thoughts ran in my head.

The first one is, it's just a random car that'll pass. Don't hitchhike. The driver might kill you.

The second one is, it's a car that kidnaps stupid girls alone at the streets at night and sells their internal organs to other countries.

I was gonna die either way.

Why is it always life and death with me?

It stopped right in front of me and the headlights were too bright for me to distinguish who it was. I squinted and looked at the three people who just came out of the vehicle.

Was I gonna die a horrible death? I just made a new friend. I can't die yet.

"Mira!" A familiar voice snapped me out of my thoughts, and a sense of relief washed over me. It was Nichole, Leo and Brandon.

I think Leo was about to yell at me when Brandon beat him to it. He held my arms so tight I thought it was gonna bruise. I couldn't even look at him properly because the headlights were still impairing my vision.

"Are you hurt?" He began, shaking my shoulders slowly, though I know he was just trying to control his strength. "Where have you been?! We've been looking for you everywhere! Why didn't you pick up your phone?! And what the hell happened?! Leo said you screamed on the phone then the line died. Tell me what the fuck happened?!"

I've never seen him so angry before. I don't know why I felt so paralyzed all of a sudden, and a lump in my throat was forming. I felt guilty.

I tried to squeak out a word of reason but my voice wouldn't come out. My eyes were so wide I couldn't even blink. My vision got so blurry. I felt my tears spilling down my cheeks, one after another.

Ah great.

I really hated it when people see me cry. I feel so weak and stupid. I turned my head so they wouldn't see but it was pointless. My tears wouldn't stop.

Brandon's grip on my shoulders loosened when he saw me like this. And I realized why he was holding me so tight earlier. I actually almost fell, my knees already gave in, and he was just holding me for support.

How did I lose so much energy? This isn't like me.

"Don't get mad at her man," I heard Leo say. "C'mon, let's go back to their apartment first."

Brandon nodded and let go of my shoulders. I couldn't say anything due to the absence of my voice. I didn't want him to let go of me. I reached out my hand but I couldn't see him because of the brightness of the headlights. I suddenly felt lightheaded, and then realized that Brandon actually carried me to the backseat.

On our way back to the apartment, I saw the two staggering guys on the window. I couldn't identify their faces because of the darkness, but they seemed to know me. They both waved their hands as we passed by them.

It was so creepy. I hid my head on Brandon's chest. Maybe he was surprised, but he held my hand and patted my head gently the whole time. Somehow, I felt kind of relieved. No, very relieved. It was so reassuring, and safe, as ridiculous as that sounds.

First teases me, then he kisses me, then he ignores me, then he gets mad at me, then he's trying to comfort me.

I don't understand him.

But what I don't understand the most is myself. Why do I feel like I forgave him when he didn't even do anything wrong?

Chapter 15

After what happened tonight, I am not going out alone again. Ever. I'm still freaked out. When I told the guys what happened, they said I was just being paranoid.

But tell me, what the hell were those staggering guys following me? Huh? Huh? Well, only I knew the answer to that.

Aliens.

"They're probably drunk dudes coming from a party," Leo sighed while making himself comfortable on our couch. We were currently in the living room of our apartment.

"Or they're injured from a fight," Nichole suggested.

"Or they just wanted to pull a prank on you since you looked so scared?"

"Or," I decided to represent my own theory as the victim of the incident. "They just wanted to rape me, kill me then sell my internal organs to other countries?" I said, pushing their suggestions away while firmly holding to my own ridiculous belief. Nichole and Leo were this close to banging their heads on the wall.

I know I sounded crazy, but haven't they seen the news these days? People are so evil. It's not my fault I think every person I meet on the streets late at night are psychopaths - staggering or not.

Leo seemed to give up, hence raising his hands in surrender and sighing profusely. He pointed at Brandon, who remained quiet the whole time and then pointed at me, who was doing the exact opposite.

I hated it when people point fingers. I want to break those damn rude fingers.

"She's tired. She's sleep-talking. She always does that. You, take her to her room and tuck her in," he commanded as if he was the chief of a tribe.

Okay, the tribe thing was not a very good reference, but it's funny since I'm using it on Leo. Leave it.

"I'm not asleep and I'm not a child. I can tuck myself in," I scoffed, standing up and preparing to leave.

I already regained my strength. Do they think I'm really weak or something?

"Just do what he says Mira," Nichole said, sounding exhausted yet relieved. I just noticed how pink her eyelids were, and her eyes were slightly reddish, as if she'd been crying. My heart sunk in my chest. I made my best friend worry so much, and here I am spouting my ridiculous theories.

I obediently nodded as Brandon went ahead to my room, not sparing me a glance whatsoever. He's been quiet the whole time. Is he still mad? I'm sure he's mad. And I'm afraid of what an angry potato might do.

When we got in my room, I left the door open and tried my best to act casual. On my way to my drawers, I heard Brandon close the door. I gulped.

I took off my shoes and changed into my pyjamas, he turned around so I could do so.

When I was through, I slid in my covers and pulled them up to my face until only my eyes were visible. I'm so scared. What'll he do? He's so quiet it's terrifying.

Staring at his back, I saw him take a deep breath and heave a long sigh before turning around again. I unconsciously concealed my whole face with my blanket. Shit.

I'm dead.

I heard his footsteps moving toward me, and I had to calm down my rapid heartbeats. I have to pretend I'm sleeping. I'll snore. I'm good at fake-snoring.

But I just got in my bed. There's no way he'd believe I fell asleep that fast. Cry.

I felt him halt in his steps. I stifled a gulp. What was he doing? And why am I so afraid of what he might do? What the heck? This isn't like me at all. Me? The girl who isn't afraid of fighting a group of men twice her size, is afraid of a potato who can't even stand spicy food and is a complete chicken toward horror films?

A weight pressed down on my mattress and I realized that he was leaning towards me. Even if I couldn't see him, I was sure that's what he was doing.

He gently peeled the blanket off my face and then revealed a very disappointed expression.

When I saw that look on his face, I felt like crying all over again. Guilt, fear, relief and hurt struck me all at once, and I have no idea why. I'm not even on my period today.

I really am weak. And stupid.

A big fool.

"Sorry," I quickly said, knowing I'll get scolded. I made them worry so much about me. That's what upset me the most. I'm such a horrible friend. "I'm sorry. Sorry."

I saw his hand approach my face and I winced, thinking he'd pinch my cheek for being so stupid again. But to my surprise, he just touched my cheek. I slowly opened my eyes and saw him tuck the loose hair away from my face behind me ears.

His hand was so warm.

"Please say something. It isn't like you to be this quiet." I mumbled before biting my lip. His gaze was so focused on my hair. I wanted him to look at me but I think I'm in no place to ask for that. "You're scaring me."

Silence was his reply once again.

I'm about to go crazy and he has no idea at all.

Lucky for me this time, my eyes didn't water. I did my best not to let the ugly tears fall and once again showcase how much of a weakling I am.

My stubbornness will kill me one day, I'm sure of it.

Brandon's disappointed expression melted and it remained stoic, I had to press my lips together just to prevent myself from crying. Why is he being like this? And why am I acting like this?

Seriously I sound so annoying in my head. I can't even explain how much I hate myself right now. And guess who's to blame?

He placed his warm hand on my cheek after he was done tucking away my loose hair. His silence was killing me.

I felt my breath hitch in my throat when he finally, finally looked at me in the eyes.

I can't breathe I can't breath I can't breathe.

He sighed quietly through his nose. "You didn't hit your head or anything right?"

I can't explain how happy I am just because he finally looked at me and even talked to me.

Gosh I'm talking like a freaking fan girl right now.

I shook my head, unable to form a decent word. He caressed my cheek. "Are you still scared of those two guys you saw?"

Truth be told, not anymore. I just found them creepy, but I think I could face them. I think.

Quiet Brandon was much scarier than two unknown staggering species.

I shook my head again. "No."

Unexpectedly, he lowered his head so his face was now buried on my shoulder. I collected the remaining oxygen from my lungs, held it in and didn't dare make a move.

I don't understand. Was he tired? Was he hugging me? Was it both?

"Good," he mumbled, his voice vibrating on my shoulder. "Then you can sleep without nightmares."

I still can't understand. Was he still mad?

He placed his hand on the bed over my body, his other hand on my hair, and his face a few centimeters from mine. I was trapped.

What is oxygen.

I thought he was going to kiss me. I was too hopeful. I stared at his doe-like eyes and felt the guilt rush to my head all over again. He was really worried. I know I should feel worse, but there's a feeling of joy bubbling inside me, knowing he got worried for someone like me.

When our foreheads brushed, he averted his gaze. "Sorry I got mad and yelled at you."

And then he pulled away.

I wonder why I felt so cold when he did. He made his way to my door and then turned the lights off. No, I wanted him to stay longer.

"Goodnight," he said before he left.

"Good morning!" Brandon cheerfully greeted me as soon as I got out of first period. I stared at him in shock and suspicion.

"Yeah, morning," I mumbled. Didn't he feel awkward after last night? I couldn't sleep for hours just thinking about him.

Ugh! I hate admitting to myself that I actually wasted precious hours of sleep just for thinking about him.

"Did you sleep well?" He asked, the smile in his face never faltered.

Of course not, jerk. And it's all your fault.

"Yeah. I slept like a baby."

A lopsided grin formed on his face as he placed an arm around me. I turned my head and looked at him - he was waiting for me to do that. He pressed his forehead against mine, just like what he did last night, and his cheerful expression suddenly turned serious.

"Let's talk. At lunch, at the parking lot where you knocked me out last time."

My eyes widened just as soon as his serious expression returned to his cheerful one again.

Just hearing the words "let's talk" made me remember all the horrible things I did to him. Shit. Oh shit.

He left just like that, leaving me dumbfounded and confused. Scared.

"Oh," a voice behind me started. It was Sam. "A lovers' quarrel?"

"It amazes me how you see it like that," I replied sarcastically.

It couldn't be considered as a quarrel since we didn't even fight. And we weren't lovers.

"Well," he said. "What can I say, I'm a sucker for romance."

I made a face similar to one that was about to puke before laughing at his face. Dude he sounded so gay.

"C'mon let's head to class," I said, still laughing a bit. Why do I find things like this so funny?

Sam smirked before adjusting his bag behind his shoulder. "Glad you finally smiled."

I pretended not to hear and went ahead. That was nothing. He was just being a good friend, but I was too embarrassed to reply.

That was nothing at all.

Lunch. My favorite subject at school in which I usually get excited before heading to the cafeteria to meet my best friends and meet food. But for now, I had no appetite.

And no, it's not the end of the world. Spiders didn't fly and I didn't get taller. If any of those made sense to you, you have a great mind like mine.

Brandon and I agreed we'd talk today, although I have no idea what about. And frankly speaking, I'm still scared.

I keep getting this ridiculous feeling like he's gonna dump me even though we're not together.

The parking lot was isolated just like the last time we've been here. Brandon got here first and was waiting on the grass under the big tree. I swallowed hard. So hard that I managed to swallow some air too, so I ended up burping.

Calm down calm down calm down.

I approached him and when I was in front of him, I stood still, waiting for him to notice I was already here, but I guess he already did. "You said we needed to talk?"

"Yeah," he replied, his tone was dull. He patted on the area beside him. "Sit."

I did, cautiously.

I waited for about a minute before he spoke again. "Those two guys you saw last night."

"Yeah?"

"They were my friends. Luke and Justin."

When the information sunk in my brain, I gawked at him. He continued.

"They were coming from a party, drunk as hell. They saw you and wanted to say hi but they said you ran away as soon as they tapped on your shoulder. They told me this morning." He hid a smirk as he revealed to me the awesome truth.

I'm so ashamed I could die! How am I supposed to face them? Did I just ruin my reputation as the fearless girl in campus?

Fart. Fearless girl my fart-y ass.

I held my face under my hands and groaned audibly. "They probably think I'm some wimp."

"Nah," he reassured me, but I wasn't sure if it was serious or not. "They were impressed actually. They never saw a girl run that fast."

"Bitch," the word naturally came out of my rude mouth. I realized I was in no position to spout profanities at him yet so I took it back. "Sorry."

He placed his hands on the grass behind his back as support before looking up at the tree's branches. And then in that position, he tilted his head over to my direction.

Why does he look more attractive tilting his head? It was both innocent yet misleading. It wasn't fair.

"Nichole cried you know," he began. I suddenly knew where he was going with this. "I never saw her cry before. Leo was frantic as well. He was about to call the cops after you called. And honestly speaking, I never saw those two lose their composure before."

I slowly nodded my head. All I could think about was... I love my best friends so much.

"But it's not your fault. So don't worry, okay?" He said. "I know you were scared. Sorry I didn't come with you. And sorry I yelled at you."

This is wrong. He shouldn't be the one apologizing.

"I'm sorry I made you guys worry," I quickly uttered. "I won't go out alone again."

Brandon nodded before the corner of his lip curled up. "If you're sorry then kiss me."

I stared at him for a few seconds, replaying what he said in my head. Did I hear him correctly? Did he just ask me to kiss him?

"And if you're really sorry," he added. "Then do so while breaking rule number three."

Rule number three: Kissing is allowed but only for a maximum of ten minutes a day. What did he mean? He wanted to go over the time limit?

I was getting strangely excited - no! He's tricking me. I can resist him.

"You said it wasn't my fault so I shouldn't worry," I reminded him of his previous statement.

"Yeah, but I didn't say I wasn't mad at you anymore."

He's mad at me? He's really still mad at me? Why does it feel like my insides are twisting into knots when he said that? He's mad at me.

"If you kiss me then maybe I'll forgive you," a smug grin formed on his attractive features. A weight got lifted from my chest. He was just fooling around again. This was just one of his sly tactics to get me to kiss him. The bastard potato took advantage of the situation.

He lied down on the grass while using his arms as a pillow. He was getting himself in a more comfortable position.

I looked around us if there were any people or cars who'd possibly see us. There were none. We were all alone in this isolated parking lot.

"I'm waiting," he said, his eyes closed and his lips resisting a smirk. Damn it, he knew I wouldn't say no to this.

I was a bit insecure since he wanted me to initiate it this time, and to keep it going for more than ten minutes - he was trying to kill me.

But I won't back down. He knew that. And I really did want to kiss him too, after what he did last night. The way he got worried to the point of getting mad at me drew me closer to him. And for that I wanted to kiss him so bad.

So I'm doing this because I want to, not because he asked me to.

I placed a hand on his chest before leaning over to his face. His lips were really... Irresistible. I never knew kissing was this addicting.

"Bipolar potato," I mumbled as I drew my face closer. This was like Sleeping Beauty in reverse. It was Sleeping Potato, and I was the Potato Charming. "See if you can resist my kissable lips."

His grin grew wider when I said that. He opened his eyes, he was shaking, trying to control his chuckles. I smiled.

"You'll never beat me," he said. I scoffed. I was about to say another smart statement when he reached out his hand and pushed my head from behind so he could kiss me already.

Impatient dummy.

Annoyed, I took his hand behind my head and squeezed it so hard he began to complain a little by groaning. I held the nape of his neck as I pressed my lips harder on his.

The warm and tingling sensations danced in our mouths and I was proud at myself. I was more than keeping up with him.

I was winning.

Chapter 16

I laid my head on Brandon's arm as I made myself comfortable on the bed of grass. We were both lying on the grass. Quite carefree if I may add.

Annoying pointy grass poked my back a few times, so I shuffled around to avoid them. Ugh.

"Stop moving around so much," he mumbled. I continued what I was doing as if I didn't hear.

After I made out with him, we called it even. I didn't have to feel guilty about anything anymore.

Or so I say.

I groaned in frustration when another blade of grass pricked me. It was itchy. Brandon wrapped his free arm around me, holding me still. From afar, it looked like he was side-hugging me.

"Stop it, you worm," he quipped. I scoffed at his not-so-pleasant remark.

"The grass is bothering me," I complained.

"It'll bother you more once it's gone forever."

"Don't be a smart ass," I punched his side. "You know what I mean."

He snickered before moving closer to me, nuzzling in my hair. The contact made me stiffen a bit. It's strange how it still affects me. "Well I'm comfortable as we are now."

I'll bet.

"Brandon." I dulled my tone.

"What?" He asked, obviously concealing his amusement. "Would you prefer taking a nap in my bed instead?"

I looked up to meet the expected smirk. I wanted to stay mad at him, but my traitorous mouth twitched up into a smile. I knew pretty damn well what he meant.

"What do you mean nap," I said flatly. "Lunch is almost over. We need to get back to class."

He stretched his arms in the middle of my sentence and groaned, his eyes were closed the whole time. "Let's skip."

"What? No." I replied as I tried to sit up and escape, but he continued holding me still. Now I'm trapped by a stubborn potato and with blades of grass raping my butt.

"Let's go to my place."

I stared at him, not at all amused. "Brandon."

"I still can't forgive you enough," he sighed, pushing my head to his chest, making it harder for me to escape his potato grip.

"What?!" I complained, trying to push him away. "But you said - "

"I'm not done with you yet." He cut me off. Now I'm getting annoyed. Why is he acting so high and mighty now?!

I groaned loudly, my voice muffled because my mouth was stuck to his chest - which I wouldn't complain about if he didn't have his shirt on.

What.

Erase. Brain, erase all that. Clear. Delete. Forget. Die.

"What do you want from me?" I said, a little hopelessly.

My head. No. Stop thinking about him shirtless. Aah.

Damn it.

"I wanna do something to you." He replied, slowly.

My mind went blank, and then it got filled with all the not-so-pure thoughts in the world. Brain, stop that this instant.

He threw his leg over my body and then pulled me up to meet his face. I have to maintain a cool expression, like I'm not affected or anything.

Because I really am not affected. At all.

I'm just thinking weird stuff because I skipped lunch and am being tempted to skip class as well.

He narrowed his eyes as he stared at me. His eyes - it was so blue, so clear. So pretty. I can stare at them all day. His eyes are just - amazing, magical. It's like he's staring at me as if he knew all my secrets.

Would it make sense if I said I felt like drowning?

Because seriously, I can't breathe.

He tucked my hair behind my ear again before resting his palm on my cheek. And then a questionable smirk formed on his face. Oh no. "You're thinking about bed things, aren't you?"

I don't know if I blushed or if my eyes widened or if my jaw dropped - I have no idea. But the next thing I knew was...

...he was already a meter away, groaning in pain.

Oh God. I kicked him away! Literally!

"Brandon!" I exclaimed, crawling on the ground after him. Why did I just use the ever so special Mira Kick on him again?

I cautiously poked his shoulder as he continued wincing in pain. He was holding his crotch and I didn't have to guess to know where I kicked him. Again.

"Sorry..." I almost cried. Seriously! I'm so stupid! "Oh gosh Brandon I'm sorry. It was a reflex."

"You've been saying sorry a lot lately," he said, his voice came out forced. He still managed to pull off a playful grin despite his wincing eyes though. "I like it, you admitting your fault. All that's left is for you to admit you like me."

My sympathy quickly melted away. I stood up and sighed heavily and loudly enough for him to notice. He did, and gave me a questioning look.

"Alright, fine," I said, looking at him. "Let's skip. We'll hang out at your place like you suggested."

"Really?" He sounded surprised, but his voice was still strangled. Huh. Must've hurt a lot.

"Yup," I popped the p. I grabbed his wrist unannounced and pulled him up with quick force. He let out a grunt from the surprise. I put his arm around my shoulder and carried his weight to his car.

I felt a wave of deja vu pass through me. This scene. Hah.

Brandon sighed as we were nearing the vehicle. Supporting him as he limped wasn't much of a challenge actually. I've carried heavier bodies than this. Don't ask.

I honestly don't know why I changed my mind. I honestly don't know why I don't know a lot of things these past few weeks actually. Maybe I just wanted to hang out? Or maybe I was still feeling bad about myself, that's why I'm doing what he wants. Or maybe I really am starting to -

Nope. Not considering that thought. I'm not even gonna think about it. Nuh-uh.

"This is so uncool of me," Brandon grunted as I helped him up to his room. I sighed, amused.

"Since when were you ever cool?"

He gave me a look feigning hurt upon clutching his chest with his free hand. His other arm was wrapped around my shoulders. "Your words sting. Stingy potato."

I rolled my eyes before I threw him, literally threw him on his bed. I bet he was just resisting the urge to start sobbing. I wouldn't mind seeing that scene, frankly speaking.

"You got some ice in the freezer?"

"Don't need it," his voice sounded more strangled than earlier. He was barely sitting up or lying down or whatever it was he was doing on his bed. I think he was attempting to crawl, I don't know.

Pitiful.

"You need to put some ice on that," I gestured to his crotch. "I'm sorry I kicked you okay? Let me at least help you."

A meaningful grin spread on his pitiful face. Here we go. "You really wanna help ease the excruciating pain you've inflicted on me?"

I frowned at him while folding my arms against my chest. I know he was gonna make another innuendo but I'll let it slide. He was hurt after all.

Brandon looked like he was concealing a few chuckles. I smiled at him innocently. "What do you want me to do?"

He tilted his head and narrowed his eyes, his grin not wavering one bit. "Hmmm. Let's see. We're out of ice because Leo didn't refill the ice-cube trays like he was supposed to, and I'm too lazy to think of other ways to get some. So let's be economical. How 'bout you start soothing the inflicted area of my body?"

I had to stop myself from gaping at him. Of course he'd say that. This was Brandon we're talking about. Something completely playful glinted from his eyes and I knew he was kidding around again.

He was always good at talking but then again, he was always weak when I actually do it to him. A playful idea sparked in my mind as well. Two can play in this game.

Before he can continue suggesting more stupid ideas, I sat on his bed and menacingly placed my hand on his leg. The left corner of my lip curled up into a smirk as he stared at me blankly.

"Umm..." He mumbled confused, shuffling over the bed. It was a failed attempt because he could barely even move in his condition.

I slowly, slowly slid my hand up his leg and bit my lip to stop myself from laughing like a psycho. I mean, he looked so nervous! It was such a nostalgic feeling to have the upper hand.

When my fingers reached his inner thigh and just an inch away from his crotch, he jumped and pulled a blanket over his whole body. I withdrew my hand and took a deep breath to calm down my laughter.

I feigned an innocent look. "What's wrong potato sweetheart? You said you wanted me to soothe you?"

Pft. Yeah. If 'soothe' is one word for it.

Beet red travelled from his neck to his ears, and his eyes were looking everywhere but me. "Yeah, well, I just remembered we still had some ice in the freezer."

I maintained my cool facade. I quickly went closer to him and grabbed his blanket. He panicked when I started tugging it. "I think it'd be better if I - "

"Nope. Nope." His voice was frantic as he held the blanket tighter. He swallowed hard and looked away again.

I couldn't help myself. It was hilarious teasing him. I cracked a smile and neared my face to his, my hand finding it's way to his leg again. He flinched. I pressed my lips on his ear and lowered my voice into something close to seductive. I'm still practicing the prestigious art. "What do you really need, Brandon? An ice-pack? Or a cold shower?"

He shuddered.

"M-Maybe both..." He mumbled before slowly sinking on his bed and hiding in his blanket. I pulled away and burst into a fit of laughter. I can't take it! It was too much! Too much!

I clapped my hands for no reason at all as I continued to laugh with all my might - I could barely feel my stomach.

"Just get the ice!" Brandon whined, sounding as embarrassed as I was amused. Oh God this was so fun. So, so fun.

I was still laughing like a maniac all the way to the freezer. I will never live this one down.

That's what he gets for fooling around.

It'd been over two hours since I've been in his room. All I did was nurse him. Well, if you call changing his ice-pack every now and then nursing, that's pretty much what I've been doing since I got here.

He was getting better. I think he was just feigning hurt again just so I can stay a bit longer. Well, I didn't mind.

I sat on his chair and grinned at him sheepishly. Ohh my mind. He narrowed his eyes at me and that just pulled the trigger on my chuckles again.

"You know it seriously hurts since you kicked it, excited it, then practically killed it?"

I raised my hands in sarcastic surrender. "Hey, not my fault I'm too hot for you."

"Yeah well." He said, then stopped. I looked at him, waiting for his smart comeback. He pouted. "Yeah you're right."

My eyes shot open and I stood up from the seat. I was grinning too much my cheeks actually started to feel numb now. "Did I just hear right? Did you, Brandon Pierce actually admit I'm right? And that I'm hotter than you?"

"No," he said, sounding stubborn yet clueless. Cute. I mean stupid. Yeah. "We're different genders. We can't compete in levels of hotness. If you were a dude, of course I'd be hotter than you."

I raised both my brows. "Well if you were a chick, I'd be hotter than you."

He was silent again for a few seconds. I snorted. "I hate it when you win in dumb arguments."

"Only when you let me," I laughed.

That marked the end of our fun debate. I flipped through the pages of his magazines out of boredom while he lied on his bed with the ice-pack still pressed on his crotch.

The silence wasn't awkward. It was actually quite comfortable. It made me wonder again how Brandon and I became close. It's still unbelievable.

"So," he broke the silence. I glanced at his direction. "How's Paige?"

"My mom?" I clarified. He nodded. "She's fine."

"Yeah, what does she do exactly, if you don't mind me asking?" He sounded genuinely curious.

"She works in a bank. She's the manager of a bank actually. Why?"

"Oh. Nothing. Just wanted to know what kind if woman raised a girl like you."

I looked at him suspiciously, but I was smiling. Gosh, mouth, stop smiling too much. You already had your fill. "A girl like me?"

"Yeah," he shrugged his shoulders as he placed the ice-pack on the bowl on his desk. Guess he was fine now. "I was expecting the mother of Mira Jadsen to be a Pro-wrestler or a Judo Master or something."

I didn't get if he was being serious or sarcastic but I laughed anyway. His sense of humor was questionable sometimes. "Well sorry to disappoint you, but my mother is normal. And if you're asking where I got my slightly violent nature from..." I paused for a moment of suspense. "Ask our principal."

Brandon stared at me for a few seconds as if letting that information sink into his brain. When it partially sunk in, he held his head. "Our principal? Principal Steele? Why, why him?"

Oh yeah. He doesn't know about our relationship.

"He's my uncle," I replied easily. Before he could ask a frequently asked question, I already answered. "He was my dad's cousin. I call him uncle out of respect."

"Okay," he said slowly, he was staring at his feet, probably surprised from the sudden revelation. "Then why'd you say your violent nature came from him?"

"Slightly violent," I corrected. "He used to be an officer for the Navy. Retired early for personal reasons and taught me self-defense. And yes, I don't hit people seriously for no reason at all. It's all just natural reflexes and self-defense."

He nodded his head unsurely. I personally don't think this was a lot to take in. "What about your dad?"

I unconsciously creased my forehead and looked down when his image hit my memories. It wasn't a pleasant one. Maybe there were pleasant ones when I was young and didn't understand a thing, but he destroyed that precious memory when he left us years ago.

He cleared his throat awkwardly when my eyes shot back up at him. I didn't realize I was quiet for a little while. He sent me a sympathetic smile while lowering his head like a guilty pup. "Sorry. I forgot he was already dead to you."

I swatted an airy hand, attempting to act cool about it. "Nah. It's okay. Do you wanna know about... My dad?"

I felt a bit disgusted. I shouldn't even be calling him 'dad' anymore. I don't know why I still do.

He gave me a look that said I didn't have to if I wasn't comfortable, but I just smiled at him. I wanted him to know. I felt like I didn't have to keep any secrets from him, and I wanted him to know every little thing about me, just as much as I want to know everything about him.

It's so weird, how I feel so open with him, aside from Leo and Nichole.

"Yeah, I want to know," he mused, looking at me. His expression looked relieved, relaxed. Or maybe I was just describing it the way I want to see it.

I stood from my seat again and sat beside him on the bed, the mattress slowly sinking in my area causing him to shift closer to me - unintentionally maybe, but I'd like to believe otherwise.

"Okay then," I breathed in. Time to let this thing out. "Listen well."

Chapter 17

Princes, castles, unicorns, fancy dresses and tea parties - mix those shit up and you got yourself a typical little girl's fantasy.

Just a fantasy.

When I was six, I was very much in love with the idea of being a princess. I mean, why not? I lived in a big house (big because I was a midget back then), we had maids clean our rooms and prepare our food everyday, I had a room full of toys and a closet full of dresses, and I was pampered by everyone in the house.

My mom was beautiful and had an aura of sheer authority, but she was kind - she still is - so she could be a queen. And my dad, well, he earned the respect and trust of his clients (which I used to call 'his people') because of his positive attitude and skillful works. I was proud of him. My dad was my king.

Was.

A few years later, I turned twelve. My life was still full of all the comfort and luxuries my parents could afford. They didn't allow me to experience any hardships because I was their precious little girl, their princess. And I believed all that.

My dad and I were very close. He used to take me downtown all the time while mom was at work. He would lift me up and carry me on his shoulders with my legs locked around his neck. It was amazing. I could see everything and everyone.

When we got home, mom would always scold us for being late for dinner and she'd get mad at dad for feeding me spicy snacks again. It was my favorite flavor because he introduced it to me.

I loved my family. My life was perfect.

But one day, things got different.

The usual jokes my parents exchanged in the living room turned into heated arguments, the warm smiles turned into frowns, the soft and loving way they'd stare into each other's eyes turned to hard glares.

They were falling apart.

I knew my parents were fighting, but they tried to keep it hidden from me. But I knew. I was twelve. I wasn't stupid.

Soon, dad would rarely come home. Whenever he did, he'd look dead tired and wouldn't even spare me a glance. He used to kiss my cheek and pat my head whenever he got home from work, now all I got from him was a cold shoulder.

Mom would go out to work, and dad and my usual trips downtown were no more. He completely ignored me.

Leo was my best friend since that time. He'd come over our house and play whenever I was alone. He never left me. He knew what was going on since his mom and my mom worked together in the same bank.

I didn't hate my dad. I was willing to understand his reasons for ignoring me. Maybe he was just tired. Maybe he was just lonely. Maybe he was just confused.

Leo and I were playing video games in my room one day when I heard someone enter our kitchen. I quickly got up and raced downstairs. I knew dad was home. I haven't seen him in weeks. I missed him so much.

As I slowly crept in the kitchen, I saw him open up a bottle of beer before he chugged it down. His tie was loosened around his neck and his hair was dishevelled. He looked older than usual because of the beard on his face.

He opened and drank one bottle after another. Soon, the table was full of empty beer bottles. And he was still drinking.

I wanted to cheer him up just like he cheered me up whenever I was sad. I walked up to him and tried my best to smile. I wanted him to smile too. He looked at me with dead eyes and then looked away like he didn't care. But I didn't believe that. I knew he wasn't always like this.

"Daddy?" I said. No answer.

I tugged his sleeve to get his attention but there was still no response. I felt so distant with him even though we were in the same room. I noticed Leo spying on me behind the counter. He was motioning me to leave dad alone and go back upstairs but I didn't listen.

I just stood there in silence, waiting for my dad to move or talk or whatever. But he didn't do anything. Just stared into space for a long time. And then I noticed that his shoulders stiffened. I looked at his face and saw his dull eyes water.

My heart broke.

My dad was about to cry. I hesitated to step forward but I did, eventually. I wrapped my arms around his neck. He probably didn't notice at first but when he did, he pushed me away. I never let go.

My hands were firmly locked around his neck, hoping to calm him down and make him feel better. I started to cry because he used a bit too much force whenever he pushed me away, but I didn't care. He needed someone right now.

"Let go of me you little brat!" He spat as he finally shook me off. I slid on the floor and almost hit my head but Leo came just in time to shield me from the crash. The empty beer bottles fell from the table and broke into pieces all over the floor.

Leo held me protectively but I took his hands off me and ran back to my dad. I couldn't leave him alone. I felt so sad for him.

"Don't come near me!" He struggled from my embrace. I didn't know what I was doing. I just wanted to hug him. He used to hug me to cheer me up back then, and I'm gonna do it to him now.

When he pushed me off once more, I fell on the ground and attempted to run back to him, but it wasn't until I heard the crunching of glass.

I didn't realize I had fallen on the broken glass. My hands and legs were bleeding, and my eyes were tearing up. But it didn't hurt as much as the intense stare my dad was giving me. I was terrified. He never looked at me like that before.

"See what you just did?" He slurred, but his tone dripping with anger. "I told you. I told you to stay away. You did that to yourself. That's the problem with you Mira. You're too spoiled! You're just a brat!"

It hurt. What he said hurt. But it was alright. I can still forgive him. He must be having such a hard time for him to act like that.

I swallowed hard to make the huge lump on my throat disappear, but it didn't. I tried to hold the tears in but I failed. I winced when he stepped forward, eyeing me with disgust.

"I should have left before you got too attached to me. You're annoying. Stop crying."

I couldn't. I couldn't stop crying because that wasn't my dad talking. That wasn't him.

Not long after, my mom came in and saw the huge mess and the blood on my hands and legs. Her eyes immediately filled with rage. She began screaming at my dad, throwing his stuff at him. Leo helped me up as my mom punched dad in the eye.

This family isn't gonna work out, is it?

I was quiet the whole time mom packed our things. We slept over at Leo's for over a month until mom found a new house for us. She and dad got a divorce and I didn't care anymore.

'Dad' was just an empty, foreign title to me now.

His cousin though, Uncle Ray, who was now our principal, visited us after he left the Navy. He apologized in dad's behalf but we didn't accept apologies indirectly. That was one thing I learned from that time. The person at fault should apologize himself, otherwise, he isn't sincere, thus does not deserve to be forgiven.

Uncle understood and left. But he came back a week later, telling my mom that he'd help take care of me, support us financially and do whatever he can just to keep in touch with me. Mom was hesitant but she knew uncle loved me like his own daughter. He took care of me when I was still a baby after all. Compared to my dad, uncle really loved me.

It was the right decision to trust my uncle. Mom and I managed to live better because of him. I told him I never wanted to feel helpless again, so he taught me self-defense so I could fend for myself. He even got a job in my school just so he could watch over me until now.

Uncle Ray was the father figure in my life. I loved him and I loved mom.

One thing I completely understood after all that's happened was this:

I'm no princess.

Brandon was quiet the whole time I told the story, at the same time reliving that day. I wasn't looking at him, I was looking at my intertwined fingers. Would he think I'm weird after hearing the story?

I hauled my knees to my chest as I reached the conclusion of my story. I felt melancholic. He put a hand around my shoulder but I still didn't look at him. I was afraid of crying. I hated crying.

"Where is he now?" He asked. I bit my lip. It would make sense if I told him I didn't know, but I did. I still know everything about my dad - where he works, where he lives, where his favorite coffee shop is, and what his new family is like.

He had two daughters and a son now.

I still keep track of him even though I should hate him. But I can't. No matter how much I convince myself that he was a bastard and we were better off without him, I still loved him. I hated feeling like there was still hope for our family to be together again. I hate being so irrational.

"I..." I breathed, hoping I wouldn't stutter. But damn me, I ended up bursting into tears. It made me wonder how earlier I was just making fun of Brandon and laughing my heart out, and now here I am crying like a dramatic teenage girl.

So weak.

Brandon pulled me in for a hug. I quickly held his chest to stop him. He looked confused but when I looked at him, it was like he was shot, judging from the pain on his face. Why would he look like that if I was the one crying?

I sniffed before cracking a fake smile, my mouth was twitching. "Sorry you had to see me like this. And witness my drama."

He shook his head before smiling himself. "You don't know, do you?"

I knitted my brows, wondering how far his reply was to my previous statement. "Know what?"

"How beautiful you really look when you cry."

I sighed and sent him a playful look, but by looking at his expression, he was serious. I didn't want to believe it. Being too hopeful caused me a lot of disappointments already. I didn't need more.

"But Leo," he said, making me look at him again. "He was kinda awesome. And Principal Steele too. Wow. I gotta give them more credit."

I laughed softly, stifling my annoying sniffles. He was right. Those guys deserve a lot of credit. Him too. I gave him a light hug before kissing his cheek. "Thank you."

"You're definitely a girl, potato," he winked. I rolled my eyes at him, taking it as a compliment. He took my hands and kissed them, much to my surprise.

He placed my hands on his cheeks. It was so warm. And then he smiled so kindly at me, I don't know why it felt so nostalgic. "You know, I don't think you're the kind of person who just tells these things to anyone. And you don't show this side of you to just anyone too. Why are you telling all these to me?"

That was a really good question. Why did I tell him? And why am I even asking myself that? I already know the answer.

I cupped his face with my hands and leaned in to kiss him gently. With my lips still pressed on his, I told him. "Because I trust you."

He looked into my eyes in surprise or disbelief or something. But I could tell he was fighting back a smile. The moment was cut short when his phone started ringing.

He took his phone from his pocket and pressed it on his ear. "Hel -"

"YOU MANSLUT DID YOU KIDNAP MIRA AGAIN?! WHERE ARE YOU RIGHT NOW?!"

He almost threw his phone away when Nichole's voice boomed from the speaker. It wasn't even in loud-speaker yet. He looked at me silly before putting the phone back on his ear.

"We're at my room. Don't worry Nichole, I'm taking good care of her." He sent me a wink and I scoffed playfully.

He turned the loud-speaker on so we could both hear what was going on in the other line. I could hear Leo arguing with Nichole. Something about an 'I told you so.'

"Well what did you do to her? Are you making her feel bad again? If you are I'm gonna rip your throat out." Nichole threatened.

"Well," a look of mischief crossed his face. "We did have some fun. And I had to put an ice-pack on my crotch instead of taking a cold shower. That answer good enough for you?"

Nichole groaned from the other line. Leo took over the phone. "Hey man. We're going there now."

"Okay."

"And one more thing," Leo added. "Mira I know you're listening. Stay right where you are. Because I'm gonna to go bitch-mode on you for skipping without telling us. See ya."

Brandon hung up and stared at me like he was gonna laugh. I stuck my tongue out like a kid before standing up and fixing myself.

Better get ready to get yelled at by my best friends in a few minutes now.

"Psst," Sam discreetly called for my attention during class. "Mira."

I leaned my back on my chair and turned my head a bit so he'll know I heard him.

"Are you having lunch with Leo and the rest later?" He asked.

"Yeah. Why?"

It took him a few seconds to reply. "Can I join you guys? There's something I have to talk to you about."

I instantly thought about Nichole, Leo and his private conversation some weeks ago. Maybe that's what he wanted to talk about?

"Sure."

I couldn't concentrate for the rest of the morning. I was worried, excited, scared and hungry for lunch.

But my hunger was winning against all the above mentioned of course.

I felt my phone vibrate in my pocket. I took it out and I don't know why I suddenly smiled when I saw it was from Brandon. Huh.

| Nichole is giving me a hard time. Help me. :(|

I snickered. It was about last night. Nichole wouldn't stop scolding him. And she told him he was a bad influence on me. I replied.

| Aww. My poor baby. :(|

Seconds later, he replied.

| I am being forced not skip class with you unless I get her permission first. |

| Good. |

| Whaaat. Whyyyy? |

| So they'll know where to find me in case you do anything naughty. |

It took him a little longer to reply.

| But you're the one doing the naughty first. ;) |

I snorted. True.

| And you're a sissy. |

| Hey! Didn't I tell you before that a gentleman is just a patient wolf? |

| We'll see how patient you are. |

| Is that an invitation? |

| Depends on how you understood it. |

I grinned secretly. I don't want to get caught smiling like an idiot in class. Brandon sent me another text.

| Can't wait. ;) |

Hm. Me too.

Chapter 18

Leo was staring at me ridiculously weird, like he was internally freaking out or something. We were at our usual table at lunch, only this time, Sam joined us.

Brandon's usual seat beside me was taken by Sam, so the original owner decided to take the seat adjacent to us. I don't think he looked all that pleased, but he managed to hide it pretty well seeing that he gave our guest a small smile.

Nichole pretended like Sam wasn't there. But her little act just made the situation all the more tense, awkward. Leo was still staring - glaring at me, silently asking why Sam was here. I shrugged my shoulders, a bit confused as to why they were acting this way. I thought they made up already?

I cleared my throat before stealing a quick glance at Brandon. He was looking at Sam carefully, as if analyzing him. What the heck is with my friends? They're treating Sam like a total leach.

Rude.

"Umm," Sam slowly sunk into his (my potato's) seat. "I get it. I'm unwanted. I just wanna talk about something."

"Don't say you're unwanted," I said, shooting my friends a sharp look each. They were being so immature right now. They should know how much it sucks to be treated like this. "What did you want to talk about?"

I was honestly more enthusiastic about what he was about to say than his own presence - he doesn't need to know that though. I was finally gonna know what the hell was going on.

Sam sent me a small smile, and I was relieved to know that he was taking this coolly despite my friends' unwelcoming auras. "Yeah, it's about what happened weeks ago. You know, when I accidentally bruised Nichole's wrists, which I apologize for again," he nodded at Nichole. She gave him an acknowledging nod in turn.

He then turned to Leo. "Like I told you before, I didn't mean it. I just wanted to know where Mira was. You were ignoring me, so I grabbed a hold of your wrist but I didn't realize you got bruised easily."

"You also didn't realize your own strength until you saw my bruises." Nichole cut in. Sam agreed guiltily.

"Wait," I interrupted, earning all of their attention. I think I'm missing something here. "Why were you looking for me?"

A barely visible shade of pink filled his face. "I just wanted to talk to you."

"About?"

"Nothing. Just casual talk. That's all."

I looked at him like crazy. "What do you mean that's all? I beat you up. You bad-mouthed me to the principal. I don't think you just wanted to talk."

I was totally unconvinced. Was what he was saying true? Was he lying? I looked at my friends' expressions to confirm if what he was saying matched what he told them weeks ago. Nichole and Leo nodded, meaning what he was saying was indeed true.

Did I just make a really big issue out of a really tiny one.

Facepalm.

"Alright then," Sam said. "I'll elaborate."

I looked at him closely, paying attention to every word that comes out of his mouth. "I got mad at you in the principal's office because, well, duh, you beat me up. Sorry 'bout that too by the way, I lost my temper. And I've had a crush on you since freshmen year. Good enough?"

I gaped at him.

Gaped at him like a freaking goldfish.

I closed my mouth and leaned back on my seat, folding my arms on the process. My brows were knitted and my eyes were focused on my untouched food. "That doesn't make sense," I shook my head. "You don't have a crush on me."

"I just said I have a crush on you," he said, firmly. "And I'm not a stalker like you accused me of that time in the office. I just happened to live in the apartment a few blocks away from yours. You seriously thought I was following you?"

I wasn't catching up at all.

This little twist in the story I came to know punched me back in the gut like a Silverback gorilla.

Sam laid his back against his chair with a shy smile plastered on his face. "This is so embarrassing. But at least I finally told you, right?"

I didn't reply - just stared at him blankly while my brain was still processing the unbelievable input.

He then glanced at Brandon, looking a bit cautious at that. "I'm not picking a fight here bro. But I want to ask you something, so I'll know where I stand."

I was nervous. What was he gonna ask and what was Brandon gonna say?

Brandon nodded, motioning him to shoot the question. Sam didn't waste another minute.

"Are you planning to date Mira seriously?"

The air around us got heavy all of a sudden. Judging from Sam's expression and tone of voice, he was, I think, serious. I was too afraid of Brandon's reply. He was quiet for a bit and so were Leo and Nichole.

I have to save myself.

"You're too serious Sam," I said, waving a hand to show off nonchalance. I hope he bought it. "Brandon and I have a deal. We're just doing stuff for fun. Of course we won't consider dating each other seriously."

My voice was shaking the whole time I said that. I don't know why my hands feel so clammy or why my heart is beating so fast. I'm scared. Did I say the right thing? It was a fact right? But why do I feel so sad after saying it?

Gosh where did my brain go?

Sam looked unfazed, as if he was expecting such an answer from me. I slowly sunk in my seat, hoping someone would agree with me so I won't sound like a total idiot just now.

I saw Brandon straighten his back from the corner of my eye. I swallowed hard. Shit why do I feel so scared? Scared? Scared of what?

"Like what she said," Brandon finally spoke. I couldn't sense a hint of any emotion from his tone. I can't tell whether he was mad or offended. Or maybe he just doesn't care and wants to get this drama over with. His tone was just, dull. "I don't like her. I won't date her seriously. Heck I'm not even taking her seriously, and I'm sure she's doing the same. We're just playing around to kill time."

A huge lump formed in my throat. I know he was just backing up what I said earlier, but he didn't have to be so blunt about it. It stung. I pinched my arm from under the table to snap myself out of my dumb thoughts.

I wanna cry. I wanna cry.

Don't, don't cry please.

Damn you Mira, your mind is a living contradiction. What the hell do you really want?

"Whoa," Sam chuckled lightly, a bit shaken after what Brandon said. Did he not expect that? Or was Brandon showing him a scary face or something? I don't know. I'm not gonna find out. "You two are the ones being so serious. It was just a question."

"And we just gave you the answer you wanted." Brandon replied. He sounded so cold. Why was he so mad? "You said you liked her, but she doesn't like you. So while you make up some sort of plan to get her like you back, I'll hold on to her in the mean time."

I bit the inside of my cheek a bit too hard, I tasted blood in my mouth. I dug my nails on my palms as I breathed heavily.

He spoke as if I was some toy they could just throw around for fun.

I finally gathered the guts to look at him, but it wasn't just a simple look, it was a heated glare. How dare he.

He met my glare with a cold stare. What. What was happening? What the hell is happening?

Nichole abruptly stood up from her seat, causing the chair to fall backwards. The loud sound silenced the whole cafeteria. Great. Way to cause a scene.

She shot Brandon and I a sharp look each before storming off. Leo's eyes were narrowed the whole time he followed after her.

Brandon stood up not long after and made his exit as well. Only Sam and I were left on the table. He was staring at me, waiting for me to say something.

I still can't believe what just happened. It was so fast. Did we just fight? I don't understand. They were so quiet. But by the way they looked at me, it was so obvious I did something that ticked them off. All I did was protect my pride. Was that so wrong? I don't understand anymore.

I grabbed my bag and left my food on the table. I left Sam without sparing him a word or even a mere glance and then went straight to the bathroom.

When I reached my destination, I lowered my head because there were two girls freshening up in front of the mirror. When they finally went out, which took almost forever by the way, I stepped forward and placed my hands on the corners of the sink. I looked at my reflection and took a deep breath.

You're alone now Mira. You can cry now.

After wasting some water my eyes produced unwillingly, I washed my face because my cheeks felt so sticky. My eyes were red and so was my nose. There was no way I'm going back to class looking like this.

I went inside one of the cubicles and locked myself inside. I closed the toilet and sat down, taking off my phone from my pocket. I'm not going out until my face recovers. I'll play some games to kill time.

Kill time.

Kill time.

Brandon and I are just doing this dumb game to kill time. He was the one who suggested it, so it's all his fault. But I agreed, so it's my fault too.

"I don't like her. I won't date her seriously. Heck I'm not even taking her seriously, and I'm sure she's doing the same. We're just playing around to kill time."

I was just about to enter my passcode on my phone when drops of water splashed on my screen. My vision was getting blurry. Shit. Stop wasting water you stupid pair of eyes.

Stop remembering his words you useless brain.

Damn it nose, stop sniffing like some drama-crazy teenager.

Heart, you douchebag, look at what you did.

Seriously, none of my body parts listen to me.

I don't know how long I was in the bathroom. Maybe too long, because my phone's battery was dying. I played games the whole time I was in there, maybe took a break so my eyes could release some more unwanted water from time to time, or so my heart could punch my chest while my jerk of a brain reminds me of all the bad things I've done.

Yup. I was fine just chilling in the bathroom. I, the stupid, idiotic, ungrateful girl. I, the confused yet stubborn girl that uses sarcasm as a shield. I, cry.

I fucking cry.

As I was drying up my eyes for the nth time, I heard a group of girls enter the bathroom.

I held my mouth so they won't know I was inside the last cubicle, and I even hauled my knees to my chest above the toilet so they won't see my feet.

In situations like this, usually I'm about to hear some sweet information from those girls. You know, like in the movies.

It's not as cool as the movies though. My legs were cramping. They were taking too long to say anything useful. All I heard were a series of compliment exchanges.

Girls.

One of them giggled before starting up a real conversation that didn't involve whose boobs got bigger over the year. "Hey do you know Brandon Pierce?"

Ah.

That definitely caught my attention. I felt a pang of hurt in my chest when she said his name. As if she was so familiar with him.

"That guy we bumped into on the way here?" Her companion asked.

"Yeah him," the first girl replied. "Didn't he look... I don't know, different than his usual cheery self?"

Girl #3 chuckled. I was labeling them based on their voices. "Maybe he fought with his girlfriend. Why do you care anyway? You like him?"

Teasing began and it echoed across the bathroom. I could only mimick their way of speaking so girly. I wonder why I feel so irritated.

Girl #1 defended herself. "I kinda have a tiny little crush on him since he sat next to me in Algebra last semester."

Again. Teasing.

"Well," girl #4 started. "He is cute. And he's part of the swim team right? He's got the looks, the personality and the body. Good taste."

Brandon was in the swim team? How come I didn't know that? Oh wait, Leo's in the swim team too! Of course. I mean, I knew he was in some kind of sport but I didn't exactly expect him to be in the swim team.

No wonder he has such a nice body. Um.

"And he just looks so dreamy. He smiles at everybody. I'm so jealous of his girlfriend."

"So he does have a girlfriend?" Girl #2 said. "Who?"

I held my breath. He does? He has a girlfriend? Then why's he sticking with me?

Girl #1 sighed hopelessly. "Mira Jadsen. She's in my Biology class."

What.

What...

What?

Girl #2 gasped. "That brute-strengthed girl managed to snag Brandon? Maybe she's just blackmailing him into going out with her or something."

HEY.

I didn't snag him. He stuck with me. It's not my fault I'm likeable.

"She's really nice," Girl #1 mused. My eyes widened at the sudden compliment. "Don't judge her. She's a really, really nice person. And she's so pretty."

Wow Girl #1, I feel so touched. I'm so sorry I don't recognize you from your voice alone. When I hear your voice again in a different time, when I'm not hiding inside a cubicle eavesdropping on you and your friends, I'll talk to you and be your friend too.

Only a few people see how friendly and loveable I really am.

"Oh," Girl #2 said. "How'd you know she's Brandon's girlfriend?"

"Well, it's kinda obvious since they're like, always together. And he looks happy with her. I even saw him kiss her in the hallways before. They looked so sweet."

I looked at the unstained tiles on the floor. We look like that to other people? No, maybe this girl was just overthinking it. Brandon doesn't like me that way. He's just a great actor.

His statement from earlier already proved that.

"Well, whatever," Girl #2 said, dismissing the topic. "If he's got a girlfriend then there's nothing you can do. I'd tell you to take him from her but that's not like you, so."

A series if giggles started and then slowly faded out. They went out now.

I put my legs down and stretched my limbs. I can't believe I actually heard something related to me in the bathroom. It's not just in the movies afterall.

I went out of the cubicle and checked my appeatance. Okay, I looked close to normal now, but my eyes were still a bit glassy and a shade of pink appeared on my eyelids from rubbing it too much.

My face looked so puffy ew.

I washed my face again before stepping out of the bathroom. I skipped two classes today. If they ask me why, I'll say I had diarrhea. That's a good excuse.

It was perfect timing when the bell rang. Classes were over. I just got out of the bathroom but I felt the sudden urge to pee. There were so many people in the hallways. I was afraid I'd bump into Brandon, Sam, Leo or Nichole.

Or worse.

I was afraid someone would notice I'd just cried, ask me what happened and I won't be able to finish explaining because I'll burst out into tears again.

Ugly-fying my face more than it already was did not sound at all appealing.

I pushed through the crowd of students and hurried to go outside, go home, eat then sleep. I need to recharge. I'm so exhausted I just want to sleep but I doubt my mind would let me.

I was already near the exit when I felt a hand grip on my arm and pull me into an isolated classroom. My eyes took some time to adjust to the sudden change of environment before I looked at the culprit.

I wasn't surprised to see who it was. More like, I was actually anticipating he'd do this sooner or later, though I don't know how he always managed to get his timing right.

"Brandon." I said.

I was nervous. I could feel the lump forming in my throat again and the tears were starting to sting my eyes.

Still, I pulled off a hard glare and composed myself, showing him how I was handling everything perfectly fine, and I still had the energy left to argue with him.

But I know he knows otherwise.

His expression showed no hate or anger. Just pure disappointment. I breathed heavily through my nose and learned that it was a big mistake because my nose sounded like it was vacuuming all the snot that collected inside it.

It's not as gross as I described it. Really.

I was hurt at the mere sight of his face. I don't know. Maybe it's because I know I hurt him too. But did I really? I wasn't sure.

But whatever it was, I wasn't gonna back down if he picks a fight because of it.

"Mira." He started, his voice cold and dull. I concealed a wince. It was like a few days ago when he got mad at me for getting lost on my way back to the apartment.

Anger boiled inside of me all of a sudden. A series of memories slapped my mind like a bitch - and they were all memories of Brandon. How dare he. How dare he treat me like this. After I told him about my dad.

He's just like him. They're all the same after all.

I was resisting the urge to punch him. His expression remained cold and the same. That ticked me off all the more.

I've had it. I'm calling this damn deal off. I've had enough. I'm done with this guy. Screw it, I'm done with guys in general.

"Listen here you mo- "

He cut me off abruptly when he quickly stepped forward, and I definitely did not expect what he did next.

CHAPTER 19

"Brandon what the hell!" I complained as I struggled off his tightly wrapped arms around me. He just suddenly hugged me out of nowhere. I'm so annoyed right now. He thinks he can sway me by this fake sweet gesture?

"I don't want to look at your damn face right now. Let go and get lost." I spat, but my tone didn't sound all that commanding at all. In fact, it sounded like the total opposite.

"Fine," he mumbled. Then he twirled me around so he was facing my back. He locked his arms around my shoulders and buried his face on my neck. "Then don't look at me. Just listen to what I have to say," he pleaded.

This is ridiculous what we're doing. It's stupid and I feel like crying all over again. I don't get him at all. What's wrong with us both?

This is getting too dramatic for me.

I stood still and remained quiet. He took that as a sign that I was listening, so he began. "I'm sorry. I just went along with your lead.

I was too harsh. I'm sorry. I really didn't mean anything I said back there."

Liar.

He's just saying that to save face and to fool me again. He's just scared of losing his only opponent in our dumb game.

"I know you probably won't believe me," he said as if he read my mind just now. "But you started it. You told Sam we were just doing stuff for fun. I mean, I know we are, but still, I don't think... I was actually..." He began trailing off his words.

I kept quiet as he mustered up the courage to continue what he was saying. He sighed. I shivered when his warm breath tickled the nape of my neck. "Before you said anything to Sam, I was about to say... Yeah, I did consider dating you seriously."

My pulse stopped for a second there. Was this another trick? A tactic? Or was this real?

How long is he going to leave me confused? I'm sick of it already. I'm sick of not being sure of anything.

"But not now," he said. I held my breath for some reason I won't admit. "I like what we have right now. And none of us confessed to each other yet, so you won't leave me for Sam, right? Right?"

I noticed how his voice showed a hint of a tremble. He was speaking out of nervousness. Like he was scared of losing something.

I can't tell if he's acting or if he's just going with the flow of the moment.

I'm scared to believe it's real. Because if it's not, I know I'll be disappointed again. I won't be too hopeful this time, I won't expect anything. Playing safe is more assuring, and this way I won't meet any disappointments.

I've had this way of thinking since my dad left us years ago. No one can exactly blame me for being what I am today.

I held the arm that was around my shoulder and rested my cheek against it. I wonder why I always lower my guard around him. I trust him, but at the same time I don't. "Do you like being with me?"

I needed to know, at least.

He stopped for a moment, maybe surprised by my question. I felt him nodding his head from behind. "Of course."

"Don't you get tired of my mean, sarcastic comments?"

"No," he chuckled. "I enjoy arguing with you even if I know I always lose."

"Don't you hate it when I punch you, kick you or harm you in anyway, conscious or not?"

He sighed. I don't know what expression he was making. He hugged me tighter from behind and somehow, I was starting to calm down. "First, don't label me a masochist for saying this. I don't hate it. But I don't exactly like it either. But it's fine with me anyway. I don't mind if it's you."

I slowly nodded, unsure whether to believe his replies or not. I still trust him. Sorta. But at least, it gave me some peace of mind for the time being.

"I want to see your face now," I mused.

He complied immediately. He gently twirled me around again, and as soon as we were facing each other, his hands fell down to my wrists.

"Sorry," I mumbled, looking at my feet. I'm so awkward at apologizing.

"I'm sorry too," he replied. "I didn't mean any of it, okay? I just said those things because I was annoyed. I don't want to give you to Sam."

I stared at him a bit surprised and a bit confused. He was misunderstanding something here. "But you don't have me."

I knew he knew what I meant.

"Yeah I do," he smiled. He finally smiled. It's just so relieving. My face unconsciously mirrored his expression. Damn it.

"Listen, Brandon," I looked down again, embarrassed to look at him in the eye for what I'm about to ask. Ooh boy. "Do you like me?"

He didn't say a word. Silence was his reply for a few seconds. I hid a bitter smile. What was I thinking? Way to make the situation more awkward Mira.

"Do I have to answer that now?" He said. My eyes were still glued to the floor until he held my chin up so he could look at my eyes. "I'm gonna lose the game if I say it, right? I'm not giving up that easily."

I don't know what to think of that. But somehow, I think I was the one losing. I'm losing. I'm definitely losing. I have to turn the tables around soon.

Brandon cupped my cheeks. He brushed his thumb softly near my eyes, staring at me with his eyes narrowed softly. "Did you cry?"

"Nope." I was quick to reply.

He knew better.

A guilt-stricken expression crossed his face as he pulled me into a warm embrace again. He ran his fingers through my hair before he pulled away to look at me. He looked down. "I'm sorry."

"Doesn't matter," I waved an airy hand. I don't want to remember my scene at the bathroom. Just thinking about how hopeless I've been makes me sick and drown myself in self-pity.

Brandon seemed like he was gonna argue, but he dropped it, probably knowing how pointless it was to argue with someone like me. He placed his hands on my waist and pressed his forehead on mine.Why was he so touchy today? Not that I mind though... "So, are we okay now?"

I don't know. Are we?

"Yeah. Sure. Totally." I replied.

"You can punch me if you want," he suggested, turning his head and pointing at his cheek. I snorted.

"You are a masochist."

He quickly returned to his original posture. "No, I just feel like I deserve a punch in the face for making you cry. I know you hate crying that much. Just punch me. I know you want to d- "

I didn't let him finish. I gave him a hard right hook on his cheek. He was asking for it wasn't he? I felt relieved after punching him. I felt like me again. Good.

He groaned as he took a step back, balancing himself and quickly trying to recover from the sudden impact. He massaged his jaw while giving me a look as if saying 'I wasn't prepared yet.' I shook my shoulders, feeling satisfied.

I took a breath before forcing a smile at him. We're okay now but it still feels a bit tense. "Now we're even."

He returned my smile.

We exited the classroom and he led me to his car. He was gonna drive me back home like the usual.

"Aren't you worried about Nichole?" He asked as he buckled my seat belt.

I shrugged again, sighing at that. "Yeah. I know she's mad because I lied to Sam - "

I stopped midway in my sentence because my mouth was saying whatever it wants. Brandon was looking at me, I gulped and pretended like I did that abrupt pause on purpose. I pretended like I dropped something and picked it up. Then I smoothly continued.

"I was just shocked because he suddenly said he liked me and he asked you that question and I just panicked. And, it's partly your fault too because you went along with it but in the extremely painful way."

Oh gosh. What was I really about to say? Did he notice?

He sighed as he started the car. He sounded so bothered. "I know. We'll apologize together. God, she's like our mom or something."

I laughed, agreeing with him. "Let's give her some time to cool down first. I'm sure Leo took her somewhere today. Wanna go somewhere too?" I asked, hopefully.

I don't know. I just felt like I lost something after that small fight. I felt the need to get it back, though I'm not sure what it was.

"Sure," he immediately replied. "I know a good place."

I stared at him in disbelief as I folded my arms against my chest. He threw his bag on the floor and collapsed on the bed as if he just had a really rough day.

"My room, Brandon?" I said. "When you said you knew a good place you meant my room?"

He grinned at me mischievously like he knew what my reaction was gonna be. Jerk. "Yeah. It's comfortable and private."

Private. Private to do what.

"Oooh," he sang. "I wonder what's running in your head."

I hid a blush before taking a pillow and throwing it at his face. Damn it, making me flustered over something like this.

I kicked my shoes off and lied down on the soft mattress. I sighed contentedly as I rubbed my cheek against my cold pillow. Ahh. My bed is the best.

He shifted from his position and scooted closer to me. Knowing what he wanted to do, I turned my back at him and slid my arm under my pillow. I'm not gonna do what he wants. No way.

I felt his body heat on my back and I admit I felt nervous. This happened several times before. Why am I still nervous?

This is so strange. It's as if nothing happened earlier at all.

I was expecting him to do something playful again but he didn't. Instead, he just quietly lied there, doing nothing. He wasn't even touching me. Or hugging me. Or playing with my hair.

Why?

I tried to steal a glance at him from the corner of my eye but it was impossible and a stupid idea.

This is so weird. He's not making any body-contact at all. He's usually so touchy. Was he restraining himself? Was he just tired?

I wonder why I want him to hug me again. What. Did I actually like cuddling?

What.

He was quiet for a while now. Was he asleep? "Brandon?"

No reply. I just heard him breathing quietly and steadily behind me. I guess he was asleep then.

I slowly turned my body around so I won't wake him up in the process. I want to play with his face and poke the spot where I hit him earlier, all while he's asleep.

When I accomplished my mission of turning around, I met a pair of open eyes and an annoying toothy grin.

Shit.

"I thought you were asleep," I concealed my surprise with a dull tone. He chuckled, the vibration from his chest sent tingles to my skin.

"Fall asleep that fast and with you in the bed? No way."

I rolled my eyes. Smart ass.

"Say," he started. His voice was so low.

I missed the way he talked like that. And I wanted to touch his cheek. The spot where I hit him was still pinkish, but I don't think it'll bruise. I feel bad for hitting him now. I don't understand why I just adored him right now. "What if you do come to like me?"

I averted from his gaze to save myself from creating another embarrassing expression. I wish he didn't ask that. "Then I lose."

He took my hand and played with my fingers. His hand was so warm. "What if we already like each other but we're just not admitting it because of this game we're playing?"

What was he implying?

I was silent, honesty not knowing what to say. What's the safest thing to say anyway?

He laughed softly. "What happens after one of us confesses?"

I don't know.

"What if none of us wants to admit it?"

I don't know.

"Will you still be my potato?"

I looked up and saw that he was grinning. I laughed at him before pinching his cheek. So he was just joking. Phew. Oh damn. I think I just shortened my life-span.

"You're so dramatic potato," I said. But I was obviously just dodging the subject.

He rested his hand on my waist and slowly shifted closer, like the tiny distance between us was still too much. "Is Sam more handsome than me?"

"What?" I giggled, surprised with his sudden question.

He shrugged. "I think I'm more handsome. What do you think?"

I couldn't control my giggles. Was he serious? "You're so vain."

"No, really," he insisted playfully. "Who do you like more between the two of us?"

Stop right there.

This was a trap.

I poked his nose with my finger - on his nose, not inside his nostrils okay? That's just gross. "I don't know. I wonder who?"

We both laughed, both concealing our questions and our answers with jokes and smiles.

We were still laughing, our gazes fixed on each other. He closed his mouth into a boyish smile before leaning in for a kiss.

It was just a slight brush on the lips. Just a tiny bit of contact.

And it wasn't enough.

Before I knew it, our lips were already locked on each other. I held his shirt and pulled him closer, his hand was on my back, pushing me closer as well.

He can't just kiss me like that and expect me not to want more.

A little while later, we pulled out to catch our breaths. We looked at each other's faces and laughed. We looked so frantic and I don't know if my eyes were playing tricks on me, but everything just looked so steamy somehow.

He smirked at me before sitting up. I watched him confused until he pressed his chest against mine. He settled on top of me, straddling my hips and making it completely impossible for me to escape.

We were fooling around again but I don't care. This was our way of releasing all the tension that transpired over the past few days, and especially earlier today. I don't want to stop now that we've started.

He began kissing me again, his hand gently playing with my hair, his other hand cupping my cheek.

Feeling his weight over me, I got more excited about what's to come next, and just a little bit afraid.

He pulled away and started trailing butterfly kisses on my neck. I sighed as I held the back of his head, then bit my lip when I felt him leaving a mark. I faintly groaned in complaint.

"Stop. Don't leave - "

I stopped when he pressed his lips on mine again, literally shutting me up. I liked it. I liked kissing him. So much it makes me wonder the hell was wrong with me.

When I felt his hand slip inside my shirt, I gasped and shivered under his touch. I felt alarmed all of a sudden. I panicked.

"Brandon," I mumbled, breaking our kiss. He didn't stop. "Brandon."

"Mm," he replied, working his way to the other side of my neck and his hand still exploring the inside of my shirt.

"The rules," I barely managed to say. I was just saying that as an excuse. I didn't care about the rules.

He sat up, looked at me with a smirk on his face and pulled his shirt off, revealing a glorious sight in which I always denied liking.

Denial was clearly not in my mind today, and especially not on my face. He leaned in to kiss me again before quickly tugging my own shirt up.

I panicked again and stopped his hand. He kissed my earlobe and I don't know what came over me, but I eventually helped him undress myself.

It was like he cast a spell on me. A dangerous spell that made me drop all the restrictions I've set on myself and between the two of us.

"Rules are just there for display," he said huskily as he dived into another big kiss.

Our bare skins were brushing against each other and it was warm. More than warm actually, it was hot. So hot it almost felt like my skin burned by his touch alone.

I felt my confidence rise back up. What's the point of rules? Everybody breaks them anyway. Why did we even create rules that were hard to follow?

I pushed his chest away and reversed our positions so I was on top. It was only right for me to be on top, right?

He had this pleased and playful glint on his eye when I started doing to him what he did to me. I kissed him over and over again as my fingers traced on his tight skin back and forth.

It still wasn't enough.

He was holding me still as I helped myself with his lips. Both of us knew this wasn't going to stop anytime soon.

I already knew what I felt about him, but because of the game, I won't admit it. Not before him. I'm afraid of what might happen when the game's over. I'll have no excuse anymore.

I'm scared of something. That's why I won't admit it to him. Not yet.

I'm not sure about Brandon. Frankly speaking I still don't get him and he still leaves me confused about him most of the time. But I was already sure about myself. I realized it a long time ago but I'm only going to acknowledge it now.

All those questions I kept asking myself. I already knew the answer but my pride wouldn't admit it. I can at least admit it to myself for now, because denial was keeping me exhausted everyday.

I like him.

I like Brandon.

But I don't want to tell him first. I'm really not sure if he feels the same. So that's why I need to keep this game going so I still have an excuse to be with him. I'm scared of being rejected again. I'm scared he'll leave me like my dad did.

Honestly, he's the only one who made me admit all of my fears to myself when I was too stubborn to accept it.

I'm just scared.

I got myself into some deep shit as soon as I agreed on playing this game with him.

"Still worried about the rules?" He asked. He probably noticed the conflicted look on my face. I shook my head and smiled at him, then softly pressed my lips on his again.

I'll just enjoy this moment while it lasts. We still have time. Wherever this thing is going, guess I'll just have to wait and see. Oh well, another heartbreak it is then.

Chapter 20

"I go to you myself with the kindness of my heart to help you sort things out in your head because I thought you cried by yourself the whole day, but what did I come home to?" Nichole scolded, disbelief and mock laughter in her tone.

"A burning sight that's seriously making me consider replacing my eyes?" Leo suggested, hoping to calm her down.

Stupid. He'd still remember it even if he does something as crazy as replace his eyes. But if he tries to replace his brain instead, I'd vouch for him.

Nichole completely ignored him. She gestured to both me and Brandon. "I come home to see my best friend pressed on a manslut, both half-naked and getting it on. Actually, I'm pretty darn glad I walked in in that moment instead of the finale."

Leo cringed. "Uh, don't make me imagine it again."

I was blushing furiously. Oh God. This was the worst. Why didn't we lock the door. Gosh. So stupid.

"Sorry..." I said in a tiny voice. Despite the guilt and utter embarrassment, I was relieved that Nichole was talking to me again. She didn't talk to me at school for nearly four hours. And yeah, between the two of us, that's already a big deal.

I'm glad she got mad for me. It just shows how much she cares. And I don't mind her scolding me for being so dumb.

She nodded, looking stubborn but I know she already forgave me. Then she looked at Brandon, expecting an apology from him too, maybe. He didn't do anything, I think he didn't get what Nichole meant when she was raising a brow at him.

I elbowed him, my eyes focused on my mother of a best friend. He awkwardly cleared his throat, finally understanding what I meant. "Oh. Um. Yeah, sorry I said those things to Mira. I already apologized to her."

Nichole nodded again, pleased. And then Brandon opened his mouth again. "You should apologize too. You walked in at a very intimate moment."

I lowered my head to conceal my cheeks. Damn why isn't this guy embarrassed to say this stuff? I know he was just pulling a joke to lighten up the mood but still.

I heard Leo groan, being the drama queen that he was. Nichole sighed heavily.

"Look, I don't care what you guys are gonna do or where this silly game of yours is headed, but Brandon, just know that if you hurt my best friend again, I'll cut you."

She was looking at him with a dangerous glint in her eye. She was serious as hell. I hid a small smile. I love her so much.

Brandon obediently nodded until Leo cut in.

"And to guarantee there's no bias here, Mira, if you hurt Brandon here for some stupid reason too, I'll..."

He looked up as if to think of a safe word to use on me. Choose wisely, fool. "I'll pinch your face so hard you won't feel it for a day."

"What!" Brandon complained. "That's not fair!"

I stuck my tongue out. Being a girl had its perks.

"The point is," Nichole said, leading the conversation to an end. "Just know when to stop. Okay? I love you guys, and I don't want our friendship to go to waste because of that game. Alright?"

At that moment I had a tugging feeling of uncertainty, some ominous or some sort. I don't know. Maybe it was my intuition, or maybe I was just thinking too much again.

Nonetheless, Brandon and I looked at each other before we returned our gazes at our best friends.

In order not to drag this tiny issue any further, we both nodded our heads in agreement.

As soon as Leo and Nichole left, Brandon and I fixed ourselves up. I mean, when they were lecturing us, we didn't look that presentable, and it was clearly obvious in our appearances that we fooled around even if they didn't catch us in the act (which they did, unfortunately.)

I hid a blush again. Oh shit I'm remembering it. We almost... Almost. It didn't happen. Well, maybe it wasn't going to happen. But it was way past third base. Ah! My heart feels like it's gonna explode. Oh gosh. My innocence...

Brandon sneaked up behind me while I was tying my hair into a messy bun. His hands crawled around my waist as he buried his face on my neck. I squeaked.

Seeing ourseleves in the mirror like that made me feel self-conscious all of a sudden, and I did what I always do whenever I didn't know what to do.

I got mad. Not really mad, just pretend-mad. Or playful mad. I don't know.

"What happened to the patient wolf?" I asked accusingly. He looked surprised, like he just remembered. Then he showed me a smug grin in our reflections on the mirror.

"A wolf's still a wolf."

I couldn't help but scoff to conceal a giggle. Gosh why am I so stubborn. I can't even show my real emotions freely without thinking about it too much. "My ass."

"Nice ass." He said.

I turned around and stared at him weirdly. His hands were still on the sides of my waist. "What?"

He was just staring at me with his lips curled up into a smirk. "What?"

Damn him. I rolled my eyes before slapping his hands off me. I walked away to put on my shoes, smiling stupidly to myself while he wasn't looking. This is bad. I shouldn't be so happy about something like this.

As soon as I was through tying my shoe laces, he grabbed my hand and pulled me outside. I complained, but didn't resist.

"Where are you taking me this time?"

He winked at me. Ugh. "To another good place."

I rolled my eyes so hard, I saw my brain. His definition of "good places" gave me trust issues. "Let me guess, the kitchen?"

He stayed silent until we reached his car. We were already on the road when I kept asking hin where we were going. He just smiled. "Dinner. We're just going out to dinner. Calm your t- " He stopped and snorted. "Never mind."

I knew the rest of that statement. I scoffed and looked out the window, but I doubt he didn't see the smile spread on my face.

And no, I wasn't smiling because of his dumb jokes. I think I was smiling because he was just so sweet. It scares me sometimes.

We arrived at a small family restaurant downtown. I could smell the aroma of the food all the way here in the car. We got out of his car and he led me inside.

"Order anything, dinner's on me," he said with a grin. We chose a table near the window, away from where the rest of the customers were sitting. A petite waitress waited patiently for my order, but I stopped and looked at Brandon puzzingly.

"But the rules?" I said. He shook his head slowly.

"Didn't we already break one of them? What's the harm in breaking another? No one's getting hurt here or anything right?"

I unsurely nodded my head. Well, whatever. I won't reject this offer of free food. I ordered what sounded like the most delicious dish in the menu and then Brandon told the waitress that he'll have the same.

When she left, it was just the two of us again. I couldn't sit still. I was so nervous. And I still feel shy about what happened earlier, I don't know. Being shy is not like me.

I still can't believe everything's that happened today. It was just so eventful. So much emotions in one day is not good for my heart. At all.

I studied the restaurant a bit and admired it's homey ambiance. It was easy to get comfortable, well, not that easy since Brandon kept staring at me the whole time.

I ignored him for a few seconds but every time I peek if he's still watching me, he is. Like he never took his eyes off me. My self-consciousness rose from 75 to 90%.

"What are you staring at you creep." I snarled. Ugh. Be nicer to the guy you like Mira. Don't be such a kid. He chuckled deeply before shaking his head.

"Nothing. I just like staring at you. Calms my nerves down."

I inhaled quietly through my nose. I need a good reply. One that won't make me sound too mean or too flustered. Just natural.

"Alright. Keep staring until you get sick of my face." Good. That was good. Strong but humble.

"I'll never get sick of your lovely face," he smiled boyishly. He had such a sweet tongue.

That was a figure of speech by the way. But he does taste sweet whenever we kiss. Maybe he eats chocolates or candies before -

What.

Mind, shh. Stop it. Stop. He's right in front of you.

"The food's here," I quickly announced. I'm glad it came at such a perfect moment.

All my thoughts were washed away in that instant because right now, I was living in the glorious moment of our food arriving.

It smelled so good, I had to close my mouth to prevent myself from drooling. I'm definitely coming back to this place with Nichole someday.

We dug in immediately without exchanging a single word or even a split-second of an eye-contact. We were that hungry.

It didn't even take ten minutes for us to finish the whole meal. It was so damn good. Or maybe its taste just increased tenfold because we were that hungry. But who cares? It was a great meal. Plus, it was free.

I lied my back against the chair comfortably as I held my full stomach. I was satisfied. Brandon smiled at me again. I smiled back quietly.

These exchanges of quiet smiles always makes me feel fuzzy inside.

He was probably about to say something but something else caught his eye and caused him to get distracted. Judging by his expression, he looked guilty and hesitant, but he was forcing a smile.

I turned around to see what was up and saw three boys coming our way. They didn't see us yet since they were so absorbed in their conversation. And their sights were fixated on the empty table behind us.

When they got a bit closer, I glanced at Brandon again. He never took his eyes off them, and it was as if he was waiting for them to notice him or something. His hand was already making it's way up to wave at them.

They finally noticed us before they sat down. All three of them looked at Brandon as if they couldn't believe it was him. To be more exact though, they looked quite cautious of him.

He waved smally before offering them a sincere smile. "Todd, Ken, Arvy. Good to see you guys."

One of them nodded unsurely. "Yeah. You too Brandon."

"How are you guys? It's been years hasn't it?" He asked, but he sounded cautious as well.

The other guy, the skinniest of the three replied. "Yeah, we're good. Hey, we're gonna sit over there," he pointed at a table which was pretty far away from ours. "Nice seeing you again."

They glanced at me and then at Brandon, and then at each other before walking away. Huh. I could've sworn they wanted to sit at the table behind us.

I followed them with my eyes until they sat down. One of them caught me staring so I looked away quickly. Why was it kind of... Tense?

I looked at Brandon and noticed how he gathered his hands and lowered his head, his brows creased and his lips were pressed together, forming a thin line.

Something was going on.

"Hey, potato?" I tried to sound as gentle as possible. He didn't look that approachable at the moment but I can't leave him alone.

He cleared his throat and placed our bill on the table. "Let's go?"

I quietly agreed and followed him back to his car. He didn't glance back at those boys but I did. They were staring at us the whole time. Creepy.

We went back to my apartment and hung out in my room. Brandon was quiet the whole time and I knew him well enough to know that something was bothering him. I knew it had something to do with those boys earlier.

I took my bun off and let my hair cascade behind my back. It's gotten quite long now, I better cut it soon.

Near my dresser, I saw a large bag of potato chips, and there was a sticky-note on it.

Mira, Leo saw this near the mall and we remembered you instantly. I shit you not, he used his own money to buy it this time.

P.S. I'm going home late, gonna hang out with Leo somewhere.

-Nichole

I snorted, but smiled. Aaw. Leo bought me something with his own money. I wonder if he wants something from me. The bag of chips is large indeed. I shook it to determine if 70% of its content was air but later concluded that only 15% of it was air.

That was good. More chips.

My grin widened when I saw the flavor. Hot chili. My mouth was watering already. I know I just ate dinner but still. I had room for one more snack.

I cradled my beloved chips back to my bed and saw Brandon just sitting there, staring at the floor.

I approached him carefully. "Hey, look what Leo got me."

It took him a second to look up at me and then at the bag of chips. He cracked a hopeless smile. "You really love spicy stuff."

I made a toothy grin. "And you can't stand them. So, more for me."

I kicked my shoes off and opened the bag easily. I was swallowing my saliva. The smell infiltrated my nostrils and brought me to an imaginative land of pure ecstacy.

Dude, it's not drugs 'kay? It's just that good judging from the smell and the appearance and the amount of chips alone. Let me describe it that way.

I made myself comfortable before I dug in. I took a fistful of chips from the bag and put them all in my mouth. My cheeks were stuffed as I started to chew, the sounds of crunching dominating the sound of anything else.

Damn, so good.

I heard Brandon chuckle beside me. I knew I made a stupid expression just now because of what I was eating but whatever. He's used to it.

"Say," I began, putting more chips in my mouth even when I still wasn't done with the current batch I was chewing. "I heard you have a trauma about spicy stuff, or something like that?"

I wasn't sure if asking that was the right thing right now. I mean, even Leo said he wouldn't tell him about it. Why should he tell me?

And why am I so interested? Well.

I guess I just wanted something to talk about. Guess I just wanted to know him better.

He sighed before nodding. "Yeah. Kinda lame, isn't it?"

I shook my head hurriedly. "No it's not lame. It's actually quite interesting. It's the first time I've heard about that."

Shit. I just said his trauma sounded interesting. Mira you're so stupid! Think before talking for once will you?!

"It's not that interesting," he chuckled quietly. "It's weird. But I really can't stand spicy stuff. Just thinking about it makes my stomach turn."

"Why?" I asked, genuinely curious and concerned. I really want to know the reason why. Maybe I can help.

He was quiet for a short moment. It actually got me worried because maybe I was being too persistent or nosy. I hope he doesn't mind. "It's a long story."

I was honestly getting excited, shame on me, I know. But he really sounded like he was willing to tell me. Or maybe it's just me thinking like that.

Maybe, maybe.

"Hey, you listened to my drama about my dad," I pointed out. I was sincerely grateful that time. I hope he knew that. "I'll listen to you talk even if it takes hours."

I meant it.

He looked hesitant. I didn't want to force him if he didn't want to tell me but a part of me said he was this close to telling me everything. He just needed a little push to open up.

"You might think differently of me after you hear it," he said, averting his gaze. Was he really so worried about that?

I stopped putting chips in my mouth and stopped chewing for a minute. I put the chips aside and gazed at him carefully. I was serious. "Like I said before, you're still Brandon."

He looked at me weirdly before laughing softly. His cheeks were heating up and I had to take a deep breath when I saw him that way.

At that moment, he just looked so vulnerable and it made me feel special somehow. Like I was the only one he showed this side of him to.

Of course, I wouldn't believe that even if I wish it were true. I already swore to myself never to expect anything that might leave me disappointed again.

"Promise you won't tell?" He asked, sounding like a little kid. He hasn't even told me the story yet and I already want to hug him. His face said it all. He went through some serious shit.

I nodded and looked at him seriously. This is it. "I promise."

He stared at me for a while, as if contemplating in his thoughts for the last minute if it was the right thing or the right time to tell me about his past.

His face lit up with a gentle smile when I gave him a reassuring smile as well. That simple smile alone made me feel trusted. He already made up his mind.

He took a deep breath and sighed heavily. I'm listening. "It started when I was eight."

Chapter 21

Brandon was shifting uncomfortably in my bed. I put my chips aside so I can listen to him clearly but mostly because I couldn't hear well with all the crunching sounds my mouth was producing.

He was staring at the floor the whole time, too embarrassed to look at me in the eye. I feel a bit guilty for having to let him tell me about his life.

He took a deep breath and quietly released it. "You already know I'm an orphan right?"

I nodded.

"Well," he said, like that word alone made him squeeze it out of himself. "What I'm about to tell you is what happened when my real parents were still alive." He showed me a faint smile, but the melancholic look in his eyes pricked my heart.

I nodded again and motioned for him to continue. "When I was eight, my parents and I lived in a lively neighborhood. The adults and my parents got along, the mailman was friendly and the other kids were all my friends, even if our age gaps were too wide."

Brandon was closing his eyes, like he was visualizing the past. It seemed like a pleasant memory for him, since he looked calm and a smile was even tugging on his lips. I smiled too, thinking about how adorable he probably looked when he was a kid.

Then his smile vanished and his lips formed a thin line when he continued with the rest of his story. "It was summer. We were watching a movie one night, a scary one, since mom loved horror films. We heard unusual sounds, like glass shattering, loud footsteps and something getting dragged on the floor. When we paused the movie to listen to it clearly, the sounds stopped. So we thought they were all just sound effects from the movie and we were just getting paranoid because dad and I can't handle scary shit."

I was breathing deeply and slowly, mentally preparing myself to listen what's about to come next.

"Mom even made fun of us. Said we were sissies or something," he hid a grin. "And then it happened."

I swallowed hard. I think I'm hyperventilating, and he's just starting. I can't help it. I'm afraid to know. Yet I want to know. But -

Shh Mira. Shh.

"I felt like something was wrong - I didn't feel safe at the moment. Not because of the movie, but because of something... Strange and unexplainable. So I stood up and went to the kitchen. I swore I heard people talking there. Mom was too absorbed in the movie to even notice I'd walked off and dad was, well, absorbed in partially covering his eyes on mom's shoulder."

I broke a helpless grin. I see the resemblance from father and son.

"All the lights were off. Mom wanted a real spooky atmosphere to match the mood of the movie. It took a lot of guts just to walk to the kitchen. It was scary as shit."

And I see how opposite his mom was to him and his dad. And how scarily similar his mom's tastes and my mine are.

Brandon's face grew dark, and I knew we were getting close to the important part.

"At first I was relieved. There was nobody in the kitchen. But what was I thinking? I couldn't see because of the darkness. I was about to leave when I heard some utensils fall. The sounds were pretty noticeable. Then all of a sudden, this hand clamped my mouth shut. My screams were muffled, I almost pissed myself from the shock."

Oh, God.

"There were two men in the kitchen. I couldn't see them, but I could hear them arguing. They were blaming each other for being too loud, and for revealing their selves to me. My parents noticed all the noise, so they went to the kitchen."

He lowered his head, slowly burying his face in his hands. He was trying to hide. I felt saddened for some reason.

"I was glad they were coming. I thought they were going to save me - but then I realized something. If these guys saw my parents, they'll hurt them. So I tried screaming, I tried to tell my parents to run and call the cops. It was impossible. All that came out of my mouth were muffles. I just made the situation worse. I was a stupid, ignorant little kid."

"Dad turned on the lights and I can't even describe the shock and horror on their faces when they saw me. My eyes adjusted to the brightness and then I just noticed those men were wearing masks. They were burglars. And they got found out. Dad tried to calmly tell them to let go of me, even though his fists were shaking. He was resisting the urge to punch them because they had me. They didn't listen. There were yelling and cursing - I don't know. I was close to fainting that time. Then those guys pulled out guns. I was crying so hard, mom was telling me it was gonna be okay but I know it wasn't. They were gonna kill us."

I listened quietly as he continued with the story. I was amazed he could tell this story so calmly, until I saw his shoulders. His tremulous shoulders. And I had just noticed how his voice was shaking, like he was about to cry.

What are you supposed to do in this situation?

"Dad took a step forward with his hands up. He was still trying to convince them to let me go. I think one of them got scared when dad moved, so he shot him."

I winced and covered my mouth after hearing that part of the story. Maybe I was visualizing it too much, because I seriously heard a gun fire after he said shot.

I know Brandon was just forcing all his words out. This story was too hard to tell without breaking down, but he was doing a good job at keeping his composure - somehow.

"I managed to release myself but only for a split-second. I saw my dad on the floor. He wasn't moving. Why wasn't he moving? That bullet can't kill him instantly... Right? My d-dad was stronger than that."

His voice was quickly breaking, and it was getting smaller until it became silent. He was quiet for a few seconds, probably trying to find his voice. I didn't know what to do in this situation. I don't know the right thing to say either. I was so useless.

He slowly raised his head and looked at me. And that quick look broke my heart. His eyes were so glassy and he was just trying his best to keep his mouth shut so he wouldn't break down.

bBefore I could even hug him unconsciously, he buried his face on my shoulder, ashamed to show his face.

I patted his shoulder as he clutched my shirt so hard I thought it was gonna tear. But at the moment, I really didn't mind.

"I was screaming and screaming and screaming. I thought I was gonna go deaf by my own voice. One of them slapped me but I couldn't. I should've. They grabbed mom by the hair and asked her where we kept the safe. Mom said that if she told them, they should leave, but they made no promises. They kicked her over and over, annoyed that she wouldn't tell them until they let me go. They were so fucked up. They weren't people. They were animals - demons. I couldn't stop crying. My mom was getting beaten and I was so helpless. I couldn't help her."

He paused again. I felt him wipe his eyes on my shirt. He pulled me close, letting go of my shirt and hugging me by the waist. Right now, he looked like a frail little boy, afraid of the world. I continued rubbing his back to calm him down somehow. It may have been pointless, but I needed to do something. I didn't know what else to do.

"They got sick of my crying so they decided to tie a cloth around my mouth or something, but they couldn't find one in our kitchen. The bastards got resourceful in that moment because they stuffed the thing nearest to them in my mouth." He took a deep breath just before releasing it exasperatedly. "It was chili. They stuffed my mouth with chili to shut me up."

Oh shit. Oh shit. This is where it all began. Shit, I never would've thought... I had no idea. No, nobody had any idea this was the cause of Brandon's ultimate hate for spices. I feel so horrible now. And a feel a deep hate for those bastards that did this to him. Shit. Shit.

"Mom was crying. She didn't want to see me get abused like that even though she was getting abused herself. She barely stood up and landed a hard hit on one of them. And as a result for her heroic actions, the guy who stuffed my mouth shot her too. And she fell. For good."

I was sniffling. God, I was crying too. It was so horrible. His childhood is so horrible and he didn't even deserve that. His family didn't deserve that. But those men deserved to go to hell.

"The next thing I knew, the cops came. I can't remember what happened during that time, all I can remember is the sight of my motionless parents on the floor, and the paramedics carrying their bodies in stretchers - but they were already gone, and nothing can bring them back."

Brandon sobbed on my shoulder and I had to force myself not to cry. I have to be the strong one here. No wonder he was so hesitant to tell Leo or anybody else for that matter. His childhood was fucked up. I never would've imagined that the cheerful Brandon had to go through those serious shit. Shit.

I can't stop the profanities overflowing from my mouth. I'm just so sad and so mad for him and I have no idea what to say so let me just cuss. Shit. Fuck.

"When morning came, I was an orphan. A psychologist came to visit me a few times a week to check on my mental health. She said most children who've undergone such traumatic experiences lost their sense of reason. She said I was lucky I was still sane and managed to get off with just a negative reaction to anything spicy. Because every time I taste that flavor, I'm reminded of that incident. Every fucking time. Even until now. I really can't help it Mira, my body rejects the mere taste of it. I don't want to hate it since it was my mom's favorite flavor, but I really, really can't help it."

He sounded like he was pleading with that fact. Like he was begging me to forgive him because he can't like the same thing I like. If that's what he's thinking then here's what I'd tell him: bullshit.

He didn't have to apologize. He didn't do anything wrong. I stroked his hair gently before planting a kiss on his head. "Of course you can't help it. It's not your fault. Stop blaming yourself, okay?"

He was quiet again. I stayed patient until he decided to speak again. My shoulder was damp with his tears now. He apologized and his ears flushed red but I said I didn't mind it at all.

Moments passed and he seemed to recover bit by bit. He never let go of me. It was like he was clinging to me for dear life, and if he let go for even just a second, I'd disappear. I was beginning to think he thought I was his mom. We were so alike, in so many ways. And I only heard about her now.

"Remember when I told you I covered for my mom when she got her period at the mall?" He suddenly asked.

"Yeah?" I replied.

He smiled at me warmly. "That's my foster mom. The one who took me in after my parents' burial."

I just looked at him, slowly sinking that information in my brain. I see...

"None of my relatives wanted to take custody of me. It was a long, boring argument in court. Until the officer that saved me from those men decided to take me in, said that if nobody in my family rejected that suggestion, he'd raise me himself. He was the only one there who wanted to take me in. My relatives agreed and signed the papers, this and that happened, and then, I became the adoptive son of a kind officer his nice wife."

Anger boiled inside me again. His relatives were pretty shitty too. How dare they ignore a kid in that situation? And they call themselves family. Family my ass.

"You must really hate your relatives," I mumbled, gritting my teeth. I was suddenly reminded of my father. It sucks to know that the people you're related to by blood are the first to turn their backs on you.

Brandon shook his head, looking strangely calm now, for some reason. He had already lifted his head from my shoulder and he was looking at me face to face. I couldn't stop looking at his eyes. They were glassy, undeniably beautiful... Like blue crystals.

"Nah. We weren't that close with our other relafives. Both my parents didn't have siblings, so the relatives I mentioned earlier are... Distant or something. I literally have no idea who they are, but the police thought it was best to contact the nearest kin. And I'm glad they didn't take me in. They looked boring and grumpy. I love my current parents. They're the reason why I got to stay sane and optimistic in this messed-up world."

I felt a smile creeping in my face. I loved it whenever he spoke fondly of his parents. Whether he was related to them in blood or not, it was obvious in his eyes that he loved them, just as much as he loved his real parents.

"Well," Brandon said, his tone almost back to normal now. "That concludes book one. Now you have to download the second book to learn about the rest of the story."

I knitted my brows while tilting my head, confused. What was he saying? "What?"

He grinned at me, the familiar twinkle in his eyes met my puzzled ones. Ah. He's back. "It's a trilogy."

I snorted. What the hell. He can still joke in this situation. This guy is definitely something. I smiled. I want to know him more, so I'll play along for him. I know he wants to tell me. His ways of opening up are just... Unique. "How do I download the second book?"

He looked at me like he couldn't believe I asked. I sent him a weird look. "Isn't it obvious already? It's not a free download. You have to purchase the second book."

What...

I sighed. Let's just get this thing over with. "What do you want me to do Brandon."

He grinned. I knew what he wanted by that grin alone. "One hug, two kisses on the cheeks and one kiss on the lips."

I chuckled at his childish conditions but complied to his requests anyway. I know he's just trying to lighten up the mood. So I gave him a huge hug, kissed his left cheek then his right, and then gave him a soft kiss on the lips.

We smiled at each other silly after that. It was kind of cute actually. I looked horrible with my tear-stained face but he looked adorable. Still, I think we looked cute.

Oh my God did I just admit that?

He made a ka-ching sound before clapping his hands. "Thank you for purchasing the second book. Now on with the story."

I tried to control my giggles. Damn this guy knew how to change any mood quickly.

I lied my back against the headboard of my bed as Brandon made himself comfortable by taking one of my pillows and placing it on his lap.

"The second book fast-forwards time a bit, so here I'm twelve now."

I nodded, eager to listen to the rest of the story. He proceeded.

"This was the time where I became the biggest bully in school."

Chapter 22

"Wait," I raised my arm and executed a silly 'stop' signal with my hand. I sent him a playful grin when he stared at me for the interruption. "You? A bully? A bully of what, potatoes?"

He rolled his eyes before taking my accusing hand and locked both our fingers together. I felt my heart skip a beat. "Shut up and listen."

I puckered my lips in a mischievous manner before motioning him to proceed. I can't describe it clearly, but I liked his expression so much. It feels like he's relaxed with all these, like he's so comfortable with me even after showing me his weak side.

I can't help but wonder if he really trusts me or if he just needed someone to talk to.

I'll think about that later. For now, I'll just listen to his story.

"Well, when I said I was a bully, that was just to catch your attention," he admitted. "I told you before that I was bullied because I was an orphan, remember?"

Now that he mentioned it...

"That's right," I said. "You even said you wanted to apologize to those bullies. But then you just said you were the biggest bully in school. I'm confused here."

I was. I really was.

Brandon's lips curled up when I said that. He loves messing with my head. Ugh. "Until I turned twelve, I was a loser. I didn't have my own voice and the older kids pushed me around because I was so small and thin back then. I never complained whenever they hurt me. Dunno why, actually. Maybe I was too weak."

He's not weak. After all he's been through, nothing about him is weak.

"So my dad - my second dad - found out about my situation in school because of my bruises and cuts. So he taught me a few tricks he learned from being an officer. He taught me self-defense."

My brows raised at the mere mention of that overly familiar term. I don't know why I felt both guilty and excited when he revealed this to me. It just got my blood boiling for reasons that didn't involve anger.

"So there. After practicing with him a few times a day, I got better and stronger. Sometimes I didn't mean it, but I fought back a bit too hard on those bullies. I couldn't control my own strength, so every time I hit them thinking it was just an ordinary hit, it was actually quite critical. I got suspended for sending them to the hospital a few times."

Aah. I think I just found my soulmate.

"And I don't know where I developed this habit of glaring at random people, maybe it was during that time so no one could ever bully me again. When I first saw you, trust me, I wasn't glaring at you. I just thought you were really pretty."

I hid a blush. No, no. Don't be so affected by something he said so naturally. "So let me get this straight," I said, clearing my throat as if I didn't just hear him say I was pretty. "You look at bullies, potential bullies and pretty girls the same way?"

"Pretty much," he simply replied. I almost fell off the bed.

"Wow Brandon. I..." I overexaggerated my speech a bit. My sarcasm switch was turning on. "I'm... I'm so honored you put me in the pretty girls category. Maybe you sensed my awesome abilities so you got confused between pretty girls and potential bullies? It produced the same result anyway right?"

He scoffed at my sarcastic remark, but then he grinned after that. "Nah. You actually belong to all three categories. A bully, because you bully me, a potential bully because sometimes I'm not sure if you're gonna kick me or not, and a pretty girl, because you're too damn beautiful. You're the whole package."

I smirked, pleased with his reply. And yeah, I was hiding another blush because of that compliment but I was playing it cool. "I'm divergent."

We laughed after I replied using a book reference. I just loved talking with this guy. I didn't have to hide anything and I felt like I can tell him everything without having to worry about him judging me. Maybe he feels the same -

Shh. Don't think about it. Just go with the flow Mira.

"So there," he said, gripping my hand a bit tighter. "The start of my career as a bully."

"Oh please," I told him. "You were just defending yourself. You're not a bully for beating up bullies."

He shook his head. "No, I was a bully. I stooped down to their level and fought back more than necessary. Whenever I felt intimidated by someone, I call them out after school and beat them up before they beat me up, you know? I was doing it ahead of them, threatening them not to mess with me. Although if I think about it now, they were pretty harmless. I was pretty much a delinquent."

I just kept nodding my head like a freaking robot. I see. I see. I never thought he was like that before. He was a Gangster Potato back then. He sure changed a lot.

"I even had enemies from other schools. They came in groups and challenged me into fights so they could feel more superior. Bullshit. I beat them to a pulp by myself, without having to break a sweat."

I released a ball of breath (let's just call it that way - I don't know how else to put it) before raising a brow. "So you're saying you're a good fighter?"

"I'm a great fighter," he replied easily.

I mentally rolled my eyes. So modest.

"So, by being a good fighter, you always get punched and kicked by me? Which makes me what, the best fighter?" I challenged, oh-so-humbly as well.

He sent me a warm smile, the kind of smile you give a kid that was being too cute for her own good. "I can't predict what you want to do next. You're different from the average guys."

Oh wow. He even compared me to the average guys. Again Brandon, I'm so deeply touched.

"Or maybe I'm just too distracted by your face, your eyes, your whole being that I don't even mind whatever you do to me."

He was smiling at me goofily while saying that, like he was reciting lines from a cheesy movie. I rolled my eyes laughing but I felt the heat rush up to my cheeks. Damn it this guy knew how to talk.

"Shall I continue with the story, or do you want a match to see if I'm telling the truth or not?" He suggested. I gave him a look. Wasn't my answer obviously already?

"Go on with your story," I said. "We'll have a match later."

"A match? Later? Right here? Just the two of us? In this bed?" He asked, sounding a bit too eager yet playful. I burst out into a fit of mock laughter.

"Sure."

He sent me a wink. "Ooh nice. I don't even want to continue the story anymore. I want to start the match already so I can win and tie you up in your own bed."

My room was filled with his deep laughter after that and I had to slap his shoulder a few times just to get him to continue with the story. He was having too much fun this brat.

"Okay, okay," he finally surrendered. Good. I have to focus, damn it. What he said just lit up a few suggestive images in my head and that was not good. Not good at all, potato. "Remember those three guys in the restaurant earlier?"

"Yeah?"

"They made fun of me because when the teacher asked me to fill a form that required my parents' name back then, I put my real parents' and my foster parents' names. They laughed at me because I had two dads and two moms. The thin one there, Arvin, told everyone at school that my first pair of parents were ghosts and the second pair were soulless bodies or something. T'was pretty childish. I hated him for that. He had no idea what I've been through. So after class, I met him outside school. He was with his two buddies. He started taunting me again and I couldn't control myself. I beat him and his buddies up. Arvin was in a coma for two weeks."

A hand travelled to my mouth. Gosh. I can't imagine Brandon like this at all. A coma?

"After that I was expelled. Dad found out about how I've been applying the things he taught me and he was very disappointed in me. I felt bad. I really did, so I decided to change. I can't erase my past, those kids I beat up probably won't forgive me but at least I have to forgive myself, right? What's done is done. I have to look forward."

I was this close to clapping. He was so optimistic. If I were in his place I wouldn't have made it this far and with such a cheerful personality too. It really is true what they say. People who smile the brightest, hide the most pain.

"It's easier said than done though," he admitted. "I still feel really guilty. And Arvin's really afraid of me after that incident. I broke his nose and fractured his ribs. It was that bad. I'm still reflecting up until this day."

I wanted to say it was Arvin's fault for being a snotty little brat. Brandon's parents were a touchy subject during that time and he just had to rub it in his face. If I was in Brandon's shoes, I would've done the same. Maybe even worse.

"I wonder why I don't feel guilty every time I beat someone up," I thought out loud.

"Because for you, it's self-defense. And it is. No arguments there," he replied. And then he looked uo as if he thought of something. "Didn't you feel bad after beating Sam up and then learning about his true intentions?"

Why is he bringing Sam up again? Seriously.

"Because I know I did something bad to an innocent person."

"What about me?" He asked, more like whined. "You don't feel bad for kicking my precious. If I can't father children in the future, I'm putting the blame on you."

I don't know why I found that so funny.

"Of course I feel bad, stop whining like a kid." I rolled my eyes. He was grinning like an idiot. I wish he'd stop smiling at me like that. I can't think properly.

He folded his arms. "If I'm a kid then you should take reponsibilty and kiss my booboos."

"Seriously Brandon?"

He was raising his brows suggestively while offering me a wide smirk. We'll see if you can keep that face up for long.

"Back when I gave you a booboo to your little precious and offered to soothe the pain for you, you flinched and backed away like a girl. If I kiss it you might faint from all the excitement."

Okay. I just used innocent choices of words for sexual references. This was awkward. Wait - How'd our conversation turn this way again? Curse you Brandon.

"First of all, my precious shall not be called little." He said.

Oh. My. God.

"And second of all, I didn't actually expect you to do that. You were being a bully and my precious did in fact get excited but - "

Make him stop! Make him stop!

"If it happens again, I'll make sure my precious and I will be prepared." He finished with a wide smirk. He knew I was getting embarrassed.

I glared at him. "Would you please stop referring to your thing as your precious? You sound like Gollum. And you look like him."

Bad taste in insults Mira. That was so weak.

He stuck his tongue out before biting back. "You called it that too. What should I call it then? Potato?"

"No! No!" I strongly disagreed as I shook my head so hard I thought it was gonna fall off my shoulders. There's no way in hell he's gonna name his thing Potato and call me Potato too. Nope. Nuh-uh.

His grin was so wide now. It probably beat the Cheshire cat's smile. I can't believe we're even talking about this right now.

"Then I'll call it Junior," he said. "Potato Junior."

Dude. I face-palmed. "It doesn't necessarily need a name you know."

"You're always torturing him so yeah, Potato Junior deserves his name." He argued childishly.

"Ahh alright call your thing whatever you want, have it tattooed for all I care but let's just drop the topic. Okay? Now where were we?"

Brandon chuckled before pinching ny cheeks. Fuck him. I mean no! Screw him! No! I didn't mean - I meant - Ugh! He's corrupting my pure and innocent mind!

"You're adorable Potato," he laughed, cupping my cheeks and bringing my face closer to his. He gave me a long kiss on the mouth and then repeatedly pecked my entire face with his kisses. "I can just eat you up."

Okay, my brain seriously needed to stop functioning right now because it was sending me all the wrong ideas.

"Brandon." I tried to sound calm. He was still kissing every part of my face. Did I seriously look like a kid to him? Why is treating me like this? Not that I don't like it but - AAH! He's driving me nuts! "Brandon."

He pressed his lips on mine as he replied. "Mm?"

I just couldn't bring myself to pull away. Damn him. He's lucky I like him so much. Damn him to hell. "What happened to the rest of the story?"

"Oh yeah," he chuckled. His warm breath fanned my face but his lips were still pressed on mine. What was he up to? "I stopped beating people up, reflected and became the me I am today. I can't get rid of my glaring habits though. The end."

"The end?!" I exclaimed, disbelief in my eyes. I would've pulled away if it weren't for his hands that had snaked to the sides of my waist. I supressed a gasp. "What do you mean the end?!"

He slowly laid me down with him hovering over me and his lips never parting with mine. I felt him make a lazy grin. "Book two is done. Now you have to purchase book three to learn more about the story. The price has been upgraded for my benefit. Do you want to purchase the third book and conclude the Potato Trilogy? Or do you want to purchase it another day? The offer stands without a deadline."

I was feeling tired already because this guy was just a hopeless story-teller and even if he did tell me the rest of the story now, I wouldn't be able to concentrate with him doing this to me.

"I'll purchase it another day," I said.

He nodded. "Then what do you want to do now? Want a match?"

I knew pretty well where this was going. My reply was the same. "In another day."

"Oh I know," he grinned at me innocently. "Want to meet Potato Jun - "

"No."

He laughed and playfully made a disappointed expression. "Damn."

It was a few seconds before one of us moved or even spoke again. It was getting pretty late. He kissed the corner of my lips a few times before diving into a real kiss. Then he trailed kisses from my jaw down to my neck. Then he just stooped, his head just buried there on my neck.

"I'm sleepy," he yawned. I yawned too.

"Then sleep." I commanded.

"You know," he began. "We're in a compromising position right now."

I had to agree. His head was buried on my neck, his hands were on my waist and my fingers were tangled in his hair. But we weren't doing anything. We were just too tired to move.

"So what?" I asked.

"Well, usually, either Nichole or Leo would walk in on us. They can sense Potato Junior's awakening, I swear. They're trying to stop it."

We both laughed at the memories where our best friends always caught us in the act. I could feel the vibrations of his laughter on my chest and it felt so warm and nostalgic. I didn't even feel much of his weight while he's on top of me. Maybe he's partially supporting himself so he won't crush me. Wow. He still had the energy to do that?

Well, either that or I had boobs of steel.

"Mira?"

Nichole gently knocked on my door and opened it before I even got to answer. Gotta love your best friends.

She released a silent, frustrated, yet mischievous groan after seeing us like that. Leo made barfing noises.

"See?" Brandon said. "Told you they were gonna walk in."

I giggled as Leo went closer to the side of the bed and started pulling Brandon's shirt like a kid. "C'mon you damn Casanova," he mumbled. "Get off my best friend. It's late and we still have class tomorrow."

"Since when did you worry about class?" Brandon lazily replied, getting off me as told. Wonder why I felt so cold all of a sudden.

"Since I found out I'm flunking Biology," he replied. "Now let's go. We're going ahead Mira."

"Bye." I mumbled, half-awake. Damn I was so tired. Maybe all the crying I did this day alone drained all my energy.

"Goodnight Potato," I heard Brandon yawn again.

After they left, Nichole pulled my covers up and tucked me in. Then she shut the lights off before she closed my door quietly. "Goodnight Mira."

CHAPTER 23

I woke up in a pretty good mood. Well, even if my eyes looked puffier than usual because of all the crying last night, I felt good. Mostly about myself.

Brandon picked me up for school. Leo had swimming practice, so Nichole carpooled with us. We were quiet the whole ride, but as I stole glances at Brandon, I could see his lips twitching, as if he was forcing himself not to grin too weirdly.

I could sense all the good vibes emitting from his aura, and Nichole did too.

"Okay," she said, breaking the comfortable silence. "I know I'm the third wheel here. Just pretend I'm air. Go on, manslut. Go flirt with my best friend."

I laughed at her accusing quip as Brandon rolled his eyes. "I don't like an audience. I like to keep things for my eyes only." And then he sent me a wink.

Nichole scoffed and waved an airy hand. "Sure. Don't you have swimming practice today too? Leo said your coach gave you a week's worth of make up practices for your absences."

"I'll come by later," he shrugged, not caring at all. "Gotta drop off some pretty girls to school first."

She scoffed even louder this time. "If you're gonna start flirting again Brandon, make sure not to get me involved. It's disgusting."

"You're disgusting." He bit back.

"At least I don't suck on stranger's necks. No matter how thirsty I am."

Defeated, Brandon released a frustrated sigh. But I knew he didn't really get mad or anything. His mood was far too great to be shaken by something like this.

After he dropped us off, he sprinted for the pool, to catch up on practice. I gotta come to their practices some time. I'm interested at how well he swims.

"Hey Mira," Nichole called my attention. I turned my look at her after I shut my locker close and sliding my bag behind my shoulder. "I need to tell you something."

This tone. That look. This was serious.

"What is it?"

She avoided my eyes as she replied, playing with the hem of her shirt in the process. "Well. Leo and I are kind of... Um. How do I put this... Things aren't going pretty well."

My eyes widened like saucers. This is the first time I'm hearing this. "Why? What happened?"

"Long story short," she sighed, meeting my eyes now, somehow hopelessly. "I'm getting exhausted. I love him, I really do and I want us to last. But he's just so overprotective. You know? Maybe that's just natural for him as my boyfriend, but I feel so trapped. He gave me a list of things I should and shouldn't do, and a list of stuff I should and shouldn't wear. Am I a dog? And he's always getting mad at me for the smallest things, and we argue all the time. I don't know Mira. I don't know where this is going."

I felt like I was the one gasping as she didn't even pause once in her explanation (despite the punctuation marks I put there for effect). She said it all in one breath, believe it or not.

I quietly nodded as all her words sunk in my brain. I always thought Nichole was the dominant one in their relationship. It was actually Leo? I never knew he had this side of him. Frankly speaking, I didn't know what to say. First, because I have no experience in this things, and second, because I got nothing bro.

"So what are you planning to do?" I asked. I was walking her to her classroom before I go to mine.

She shrugged her shoulders. "I don't know. I'm happy with him though. I guess I can still tolerate the small stuff."

Small stuff. What if that 'small stuff' turn into something big in the future just because she kept tolerating it?

But I didn't speak my thoughts. It was risky. And it's her decision to make. I'm not even qualified to give advice yet.

"Well, whatever it is you're planning to do, I'll support you. If Leo does anything stupid, just know I'll punch him without hesitation, even if he is my best friend too. You know that."

"Yeah," she smiled at me. Then she gave me a tight hug before pulling away and entering her class. "Thank you. I love you. See you at lunch."

I nodded and then left for my own class, still thinking about what Nichole just told me. I don't get it. Are relationships that complicated? But she and Leo looked fine these past few weeks.

I feel so dumb and useless. I didn't even realize what my best friends we're going through. And I don't know how to help. I'm afraid I'll only make it worse so I'll just support them from afar. I don't intend on taking sides. But considering the gender and friendship advantage, I can still punch Leo if he's done something stupid enough.

Relationships. It's kinda scary.

"Hey," Sam gave me a brief nod as I placed my bag on the floor and sunk in my seat. Oh great. I had this to deal with too.

"Hey." I replied.

"Listen," he leaned over his desk to speak to me in a whisper, so only the two of us can hear. I felt a bit uncomfortable since he practically confessed to me yesterday. "I'm sorry for my careless mouth. I was just curious, and I wanted to see if I had a chance. Now I know that I clearly don't. I promise I won't make any moves. I swear. If I do, though, and that's probably by instinct without me knowing, smack me. I'll stop." He halted in his words and lowered his head all the more, sincerity clear in his eyes. "So... I hope you'll still be my friend?"

Well. He's quick to volunteer as a friend before I can even put him in the zone. Oh well. At least he's mature about this. I felt like a weight lifted from my chest all of a sudden. And I was too occupied in my current thoughts to let this thing with Sam drag on, so I decided to forgive him.

"Sure Sam." I gave him a soft smile. He looked relieved before sinking back to his seat.

"Thank God. I thought you were gonna ignore me." He laughed quietly. Then he looked down once again, a hint of a grimace crossed his face for a split second before he put up a smile again. "I can't beat that guy anyway."

I pretended not to hear and focused my attention on the black board. What did he mean, beat? There was no competition.

I suddenly thought about Brandon. A small grin lit up my face and then I quickly shook it off. I look stupid smiling to myself. And then I thought about Leo and Nichole.

What if they break up? Then we can't hang out anymore? Then I'll have to choose who to be with, between the two of them? Both of them are precious to me. I really don't want to choose. And if they do break up, and if Leo stays away, will Brandon stay away too?

I shook my head again. Shut up thoughts. That's not gonna happen. They'll figure things out. I trust them. Yeah.

"Yo, Mira!" I heard Leo's voice somewhere. I glanced over my shoulder and saw him running towards me. I took a deep breath and held it in until he was already a step beside me. "What's up?"

"Hungry," I replied, quickening my steps. I don't even want to look at him right now. I feel like I wanna punch him but I also want to beg him to please work things out with Nichole. I don't know why I'm so worried. Maybe it's not that big of an issue. I have no idea. That's the problem though - I have no idea. "Where's Nichole?"

"Bathroom," he replied. "Did you see Brandon anywhere? I didn't see him after practice. He was the last one to come in and the first one to go out."

I shrugged my shoulders. "Dunno. Didn't see him."

"Okay," he said. "Well, see you in an hour. Bye!"

An hour - Lunch. Ahh. I nodded and then he dashed outside the door of the women's restroom. I observed him sneakily as I pretended to blend in with a group of girls. I'm a super spy with a samurai's reflexes and the stealth of a ninja.

I watched how Nichole went out of the restroom, met up with Leo and then they chatted their way to their next class. Even if I know they're fighting, they look so normal, I mean, the usual. I can't tell the difference at all. Am I that dense?

Occasional fights are normal in a healthy relationship right? What if that's just the case? I then whined to myself. But what if it's not?

I just realized that the group of girls I was blending in with were staring at me weirdly. They offered me a polite smile before walking away. They probably thought I was a weirdo. Heh. Whatever.

Finally. It was lunch.

We sat at our usual seat but Brandon wasn't here yet. I discreetly observed Leo and Nichole and again, left myself get confused. They looked like the usual. I can't sense anything wrong at all.

As the two of them bickered about who's gonna pay for their lunch again, Leo's eyes found mine. He stopped his little argument with Nichole and cocked a brow at me.

"Why do you look like you're planning a murder behind my back?"

I scoffed before I chuckled lightly. Nothing wrong here at all. Maybe Nichole was just overthinking it all? It's none of my business but I'm so curious.

"Relax, it's just my face."

He grinned mischievously. "Thought so."

Moments later, Nichole managed to persuade Leo into buying their lunches with his own money, well, with my help of course. I even got him to pay for mine too. The perks of being his snack-provider in middle-school.

He was grumbling as he returned to our table balancing three trays. Nichole and I just flashed him sarcastic appreciative smiles.

As we ate, Leo inquired again, his mouth still full. Bits of chicken sprayed all over my face. "Brandon's not here yet?"

I whined a complaint as I wiped my face and kicked his feet under the table. Nichole was hiding a giggle. "Obviously."

He himself smirked when he saw how disgusted I looked at him. I recovered easily though, seeing as I was used to it. Seconds later, he released the longest burp I've heard in my life. He was facing directly at Nichole too.

I was laughing hysterically but not before rolling my eyes so hard it hurt. Nichole shrieked in protest and punched his arm. "Damn it Leo! That's so gross! Shit. Ugh!"

Her boyfriend just snickered like a little kid who got away with something.

Nichole then extracted revenge by calling his attention, her hand crawling up his leg. I was about to cringe when I saw the glint in her eye.

Oh, something amusing is about to happen.

Leo turned to look at her at once. She leaned closer as if to kiss him, and when his face was close enough to her liking, she released an equally loud and long burp as if she collected all the air from the pits of her stomach and released them all at once and at will.

I was not surprised. Nichole and I had burping contests back at our apartment when we were bored enough.

Leo's expression looked like he was slapped with a stick. After that, people around began to stare and laugh at the horrendous exchange of burps. Nichole and I fist-bumped while Leo was still in a trance, as if he couldn't believe his girlfriend just did that.

We were sitting idly at the table, half an hour already passed. And Brandon was still a no-show.

Silence wasn't normal among the three of us so someone had to break it, and that someone was Nichole.

"So, you and Brandon are getting along pretty well now."

I stiffened. I hope she doesn't blurt out the fact that I like Brandon. Leo doesn't know it yet.

"Yup."

She sent me a small grin as I gave her a warning look. Leo looked oblivious to our silent signals though.

"Listen," she said, her voice sounded serious now and I somehow straightened my back and leaned closer so I could pay more attention. I don't know, she felt like my mom sometimes. "From the start, I really wanted you and Brandon together. For real, I'm not shitting you here. And I didn't expect you two to come up with that ridiculous game of yours about who's gonna like who first. I'm not butting in, I just wanted to tell you to be careful again. I know, I said this before but I really mean it. I want Brandon for you. I've known him for a while now and he's a good guy. I just call him manslut for the heck of it. Because face it, he is."

I snorted at how she emphasized her point. Leo was quiet but was nodding at her words, like she was taking the words right out of his mouth.

"Yeah," I slowly mumbled, a bit shy. Heh. Shy. It's true though. I am feeling shy. It's such a weird and foreign feeling. I tried to slightly dodge the main topic and focus on her last sentence. "He is a manslut."

"He is," Nichole said it again. We exchanged laughs but I was feeling tense inside. Suddenly, a rush of uncertainty washed over my guts. I don't know what it is. "Seriously though, when you two are together, I think I can sense his, ugh… Masculinity."

"What?" Leo asked, confused. He's so slow. And he calls himself a guy.

I snorted at the term, but knowing exactly what she meant. Brandon and I discussed this last night. "You mean you sense the awakening of Potato Junior?"

"What?" Leo asked again.

"Exactly." Nichole slammed her fist on the table. We laughed again, ignoring poor Leo guessing what the hell we were talking about.

"What about my Potato Junior?" A familiar voice startled both me and Nichole. We halted in our laughs too abruptly you'd think we got shot cold-blood.

"Where have you been?" I asked, attempting to quickly change the course of discussion. Brandon sent me a sly grin before he sat beside me. He didn't even buy lunch anymore. In a few minutes, class was gonna start.

"I had to go back to the apartment after swimming practice. I forgot my phone."

"No wonder you weren't answering my texts," Leo grumbled. Nichole rolled her eyes at him.

"You sound like a pissed off girlfriend."

Leo mimicked her way of saying that and so, another childish argument broke out between them.

I noticed Brandon stealing glances at me though. It was so obvious. I felt so confident all of a sudden, I don't know. I actually felt pretty. Somehow. I don't know, I must lack sleep for thinking like this.

It was silent between us, no words were exchanged - only quiet smiles. It felt fuzzy actually. But the thing in my chest was going on a rampage, just because he was staring.

Was he thinking about last night? Was he just simply staring at me? Was he starting to like me?

I panicked at my last question and stood up, saying I was gonna buy another drink as an excuse. Oh God, stop thinking about it. I was in such a hurry that as soon as I stepped out of my seat, I bumped into somebody passing by.

Not just bumped this time, I literally knocked the poor girl down. I quickly apologized before helping her up.

"It's fine. I'm sorry, I was spacing out while walking," she made a nervous laugh. I looked at her from hair to foot and almost gasped at how pretty she was, momentarily forgetting about my thoughts a little while ago. My gosh can someone be this pretty? She looked like a model. Then my eyes widened when I recognized her voice.

"Girl #1!" I exclaimed, remembering her voice in the bathroom when I was bawling my eyes out like the pathetic loser that I was. This girl called me nice and pretty!

Oh my God. She called me nice and pretty even though she looked like a model. Her black hair was long and straight, her complexion was soft with just a hint of make up to emphasize her symmetrical face, her teeth were perfect and the clothes she wore fit her perfectly. I feel like I've been complimented by a celebrity.

"I'm sorry what?" She asked, smiling unsurely. My friends stopped what they were discussing and stared at the both of us.

I smiled at her before shaking her hand. Her hands were so soft. She was so girly. She even smelled nice. This is what I wanted to look like. Well, not really, but man if I were a guy -

What. Shut up thoughts.

"Hi, sorry again. I'm Mira," I said. I can't help it. I took an immediate liking to her because she called me nice and pretty. Nobody ever called me that before, well, besides my mom, Nichole and Brandon. Well, maybe she just called me that because she didn't know me yet.

I'm not sure why but I want to be friends with her. She bobbed her head like she already knew who I was. She looked so polite too. An angel. I'm shaking hands with an angel.

"I'm Emma." She said.

Emma. Emma. I'll remember that name.

I remembered my friends were still staring at us so I introduced them to her, and her to them. I don't know why I feel so proud and excited.

"Hey Em," Brandon smiled at her.

Emma's cheeks lightly colored. "Hi."

Oh yeah. I remember her saying she sat next to him in Algebra last semester. So that's why they already knew each other.

Wait. She said she liked Brandon too.

I stared at her and she looked so nervous just standing there. Was she shy because the guy she liked was there?

I shook my head. At the bathroom, she said she thinks I'm Brandon's girlfriend and she's not the type to steal someone else's boyfriend.

Even though he's not my actual boyfriend. But still.

She glanced at me and smiled. Nothing about that smile was fake. It was purely innocent. I've seen some pretty fake smiles from girls here at school and this wasn't one of them.

"Emma, you coming?" A girl called her from the other table. The voice was familiar too. Maybe it was one of her bathroom buddies.

Oh wait. Those were the girls I tried to blend in with earlier when I was spying on Leo and Nichole. Small world.

"See you in class Mira," she smiled at me again before going to her friends. Even the way she walked was so girly. A model. No, an angel. She was perfect. And I just met her today. Her aura was completely feminine. How does she do that?

Wait. See you in class? We're in the same class?

"You're terrible," Leo said, making me stop admiring Emma for a moment. "You're in the same class as her and you just found out her name today?"

Oh God. Oh right. She said she sat next to me in Biology.

"You know I can't recall that many faces." I defended childishly.

My best friends just laughed and shook their heads knowingly. My attention was still on Brandon though. Having a crush on your close guy friend is so inconvenient.

And risky.

The bell rang, signalling the start of the afternoon classes. Leo and Nichole went ahead and Brandon said he'd walk me back to class.

I was excited of course, but I kept my cool façade. I have to keep my breathing steady too so he won't notice. He must not notice.

"Let's go?" He teasingly hooked his arm with mine. I took a sharp breath at the mere touch. Breathe, Mira. Focus. You can do this. It's just this small thing, you should be used to it by now.

I flashed him a smile before patting his arm with my free hand. *Don't notice. Please don't notice how much I like you.* "Let's go."

Chapter 24

"For real?" Sam's face twitched into a look of disgust as we both watched the video I saved on my phone last night. "Oh shit. They're really eating it."

"Yup," I replied, pausing the video at just the right moment, it was enough to make him vomit everything he ate since last week.

"That's just sick. Why. Why did you show me this. Just. Why." He cried, not blinking the whole time. I practically just scarred his eyes for life. He groaned before rubbing his eyes with the back of his palm, as if he was trying to erase what he just saw.

I just showed him a video I saw last night about two girls eating their poop in a cup. Yes, when I first saw it, I almost puked too. So in order to recover from its horror, I decided to pass it on to another poor victim.

"Be a man," I chuckled, shoving my phone back in my pocket. He sent me a glare.

"Be a girl and don't keep videos like that in your phone."

I shrugged my shoulders, not considering his suggestion for a second. I was secretly happy inside. I'm so glad Sam and I are like the usual again. Not awkward at all. He's such a nice guy.

"Hey Mira," I heard a chair being moved beside me. When I turned around, I met a smiling Emma. My face brightened up as soon as I saw her. She's so pretty. So girly. So not me.

"Hey," I returned her smile. Sam also greeted her with a nod, and then he turned his head to shoot me a teasing grin. My brows automatically wrinkled in disapproval. Here we go.

"Heard you just found out about her name yesterday. And she's been sitting right next to you the whole semester." Then he turned to Emma and gave her a dramatic sigh with a matching hand on his face. "I know how you must feel, Em."

Jerk.

I rolled my eyes and crossed my arms against my chest. "How come you know about it?"

I was thinking stalker.

He grinned at me. "You don't know how news travels in this school. And you definitely don't know how watched you are."

I eyed him in disbelief. "What do you mean watched?"

"You're pretty popular Mira," Emma joined in the conversation. I turned my gaze towards her. I didn't believe it when Sam said it, but when Emma backed him up, I was starting to. "Especially with your fights. People talk a lot about you. But I think it's because you're so pretty."

People were actually listening to us in the cafeteria that day?

People actually watch me in my fights?

I felt my cheeks heating up. Oh my God. And she just complimented me again. Why is she complimenting me? I feel like I don't deserve to be acknowledged by a girl like her.

She's way prettier, but I was too embarrassed to tell her. I mean, I just can't. It's not like me.

"People are just nosy," I quickly brushed it off, discreetly hiding my cheeks with my loose hair. Shit I'm getting flustered over nothing.

Sam was just looking at me, like he was feeling sorry for me or something, while Emma just continued smiling. Gosh she's such an angel. But pertaining to what they just told me, it sent shivers to my spine.

I'm being watched?

Dude. That's just creepy. I don't even have that many friends to be deemed 'popular'. What they're saying is ridiculous. They're just trying to flatter me.

We stopped our small discussion when the teacher arrived. We moved our seats back to their proper places and all of us in class gasped in horror when we saw the stacks of paper our teacher was carrying. Oh shit, a pop quiz.

A week passed, and Emma and I became great friends. I mean, she's just so approachable, and she's so honest. I still can't believe I'm walking side by side with a deity.

She hangs out with us from time to time seeing as she already has her own group of friends. I admire her. So much that I get jealous, but not to the extent of trashing her or anything.

And these days too, I've been feeling more and more insecure about myself. Maybe it's because I'm so conscious being around a really pretty person.

I logged into my facebook account one night and checked my notifications. Emma Pressman sent me a friend request. Before I accepted, I checked her profile. Man, her pictures. The likes were skyrocketing! Was she always this popular?

My ego was sinking lower and lower as I scrolled down her profile.

I saw some of her albums - she's done a few photoshoots in the past, she's even done some modeling. Amazing. Just, amazing. I'm friends with an amazing person.

As I was about to click the 'accept friend request' button, I noticed that we had a lot of mutual friends. I don't know why, but I felt something sink in my chest when I found out that one of them was Brandon.

What am I getting so jealous for? It's just facebook. And I've no right to be jealous. Plus, this is nothing. Why should I be jealous? Am I jealous? Damn it, I am jealous.

These dumb emotions are so pesty, I hate having to feel them. I never even thought I'd ever feel them.

I sighed before clicking accept, then I shut my laptop off. I'm so upset and I don't understand why I have to feel these girlish emotions I always made fun of before. It came back biting me in the ass.

Emma and Nichole were chatting animatedly on our usual table at lunch. Brandon was already there with Leo too. As soon as they saw me, they called out to me.

I sat down and put on a big smile. I'm glad I became friends with Emma. She's so cool. And she gets along with everybody. Why. Why can't I be like her? And again, she's so pretty. I want to hide my face just for sitting right next to her.

"How's Biology?" Leo shot that question at me. As a reply, I groaned and nearly slammed my head on the table.

"Need I express my hatred for that sorcery we are being forced to learn?"

Leo gave me a weak grin. "Yeah I'm flunking it too."

"I didn't say I was flunking it," I said, straightening my back. "I managed to pass everything with the help of Sam."

His face fell, as if he just lost a flunking-accomplice.

"Cheater," he snarled. I stuck my tongue out. Don't laugh. Just pity the fool.

"You're just jealous because I'm a ninja-cheater. And you just have bad luck with your seat mates since they're in the same situation as you."

And I have great luck since I always sit next to the brightest kid in class. Plus, with the help of my assisstant Sam, things just got easier.

He just grumbled in reply, showing just how right I am. I know I shouldn't be proud of it (cheating that is) but like I said before, I need it to survive high school.

Kids, do not imitate me. I am setting a bad example here.

"No shit!" Brandon laughed at what Emma just said.

"Really, really," Emma replied, holding her stomach to keep herself from laughing too much. "He told me..."

From the corner of my eye, I saw Brandon and Emma conversing excitedly. A pang of hurt pricked my chest just because of that.

I wanted to eavesdrop on what they were talking about but Nichole just started a new topic of discussion. She was complaining about something Leo did earlier or something like that. I couldn't pay much attention, and I couldn't hear what Brandon and Emma were discussing since they lowered their voices so only they could hear, like they were sharing a secret or something.

Of course they'd be like this right? They were friends even before I met the potato jerk. I remember her saying she liked him, but she wasn't going to take him away from me. They're just having a friendly chat.

So why do I feel like I'm being deprived of air?

I observed them quietly. She was good-looking. He was good-looking. They were such a great fit - a good-looking couple. The perfect match. A power couple. Me, on the other hand...

Now that I think about it, Brandon and I don't match at all. No wait. I don't want to think about it. It'll just make me feel worse.

Unconsciously, I started to examine myself critically, as well as Emma. And I began comparing.

Emma was slim, I was kinda like the curvy type. But I think my thighs are too big.

Her face was gorgeously symmetrical. My face was shaped like an awkward potato with my chubby cheeks.

Her teeth were so perfect. I used to have crooked teeth. It looked fine now but still.

She had a great fashion sense and had a way with people. Me, I pick whatever I see first in my closet. And I'm not so friendly.

She's lady-like. I'm part-gorilla.

Her waist was so tiny. Mine was... Fine. I have stomach fat I'd like to get rid of.

On the brighter side, I had bigger boobs than her. And my butt was bigger.

Wait.

Stop. Stop comparing.

Shit. This is horrible. I'm horrible. Why am I thinking this? Why am I getting jealous? Of Emma of all people! She didn't do anything bad. I mentally smacked myself with a brick for thinking stupid things. She's my friend. She's a good friend. I'm such a horrible, horrible person.

I sunk in my seat as the two pairs of couples got lost in their own little worlds. Well. I lost my appetite already. I don't even think this table likes me anymore.

"You okay?" Brandon asked as we both walked to his car. Like the usual, he was gonna drive me back to my apartment.

"Yeah!" I faked my enthusiasm, unintentionally sounding too obvious that I was in fact, not okay. I cleared my throat before he could point it out. "Don't you have practice today? It's okay, I can walk home by myself today."

"Nope," he quickly disagreed. "You can't go home by yourself. Just not happening. I'll just text coach I'm sick or something."

I narrowed my eyes at him. "Aren't you afraid of getting kicked out of the team? You have so many absences now. I doubt he'll believe your excuse anyway."

He then puffed his chest to seem bigger and gave me a proud, confident grin. "He should be afraid if he's gonna kick me out. He'll lose one of his best swimmers."

Cocky.

"You should come to the pool and see me swim some time. You look like you don't believe me," he added, flashing me a warm smile.

Don't smile at me. Damn you. I hate why I'm feeling down again. What the heck is wrong with me?

I don't know if he noticed I was upset during lunch. I don't know if he knows I'm not myself today. I don't know. But the important thing is, he shouldn't know. At least not yet.

"Hey," he suddenly took my hand. I looked at him, forcing some expression on my face but I was too tired to fake one. I hate this. I'm getting so greedy. "Want to spar?"

What? That was so out of the blue.

"Let's spar. I'm going to show you how cool I am." He executed a weird stance, an overexaggerated imitation of Bruce Lee or Jackie Chan or some famous martial artist. A giggle escaped from my lips and he smiled as soon as it did.

Was he trying to cheer me up?

Did he notice?

Shaking my unusual thoughts aside, I brought back myself and gave him a challenging smirk. "You sure potato?"

"Hell yeah. I'm not holding back just because my opponent's someone as pretty as you."

A nerve twitched when he said the word 'pretty.' I don't know. I just felt irritated all of a sudden. I attacked him first, venting that feeling just now and he blocked it perfectly, much to my surprise.

I continued throwing punches and kicks at him but he dodged all of them. His form and his footwork were amazing, like he's memorized my pattern of attacks a hundred times before.

I managed to land a hit on his stomach, and when he recoiled from the surprise, I dropped down on the ground and attempted a leg-sweep, but he jumped away just in time.

For an experienced person, that was a pretty basic and predictable move. I still can't believe he was serious when he said he was good at fighting.

I'm not sure how much time passed, the sun was already setting. I didn't notice at all. We exchanged equal blows and dodges, and nobody seemed to back down. He was pretty damn good. When he grabbed my fist as I was about to send him a right hook, he grinned.

Intimidated, I used my free hand to punch that damn grin off his face but he caught it too. He tightened his grip on my fists while I struggled to break free. He's, well, strong.

No shit dude, he's a guy.

I was thinking of a plan on to what to do next when he suddenly pulled me into a hug. I stood still because of the shock. What.

What was happening? Was this a part of his attack?

"Brandon?" I asked, unsurely. He dropped my hands slowly as he wrapped his arms around my shoulders. Was he okay?

"You're so pretty." He said. I couldn't contain my scoff. Here he goes again. I lifted my leg to knee Potato Junior but he blocked just in time, as if he predicted what I'd do.

"Are you okay?" I asked, a bit irritated, a bit concerned. He chuckled, his breath tickling my neck. I just noticed we were covered in sweat, and both of us were breathing heavily because of the little spar just now. And we were hugging. Oh, gross.

"You're pretty. You're beautiful. You're amazing." He said. I resisted the urge to roll my eyes. What was this tactic? It was so lame. But somehow, it got my heart racing a bit there. Wait no. I mean - ugh. Never mind. "I can't believe I'm always hanging out with this beautiful potato."

I sighed, giving up on trying to free myself. Not like I hated his hugs or anything. I felt myself take a deep breath. I feel so pitied right now. "You're always calling me pretty."

I know you're just saying that to flatter me anyway.

Emma is way prettier than me. And she's better than me in so many ways.

He pulled away a bit, just enough for our eyes to meet. He sent me a genuine smile. He wasn't smirking, he wasn't teasing. My heartbeats were getting irregular just by his looks alone. Someone give me a defribillator so I can return my heartbeats back to normal.

"I don't know. I just feel like you need to be reminded everyday." He said as he took the loose hair that stuck to my face from the sweat. He tucked it behind my ear before smiling again. "You don't know just how beautiful you are. And while we were sparring just a moment ago, I was trying to hold back from hugging you. I failed, though. I love the look on your face when you fight, when you cry and especially when you laugh. You're wonderful, beautiful, amazing, potato."

His sweet words were killing me.

I wanted to complain and roll my eyes, but I couldn't. I was stunned. Did he mean all that? Why do I feel relieved all of a sudden? So reassured? Even if it's just a lie he made up to cheer me up, it worked. I don't know how it did, but it worked.

Does he know I like him? No. Impossible.

Did he know I was jealous at Emma for talking with him at lunch? Um. Probably.

I didn't reply. What's the right thing to say after receiving full-blown compliments like that?

Brandon lowered his head to conceal his cheeks. I hid a smile because I know it was because he was flustered. He looked surprised himself after he said all those things.

Was this real?

No.

Mira. Don't expect too much.

"So, are you okay now?" He asked slowly. I nodded, forgetting that I was actually trying to deny the fact that I wasn't fine. He sighed, relieved. "Good."

Was it okay to feel this happy?

Brandon lifted his head and smiled again. My face mirrored his.

I'm scared of being too happy. I can't be too happy. I can't. Because being too happy means that life is preparing to take something away from me.

I know from experience that people can fucking leave. It's just a matter of time.

And I don't want him to leave my side.

I need to keep my emotions steady, and at a safe level. Liking Brandon is fine, but going over that is a red flag. A dangerous zone.

I need to control myself and supress the unwanted feelings growing inside everyday. I shouldn't care too much. If I want to be by his side forever, the best way - the safest way - is to just be his friend.

But right now, right this moment, I want to embrace this warm feeling just before I let go and get back to the harsh reality. Even if it's just me feeling this way, so be it.

I stood on my toes and planted an innocent kiss on his lips. Then I hugged him again.

This is only temporary happiness. I shouldn't get used to it.

"Thanks," the word slipped out my mouth. Luckily the rest of my thoughts decided to remain in my head.

"Anytime potato love," he chuckled as he rubbed my back soothingly.

No. Stop.

Don't you dare get used to it.

Chapter 25

"Awesome!" Leo and Brandon fist-bumped as soon as the announcer finished saying that the afternoon classes were to be cancelled because of some seminar the teachers were required to attend.

Nichole and I cheered ourselves, bumping our chests the hard way like the guys always did. Only, we forgot we had boobs. And it hurt.

"Ow," I said, slowly hugging my chest with my arms. Nichole nodded, doing the same.

"We are so not doing that again."

We saw Brandon and Leo staring at us weirdly. Brandon, having an unexplainable look on his face, as if he was supressing his laughter, and Leo, managed to present his own version of a pedophile's smile.

"Get away creep," Nichole said. Leo quickly put an arm around her and guided her to the pool.

"You girls can watch us practice today," Leo said, peering over his shoulder as they continued to walk forward, away from us. Brandon and I looked at each other.

"Can we?" I asked. He nodded.

"You're finally gonna see my awesome side." I laughed quietly. He took my hand and pulled me to the same direction Nichole and Leo were heading.

I didn't see the point of holding hands, but I didn't mind. I didn't mind at all.

When we entered the gym, huge splashes of water could already be heard and incoherent shouts were echoing throughout the place. As soon as our presences were made known, a group of guys went up to us, sending knowing grins to Brandon and Leo.

"Hey slackers," a tall, tanned guy approached us. "Why'd you bring your chicks here today?"

Before Leo could reply, Nichole and I stepped forward out of instinct. We didn't really plan on it, but we said the same thing at the same time. "Chicks my ass."

We looked at each other quite surprised, and then we burst out laughing. She gave me a high-five as the guys followed our laughter.

The tanned guy then gave Nichole a funny smile. "I was kidding Nic." Then he looked at me. "Oh. Hey."

"Hey," I replied shortly. It was my first time being here, so I understand why he didn't know me. Nichole, on the other hand, had been here a few times because of Leo, so no wonder the guys were already familiar with her.

Brandon came up behind me, putting a hand on my shoulder. "Guys, this is Mira."

I hid a smile when he introduced me to his team mates. I don't know. I just felt giddy. Ugh. Such a girl I am.

They all smiled at me and to be honest, I was having a hard time returning the smile. Well, they were all shirtless and wet from hair to foot. There's no denying their bodies were fit for swimming too.

A guy with blonde hair suddenly raised his arms and gestured to all of me. "Boys, here stands the sole reason for Brandon's many, many absences."

A deep chorus of laughter filled the gym as Brandon nudged his arm. "Knock it off."

"We actually already know you, Miss Mira Jadsen," another guy came up, flashing me a business-like (or Cheshire-like) smile, though his eyes were twinkling of playfulness. "You're pretty popular for beating people up."

I wanted to hide. Oh God. I had this bad a reputation at school? Brandon chuckled, and then followed everybody, including Nichole.

"Our best friend, boys!" Leo mockingly announced, dodging a swift kick from me - which just added to their amusement. This is so embarrassing. My sole existence is embarrassing. I want to dig a hole and hide in one.

"Where's coach?" Brandon asked, changing the course of discussion smoothly.

"He went with the rest of the teachers at that seminar or something," the tanned one replied. "Today it's self-pracrice."

"Alright," Leo grinned when he heard the news.

"Do you swim, Mira?" Somebody from the group asked. I avoided their eyes as I replied. I still can't get over my embarrassing self.

"A little bit."

They all grinned in unison. Oh no. "Then get in the water."

I was about to protest when Brandon explained the reason why we were here. "She just came to watch guys. It's okay Mira, you and Nichole can sit over there."

They booed.

"C'mon dude, coach's not here anyway. Let your girl have some fun."

Brandon was firm in his decision. "No."

And then teasing came. The tone of their voices made me want to kick all of them. I hated getting teased.

"You're so possessive. If you keep that up, she's gonna leave you."

My breath hitched in my throat. Hey. They thought we were..?

"We're not together." Brandon coldly replied, walking away now to drop his bag near the bleachers.

I suddenly had the motivation to swim now. I mentally cussed that damned potato. He has no idea how what he just said punched me in the gut. I know he was just being honest, but still.

I glanced at Nichole, she was already looking. Then she gave me a nod like she understood everything.

I want to get back at him for some reason.

"Do you have some spare swimsuits for girls here?" I asked one of the guys. They all cheered when I said that, and I saw Brandon stiffen. Even when I was just facing his back, I know he was making another disappointed face because I didn't listen to him.

Whatever. We weren't going out anyway. Why should I listen to him?

"This is my sister's. I'm sure she won't mind," the tanned one handed me a small bag. I opened it and pulled out the black piece of cloth.

I eyed him weirdly. "This is a bikini."

"Yeah," he replied, as if it was the most natural thing to say. Then he started to explain why he had it. "She bought it yesterday. Her guy got mad at her so she asked me to give it to someone as a present since it was a waste to just throw it away. Lucky you're here. Must be fate."

Yeah. Guess fate finally paid its debt. Although I preferred cash but this was alright.

And her guy got mad at her? Maybe because it was too sexy? Jealous boy. Nichole told me Leo didn't want want her wearing clothes that showed a bit too much skin. Are all boyfriends like that?

I wouldn't know.

Nichole studied the bikini as well, her head bobbing on approval. "It's nice."

It's not like it was gonna be my first time wearing a bikini. But it felt weird. Well, it was the only one I can wear anyway. I just wanted to swim. I miss swimming. I'll show that jerk.

"So you're giving it to me?" I asked, fiddling the bag on my hands. He nodded, looking relieved that he finally accomplished the mission his sister entrusted him with. I gave him a grateful smile. "Thanks dude."

"I'll be sitting in the bleachers," Nichole said. Leo and Brandon already changed into their swimming trunks. Leo was even looking at me worriedly. Brandon, well, didn't meet my eyes. Whatever. Let him be mad.

I checked myself out in the mirror. It was a perfect fit. This is so convenient. I mean, what a coincidence that guy had this when I needed it. And I don't even know his name.

I'll just call him The Tanned One in my head.

I had a slight problem with the top though. It was a bit fit - maybe I tied the knot too tight. The cloth hugged my boobs together lovingly, forming a daring cleavage.

I used my hair to cover it up, although it was still teasingly peeking from its concealment. We were gonna be underwater anyway, so there should be no problem.

As soon as I stepped out of the changing rooms, the guys were already near the pool waiting for me. They surrounded Brandon and they were like discussing something, and then stopped when they noticed I was approaching.

The Tanned One raked my appearance up and down, but his expression showed no change. "It looks good on you."

"Yeah, thanks again," I replied, discreetly attempting to cover my chest. I was so conscious. I just realized I was the only one with a vagina here.

Gasp.

Gangbang!

What. What!!! What the hell did I just think?! Shut up you filthy mind! Oh, gosh. Oh ew. If they could read my mind right now I'll freaking drown myself. Curse Leo for tricking me into watching that indecent video back then.

I glanced at all of them swiftly, and took a deep breath. Maybe I'm just overthinking, but were they all staring at me?

Wow. I'm so not conscious about the fat on my stomach at all. I'm just stomaching-in the whole time. Maybe they noticed.

I felt weird when I met Brandon's eyes. He looked disappointed, as expected, and I felt bad about it but whatever. Ugh. Whatever.

I was so busy being tough in my thoughts that I didn't notice him stepping forward, towards me. I felt my cheeks heat up when he held my shoulders. That look on his face was so scary.

I'm not so tough now, am I?

All of a sudden, he lifted me up and threw me to the pool. I didn't realize everything that happened until my butt touched the floor of the pool. I swam up and yelled at the damn potato.

"What the hell Brandon?!"

The guys were laughing so hard. He just sent me a sly grin, but I know there was a deeper meaning to that. "Let's race."

"What?!" I almost sounded hysterical, splashing all of them with water while I was at it. "You're a real swimmer! That's not fair!"

"Hey manslut!" I heard Nichole yell all the way from the bleachers. She was stepping on his bag and belongings mercilessly as she continued to get mad at him.

Brandon cringed.

"How is that not fair?" Leo asked, innocently. "Mira's pretty good at swimming. She beat me a lot of times back in grade school."

An argument broke out among all of them, but Brandon and I just stared at each other. It wasn't just a stare. I can't explain if it was a heated glare or an icy gaze or whatever. One thing's for sure though: it was unpleasant and it gave me enough motivation to accept his challenge.

"Fine," I said, silencing all of them. It was my decision after all. I never tore my eyes off him. I raised my arm so he could pull me up from the pool. When I was finally back on dry ground, he squeezed my wrist before letting go.

He's mad at me.

I got mad at him because he's mad at me. It makes sense, I swear. As for revenge and a little demonstration of my sudden rush of confidence, I irritatedly pushed my wet hair off my shoulders and let them flow freely behind my back. The revealing top that I was trying to cover-up earlier was now exposed.

I was satisfied when his eyes shot open from the surprise. He didn't expect that now did he? Bitch.

To add more effect, I straightened my back and put a hand on my waist, showing off the S-line I was always so conscious about.

I don't even know what I'm doing anymore. I'm just so pissed at him. I don't know why I'm even pissed at him. I want to piss on him.

Forget that last part. I'm so mad I can't think like a human anymore.

"First one to finish wins?" I stated obviously, stretching my arms and legs. The guys were howling and cheering me on. Brandon's eye twitched. Good.

"Yeah."

Both of us stood on the springboard, now in position. I was serious as hell in winning this. My back was arched and my arms were outstretched over my head - my most comfortable diving posture - I could clearly see how much I just emphasized the two balls of fat on my chest. I glanced at Brandon and saw him already staring at me with a really annoyed look.

WHAT. EVER. My form was awesome.

One of the guys shot the starting pistol, and before the sound could even echo throughout the whole place, Brandon and I dived into the pool.

I kicked my legs with full strength, my arms were a bit relaxed at first so I wouldn't get too tired before I even reached the goal.

I glanced at Brandon as I breathed on my right. He was a little ahead of me damn it. With newly found strength, I kicked my feet faster, and I was gaining on him.

He was really good, but I was keeping up with him. Damn. This will hurt in the morning.

As soon as I slammed my hand on the wall of the pool, I could hear the boys cheering and clapping. And howling. Well, it was Nichole who was howling.

I was breathing heavily and so was Brandon. I didn't realize we were so close until I felt his breath on my cheeks. Or maybe that was just my cheeks.

He was so quiet, just staring at me. I hated quiet Brandon the most. It makes him so hard to read.

"Brandon won by three seconds!" One of them exclaimed.

"How could you say you just know how to swim 'a little bit'? You were awesome!"

"You actually kept up with him! Damn, girl."

"I want you in the team, now!!!"

I was laughing at their remarks, not knowing what other way to respond to their flattery. For me, it was no surprise I kept up with this potato. Rather, I was disappointed I lost. Back when we were kids, Leo took swimming classes, and I tagged along. I wanted to try all kinds of sports that time.

Our coach saw how well I performed so he made me join a few competitions but not as an official player. I won a lot but in the end I got tired of it and I was itching to try softball so I left Leo and joined the softball team.

Speaking of Leo, while all of their team mates were applauding me, he was just giving me a worried smile. I knew what he meant. He meant 'congrats, but Brandon is still mad at you.'

They started training on the other side of the pool while I stayed a bit further away from them since I didn't want to be a disturbance.

Brandon separated from his team and swam towards me. My stupid switch turned on and I began running underwater to get away from him. Why the hell didn't I just swim away like a normal person would?

When he finally reached me, he grabbed my wrists and pinned them on the wall. I gulped. He was glaring at me so hard now I almost wanted to cry. But at the same time, my own anger increased.

He didn't say anything. After a small glaring-contest between us, his eyes softened and his tight grip on my wrists loosened as well. He sighed before resting his head on my shoulder. I almost thought he was trying to drown himself.

"Please stop doing this," he breathed, almost sounded like he was pleading. Before I even got to ask him what (although I already knew the answer) he got out of the pool and lifted me up like a rag doll, pulling me out of the water as well.

He grabbed a clean towel on one of the small cabinets near us and threw it on my face. "Cover up."

I fumed in annoyance, but kept quiet. Honestly, I was scared of him. He's so scary when he's quiet. And when he's quiet, I know he's either mad or upset. Most of the time, with me.

After I wrapped it around my body, he pointed at the girl's bathroom. "Go change."

I couldn't resist rolling my eyes and stomping my way there. I'm acting like such a kid. He wasn't my boyfriend, we weren't going out. Why should I listen to him? But still, I was following his orders. I hate this so much. It's like he's got complete control of me.

On my way to the bathroom, I heard a multitude of voices, which I know belonged to the team. I peered over my shoulder and saw that Emma came in. I remember her mentioning her brother was in the swim team too.

They all looked excited when she arrived. They were laughing about something I couldn't hear because I was too far away. When I saw her chatting with Brandon again, and when I saw Brandon gleefully enjoying her company, my heart sunk.

I didn't watch any longer. I entered the bathroom and showered. Jealousy is such a stupid thing. It shouldn't even exist. Especially not in me.

I took a shower and just stood there under the hot water raining down my hair and body, washing off the smell of chlorine, and hopefully all this negativity.

I thought about Brandon's face. About what happened. Just earlier we were okay. Did we just fight again? I don't know if we did. I just feel so sad.

I don't know how long I was standing there, just thinking about him and Emma. Does he smile like that when he's with me? Why can't I be as pretty as her?

I bet he tells her she's pretty and amazing and all the things he told me yesterday too.

I can't even tell if I was crying because the hot water was starting to sting my eyes anyway. Yeah. It's just the hot water.

"Mira?" I heard Emma's voice outside the bathroom. I quickly rubbed my face as if there was something wrong with it before calling back to her.

"Yeah?"

"You forgot your bag."

I slapped myself. Oh right. My bag. My clothes.

I turned the shower off and wrapped myself with only a towel. I wrung the bikini dry and placed it inside a clean plastic bag I found in one of the lockers.

"Thanks Em!" I said, rushing to get my belongings. Before I even got to the door, I saw Brandon standing in front of me, holding my bag. My face fell.

"Where's Emma?"

"Out. She gave me your bag." He said.

He was still wet, probably just came out of the pool. He stepped forward and closed the door behind us. I gulped.

"T-This is a girl's bathroom you know," I stammered. Just so you know, I stammered because I was shivering from the cold, not because he was advancing me slowly with that unexplainable look on his face.

I gripped the towel around my chest. I'm stark naked under this thin piece of cloth. I think I'm gonna die from embarrassment.

"Where's that swimsuit?" He asked. I looked at him unsurely before pointing behind me.

"Over there."

"Throw it away." He said. My face went red with anger. How dare he?

"Your friend just gave it to me. It must've been expensive. How could I just throw it away?"

He quietly glared at something on the floor. I just made him angrier. Great. But then his expression softened again, kind of hopeless. Do I really stress him out this much?

"Then don't wear that thing again," he said, his tone firm and commanding. And then he looked up to meet my eyes seriously. "At least not with a lot of guys around."

He said it a bit unclearly but I heard him perfectly. Was he jealous? Maybe? I didn't know what to reply so I just kept quiet. He stepped closer again and I unconsciously took a step back. I forced my legs to get away but my feet were glued to the ground.

He held my arms to keep me from escaping. He looked annoyed. "Seriously. You're just making me too greedy for your own good."

I stared at him in shock. What... What did he mean by that? Can I be hopeful?

He lowered his head again. He slowly pulled me into a gentle hug, his mouth resting on the nape of my neck. I can't get over the fact that I was only in a towel, and he was in his swimming trunks.

"Only wear things like that when you're with me. Only me."

If I was my usual self I'd protest and complain why I should, because we weren't even in a relationship. But since I felt drunk, maybe because of the long hot shower, or maybe because of Brandon, I nodded obediently. "Okay."

After that hug, he couldn't bring himself to look at me, so he quickly turned around. He gave me back my bag with his head facing somewhere away from my direction. I could see how red his ears were. I think he just realized our lack of clothes during that hug.

Now I'm wondering if he felt my boobs or something. He looks so flustered.

"After you change, let's go downtown." He said.

"Why?"

I was still facing his back. He was making his way to the exit. "Because you look so down lately."

So he wanted to cheer me up again?

I didn't want to admit that I really wasn't myself lately, but I don't think I can ever lie to this guy. I gripped my bag and forced myself to keep a straight face even though he wasn't looking. Shit I can feel a silly grin coming. I'm so relieved somehow.

"Okay."

He nodded. He peeked at me over his shoulder and quickly turned his head forward while covering his cheeks with the back of his hand. Then he went out.

When I was sure he was already gone, I smiled so widely at myself. I covered my face and suppressed the girly giggles that were threatening to escape my lips.

Damn it. Damn it all.

I like him way too much.

Chapter 26

It was kinda awkward on our way downtown. The whole time Brandon was driving, I was too occupied pretending to be occupied.

Yeah. The feeling's just like the first time we met. It was awkward.

It was a quiet drive, and as soon as he parked the car, he killed the engines and sighed. His hands were still on the steering wheel and I was slowly sinking in my seat.

Why do I feel like I'm gonna get scolded?

He turned his head to my direction as I not-so-discreetly watched him from the corner of my eye.

Gulp.

"Look," he started, a bit to my discomfort. "I have no idea why you're mad at me. But whatever it is, I'm sorry. I don't want us to fight, and I hate it when none of us admits why we're mad at each other."

Breathe in. Breathe out. Breathe in. Breathe in... In... In... In...

"Mira?" He called my attention before I could kill myself. I let out a long exhale. Keep calm my poor chest. Keep calm. "Are we good?"

"Yup." I replied, a bit short of breath. Why did just I irregularly control my breath (read: attempt to murder my lungs).

He looked at me unsurely before stepping out of the car without a word. Why am I making such a big deal out of this? He's already apologizing - and he didn't even do anything wrong! I'm just terrible. I clutched my chest before I went out myself, but I was surprised when the door opened by itself.

Dumbfounded, it took me a few seconds to realize that Brandon had opened it for me. I looked at him strangely - he was just offering me a small smile and he was expecting my hand.

I feel like such a lady.

I snorted as he took my hand and pulled me out of the car as if I couldn't do it myself. After he shut the door close and locked the car, he dragged me forward, not letting go of my hand the whole time.

I lowered my head as he just kept leading the way. We passed by a small, familiar restaurant, and before I could recall it, Brandon squeezed my hand and pointed at it.

"Ah, spicy burgers."

Oh that's right. I couldn't help it. I made a sneaky grin and wagged my brows at him. "I beat you in that contest."

He rolled his eyes laughing, pulling my hand again. Where was he taking me?

These days, he's been holding my hand a lot. Honestly, I didn't mind, but why is he doing it? Is it purely out of instinct so I won't get lost or something?

Does he do this with other girls?

"Where are we going?" I asked. It took him a while to reply. I was staring at him the whole time, waiting for an answer. He turned his head and flashed me a sickly cute smile.

"No idea."

"What!" I almost pulled my hand back.

"Relax!" He laughed, tightening his grip on my hand. "We're just taking a walk."

"You took me downtown to take a walk?" I asked, sarcasm dripping from my words like venom. I don't know. I just needed a reason to get mad at him. I want to be mad at him for being too nice to a horrible person like me. I want to stay mad at him even for just a little while.

But I can't.

"Of course," he replied like it was so obvious. "Your fat is piling up in your stomach. You really need to work out."

I stopped and stared at him with shock written all over my face. Screw you Brandon.

"Yeah," I said, barely suppressing my disappointment. I can't explain how humiliated I am right now. And insulted. "Maybe I really should join the swim team."

Saying that was like dropping an atomic bomb. Brandon halted in his steps, and so did I since he was holding my hand. He wasn't looking at me directly, but he was facing me - his slightly damp hair framing his face as he looked at our feet.

"Just not the swim team." He said, his voice low. It sounded like a harsh whisper or some sort. One thing's for sure. It made me regret I suggested it even when I wasn't even half-serious about it.

We were both quiet again. Great. Just when the awkwardness already faded, I welcomed it right back. My unnecessary skills of being stupid never fails to amaze me.

"Sorry," he said. He raised his head just a little bit, but his eyes couldn't meet mine. "I didn't mean it with the fat thing. You're perfect. I just didn't know what to say. Sorry."

I just stared at him blankly. Wow. He looked so conflicted. Why was he taking this so seriously? Wow. I'm one to say. Instead of saying it was okay, I ended up laughing, releasing all the tension I held in my chest. Well, part of it.

This is one of the things I liked about him. Even when it's my fault, he's the first to apologize. It's like he's losing the arguments and fights on purpose just so we won't...

We won't what?

"Such a serious potato," I mumbled, trying to hold in my laughter. I'm in no position to laugh in this situation.

To my relief though, Brandon's face brightened, and he sent me a big smile. I have no idea how I'm going to explain this but...

We were okay now.

This is so confusing. I don't even understand what just happened. But yeah. We're okay now.

"Wanna grab a bite?" He asked. I looked at him with a wide grin on my face.

"You need to ask?"

He stuck his tongue out before pulling me somewhere again.

We ate at a small snack house and we chatted casually like nothing happened. The serious questions are right at the back of our minds but none of us wanted to shoot it. I doubt one of us are even prepared to answer it anyway.

After that delightful snack, we went out for another walk. He took my hand again and this time, my curiousity took over and I didn't hesitate to ask.

"Why are you always holding my hand?"

Shit. He's gonna think I don't like it and then he'll withdraw and then I won't have an excuse to hold his hand again. You're such a dick, Mira.

He smiled, raised our intertwined hands up to his face and planted a kiss on the back of my palm. "Because your hands are soft. Because I like holding your hand. And because I want to hold your hand, always. Do you hate it?"

But what if I poop will he still hold my hand oh wait.

Shut up.

Breathe. Breathe. Breathe. Breathe.

How the hell can he be so smooth? That's not fair. And here I am trying to tame my stalling thoughts and the badass creature inside my chest.

I presented my calm and composed facial expression before nodding stiffly. "No I don't mind."

Facepalm.

Stop acting like a bitch. Ughhhh. Why can't I just tell him I like him already?

He smiled again as if he knew what I was thinking. That smile was so contagious. I didn't even realize my lips tugging up until he kissed me.

Please wait a moment before I describe my reaction. My soul went on a surprise vacation and I don't think it's planning to come back.

Ah, no, wait. It just came back.

I looked at him wide-eyed, he was still smiling, grinning like a happy kid. My cheeks flushed and I felt something weird stir inside my chest.

It was sorta bubbly, sorta hot and sorta fast. I don't know. I'm horrible at describing my feelings. And my brain isn't even making any effort to help.

As I watched his eyes carefully, as if it was pulling me in, my own eyes drifted down to his lips. He was smiling. My heart just stopped.

I want to tell him that I like him.

Maybe I'm just caught up in the moment or maybe I'm just mesmerized by his charm, but I had this persistent urge to tell him. To finally confess. Because if I don't right now, I might regret it. Or I might regret telling him. Or I might regret my whole existence.

Whoa. Getting deep there Mira. Loosen up.

I know I said it was risky and I wouldn't say it until he does first but my patience is already running out.

I like him. So much it hurts.

"Brandon," I said his name shyly. Gosh shyly. He was paying close attention and I don't even want to imagine how red my face was right now. "I have to tell you something."

Am I doing the right thing?

He raised his brows and waited for what I was about to say.

Breathe, Mira. You have to do this. You already made up your mind. Well um, partially. Your mind is still as reckless and suicidal as usual. Maybe he likes you too and then you'll live happily ever after.

Cry. That will never happen.

I will die alone.

No! Shoo negative thoughts. Shoo!

I tugged his shirt and leaned closer. I want to tell him in a whisper. I want only him to hear the words I never thought I'd ever say. We were in a public place but I don't care. The people passing by don't seem to care too.

He noticed what I was trying to do so he stepped closer, minimizing our distance more. Now that we were just centimeters apart, I took a deep breath.

I looked at him. I looked at those beautiful blue crystals I liked ever since I got to know him for real. I looked at those lips, those damn sweet lips that traitorously claimed mine and made me want more, made me addicted to his wonderful kisses.

"Brandon," I said. My hands were shaking. What if he laughs at me? Or rejects me? Should I really be doing this? But... I won't know if I don't do something about it, right?

Please. Don't let anything interrupt this moment. I may never be in this state of temporary insanity again.

I pulled his shirt out of instinct or out of anxiety. I can feel his body heat. He was looking at me seriously, as if he already knew what I was going to say, but if I'm in my right mind right now, I'd describe his expression as frantic, impatient, flustered, confused - scared.

But maybe I'm just projecting my own current feelings into him.

I sighed, looking at him intensely to conceal how afraid and flustered I was. Here goes my pride. "Brandon, I li - "

"Mira?"

I stopped.

No.

No.

That voice.

No no no please not now.

I turned around and felt my heart squeeze in my chest. I could already feel the huge lump forming inside of my throat, so huge it was hard to simply swallow it.

He was standing right in front of me, really surprised. His hair had grayed over the years, probably from the stress of work, and there were wrinkles on the corners of his eyes too.

His sense in clothing were still the same - a dress shirt tucked inside his black pants and a pair of polished shoes. His necktie was loosened around his neck and his hair was dishevelled. I'm guessing he just got out of a stressful day at work.

I swallowed my hardest when I saw the little girl riding on his shoulders with her legs locked around his neck.

Brandon didn't know what was going on, but he held my hand as I just stood there frozen like an idiot.

Say something. Talk. Fuck it Mira, you're tougher than this.

My mind was screaming and I was just trying to hold back the ugly tears. Damn it. Damn this day to hell. Why does nothing ever go right in my life?

"Hi dad." I said, trying to keep my voice steady. I hope he didn't notice. Please voice, don't betray me now. Please.

He smiled at me. I sucked a deep breath. I haven't seen him smile like that since I was a kid. Scratch that, I haven't seen him since he left when I was a kid.

"Daddy, who's that lady?" The little girl sitting on his shoulders asked. I stared at her and pictured myself back then. She's just an innocent kid. I can't hate her. It's not her fault.

"Pretty isn't she?" He told her, his voice gentle and loving. Like how a father should sound like - but how should I know? His fatherly way of speaking is already foreign to me. "She's Mira. Mira, this is my daughter, Laura."

I clenched my fist so hard I thought it was gonna break. Fuck. Fuck. Don't cry. Don't cry.

"Hi Mira!" The kid waved her little hands. My father gave me a look that said just go with it. How dare he. He just introduced that kid to me as his daughter. And what am I to him then?

"Hey." I said, trying my best not to look at them. I can already feel the damn waterworks coming. I need to leave. I need to leave now. "Listen, I still need to go somewhere."

"Is that your boyfriend?" He looked at Brandon from head to toe. "What about Leo?"

I shook my head vigorously. "Dad..."

"How's your mother?" He asked, not listening to me at all. I cringed and tried not to blink. If I blinked, I know a tear would fall down.

"She's fine. We're all fine. Now dad, we really should be going now." I didn't realize I was squeezing Brandon's hand so hard right now it was turning purple. He didn't mind though. He put a hand over it, attempting to calm me down.

"We should meet again and talk sometime. I miss you Mira," he mused.

I don't know if he just said that because he pitied me or just out of common courtesy. Whichever it was, it didn't matter.

I feel like I'm getting stabbed in the chest a million times and at the same time, I feel like I'm drowning. Only, the people around me were breathing.

I pulled Brandon by the hand. I was already turning my back, just in time for me to blink back the tears. It was rude, but there was no way in hell he's gonna see me like this. "Bye dad."

I quickened my steps, squeezing Brandon's hand with all the strength left in me. I wish I could run, but I couldn't even feel my legs anymore. And here I am dragging Brandon along my problems, my drama. I'm always a bother to people, aren't I? They're already sick of me right?

I'm sorry. He noticed that I was barely walking straight because my knees were already numb. So he held my shoulder for support until we reached his car.

As soon as he slid me in the back seat, he sat right next to me. And as soon as he closed the door, I buried my face on his chest, my hands squeezing his shirt so hard. I don't know if I squeezed some of his skin too but I wasn't in the proper state of mind to consider anything other than myself right now.

I'm so selfish. So selfish. So stupid.

And just like that, the tears flowed nonstop. I was biting my lip to prevent myself from hiccuping but I couldn't help it. I wailed like a child. I wailed like a useless, helpless little girl who just lost her father.

Even though I lost him years ago, seeing him again after all this time still hit me hard. It was the first time I saw his new daughter in person too. Seeing that... Seeing my replacement... Was awful.

Brandon was rubbing my head as I cried on his chest. I'm so ashamed. His shirt was so wet with my fat tears.

"I'm sorry," I hiccupped, distancing my face from his shirt. I made such a mess. I'm such a mess. I'm horrible, horrible. "I'm sorry. I'm sorry. I'm sorry. I'm sorry."

He gently pushed my head back to his chest. "Shh. Stop apologizing."

I kept crying. Damn it. I hate feeling so helpless. "I'm sorry. I'm sorry you had to see that. I'm sorry you had to meet that jerk this way. I'm sorry for your shirt. I'm sorry I got mad at you. I'm sorry you had to be with me. I'm sorry. I'm sorry."

I can't stop apologizing. I feel like if I don't apologize enough, Brandon's gonna hate me and leave me. I hate this. I hate this. I hate myself.

He continued rubbing my head soothingly. My hiccups were uncontrollable and I couldn't even speak clearly anymore. When he pulled my face from his chest, he looked at me. I turned away and closed my eyes.

Don't look. Please. Please don't look at my miserable face.

I don't know what expression he made. And I don't want to.

Like a big baby, he lifted my weight and placed my body on his lap, my back resting on his arms. I locked my legs on the sides of his waist and wrapped my arms around his neck. He pulled me in for a warm embrace, and I buried my face on his neck.

I don't know why I even did that. I just wanted something to cling on.

I'm so pathetic.

But the contact was calming me down. A lot. He rubbed my head again in a soothing manner as he tried fixing my hair with his free hand.

"Stop apologizing. You didn't do anything wrong. Your dad's just an asshole. He doesn't deserve you. He doesn't deserve you at all Mira. So don't waste your tears. I'm here. I'll stay with you until you calm down. Don't worry. I'm here."

My heart was fluttering in my chest and I don't know for which reason anymore. I couldn't think properly and every time I blinked, tears fell even if I willed them not to.

Brandon held me like that for hours. This is so embarrassing. I clung to him like a baby. Shit. Shit.

When he noticed I'd calmed down (read: my hiccups were slowly fading away now), he broke our hug and held my face, looking at my face like it was a broken piece of art. I felt the tears coming again but I sucked in a deep breath and held it in. My chest hurt. And my eyes were stinging.

My tears and snot got mixed on my face disgustingly but I wiped it on his shirt so my face was dry now. He's seen me in my ugliest. In my weakest. He's seen lame, weak me.

"I should have left before you got too attached to me. You're annoying. Stop crying."

My father's words screeched like nails on a chalkboard in my ear. I was in the same situation I was in years ago. I showed my weak side, and that made dad leave. And now Brandon.

He's going to leave me too.

My brows creased and my lips quivered - his face softened. Shit Mira, stop remembering bullshit. Stop crying already.

He pushed the awkward tangles of hair away from my face and placed them neatly behind my ears, just like he always did. He cupped my cheek and I couldn't help but enjoy his touch because it was so warm and comforting.

After staring intensely at me for a few more seconds, he sighed and buried his head on my chest. I gasped from the surprise. My heart...

"Aah," he mumbled, wrapping his arms around my waist and pulling me closer, as if the tiny distance between us was still too much. "I'm done for."

What? What did he possibly mean?

He pulled away and stared at me again. I gulped. I just realized I was still sitting on his lap. But I didn't want to go just yet. "Have you calmed down?"

I looked at his expression unsurely before bobbing my head weakly. I'm so exhausted. He leaned in, cupped my cheek and gave me a deep but quick kiss. Then he kissed my forehead before hugging me again. "Thank God. I had no idea what to do. I'm sorry for being so useless."

I hid a smile. He didn't know he practically saved me.

I returned the hug with equal force, but I could feel my strength leaving. I'm so tired. So sleepy. My lids were like heavy weights and my head was so light.

"Thanks," I mumbled. He smiled at me gently before kissing my forehead again. I think I said something else but I can't remember. Everything turned blurry.

Then I was out.

Chapter 27

I could hear faint sounds as I struggled to open my eyes. My head ached when I realized that some kind of light was directly, unpleasantly shining on my face.

I groaned while wrinkling forehead, my nose and my mouth - making the ugliest face but who cares. It kinda helped ease the throbbing. Or, well, I just did it for dramatic effect.

"Turn off the lights," I said to no one in particular. I wasn't expecting a reply. I was just out of it, and I wanted more sleep. I don't even remember anything. How did I get to my bed? Wait. Is this even my bed?

"Mira?" A sweet, warm voice called my name in such a tender way. I squinted at the sight before my bed.

"Mom?"

She smiled at me as she held my forehead. Mom's hand was so warm. Her hands were so soft. I held her hand on my forehead and smiled. I miss mom. Her presence alone was so comforting. Is this a dream?

"Are you okay? Are you hurt?" She asked, purely nothing but concern on her tone. I shook my head slowly. She sighed. Then she looked at me worriedly. "I heard you met your father yesterday."

My eyes shot open. I remember. Oh yeah. That happened. I sighed heavily, taking my mom's hand and burying my face under her palm like a spoiled kid. "Yeah."

My mom's soft scent filled my nostrils with so much nostalgia and familiarity. I can't believe she's here. I can't believe she made time for me even when she was so busy. She definitely is the best.

"I'm so sorry I wasn't there to kick his ass for you sweety," she said, strictly. I hid a giggle. That's my mom. "Brandon told me everything. I feel horrible for you, and I'm resisting the urge to call your father and tell him not to bother you in any way again. Tell me what you want to do Mira."

I was quiet for a while, thinking.

"I don't know," I replied. "I don't want to run away from him mom. I want to face him. And when I do next time, I just want to face him with a smile. Prove we're doing damn well without him."

My eyes closed and I was slowly drifting into fluffy wonderland. I wanted to use my mom's hand as a pillow but I understand she had to let go sometime soon.

"Okay, if that's what you want," she sighed, sounding a bit reluctant. "But tell me if he does anything to you. Anything. You know I won't hesitate to give him my infamous Paige Kick."

This time, I laughed out loud. My mom is so awesome. "Thanks, mom."

"Oh and by the way," she added, fixing my hair and pinching my cheeks gently on the process. "It was Brandon who carried you here back in your room. I was surprised when he called me using your number. He sounded so panicked and all - such an adorable boy. I'm happy you met a nice guy who's always protecting you. I trust him."

Brandon? Panic? I recalled his various expressions on various occassions I got myself in trouble. Not surprising at all, but definitely, definitely adorable.

"We're not dating mom," I clarified just in case she got the wrong idea. She gave me a look of disapproval.

"Why not?"

I shook my head, not knowing how to reply. "Well, it's complica ted..."

Mom stared at me for a bit and I discreetly tried to cover my face with my blanket. My face was getting hot.

"You like him, don't you?" She asked. Well, more like stated. She looked like she already knew the answer to that question, but still needed to hear my say anyway.

I concealed my face, only allowing my eyes to be seen from my blanket. I couldn't look at her. This is the first time we had this kind of conversation. And I can't lie to her. "Yeah. A lot."

She laughed merrily. "Then tell him."

"It's not as easy as it looks mom," I said. And then I sunk in my bed. "And besides, I tried to tell him. But well... Dad happened."

Mom nodded her head in understanding. "So tell him the next time you see him."

"Whoa mom slow down," I finally released myself from the blanket and looked at her in the face. Her brows were raised, as if she didn't see the problem with what she had just suggested. "I'm not even sure he likes me back."

My mother sighed, shaking her head and clicking her tongue. She folded her arms while leaning her back against my chair beside my bed. Uhh. "How dense is my daughter? I thought you were exposed to enough boys in your life to understand how their minds worked. Your mind works like a boy. I thought it was obvious."

Well maybe it was obvious for you mom, but me being the one close to Brandon - it isn't so obvious to me. It's making me even more confused actually.

"Yours work like a man," I said, laughing. It was true though. She rolled her eyes, waving her hand and dismissing my pointless attempt to change topic.

"Honey, I've seen the way he looks at you. He respects you, he protects you and best of all he makes you happy - unlike your father. I want that boy as my son-in-law."

"Mom!" I complained, hiding my face behind my hair. Oh gosh, was she serious right now? "Mom you're getting way ahead of yourself!"

"I don't even understand why you two still aren't dating. I thought you already were. It was so, so obvious."

My heart was beating so fast and I don't even want to know if my cheeks are beet red or not. This is so embarrassing. "We're not."

"I totally ship you guys. Mira. Brandon. Mirandon. Hey, Mirandon sounds cute," she said, and then laughed at her own joke. I facepalmed.

"Aah mom stop it!"

Seriously! I'm glad I can be open with my mom about this but still! She's having way too much fun teasing!

She laughed again before leaving her seat and coming towards me to pinch my cheeks again. "My baby is so cute." I complained while swatting her hands off my face but couldn't resist laughing. My mom is such a goofball. Her eyes fell on her wristwatch and she instantly cringed.

She gave me a sad look. "Mira, I gotta go now. I left in the middle of a board meeting. I'll call you later honey, I'm so sorry."

She kissed my cheek hurriedly and gave me a huge hug before quickening her steps to my desk to get her bag. She looked like she was still struggling in those heels even though she'd been wearing them for more than ten years now.

"It's okay, it's okay," I said. Seriously, it was. I kinda felt bad she had to leave work for me though, but very grateful. I know how hectic her schedule is.

She glanced at her watch again. "Shit. The board is going to skewer me alive then post about it on facebook. I knew I shouldn't have accepted that old perv's friend request. Ah. Sweety, I'm going now." She ran back to my bedside and gave me another kiss on the forehead. "Take care bye!"

I was laughing the whole time my mom ran back and forth in my room then finally out of it. When she was gone, I felt a bit lonely, but nonetheless relieved. If she wasn't here when I woke up, I would've remembered those things and cried like a baby again. Thank God for giving me my mom.

I took my phone from the under my pillow and winced when I saw the time - er - the date. A day has already passed since that incident, and it was way past noon. So I slept for more than a day and still woke up looking like Shrek. My eyes are so puffy. So-called beauty sleeps are pure bullshit.

I noticed an unopened text message so I tapped on the icon and read it. I smiled.

| Mira, if you're awake then get your butt out of that bed and wash up. Brandon's taking you out tonight. Talk to me after your date. Love you mwaa. | From: Nichole

| Hey Mira, heard you met that douche again? Need to talk to someone? Well, Brandon's there but me and Nichole are here too. Get better. You look ugly when you're miserable. Btw, I'll treat ya something cheap when you're done with your date. Have fun. | From: Leo

| Anddd, the traitors we call our best friends have spoiled my plan. Real cool. Call me when you wake up. | From: Brandon - Scaredy Potato

I love my friends.

I quickly obliged to that last text and called Brandon. There's a lot of thanking for me to do. As soon as he picked up, my heart skipped a beat. Why am I so excited?

"Potato!" He said from the other line. "You're alive!"

I rolled my eyes laughing. "Well of course."

I heard some ruffling and then some crashing and a few cusses. It got me worried there. "So, you free tonight?"

"What are you doing?" I supressed my giggles. He chuckled himself before sighing heavily.

"Well, I was kinda fixing the light bulb. And I definitely didn't expect you'd call right now. And.. Here comes the lame part... I fell off the ladder."

"Oh shit," I said, more concerned than amused. Well, the two feelings were fighting, actually but the concerned one was winning, so. "Are you okay?"

"Yeah," he said, and then I heard a groan. "It'd be great if you come over and soothe my pain though."

I rolled my eyes, remembering the last time he asked me that.

"Brandon." I warned. He chuckled again before shooting a defensive reply.

"Hey, don't take it the wrong way. I just wanna see you. Come over, then we'll have dinner."

Oh yeah. Nichole and Leo said he was gonna take me out tonight. I checked my watch - it was still a quarter to three.

"Where are we eating?" I asked, already choosing what to wear in my head. I've been so conscious with my clothes lately. Guess I just want to look good for a certain potato.

"Somewhere we haven't eaten dinner before. A special place." He said. I smiled. I'm more excited about dinner than meeting with Brandon. I can't wait to taste new food. "But before that, just come over. Please?"

I bit my nails in the midst of concealing my smile. I'm smiling too much. I'm too happy right now. Stop it. Stop it. You know what happens if you're too happy.

I took a deep breath and silently released it. "Okay. I'll be there in twenty minutes."

After that I hung up and went straight to the bathroom. While I was washing my hair, I wondered what restaurant he was gonna take me to this time. He absolutely knew my taste in food. And that's definitely what I need right now. Food.

I haven't eaten in so long. Yes, for me it was already so long. Plus, I can't wait to see Brandon. I'll admit I was a bit aftaid and embarrassed because I was so clingy yesterday, but he didn't seem to mind.

In the shower, a lot of things came to mind. What mom said earlier. She thinks Brandon likes me? I think she's just overseeing things. She's a die-hard fan of soap-operas and teenage-drama series, so no doubt that's where she got the amazing idea.

And how were Leo and Nichole? They look like they're in good terms everyday. Are they really fighting? Or is there something bad happening behind our backs?

And what the heck is Brandon thinking? How does he feel about me? I considered mom's suggestion. If I try to confess again today, will it be the end of us?

What if he says he likes someone else and just sees me as a bro? What if he says he's liked Emma for some time now? I wouldn't be surprised if he'd say that. But still, just thinking about it hurt.

Negative thoughts please get the hell out of my mind. Today should be a happy day. It's this damn shower's fault, making me think too much.

Oh yeah, blame the shower Mira, very mature.

I got out of the shower and changed into my best clothes - a red blouse that was tight enough to show off my curves but loose enough to be decent, skinny jeans and my customary pair of sneakers.

I adjusted my bra and took a deep breath. It got a bit tight. It's either I got fat or my boobs got bigger. Or my bra shrunk. Or this isn't my bra. There are so many possibilities.

I let my hair air-dry and put on a little lip gloss. My lips were getting dry. I checked myself out in the mirror and smiled.

Alright. I don't look Shrek-like in any way anymore. Time to go.

"Hey!" Brandon cheerfully greeted me as he opened the door. He was dressed in an old shirt and a pair of jersey shorts. He was wearing slippers. His hair was a mess too.

"Um..." I mumbled, realizing how overdressed I was. "I thought we were going out to eat?"

"Oh yeah," he said as he led me to his room. "We're gonna have dinner in a special place."

"And that place is?" My suspicion was already rising. Oh hell. I think I know where this was going, just judging by Brandon's appearance alone.

He sent me a playful grin. "My kitchen, of course. You're gonna cook dinner for the two of us."

I looked at him wide-eyed. I didn't know what to say. I wasn't prepared for this! And aah what a waste of clothes! I could've worn this for school on Monday! "You said... You didn't say... I wore this and... I could've... Ahh! I wore a bra for you today Brandon!"

Oops. My suffocated boobs have spoken.

He looked surprised from my sudden outburst that he slowly took a step back and raised his hands in surrender. He looked at me unsurely. "Well um... You can take the bra off if you're so bothered about it? I won't mind."

I scoffed. Sure he wouldn't mind. He'd be more than delighted in fact. Well I'm not giving him the satisfaction. I feel so ridiculous dressing up. Wait, why am I even making a big deal out of this? Gosh my hormones are so out of control lately.

And I mentally smacked myself. Why'd I get mad? He actually deserves this after saving me yesterday. I'm such an ungrateful bitch.

"Never mind. What ingredients do you have here?" I said, casually making my way to their kitchen. Their apartment was a lot like ours, but the style was more boyish compared to ours, of course. And ours was cleaner. Definitely cleaner.

Brandon followed me inside. "Chicken. And... Stuff."

I opened their fridge and took out a pack of chicken drumsticks. Then I took some flour, eggs, salt, lemon and oil from the cupboard. I knew where everything was. Leo arranged all these, no doubt.

I placed the ingredients on the counter and instructed Brandon to get me a bowl and a wooden spoon. "I can only make us some fried chicken since the ingredients are limited."

He returned with the things I asked for. He was grinning at me. I glared at him. "I didn't really expect you to be willing to cook."

"Oh, so should I just leave then?" I asked, my tone serious but trust me, I was just having my fun.

"No! No!" He waved his hands frantically. I hid a grin. "Please, stay. I wanna watch you cook. And I wanna eat your food."

I stared at him for a bit before clearing my throat. I have no reply damn it. I mixed some of the ingredients quite nervously since he was staring at me work. I have to start a conversation or something. I can't do well if people stare at me while I work. Distraction. I need to give him a distraction. "So, do you know how to cook?"

I was glazing the chicken with a thick coat of the mixture I just made. I stole a glance at Brandon and he was smiling at me. I looked away quickly. "I know how to fry an egg. And some spam. And hotdogs and bacon. Hm. That's about it."

I laughed. Well, at least he knew how to fry. He walked behind the counter, to the stove, to me, and observed what I was doing. I had to control my breathing. "What about you? You look like you're used to cooking."

I nodded as I placed the pan on the stove and turned the fire on. "I am. Uncle taught me, and I did most of the cooking when I was in middle-school. Mom was always busy so I learned to cook for her and myself."

I was actually proud of that fact. At least I was useful back then, despite all the shit that's happened.

Brandon hummed an understanding tune. Was it getting hot in here? I feel faint. Maybe it was because of my tight bra? Yeah, it's definitely the bra. No, he was too close.

Minutes later, I was done frying the chicken. I aligned the drumsticks neatly on a plate. There was something missing.

Ah. The lemons.

I grabbed a knife and began slicing them evenly. As I was doing so, Brandon asked me what I was gonna use them for.

"Nothing. Just decoration." I simply said. He snorted.

"You're like a potato masterchef. A really short potato masterchef."

I glared at him. Did he just make fun of my fun-sized height?

"I'm holding a knife right now, Brandon. Nothing good ever happens if you bother a person holding a knife."

He raised his hands in surrender again. He was so adorable. "Hey, I was complimenting you just now!"

I laughed, shrugging it off as I finished slicing the lemons. I put them on the plate beside the drumsticks and smiled at my pleasant presentation. It looks good enough to eat now.

"What're our drinks for tonight?" I asked as I made my way to the small dining table, placing the plate on the center. I also prepared our placemats, plates and the utensils. I can't wait to eat.

"Is root beer okay?" He called. He was checking the fridge. I shouted back a yes before taking my phone out. I gotta take a picture of that chicken. It looked too pretty to be eaten.

I took a few shots, and while I was trying to get a better angle, I felt a pair of strong arms wrap around my waist and I squeaked, almost dropping my phone.

I quickly turned around and felt my butt hit the table as Brandon took a few more steps toward me. God, what was he gonna do this time?

His left hand was on one side of the table and his right hand - which was holding the bottle of root beer - was on the other side of the table.

For short, I was trapped.

I looked at him confused, but inside I was panicking. Dude. Dude. The way he was looking at me right now was frighteningly hot. I mean, he looked so cool with those narrowed eyes. No, no. His jaw-line was... I mean... I mean...

What? What was I saying?

He cocked a grin before pulling his face closer to mine. "Did I tell you you look beautiful today as well?"

"Stop that," I mumbled, embarrassed. Man. My cheeks. Please don't turn red. Heart, damn it, calm down. And brain, cooperate with me please.

He touched my cheek and smiled at me. "Stop what?"

I can't say.

Seeing no way of escape from left and right, I slowly decided to sink to the floor and hopefully get away. He's making me too nervous. I just remembered we were alone in his apartment right now. He looks like a hunter - and me, the helpless prey.

Upon sinking to the floor, which I realized was quite a dumb idea, he followed my pace down as well. And when both of us were squatting on the floor, I avoided his eyes. How can he stare at me for so long and not get sick of my face?

I tried to laugh to ease the tension. "What the heck are we doing?"

He laughed softly in reply, his eyes narrowing down to my lips. Gulp. "I don't know."

I was having a hard time breathing. Why was he looking at me like that? When his eyes met mine, I bit my lip. His eyes were so beautiful. I can't explain how anymore, but it was just so beautiful.

Memories quickly flashed in my mind like a montage. Our encounters before we met, the glaring, the day we met at that restaurant and him ridiculously sucking the remains of my milkshake on my neck because he ate my spicy burrito, our little movie dates, our fights, our talks about our pasts, how he got along so well with my mom, how he always saves me, how he's always there when I cried, how he made me feel horribly sad but exceptionally happy too.

I'm afraid. I don't think I just like him anymore. I think it's growing into something scary. And if I fall completely into that scary place, I don't think I'll be able to go back anymore.

Shit. Am I falling for him already?

No. Stop it.

"Hey Mira?" He called, as if to snap me back into reality. His eyes were narrowed again and his hand was already cupping my cheek. My eyes fell down to his lips, like I was getting tempted. "Can I kiss you?"

The room was so quiet. I hope he doesn't hear my loud heartbeats. I bit my lip again and noticed him take a sharp breath when I did so. My heart fluttered. I slowly nodded, feeling the need of his warmth right now.

"Yeah," I barely said in a whisper. He wasted no time and pressed his lips on mine, pushing the back of my head gently, to get better access.

I'm really not sure if he does like me. Even if it seems obvious to other people, it's not to me. But I want him to like me. I want him to feel the same way I feel about him.

Damn it, Mira. You're killing yourself here.

My fingers found their way to his hair and I happily played with it as we continued to share this blissful kiss. Even though his hair was already a mess to begin with, it was still so soft. He's amazing. He's so amazing.

Ah, the chicken's gonna get cold. But for now, my potato comes first.

Chapter 28

One of the best feelings in life is taking off really tight bra after a long day.

In case some of you get any ideas, I'm already back in my room. Brandon and I talked a bit after dinner, watched a movie in his room, and then he drove me home.

That's it.

Now I'm not dismissing the fact that we had a heated session before dinner, but just so you know, that session ended abruptly with my stomach imitating the sound of a barfing bulldog.

I was wrong. I needed the chicken before my potato. Sorry.

So yeah. He laughed and we both ate dinner. Then fast forward, I'm back in my room, dancing around naked because my boobs were finally free.

As soon as I washed up and changed into my pyjamas, Nichole barged in my room. I wasn't surprised to see her, but I was surprised when she suddenly pulled me into a hug.

"Umm?" I mumbled unsurely. She was hugging me so tight. She let out a short wail.

"Are you okay now? Are you still hurting? Do you need anything?"

It took me a fraction of a second to realize what she was saying. She meant my encounter with my dad yesterday. Knowing my best friend, she must've felt horrible the whole time I was out.

I offered her a reassuring smile before giving her an extra hug to show how relieved I am to have her. "I'm okay. Brandon was there. Mom talked to me. You and Leo are here. I'm perfectly fine."

We broke the hug and I concealed a gasp when I saw how her eyes were glassy with tears. She quickly wiped her face with the back of her hand before laughing. "Sorry. I was pretty useless. Brandon and I fought about who should take you out and cheer you up when you woke up. He put up a really big fight."

I smiled, feeling giddy. But then I forced my lips into a thin line because I shouldn't feel so happy when my best friend looked so miserable.

"Really? You two fought? Wow. Why am I not surprised?" I said. Nichole giggled before punching my shoulder.

"Yeah. Rock-paper-scissors. He had two out of three wins."

This time, I burst out laughing. It was ridiculous but sweet at the same time. Nichole rolled her eyes at my laughing fit, but she was laughing as well.

"Leo proposed that game. Ain't he the peacemaker." She defended herself. And then she sent me a small smile. "But are you sure you're okay now? Did Brandon cheer you up?"

I'm glad they're so worried about me, but I don't want to be treated like I'm gonna break any second. They know I'm tougher than that. But since it's about my dad this time, I get why they're all so flustered.

"Yup." I smiled, a bit too widely. Before I could hide the huge grin on my face, Nichole raised a brow at me.

"I see. Did you tell him already?"

She meant if I confessed to him already. I shook my head slowly. "No. I'm just waiting for the right time. I'm still hoping he'll tell me first though. To tell you the truth, me confessing to him... I think I'm getting way ahead of myself."

She gave me a look I couldn't decipher and then sighed. "Well, whatever. Just know I'm always here okay? Call me if you need an extra hand in beating up some jerk who'll break your heart, I'll be of assistance."

We exchanged ridiculous grins to cool the tension a bit. I always feel at ease whenever we have these conversations. I don't know. I'm just so grateful I have such an amazing best friend. She hugged me again before heading for the door. "G'night."

Brandon drove me to school this morning like the usual. I hid my smile and pretended to be cool when he pecked my lips as a 'good morning' greeting. And when he smiled...

I felt like my heart was gonna burst.

How. Just how does he do that?

We went to our separate classes and I couldn't even concentrate anymore because I couldn't stop thinking about him. There was a tugging feeling in my chest. A feeling of caution of some sort - as if it was sending me a signal, a storm warning.

He just kissed me this morning. He's kissed me several times before, kisses even deeper than that innocent one earlier. But why do I feel so flustered? It's like I'm drowning, but I'm enjoying it.

I know. Ridiculous. I'm so horrible at describing my feelings. I'm just good at rambling. Like what I'm doing right now. Blah blah blah.

"Mira!" A voice boomed into one ear and out the other. A pair of heavy hands slammed loudly on my desk, causing me to stand abruptly from the shock.

I was a bit confused at first because more than half the class was staring at me with weird grins. I only realized what it was when I heard a low groan beside my table.

Sam was holding his jaw while he knitted his brows so hard it almost became one.

"Seriously," he hissed, getting himself up. "You're gonna kill me someday."

I'm kidding. I had no idea what happened. I didn't realize anything. I'm not realizing anything. I can't realize anything. I want to realize it. But maybe I already realized it. Realize... Realize what? Brandon. My feelings. Realize the potato. I mean. What? Wait. What's happening again?

Oh yeah. Sam.

"What's wrong?" I asked, shrugging my messy thoughts aside.

He groaned again. Emma was giggling beside me. Sam sent me a semi-glare but it quickly softened into a hopeless look when he saw how I had no clue on what was going on.

"You were spacing out. I kept calling you a few times but you were ignoring me. Then you stood up and hit my jaw. Thanks, by the way."

I held my head and wondered how I didn't feel any pain at all. Maybe he's just really weak. Or my head's as hard as... something really hard.

Ughh. I can't think properly anymore. Brandon. Brandon. Brandon. Potato. Potato. Potato Brandon. Damn it. It's only been a few hours but I want to see him already.

I used to think the nickname Potato was ridiculous and corny, but why do I like it so much right now? I like it. I like Brandon too.

Am I clingy? Is this clingy? What is clingy?

Ughhhhh. I hate being a girl.

"Hey," Sam called my attention once again. "Are you sure you're okay? Your mind's like, in vacation."

Before I could shake my head, Emma joined in our conversation. She was just a seat away anyway. "I bet she's thinking about Brandon."

Dead.

"Why would I think about that potato." I mumbled like a kid. But Emma knew better. She sent me a quiet grin as Sam shrugged his shoulders and made his way back to his seat.

I drifted into my thoughts again. I don't care. I just want to think about him. I can't wait to see him at lunch.

"Mira," Emma whispered, making sure Sam couldn't hear and butt in our conversation.

"Yeah?"

She smiled shyly as her eyes met the floor. She was just too lovely to look at no matter what she did. "Well. Nothing really. I just... Kinda wanted to tell you something. But it's not that important. Sorry. Never mind."

I raised a brow before twisting my body on my seat so I could face her directly. I placed my elbow on my desk as my cheek rested comfortably in the palm of my hand. "You got me curious already. Too late to back out, Em. What is it?"

She supressed a laugh before changing her position to face me directly as well. The teacher already came in a few minutes ago but we didn't care. "It's about my friends."

"And?"

Her eyes found the floor so interesting all of a sudden. Something tells me it's not about who's boobs got bigger this time.

"You know, they're kinda fake?"

My eyes popped. She took in the shock in my face and nodded her head, confirming what she said previously.

"I hang out with them, yeah, but it's because they're the first friends I made since I got into this school and we kinda stuck. But honestly, I really wanna stop hanging out with them. I feel like I can't be myself. But if I leave the group I'll be a loner. I don't know." Her voice was starting to fade off.

I can't believe what she just told me. She looked so close with her friends. What's actually happening behind the scenes then? And a loner? Please, she wouldn't have any problems making new friends. The real problem though was finding the real ones.

"It's really none of my business," I mumbled unsurely. "But if you feel like you don't belong in that group, even if you'll be alone, just leave them." I said. "You can always hang out with us. Don't worry. You can start over if you want to, everything's up to you."

I didn't like giving advices because I don't wanna get blamed in the future if they screw up because of what I told them to do, that's why I add 'I don't know' or 'everything's up to you' in the end of every advice.

As usual, I play safe.

She sighed and then smiled. It sounded like a really hopeless sigh, but her smile looked relieved or something. "You're really,

really nice Mira. I'm so glad we're friends. You're not fake and you never lie. You always say what you feel and do what you want to do. You're so cool, I swear. Thanks for the advice."

I just stared at her in silence as she sent me another smile. This person is an angel. I feel like I just sinned big time.

I'm not any of the things she mentioned.

I'm not honest. I even lie to myself just for the sake of saving my pride. I always play safe because I'm afraid of losing a lot of things. I don't do whatever I want - I hold back on everything because I'm a wimp.

A pathetic wimp.

I'm a horrible person, and she doesn't deserve a 'friend' like me. I even made comparisons between our bodies before since I was pathetically jealous of her just because she was talking with Brandon. I'm jealous at how perfect she is without even trying. I'm jealous at how effortless it is for her to smile at people and make a lot of friends.

My insecurities are biting my ass in huge chunks and it hurts so much I want to poop but I can't poop because my insecurities just theoretically ate my ass.

It's creative, I know. Let me ramble, I'm panicking here.

I couldn't even return her smile when she told me those things. No, Emma. No. I'm practically a demon. You'll only get hurt if you stick with me. And you definitely don't deserve that. I'm probably worse than your friends.

A beautiful angel like you should stay in the light and stay away from a demon like me.

And yet, I couldn't tell her any of the things I just thought about. I really want to be her friend too. She's cool and she's real. But I feel so guilty just being around her. If I'll be blunt about it, she might hate me.

It's been a while since I've made close friends after Leo and Nichole.

Brandon, Sam, Emma.

I just gained more things I could lose.

Emma hung out with us during lunch. Sam decided to stop by our table and told our friends his lame story of me hitting his jaw earlier at class. Maybe he was expecting some looks or words of sympathy.

He received none. Instead, he received a few laughs.

He left shortly after that. Emma was having small talk with Leo and Nichole, I was quietly eating my food.

Brandon arrived as soon as I was finished. He slid in his seat beside me and our friends just gave him a nod of acknowledgement. They were too absorbed in their little talk. I wasn't paying attention so I had no idea what it was.

My heartbeat quickened when I became fully aware of Brandon's presence. A mixture of happiness, relief, guilt, uncertainty and panic washed over me.

Maybe I shouldn't confess to him after all. I don't want to destroy our friendship. I'm afraid of risking that. The thought of Brandon ignoring me or pitying me makes me sick to my stomach. I don't even want to think of those things.

I felt him intertwine his fingers with mine under the table. I looked at him, wondering what the deal was, but he just flashed me a smile.

Stop it.

"You look down. You okay?"

Stop noticing every little thing.

"I'm fine. Just a bit tired," I replied.

I'm tired of overthinking.

He squeezed my hand and discreetly planted kisses on each of my fingers - quietly enough so our friends in the opposite side of the table won't notice. After that gesture, he hid our hands under the table again and placed it on his lap. "Whatever it is, it's gonna be alright. It's okay if you don't wanna tell me. Just know I'm here if you need me. Okay?"

Please. Please.

Please don't let me fall. Please. Please. I hate feeling hopeless. I'm tired of being sad. I'm sick of these one-sided feelings already.

Mira, you stupid idiot. What have you gotten yourself into? Stop it. Stop feeling. You will get hurt. You will get hurt.

I nodded. He probably noticed how stiff I was, so he shifted closer to my side, to comfort me probably. Like what he did when I broke down after seeing my dad.

Stay away.

"Hey," he whispered before putting a hand over my shoulder. He pulled me into a small hug and kissed my forehead. "What's wrong?"

Nothing's wrong. Nothing's right either. Nothing's ever right for me. I don't know what to do.

I couldn't say what I was thinking. I was just quiet. He rubbed my head gently as he stared at me with worried eyes. He's just like this because he's a great friend. And because I'm so selfish, I don't want him to give this exact same treatment to anyone else.

Not even Leo. I mean, c'mon.

"Is your dad still bothering you?" He asked. I bit my lip. He thinks I'm like this because of my dad? Well, it's better than him knowing about my conflicted thoughts about him.

I didn't say anything. Instead, I forced a smile, a painful smile just for him. I like his attention, but I feel bad for lying to him again. As I've said, I'm a horrible person. Why do I even wonder why people always leave me?

Brandon's expression softened a lot after I gave him my response. He gently pushed my head to let me rest on his shoulder, and then he patted my hair soothingly. It felt nice. "Everything's gonna be fine. As long as I'm here, I promise you won't get hurt."

I wanted to cry.

Just how sure was he about that?

Didn't it even occur to him that he may be the reason why I've been so emotional this last few weeks?

I pressed my lips hard.

Fuck this. I'm terrified. I'm terrified of the way this guy makes me feel because honestly, I don't want to feel anything. I wish I can't feel a damn thing. But I can't help it.

I'm falling.

I'm falling for Brandon.

Damn it. He just makes me so happy, so relieved and at the same time he makes me so sad I want to punch his face.

I can still control this, can't I? I'll stop. I'll stop thinking of him. I just like him. Like a crush sort of thing. That's it. That's it. That's the line, Mira. Don't cross that line. Don't kill yourself now.

"Too much PDA guys," Leo was waving his hand, signalling us to go away as he covered his eyes with his other hand. "And yeah, we saw everything no matter how subtle my dear roommate was."

Nichole and Emma were giggling at Leo but Brandon didn't care. He placed his hand on my head and pulled me closer, so close it looked like a side-hug.

"Don't bother us. Shoo. Shoo."

I smiled, laughing a bit as well. I love it when he does that.

"Ew. Whatever," Leo rolled his eyes. He was about to say something else until he noticed something off about me. "Hey Mira, is something wrong? You feeling okay?"

I don't know what I'm feeling Leo.

"I'm fine," I said. "Just sleepy. Tired."

My best friends didn't look convinced. I'm guessing they think it's about my dad again, but it's okay. I'll just make everything awkward if I tell them the real reason.

Nichole checked her watch before calling my attention. "We have three more classes to go. Wanna skip?"

Before I got to say anything, Leo second the motion. "Yeah, let's!"

Emma raised her hand jokingly. "I'm in."

I was laughing at their excited grins. I know they're doing this for me. That's just how awesome they are.

"Alright." I chuckled. When I gave my answer, Brandon said he'll drive.

They already made a plan. They were gonna try their best cheering me up today, and even though Emma had no idea why, she still gave a hundred percent support.

I feel glad and feel bad at the same time. Do I deserve to be friends with these people?

I sighed. Whatever. I'll continue being pessimistic later. For now, I'll just go with the flow and accept everybody's kindness.

Chapter 29

It's been over a week since my friends and I got caught skipping. Our detention just ended today, and as soon as we left the room, all of us shouted FREEEEDOM!!!

Including Emma, mind you.

So right now, all of them are in my room - the girls are destroying my neatly folded sheets because of their jumping around like little monsters and the guys are emptying my fridge as of this moment.

I'm not even gonna speak my complaints out loud anymore I know they won't have much of an effect anyway.

"Do you have any movies we can watch?" Sam asked as he stuffed his face with the chocolate I tried to hide so much.

Before I could give him a decent reply, I sent him a wild glare. I may even have gritted my teeth and growled like the uncivilized gorilla that I was, who knows. But dude. That was my chocolate he was eating. My. Chocolate. He showed a faint sign of a flinch. "Ask Nichole."

Nichole cringed when she saw the murderous intent in my eyes. She nodded in understanding when she saw Sam eating my precious chocolate.

"Okay guys, let's move to my room. I got a lot of new movies in my laptop. Move! Move! Before Mira kills us all."

They were all too hyper. They screamed and laughed then ran to Nichole's room. Seriously, our small apartment can't handle six gorillas at once.

I left my messy room as is and went to hide more of my stash of food (read: I don't trust Leo and Sam) before I followed after them.

As soon as I entered the room, they were arguing whether to watch Crazy, Stupid Love or Ant Man. It was getting really loud until Leo suggested we watch Magic Mike. All of us shut up and stared at him weirdly.

"Dude. Really?" Sam said. Emma burst into a fit of giggles, and then everyone else followed. Leo had no idea why we were laughing. He didn't know what Magic Mike was about. He thought it was about basketball.

To make fun of him, they decided to watch that. Nichole was failing miserably at controlling her laughter as she played the movie. And that marked the end of their argument.

"No! No!" Leo screamed, squirming under Nichole's arms. "Stop it! Stop the movie! No! Oh fuck no!"

I couldn't even produce any sound because of laughing too much. I could already feel a six-pack coming, oh man.

"You wanted to watch this!" Nichole giggled as she held her overdramatic boyfriend still. Leo was trying to cover his eyes but Sam and Emma prevented that by holding both his arms. When he tried to shut his eyes, Nichole forced them open.

"No! Dude stop! He's... I... Oh God, he's stripping. He's stripping! I can see his ass! Motherfu - Make it stop! Make it stop!"

I don't know if I should join them in detaining my poor best friend or if I should pity my poor best friend, or if I should just leave the room.

"Leo, it's Channing Tatum!" Emma squealed. "If he moves like that on the floor, imagine him moving like that in be - "

"NO! NO! NO!"

Okay, I think I'm going to leave the room for a bit.

I quietly closed the door as my friends continued to torture the drama king named Leo. I admit though, I was still giggling. Poor kid.

I was smiling to myself as I did so. Since when did our group get so big? Since when did it get this fun? When I first met those freaks, I never thought we'd hang out like this. Ever.

I chugged down a glass of cold water and then sighed in relief. I stared at the empty glass on my hand and sighed again. Until when will this last?

A few seconds later, I snorted to myself. Way to go all sentimental again you loser.

"Mira?"

Brandon.

"Hm?"

He walked towards me and I had to breathe slowly to control my rapid heartbeats. Dude, I'm going to develop a serious heart problem if I keep this up.

When we were finally face to face, he smiled at me.

My heart hurts ow.

"You okay?"

I feigned a laugh to release the tension building up in my chest. "Why do you always ask if I'm okay?"

He put an arm around my shoulder before pulling me in and pressing his lips on my ear. "I don't know. I'm just making sure you're not being sad on your own again."

All the hairs on my body stood up. Maybe it's because of what he did. Or maybe it's because of what he said. Who knows. All I know is that he's killing me.

And why was he getting too close? That was totally unnecessary.

I slowly pushed his head away from me and sent him a quiet smile. "I'm fine. Thanks."

He tilted his head and gave me a look that meant he didn't believe a word I just said. "These past few weeks? Nuh-uh. Something's bothering you. What is it? You can tell me."

I bit my lip as I stared at the floor. Wow I really need to mop after they leave, it's not as sparkly as -

Shhhh. Focus, focus.

I shook my head slowly and forced a smile. "I'm really okay. Thanks for worrying about me though."

He looked hurt. Or something. I don't know. But I feel like he made that expression because he thinks I can't trust him even after all that's happened.

But the truth is, I trust him, and I don't trust him. It's... It's complicated.

I just want to tell him I like him already and get this over with but I know it'll just make things awkward, especially with our friends in the other room.

"Well," he stepped forward and held my waist. I flinched but I still didn't look at his face. I can't. "Let me at least try to cheer you up?"

I wanted to scream and run away and hide and cry. He can't cheer me up. He'll only make me fall for him more and then I'll beat myself up real bad afterwards. No, that's not cheering up bruh. That's only salting the wounds.

"Hey," he tried calling my attention. Seeing that I wasn't responding, he pushed my chin up so I can look at him in the eyes. I took a sharp breath.

He stared at me for a moment until his expression softened into something familiar, something... something heartbreaking.

"If you don't want to tell me that's okay. I won't force you. Just know I'm here, always. If you wanna talk about anything I'm just here. Okay?"

No no no stop making me believe like you like me as more than a friend. Because I'm not really sure if you do. Maybe you're just being a really good friend. Ugh. It's dangerous to assume. Damn I hate my thoughts so much.

I couldn't help it. I glared at him. He was confused and a bit panicked when I did so. This guy has no idea. No fucking idea.

I was pissed. And I'm too pissed to explain why. Seeing his height towering over mine, I got more annoyed, so I punched his stomach. His eyes shot open from the shock and as he arched his back from the hit, his current height worked for me, so I grabbed a fistful of his hair and kissed him.

He couldn't even make up a clear expression.

Now why the hell did I do that? Maybe because I just wanted to kiss him? Maybe because I just wanted to punch him? Which is it?

I let go of his hair and broke our kiss. His eyes were still wide open, he probably never closed them. I gave him a lovely smile before heading back to the room. "Thanks. I feel better now."

After watching three movies, the gorillas went home. Nichole's room was trashed and our fridge was empty. Nice. Very nice.

Brandon didn't say a word to me after that incident in the kitchen. I don't know if I made things awkward or anything but whatever. I always act on impulse.

After cleaning up a bit, I returned to my room and dived into my heavenly sheets. Aahh. We didn't even do much today but I feel so tired. So burned out.

I hesitantly got up to take a quick bath and change into my pyjamas. After all that I fell to my bed once again.

Sigh.

Why do I feel so distant with Brandon? What happened? What shit did I screw up this time?

I rolled to the side in frustration and just kept thinking and thinking and thinking and thinking and thinking.

No, I don't overthink.

Yeah, I pretty much do.

Aaaargh!

In the middle of my mental, gibberish rant, my phone rang. I stopped abruptly, knowing exactly who could be calling at this hour.

I took deep breaths while patting my chest, forcing my body to listen to my brain and calm the shit down. Calm down the shit. Shit down.

Shit.

Just answer the phone!

"Yeah?" I said as soon as I pressed the answer button. I hope my voice sounded cool and composed but not too bitchy, and I really hope I sounded like I wasn't anticipating his call or anything.

"Um, hey. Hi. Hello." He mumbled.

Oh. Okay. So he needed to say hi three times. Should I reply three times as well? No, I should not.

And I'm answering my own questions. Very normal Mira.

"What's up?" I asked, sliding in my sheets and covering my face with a pillow. Might as well get comfortable.

I heard him sigh as I quietly swallowed hard. "About that kiss..."

"Nope." I quickly interrupted. Oh no he won't. "We are not talking about that."

There was a slight pause.

"We aren't?" He asked.

"We aren't." I deadpanned.

Another pause.

"Oh, okay." He mumbled unsurely. I cleared my throat and thought of something to talk about since I just rudely dismissed our would-be topic for tonight.

"So, what're you doing right now?" I asked.

"Talking to you, scratching my butt." He replied.

"Oh," I sighed. "I'm scratching my boobs."

Long pause.

"Ooookay," he snickered on the other line. "So we're scratching."

I concealed a laugh. Dude. Awkward. Why did I just admit I was scratching my boobs. "Yeah, we're scratching. And it feels nice."

"How about you make some funny noises while you're at it?" He suggested, barely finishing the sentence because he was chuckling so hard.

I quickly said no. "Dude, I am so not gonna phone sex you."

He burst out laughing and I couldn't help it, I did too. I don't know. Was it really that funny? I'm just laughing because he's laughing. Honestly, that's funny enough as is.

When his laughter slowly calmed down, he spoke again. "I miss having these conversations with you."

I smiled warmly to myself, pressing my ear harder against my phone. "Me too."

I don't understand. Whenever we talked on the phone before, the feeling was light, it was heart-pounding at times yeah, but it was light. But right now, why does it feel so heavy? So tense?

It feels like I'm losing something. And it's more than just the game.

"I have a question," he suddenly spoke again, his tone serious this time. My soft hum signalled him to proceed. "Do you feel... um. Comfortable with... me?"

I was silent for a while, thinking about what I should say. What's the right thing to say? Do I feel uncomfortable with him?

Well duh, of course. I like him. I'm conscious around him. I'm a clumsy uncivillized gorilla around him. I overthink a lot of things around him. My brain does not cooperate with me when I'm around him. I like him that much.

But at the same time, yeah, I feel comfortable around him. I can tell him anything, I feel safe when he's with me, I'm confident at my skills and I can be at my best with him. I can goof around all day with him without him judging me, he's best friends with my best friends, and he's always there for me. Always.

So what's the right thing to say?

"I only accept two answers," he said, breaking my thoughts for a second. "Yes or no. There's no 'maybe' option here. Just tell me. Honestly."

Isn't he putting a bit too much pressure on me?! I'm confused enough as is!

Alright Mira, you played safe all your life. What should you say? It should be an answer that doesn't put anything in jeopardy. It should be an answer that won't hurt anybody.

But shit man, I only get two options?

If I say yes, he'll think I like him, which I do, but don't want him to know yet. More like, I don't want to accidentally confess over the phone. But if I say no, he might get crushed and I'll only make things more awkward between us. Damn it, is this a trick question?

"It's a yes and a no." I replied.

"What?" He said. "No, I can't accept that. Just tell me if it's a yes or a no."

"Why are you asking me this?" I asked, feeling tense and a bit frustrated.

"I just want to know."

I sighed heavily. "I told you, there's no absolute answer. It's a yes and a no. I can't elaborate any further."

Stop it.

"Mira, just tell me. Which is it? You can't give me that. That's just unfair."

Unfair? Wow, unfair. And what about me? He thinks this is fair for me?

His tone turned cold and I felt the pressure get into my head. I hate it whenever this happens. "I ask you a simple question and you can't even give me a certain response. I'm not even asking for anything big, just a simple yes or no. You can't say yes and no, or half-yes half-no. I wa - "

Fed up, I cut him off. I hate getting told off. "Fine, no." He shut up. I didn't realize that I raised my voice. "You want a simple answer? No. No is my anwer. No, I am not comfortable around you. No, I will not elaborate. No. There, I said it. You happy?"

There was a long and heavy silence. Even if we were just talking on the phone, I could feel the air weighing heavier than whatever I can't think straight anymore.

Fuck. Fuck. I said something stupid. Shit. I offended him didn't I? Did I hurt him? Why the hell couldn't I keep my mouth shut? Why the hell did I get mad? And now I'm meeting up with my old friend regret again. Hi there buddy. Wish I could tell you to go fuck yourself.

After that silence, I heard him breathe on the other line. It was the longest five seconds of my life. I'm scared. Shit.

"Okay." He said.

Okay? Okay? He does not sound okay. He definitely does not sound okay at all. I screwed up again.

"I'm sorry," I said, my voice so quiet I wasn't sure if he even heard me. But he did.

"No, no." He said. "Don't feel bad. You shouldn't feel bad at all. I'm the one who asked."

Another heavy silence fell. What the heck were we supposed to say? It got so awkward and tense. I don't know if I regret my answer or not. But why did he ask me that? Was he genuinely curious, was he testing me or was he just confident I'd say yes?

Should I even be making such a big deal out of this? Damn it, thoughts. Shit.

"Um..." I dumbly mumbled. I had nothing to say, but I wanted to say something. I don't know.

A few seconds of silence passed. I was about to open up another topic so we could just forget about the last one until he replied.

"Yeah. Um, so. Goodnight?"

My heart clenched inside my chest as I gripped my phone. That's it? I hate myself.

"Hm, goodnight."

Then I hung up.

Chapter 30

Toss. Toss. Turn. Toss. Turn. Turn. Cry.

I hesitantly opened my eyes at the rays of light peeking from my curtains. Grumbling and squinting at the blinding light, I earnestly thought about how useless a human being I was. "Ah, the sun."

It's morning already. Wow. I didn't sleep a wink. Wow. I'm still alive. Wow. Wow.

I'm so tired and my face feels sticky.

I got up from bed and walked like a zombie to our bathroom. Lucky it was Saturday. But regardless whether it was a weekend or not, I still wouldn't go out today.

Today sucks.

My life sucks.

I suck.

After splashing my face with some cold water, I somehow felt a bit bitter - I mean better. Ugh. I'm so tired. But I still can't sleep.

I was on my way back to my room when Nichole flicked my forehead. I jumped from the shock because 1.) Where the hell did she come from? And 2.) Ow, that hurt.

Instead of saying my usual complaints, I just stared at her while rubbing my forehead. I didn't have the energy to be myself today. I just want to sleep.

She folded her arms as she studied my face. "What happened to you?"

I shook my head, meaning nothing. I just didn't feel like talking. Uuugh.

A few seconds later, her expression softened, almost as if she was about to cry. But maybe that was just me. She suddenly sighed heavily before hugging me so tight you'd think I was gonna die tomorrow.

Which, I probably will if I keep living like the useless human being that I am. No, gorilla would suit me better. Let me rephrase that:

I might die tomorrow if I keep living like the useless gorilla that I am.

Better.

But my nonsense can wait. Let's get back to Nichole. She groaned and sighed and grumbled. I don't know what's up with her. "Mira, hit me."

It took me a good five seconds to let that sink into my brain. "What? Why?"

"Just hit me." She said firmly after she broke the hug. Confused, I punched her lightly on the shoulder, because I know that's the only way for her to tell me what's going on.

She gave me a look that said 'did you even try?' but didn't ask me to hit her again. Actually, I could've hit her harder, but like I said, I had no energy today. What time was it anyway, like six in the morning?

"Oh, God," she sighed heavily again, burying her face in her hands. "I'm so sorry. I'm horrible. I'm sorry."

What? What?

"What?" I asked. She slowly lifted her head and didn't bother forcing a smile. She knew better than to pretend to look okay in front of me.

"Leo and I fought again last night."

I looked at her strangely, something pricked the little monster inside my chest. "Over the phone?"

She shook her head. "No, after the movie when everyone left, he stayed behind for a few hours. We were in my room, you were kinda out of it last night so maybe you didn't notice us."

I nodded, smacking myself mentally. I always pick the perfect times to be stupid. She continued.

"It was just a small fight. A stupid fight. I'm so stupid."

I'm confused here. And my brain wasn't actually in perfect condition to process anything properly. I looked at my best friend. She looked so down and guilty. And here I was, feeling the exact same thing, for an entirely different reason. "But why'd you apologize to me?"

She stared at me for a while, her expression turning softer and softer, like she felt really bad by just looking at me. Did I do something wrong? Did she do something wrong?

"Because I'm a horrible friend." She mumbled.

What? What did she mean? She's not making any sense now. What happened? I have no idea. My thoughts are still floating in a giant mess in my mind right now. I can't understand the situation.

Before I could ask her, she waved her hand and dismissed the topic. She laughed nervously before giving me another tight hug. Kinda made me feel better, but it kinda gave me the feeling of uneasiness as well. "Never mind. Sorry I bothered you. Get some sleep Mira. You look like you tried on every drug in the world."

It took me another five seconds to let that joke sink in my brain. When I was about to retort with an idiotic response (read: without the help of my uncooperative brain) she already went back to her room.

What the hell was going on today? They fought? She apologized? Yes? No? Comfortable? Brandon? Brandon? Brandon?

I let out a frustrated groan and then a silent wail as I made my way back to my room. My mind's a mess. My heart's a mess. Damn it, my whole life's a mess from the start, why am I still surprised? I just want to sleep. Damn it.

So, I couldn't sleep no matter how much I tried.

It's sad, I know.

But I'm not sad. I'm not sad at all. Psh. Who's sad? Definitely not me. Maybe you're sad. Stop pushing it on me because I know I'm not sad. I'm really not.

The door opened in front of me, revealing the most ridiculous scene I've seen all week.

Hold on. Let me describe it and give you the perfect picture:

A grown man with dishevelled hair and a beard that was growing like a cactus on his face was staring at me ridiculously while holding a mug which I assume was coffee. He was wearing a white shirt and a pair of gray boxers, and as for his footwear, he was wearing socks that didn't match and a pair of pink bedroom slippers.

Ah, the sight pains my eyes.

"Mira?" He said softly, looking a bit surprised that I was on his doorstep. I haven't been here for at least a year already.

Hearing his voice and seeing the worried look in his eyes, I recalled my previous thoughts. I suddenly bit my lip before I forced a smile to greet him, but it was useless. My face was gonna crack.

"I'm..." I barely said in an audible voice. "I'm... not sad. I'm not sad at all. I'm not. I'm not."

Why the fuck did I just say that?

Seeing me in this worthless state, uncle Ray, who was also our school's principal, opened the door wider and let me inside. But not before hugging me first. I grunted.

"Your beard itches."

He ruffled my hair before pushing my back and guiding me into his house. "Deal with it."

I sat on his couch and made myself comfortable. This place was like my second home. He made sure I wasn't breaking down like some over dramatic teenager as he gave me a mug of hot chocolate. Yay.

"I'll be right back. Gonna change into something appropriate first." He said.

I snickered at his attire again. It wasn't the first time I saw it, but my reaction every time I did never changed. Yeah, he hated that. "But uncle, you rock the 'just got out of bed' look."

He clicked his tongue and striked a pose. "I know. I'm fabulous."

I laughed at him as he grudgingly made his way to his room. His sarcastic-switch automatically turns on whenever I make fun of him. Except when we're at school of course.

While waiting for him, I observed the house. I felt nostalgic just sitting here again, and felt guilty for not visiting more often. Uncle helped my mom and I so much for the past few years. I feel like I can't thank him enough whatever I do.

I saw the familiar picture frames aligned on top of the fireplace. It was arranged in order, starting from when uncle was still in the Navy, when he got promoted, when his girlfriend said yes to him, when they got married, when they got pregnant...

The last pictures that followed were of me and mom.

I felt sad. Not for personal reasons anymore, but for uncle. I still can't get over it even though it's been years already.

Uncle Ray's wife, Susan, was four months pregnant when he was still on duty. She got involved in a car accident and after that day, she lost the baby, and she never opened her eyes again.

All of that happened before dad left. My pain doesn't even compare to his. And yet, he still had the courage to live on and even help my mom and I through all those shit.

He's a true soldier. A real hero.

"Alright," uncle appeared, now dressed 'appropriately' which also translates to a 'pair of pants.'

I snickered silently. He didn't bother fixing his hair or wash his face or anything. He knows I was used to seeing him like this, and he knows I won't actually care even if a bird died on his head.

This is how I show my love. Hm. Hm.

He nudged his head towards a certain direction and my face lit up when I realized what he was planning. I quickly chugged my hot drink down and got out of my seat, following him to our favorite part of the house - his own personal gym.

Well duh, uncle still works out to stay fit. I don't know if it's out of habit or if it's just his way of relieving stress. Being a principal at a high school like mine can be stressful. I know, because I'm usually the primary cause of his stress.

Shame on me.

When we arrived, my smile couldn't get any wider. I missed that huge punching bag hanging on the ceiling, the weights placed in order of size on the floor, all kinds of gym equipment and oh look, the threadmill I almost died on a few years ago.

Don't ask.

I went to my favorite punching bag, which looked sort of worn out already, and hugged it. I hugged it before I punched it, testing if it's still as tough. Yup. Still in perfect condition.

Uncle walked up behind me and offered me a kind smile. "I don't know about teenage-girl-drama, but I do know for a fact that you'd rather punch something than rant about it. It's good if you tell me about it, but just after you sort things out in your head - by going violent and bat shit crazy on non-living objects. So, go knock yourself out."

I rolled my eyes, but smiled back. He knew me too well.

"Oh," I supressed a gasp when the rip on the punching bag expanded, revealing a second layer of something I'm too lazy to describe. I didn't mind it though. I focused all of my unresolved and confusing emotions in each of my punches. I didn't fully react or even realize it when the punching bag gave up and fell heavily on the ground. The hook snapped because of my force, probably, but at least I didn't get hurt.

Hehe.

Okay, I felt a bit guilty for that. Uncle will have to put it back again and it's quite a hassle doing it alone. I sighed. What a good for nothing gorilla I am.

"I knew you'd be here," I heard a familiar voice behind me. I spun on my heels and grinned so wide my cheeks hurt when I saw my mom.

I got so excited and relieved and sad and blah blah blah you get the picture. I ran full speed towards her and jumped in for a big hug. Yeah, like a five year old. Be jealous.

She chortled as she ruffled my hair gave me a kiss on the forehead. I can't believe she's here! Oh God. God. Thank You so much for bringing my mom here!

"I see you've met your equally violent companion for today," uncle mused, standing beside us holding some bags of food and stuff. I'm pretty sure those stuff were mom's.

Mom gave him a look before rolling her eyes. Uncle just shrugged his shoulders and went out to do whatever it is mom instructed him to do with those stuff.

I supressed a giggle as mom laughed at his retreating back. Mom and uncle were the best of friends since high school. Uncle was the one who actually introduced my dad to her back then, and long story short, uncle got kicked to the friendzone as soon as my parents were introduced.

I'm just kidding. Uncle doesn't see mom that way. I think. Oh shut up brain. He's been through a lot. Don't push it.

We went for a place to sit and talk, walking over the dead punching bag on the ground, and ignoring uncle's whines all the way from the kitchen.

Seriously, he's like Leo sometimes.

"So tell me," mom said as soon as we sat down on the long benches at the side. "What's this teenage-girl-drama you're currently undergoing?"

I almost face-palmed. "Uncle ratted me out?"

She shrugged her shoulders. "Uh-huh. I'm kinda jealous you went to him instead of me though."

My heart pricked with guilt all of a sudden and I quickly and honestly said my reasons. I really don't want to disappoint my mom of all people. "I thought you were busy with work. I just didn't want to disturb you. And uncle was always free on weekends so... so... um... Mom, I'm sorry."

She laughed light-heartedly. I don't know what to think. "There's nothing to be sorry about." Then she gave me that tender look in her eyes that always made me feel secure and comfortable. I can tell her anything and everything. "Now tell me what happened between you and Brandon."

I stopped in my thoughts and stared at her wide-eyed. "But I didn't even - "

"Oh I know it's about that boy," she interjected. "I knew you were gonna be bothered about this soon enough."

A shiver went down my spine. It's scary how mom always knows me so well. Uncle too. And Leo, and Nichole, and Brandon, and... am I a walking open book or something? That's just sad bruh.

I took a deep breath and let out a heavy sigh. I couldn't look my mom in the eye. And I can't explain exactly what happened since I don't know myself. I'm embarrassed to tell her about this boy stuff. It's so awkward.

"It's a really long story. And I suck at telling stories," I said, honestly, but hoping she'd listen anyway. She patiently nodded and smiled.

"Tell me everything."

So I told her.

I told her about my first impressions of Brandon was, our first encounter with the spicy burrito and the milkshakes, our stupid game, our dumb fights, our deep conversations, how I met Emma, how I'm envious of Emma's perfection and how insecure I am of her and Brandon's friendship, and how confused I am about shit, and about Leo and Nichole's current status, and about Sam and... and...

I didn't realize I was running out of breath when I was telling her the whole story. I had to swallow my saliva a few times (read: gross, but I know you feel me) just to continue my long rant. Mom was just quietly listening and paying attention to every word I said without interrupting even once. She knew that if she interrupted, I'll never be able to continue, knowing my stubborn personality.

I just realized how difficult I am. Ugh. I hate myself.

As soon as I was done, I closed my eyes and breathed. Did I tell her everything? Did I forget something? How will my mom react? Will she be disappointed in me? Will she laugh at how emotional I am and how I'm making things into such a big deal?

Instead of those things though, she pulled me into another hug before kissing my cheeks several times. "I'm so proud of my baby. Do you feel better now that you let it all out?"

A bit surprised and a bit glad at her reaction, I couldn't say anything but just nod my head like an obedient little girl. Mom smiled at me gently, her warmth soothing the ache of my damn heart.

"You didn't cry though. Are you still holding back? Did you use up all your tears already?" She asked, genuinely worried. I giggled, releasing the remains of the tension in my chest.

"I don't know. Maybe I used them all up since I met with dad again. Or maybe I'm just numb."

She stroked my hair while holding my hand. "I know you, Mira. You're exactly like me. And based on what you just told me, I think you have great friends. And honestly, no bias here since I'm your mom, I think Brandon really likes you. For real, honey, think about it. Friends don't do what you potatoes do. C'mon."

I snorted. My mom was really paying attention.

"Here's the only thing I can say," she said, sighing quietly, probably reminiscing her the days when she was my age and preparing to give me some tips. "Trust your gut. You see, girls like us, we rely on our guts. Why? Because we don't let our emotions take control of us. Because that simple, tiny gut feeling already knows what our dumbass heart hasn't figured out yet."

I nodded, taking in what she said, but offering a small laugh to lighten up the air. "I thought the saying said that we should follow our hearts?"

Mom groaned and rolled her eyes as she held my shoulders and looked at me seriously in the eyes. "Our hearts are as stupid as fuck - sorry for my language - but it's true. Look where that got me."

Oh. Ohh. This makes a lot of sense. I mean, for us, since we're not normal people. I don't know about the rest of the female population, but I kinda agree with my mom. Our hearts are confusing as shit. And we're quite the stubborn types so it's easier to follow our guts.

I shifted uncomfortably in my seat. I'm still not sure. Even though I am quite enlightened, I'm still not sure what to do.

"But what if I follow my brain?" I asked mom curiously.

She didn't even have to say anything. Her face said it all.

"You know me too well, mother. My brain hates me."

We exchanged a few laughs before I squeezed her again. God, I can't thank You enough for giving me my mom.

"Thank you," I whispered in her ear, not planning to break this sweet embrace any moment soon.

She kissed the side of my head. "Anytime baby. I'm so proud of you. You know that, right?"

I nodded, squeezing her some more. She laughed before pinching my cheeks.

There was still a bit of uneasiness resting in my heart, but that's already up for me to figure out. I'm just glad that I got to put a load off my chest and frankly speaking, it feels amazing. Why have I not done this before?

Mom and I were still in the middle of our squeezing battle when uncle once again appeared out of no where.

He was in his blue pyjamas and unmatched socks in his pink bedroom slippers. You'd think he was about to go to bed. And it was still just the middle of the day. He gave mom and I a silly grin. "Ooh. Are we still talking about boys?"

I laughed at him, wishing my phone wasn't dead so I could take a picture of him right now. Mom was shaking her head.

"I still find it hard to belive that you're an ex-Navy seal." She said.

"Buzz off Paige," he mumbled, then turning to me with a small smile. "The food's ready. Let's eat lunch while watching some movies."

I got excited. Oh goody! Food and movies! Uncle Ray is the best!

"Don't forget to mention who brought the food and the movies," mom sang, standing up and linking her arm on uncle's, teasingly. He was groaning in mock-annoyance, but I could see the smirk tugging up from the corner of his lips.

I missed this scene. It's so heart-warming how mom and uncle Ray are still best friends. I hope Leo, Nichole, Sam, Emma, Brandon and I will be the same way years from now.

I got up from my seat, temporarily putting my messy thoughts aside and decided to enjoy the day with my family.

I know for a fact that whatever happens, my mom and uncle will never leave me. And that's good enough for me.

Chapter 31

"Damn it Ray!" Mom kicked uncle's leg when she found out he ate the bag of Cheetos she brought and didn't leave some for us. They were currently sprawled on the couch, with uncle sitting on the edge and mom lying down on the opposite side, her legs placed on his lap comfortably.

Uncle Ray was snickering as he swatted mom's feet away, but my mother was persistent. A short battle of the feet and hands went on, and in the end, uncle got kicked in the face.

I laughed out loud, in the middle of that gory movie.

Not particularly new in any case.

"Damn it Paige!" He whined, rubbing his jaw. Mom withdrew her legs and rubbed her feet as well.

"What's your beard made of? Cactus? It itches."

I sighed happily on the floor and tried to ignore my lovely guardians behind me. Mom kept shooting sarcastic comments about uncle's beard and uncle kept whining about his jaw and how he felt sad about getting kicked around by his best friend since high school.

I kept quiet the whole conversation, slowly sinking into my own conscience. Do I kick Leo around and stuff? I think I'm pretty nice to him.

And as soon as I thought that, I get hit by a shitload of memories where I was not at all kind to him.

Well. Damn.

I am my mother's daughter.

The movie was pretty much forgotten. All of us cleaned the mess afterwards and went to the kitchen to find something to eat. Again.

Mom grabbed some bacon in uncle's fridge and went to fry them. She knew exactly where everything was.

Me, at a loss for words in front of my very mature mom and uncle, decided to be an obedient little potato by patiently waiting for the wonderful bacon to get served.

Uncle sat beside me on the dinner table and then he gave me a sheepish grin. I eyed him knowingly, because I know he was gonna say something that'll get me worked up.

"So," he started, flashing me his perfect teeth. Sometimes I wonder if he wears dentures. I adjusted my position in my seat to face him directly. "You and Brandon."

I didn't realize my cheeks flame until I felt the heat rise in my face. How did I know my traitorous cheeks flamed? Why, the damn smug grin on my uncle's face said it all.

I nonchalantly avoided his eyes and hid part of my face in my hair. Like, yeah, why wouldn't I? It's not like I'm gonna make it any more obvious. I mean. Why the hell am being so awkward?

He chuckled softly, looking very pleased with my reaction. "I knew there was something going on between you two the moment you kicked his nuts and went straight to my office for some ice."

"Uncle!" I whined, literally shutting him up by slapping his mouth with the table napkin. My hand moved on it's own accord. Swear.

He was unfazed. He was probably used to the same treatment from my mom since they were my age. I don't know why I keep feeling so bad for Leo every time I acknowledge mom and uncle's relationship.

"So?" He pressed, ignoring the fact that I just napkin-slapped him. "Are you going to talk to him?"

"Uugh..." I buried my face in my hands. Not for the reason that I was flustered by my uncle's choice of subject, but because I know how much of a coward I am to even look at Brandon, much more talk to him. "What's the point of talking about this?" I told the man dejectedly. "I know I screwed up. It was such a tiny issue, I don't know how it got so big. I don't know how one minute we were laughing, and then the next minute, it was so tense and cold. It's my fault. I screwed up big time."

I groaned internally. Why. Why am I blowing another bubble of negativity? What was I thinking, 'temporarily putting my problems aside'? I didn't put them aside at all. They were stuck in my mind the whole time since this morning, I just didn't want to confront them.

Uncle offered me a smile as he pinched my cheek. I winced and stared at him weirdly. "Our baby's finally turning into a girl."

"What." I didn't know if I should feel confused or offended.

"You finally talked to me about a boy in a non-violent way. And that boy made you like this. You really like him. This is great. Fantastic."

I stared at him again, my brows creased to their extent and my hands doing weird motions in the air. "Did you hear what I just said? We got into a fight! We might not talk to each other anymore!"

"Yeah," he replied patiently, which was actually starting to piss me off. "But that's only for now. You two always make up, right?"

I stopped and thought about it.

Looking back at all our dumb fights and arguments and fights that didn't seem like fights, we always made up. It lit up a bit of hope in me but then I remembered. Last night was different. I don't understand. It was just a small thing, just a small, simple question. How did it get so complicated?

"Bacon's done." Mom announced as she placed the plate in the middle of the table and gave each of us a fork. She gave me a worried gaze before she flicked uncle's forehead.

"Ow!" He shot mom a glare. Whoa dude, that sounded painful. Mom's flick was pretty deadly. A hundred times worse than mine. "Why'd you do that?"

"Just felt like it," she shrugged her shoulders. I stifled a giggle, knowing that she did it for me. But despite that, I know uncle had a point. I was just too stubborn to admit it.

A lot of things spun inside my head. Emma with Brandon, Leo and Nichole's fight, Nichole's weird apology, my buttheadedness, the chocolate Sam stole from me, uncle's tasteless choice in clothing, dad and his new kid, Brandon, mom's advice, Emma's so pretty, my paper due on Monday, Brandon, how to talk to Nichole later, need to buy more chips, Brandon, potatoes, should I eat mashed potatoes for dinner, Brandon, cheese, Brandon, Brandon, Brandon...

Help me God. I need a new brain.

"Ah, I can see the smoke coming out of her ears," uncle said with a full mouth. "Her mind's overloading. Reminds me of you, Paige."

"Har har," mom mused, holding my shoulder at the process. "She's so much smarter than me. She'll know what to do."

I almost broke out a wail. I hope so mom. I hope so.

No matter how much I prayed, no matter how many times I begged, the dreaded Monday still came. I know it was an impossible wish but I tend to be very illogical in logical situations.

I didn't speak to Nichole about her weird behavior two days ago since opening up such topic will probably lead to more awkwardness.

It's not like I'm gonna bury it. I'm just gonna wait for the right time to ask her about it. She and Leo looked fine now, but even I could feel the slight change of air between them.

Brandon didn't pick me up today, just as I had expected, but I still felt disappointed and guilty. It was my fault. I shouldn't feel so disappointed. I should be disappointed at myself.

Second period was almost over, still no sight of Brandon. I was so paranoid, looking left and right, wondering when he'll appear, and what I'll say when I see him, or what I'll do if he ignores me.

I hope I don't cry.

Cry.

"Psst," Sam called my attention in the middle of the lecture. I looked at him to ask what it was when he threw me something. I didn't know what it was until I caught it with a single hand. I was pretty good at catching stuff seeing as I used to play softball.

I snorted when I realized what it was. It was the same brand of chocolate he stole from our fridge last week. Nichole probably told him and made him feel guilty about it or something.

At the back of the chocolate bar, there was a tiny note that said: Sorry Mira. And insert sad face.

I supressed my laughter. I can't believe I think this is so adorable. I looked at him and gave him a smile. He looked relieved and then he sighed as if he was holding his breath the whole time. Sam was so nice, in his own way.

"Hey," I whispered as soon as the teacher turned around to write something on the board. "Did you see Brandon today?"

Sam nodded. "I think their coach called him and Leo. Last I saw them, they were heading for the pool."

I see. I see. They must be in trouble for skipping so many practices. So that's why. That makes sense. Yeah. Hm. Hm.

"Mira?" Sam said. "Did you guys fight?"

I stared at him in shock. Did Brandon tell him? "How did you know?"

He snickered. I glared. "I don't. I just asked. You always look so lost whenever you and Brandon fight, so I figured this time, it might be because of him again, and oh look, I'm right." I knew I couldn't fight back because he was, but I was too stubborn to admit it. I just glared at him because I couldn't come up with anything good in my defense. So I did the mature thing.

That is glaring at him until my eyes hurt.

"Aww," he cooed, much to my annoyance. "She's upset."

I can't explain how much I want to kick his face right now. I don't need to hear that from him. In fact, I don't need to hear that from anyone. Ever.

The bell rang, and class was over. I hurriedly grabbed my bag and made my way outside the room. I need to find Brandon and talk to him.

That is assuming I could still talk properly when I see him.

"Want some help finding your boyfriend?" Sam offered with a teasing tone.

I rolled my eyes. "He's not my boyfriend."

He snorted. "But you're dating him."

"We're not dating - for real." I mumbled the last part. Well, we weren't right? I mean he did once say he wanted to date me seriously but he also said not now. So that means that technically, even though we're together doesn't mean we're together together and since that call that night, we can hardly call ourselves together and just by thinking how much I want us to be together together and not just together, it makes me want to punch myself in the gut and cry my eyes out altogether but I can't because right now I have to pull myself together.

Wow. That's a whole lot of togethers. I don't know how I made so much sense to myself in that mental ramble. Usually I talk nonsencial science in my head but now I think I deserve an A in English.

"Ow!" I yelled like the lady that I was when something flicked my forehead. More particularly, when someone hit my forehead.

I glared at Sam.

"What?" He said, a bit sceptical, hiding his hand behind his back. "You were staring into space again and you were gonna walk straight to the men's bathroom."

He motioned in front of us and I even noticed a group of boys staring and pointing at me, as if waiting to see if I'd really walk in the men's room with Sam. I concealed my blush with another glare.

Humiliation. Humiliation. Utter humiliation. Shit.

"And," he added. "Brandon's right over there."

As soon as I heard his name, all thoughts dissipated in my mind. I turned to the direction Sam's eyes pointed and I literelly felt my insides turn.

How can I clear things up with him? Should I just confess and get this all over with?

Still debating in my thoughts, I already left Sam and started walking towards a certain potato.

I don't know if he noticed me walking towards him or not. If he did, he was pretty damn good acting like he didn't.

Now that I was only a few steps closer to him, I felt my knees shake, and then the memories of our last conversation on the phone flooded my mind.

I'm such an idiot.

I was about to call his attention when his head slowly turned my way. My mouth was already open to call him, but as soon as he saw me, I shut my mouth and bit my tongue inside.

Genius.

He offered me a quiet smile and I couldn't help my brows crease in guilt. Why did he have to smile if he didn't mean it?

Both of us were waiting for the one who'll say something first. Me, being the one at fault, knew it had to be me to say something first. So I did.

"So..." I mumbled unsurely, nervously, pathetically - wow, the floor looks so interesting today. "What's up?"

Can the floor swallow me whole right now? I don't mind being part of the floor for a day. Or maybe like, forever.

He released a small sigh, but I think that was some kind of a forced laugh. I hate seeing us like this. So stupid.

"I'm fine, Mira. Hey listen, I gotta run. I just went to get a few things from my locker. Coach's waiting for me."

I quickly nodded my head, afraid he'll get mad at me if I asked him to stay. "Sure. See you at lunch?"

Again, he sent me another fake smile. "Yeah."

As soon as he walked away, I could feel my legs giving out. I couldn't help it. I felt like my heart was gonna explode. But if my heart did explode though, then my guts will be all over the floor. And then the floor won't be so nice and sparkly anymore. And then I'll have nothing to swallow me whole if I ever get into a situation like this again, which will probably be in the next few hours.

"Whoa there," a familiar, annoying voice said behind me. I felt something hold my shoulders firmly. When I turned around to see Sam, I realized that I couldn't feel my knees anymore, and I had no strength left in my hands or legs. He was holding me for support.

I gave him a pathetic look, one that roughly translates to I suck, I'm stupid, I'm a good-for-nothing gorilla and I'm gonna regret my whole existence.

He offered me an amused smile though, and then a kind one. He shook my shoulders gently as if to knock me out of my stupid thoughts and a good attempt to bring me back to my senses.

"You did great." He said, like he was praising a kid for passing a hard test. It sounded weird, but honestly, it was comforting to hear at the moment. I needed that.

"Thanks." I said, smiling at him.

He finally let go of my shoulders when I quickly regained my strength. "Any time. But are you just going to leave things like this between you two? He looked really torn to me."

I could feel my smile fading out my face. So even he could see it. I really am an idiot. I had to resist pulling my own hair and use it as a mop to clean the floor I theoretically messed up with the explosion of my guts earlier.

This is one of the moments where I hate my brain more than myself.

"There's still the thing with Nichole and Leo," I mumbled, remembering we were having lunch later. All of us. And Brandon. This is gonna be so awkward. The first time it's gonna be this awkward. I looked up at Sam with my regular pathetic look and I think he already knew what I meant. "Come with me please?"

He thought for a while. "Is Emma coming too?"

"Yeah well, she's with Brandon." I absent-mindedly replied. When I noticed that the tone I used was far from an non-bitter one, I quickly averted my gaze from Sam and attempted to be nonchalant about it. "So, you coming?"

"Alright," he sighed, but he sounded like he was supressing a laugh. Was he enjoying this, damn it? Well, whatever. He's helping me out in some way, in his own way. And that's good enough for me.

We still had another class to go before lunch. I'm so excited...

...to become floor-food.

God, help me overcome lunch please. Help me not to say anything stupid that'll jeopardize my relationship with my friends. Help me ignore the dumb part of my brain that'll make me think nonsencial science in hard situations again.

Help me resist offering myself as floor-food for the cafeteria, because the cafeteria floor stinks.

I stink.

Not literally of course.

"We're gonna be late. Are you gonna stare at the floor the entire day or?" Sam tugged my sleeve.

"Sorry I can only stare at something I can't be a part of," I said sarcastically, directing that statement to the lovely floor, and knowing Sam won't get what I meant. But looking at his expression, he looked like he was agreeing with me. Was that a bitter smile I see?

I faced the floor again as we made our way to our next class. Things are getting more and more confusing.

Chapter 32

"Hey," I smiled at Nichole and Leo as Sam and I sat down. It was lunch already, and I can't explain how my insides feel right now.

Even if I did try to explain, I doubt I'd make any sense.

I scanned the crowded cafeteria for a certain person. I didn't even try to be discreet. I was this anxious already. "Where's Brandon?"

The question was directed at Leo since they were together just a while ago at swimming practice. He avoided eye-contact and shrugged his shoulders.

"He'll be here. Don't worry."

"Worry? Me? Psh. Why would I worry? I'm just genuinely curious as to where he is, since, you know, the table's not as noisy as the usual."

Yeah Mira, you sounded so nonchalant. Not obvious at all.

"Sure." He replied sarcastically, but his tone sounded weak, like he wasn't even trying to piss me off like he always did.

Something's wrong.

I glanced at Nichole beside him and noticed how she also averted her eyes. She was quiet since I arrived and I didn't miss the part where there was now a decent space between her and Leo's seats.

That was weird, seeing as their shoulders would usually be stuck together, but now... It's like even the briefest physical contact between them was lethal.

I cleared my throat and looked down. Well. This wasn't so awkward. Were they fighting just a minute ago?.did we come at a bad time? I have no idea.

Sam was busy scanning the cafeteria, probably because he was gonna alert me as soon as he sees Brandon. I gave him a nervous smile as he gave me a reassuring one in turn. Good thing I have back-up.

I was busy trying to figure out what was going on between my two best friends, and if I should ask them or not, but Sam suddenly nudged my arm a few times.

"He's here, he's here."

"Where? Where?"

"There, there."

"Shit. Shit. Shit." I mumbled. I wasn't ready yet!

"Aw," Sam said. "You broke the chain. You're supposed to say your reply twice, not thrice."

I pinched his leg under the table and he snickered. "Stop joking! I'm freaking out! Help me!"

"Just act natural, Mira." He said as if I was being so overdramatic. Well I wasn't.

"Okay," I mumbled in reply as I nonchalantly turned my head so he won't notice I'd been anticipating his arrival. Because I wasn't.

His usual seat was beside me, but since Sam was sitting there already, he grabbed another seat from a vacant table and sat down across from us.

Our eyes met for a second and I was about to give him an acknowledging smile but before my lips could even twitch, he looked away. I grabbed the hem of my shirt and faced the unusually empty table. Seemed like nobody felt like eating today.

"Where's Emma?" Brandon suddenly asked. A sharp pain went through my chest but I just ignored it. I deserved it anyway.

"I saw her in the bathroom with her friends a little while ago," I replied. Now that I think about it, Emma told me the girls she usually hung out with were fake. I wonder if they were still being fake around each other, or if they're just tolerating each other or something. I hope she's okay.

Brandon didn't say anything. He just briefly nodded while his eyes continued to scan the cafeteria. Did he want to see her that much?

Hurts. It hurts. But I deserve this.

Sam softly kicked my foot under the table and gave me a look that said just talk to him and get it over with.

I wasn't so sure about that suggestion. I'm scared he'll ignore me or give me evading replies. He can't even look at me right now. And the only thing on his mind right now is probably Emma so why should I bother?

Sam glared at me, as if he sensed my pessimistic thoughts and conclusions. I took that as an encouraging look. Alright, fine.

I glanced at Brandon - he was still looking everywhere but me. Leo and Nichole were quiet too, but I know it's because of their own problem. Man. How did we end up in this lame situation?

I took a deep breath. Here goes. "Brandon - "

"Brandon!" We heard an all-too-familiar voice behind us. Emma was running towards our table with an unexplainable look over her face. I turned around to see Brandon's reaction. Maybe he was smiling at Emma. Maybe his face was beaming with joy now that she's here. Maybe he's grinning widely. Maybe he's showing her all the expressions he used to show me.

I was expecting myself to see him give her those looks so it would hurt less, but to my surprise, he was staring at me. Me.

You can say I forgot how to breathe at that moment.

His stare was dull and empty. Or maybe that's just me projecting my feelings into him. Whatever, I don't care. I shouldn't assume anything that'll comfort me. All that's waiting is disappointment, as always right?

Maybe he just looked at me because he heard me call his name first. I glanced at Emma again, she was a few feet away from the table. When I turned around to look at Brandon again, he wasn't looking at me anymore. And my initial guess was right. He was smiling at Emma as she approached. Maybe I was just imagining things earlier.

Whatever. I deserve this.

"Oh my God!" She exclaimed as she slid on the seat right next to him. "I did it Brandon! I told them. In the bathroom, of all places, but I told them everything I wanted to say. I feel so light now. Oh my God my knees are still shaking."

She let out a nervous laugh, and I noticed how pale her skin was today. She must've been really anxious. So that's what happened. I see. That's good. I'm proud of her.

I wish I can say those words wholeheartedly. But that was their conversation, and I have no right to intrude.

Brandon patted her head before running his hand over her beautiful hair.

Sting.

"Good job," he said, while giving her the most genuine smile I've seen since our little issue.

Sting.

"Thanks." She sighed, taking his hand off her head and giving it a quick kiss. "I mean it. Thanks for helping me."

Sting.

And then they smiled at each other, gazed at each other's eyes and got married and got babies and named them all Potato and then they watched their kids grow up and go to college and then they grew old and kissed each other without teeth and did some shit my mind is making up to make me feel even worse.

Fucking sting.

I wonder why my chest is stinging. It's stinging or pricking or most likely stabbing the dumb shit inside my cage. Dumb. Stupid. Shit.

Oh look. My knuckles had already gone white from clenching them too hard for some time now. No wonder Sam's been giving me that look. I must look pathetic. But he said nothing.

Ahh.

It hurts. It fucking hurts seeing them like that. And fine I admit it. I am jealous. I am so fucking jealous. I have no right to be since he's not mine, but I am, so just let me feel jealous like the stupid human being that I am.

But still. Why?

Why would he do that? In front of me? Why do I deserve all these? Why? Why?

"Um, Mira?" Nichole finally said something. I turned to look at her weakly; she was giving me a really worried look. I feel even worse. She had her own problems to deal with and she had to worry about me being stupid as well.

I gave her a smile, but anyone could tell it was forced. I don't know if I even smiled. I mean, I tried. Did my lips tug up? I don't know. I don't think I even care anymore.

Nichole creased her brows as she stood up from her seat. She went behind me and pulled my arm, making me stand up.

"What is it?" I asked, wondering why Leo didn't move an inch. Every time Nichole stood up or went somewhere, he always went with her, or at least asked where she was going. Now it's like he didn't even notice her presence the whole time she sat there beside him.

I don't know exactly what's going on. But I hate it.

She sent me a dull smile. I was quickly alerted with that smile. I know that smile. It was that smile. That was a sign. She was gonna break down any moment now. Shit. I have to get her out of here before anyone sees her cry. Both of us hate it when people see us cry.

Fuck my problems, I'll deal with them later. My best friend comes first.

I quickly stood up and told Sam we were going out for a bit, even if class was only half an hour away. I didn't feel like attending anyway. I only told Sam, because Leo was too preoccupied staring at air to care, and Brandon and Emma were still stuck in their little bubble of happiness. They're probably deciding what type of potatoes they're gonna name their beautiful babies.

No, that didn't sound bitter at all. If it did, you read it wrong. Read it again. Without feelings.

Nichole grabbed my hand and pulled me outside the school. She couldn't control her strength every time she was in this 'mode' so she was gripping my hand a little too tightly, but honestly it didn't matter. My hand had already gone numb from clenching my fists too hard at that scene in front of me earlier, so it's not like I could say it hurt as much as the dumb shit inside my chest.

I know, it doesn't even deserve to be called its normal name anymore, because this dumb major organ inside my dumb body got us into this dumb mess.

Our apartment wasn't so far from school so we just walked since our usual rides home weren't actually very friendly at the moment.

The whole time we walked, she just kept pulling my arm. I couldn't even see her face because she was in front, just walking straight ahead, her grip tightening on each step. All I could see was her back, and her shoulders were unnoticeably sinking from time to time, but she managed to keep her back straight. She was holding it in until we get into our room.

Even I had the sudden urge to cry; my throat growing a huge lump inside of it all of a sudden. My best friend had to deal with that back there. If they were fighting, why did they still sit in the same table? They should've given each other even just a few hours of space. That must have been torture. Silence was torture.

I'm qualified enough to say that's true.

As soon as we got in and shut the door, she knelt down on the floor like all the strength already left her legs. Her grip on my hand loosened until her hand slipped away and landed heavily on the floor.

She didn't say anything at first. She just let the tears stream down her cheeks. Her lips were quivering, as if she was forcing herself not to cry, and she angrily wiped her tears off her face with the back of her hand. She hated crying so much. And so did I.

But I couldn't help it. It triggered the tear sacs. I cried as well.

I cried for my best friend. I cried for Leo. I cried for Brandon. I cried for being jealous of Emma. I cried for my dad. I cried for my uncle. I cried for my mom. I cried for being sad. I cried for being so disappointed with myself. I cried for the horrible memories that suddenly came rushing in to make me feel worse. I cried for the dumb shit and I cried for myself.

There was a lot of things I cried for now that I didn't cry for before. When did I become such a baby? I thought I could handle all these things. Was it too much already? Tears are just unwillingly spilling out of my eyes.

And they won't stop no matter how much I convince myself that it was pointless to waste tears. It wasn't going to change anything.

It was a few minutes of angrily wiping away tears, sobbing, punching floors and walls and anything hard enough.

Our knuckles were bruised. But who cares?

Obviously not Brandon or Leo.

Nichole and I looked at each other, faces flushed, eyes red, snot running, and hairs putting birds' nests to shame.

She sniffed. "You look pathetic."

I nodded, agreeing with her though I haven't met with a mirror yet. I know how horrible I look after every time I cry. There was no need. "Well you look like you tried on every drug in the world."

We laughed for a bit, which was the only laugh we could force out of our systems at the moment. We looked like shit. Heck, we felt like shit.

We decided to be normal humans and left the floor beside the door to go talk in my room normally. Because we were normal. Definitely normal.

Nichole sat comfortably on my bed, her gaze so faraway. I sat in front of her, taking her hand in the process. I didn't waste another minute. I asked her.

"What happened?"

She wasn't crying anymore, but she looked like she was still crying - without tears. She took a deep breath and forced it out of her lungs. She kinda shouted it out actually, and I understand why she did that.

She wasn't looking at me as she slowly raised her head. She was just staring at my wall. And that was fine. I patiently listened as she began her rant.

"You know that small fight we got into the other day? Yeah, it wasn't as small as I had thought. The fight was actually about this girl Leo liked before. He just mentioned her name and I was so surprised and I tensed up and I was flooded with jealousy and all I could think of was hurting him because when he told me about her, it hurt me. I mean, when he talked about her, his eyes were different. I told him he might still be in love with her, and he said no, and I said I didn't believe him and then he said I didn't trust him enough and I said maybe I didn't and and..."

She was this close to hyperventilating. Luckily I had a bottle of water near my desk so I grabbed it and gave to her. She drank it in one gulp, crumpled the bottle then threw it in the trash can. She missed though.

She was still avoiding my eyes, her face growing darker and darker with guilt and regret. I was getting anxious as well. I think I knew who she was talking about. Leo told me about that some years ago, before he met Nichole.

"S-Sorry... So after that, both of us got worked up and decided to not speak of that again," she continued, her expression getting more furious at the memory like she was really regretting her actions. "But that only made things worse. All the small things, both of us would make a deal out of it. Remember when I told you that he forbid me to wear anything close to revealing or that I wasn't allowed to talk to other guys - even the teacher! I told him he didn't trust me enough since he was always getting mad at me for some stupid shit and I said that I've had it. And then he repeated the exact same words I told him when we fought about that girl he used to like. He told me that yeah maybe he didn't trust me. And then I told him to go after that girl if he wanted her so much, and he said I was unreasonable and he told me to go and date other guys if I wanted to talk with them that much. I said it was just talking! And... And then we fought about that girl again. And after a long while of not talking to each other, he asked if I wanted to break up. I was too surprised to say anything. So I didn't say anything. I don't know how he understood that silence. And then you and Sam came."

I nodded slowly, but quickly processing everything she said in my head. So that's what really happened.

We really did come at a really bad time. I'm surprised they still sat on the same table after that heated argument. I'm guessing it was the pride.

"I'm... I'm sorry..." She mumbled mostly to herself, but I heard her clearly. Why was she even apologizing? I don't even know if that was directed at me or Leo. Or herself.

I looked at her, honestly not knowing what to say. I don't know what to tell her to make her feel better, or what advice I can offer. And I don't want to take sides. I mean, both of them were my best friends.

"Well," I said, still sniffing. My nose was congested. Damn I wish the evidence of our little episode earlier would just go away. "Both of you are at fault. You lack trust. I think you lost more trust after those fights since you didn't resolve it. You guys just ignored it, and now it got bigger. I love you, and I have no idea about relationships, but I'll help you go through whatever's making you sad. I promise. Both of you have to fix this if you want to save this relationship."

It was the safest and most honest reply I could give.

She snorted a bit, giving me a kind smile. A rather forced one. I know she didn't feel like smiling, but she still did so anyway. "Great advice. But did you ever try that out yourself?"

Guilty.

"Thought so," she sighed, looking like she had calmed down after telling me everything. It was her turn to listen to me rant. "Now tell me what the fuck is wrong with Brandon?"

I told her everything too. The same way she told me, without pause and without stopping for enough time to breath between sentences. Words were just spilling out of my mouth. A few tears spilled too, but I quickly rubbed them off.

After I told her everything, a furious look crossed her face. A murderous one, to be more specific.

"That dipshit," she said through gritted teeth. "I told him I'd cut him if he ever hurt you."

I held her hand tighter and sighed heavily. The dumb shit in my cage was beating so fast. It really hurt. Physically.

"But I think I hurt him too," I honestly said. "Because of my stupid mouth. And stupid pride."

"You and me both," my best friend replied.

We shared another bitter laugh, but felt a tad bit better after letting all those things out of our chests. Now we just have to deal with them. I'm scared to walk out that door and face reality. I mean, reality stinks.

"What time is it?" Nichole asked. I checked my watch.

"Time to not go to school and to skip the whole day because we're sick." I hid a grin. We can't go to school looking like this. Our eyes look like they were poked a hundred times by a dull blade.

Ugh. I watch too much gore.

She agreed and both of us hid under my covers. We were tired. Never did understand why we felt sleepy after every time we cried. Nichole decided to sleep in my bed today, like we always did whenever we went through shit. We were always there for each other.

And I have my mom and uncle too. I wasn't alone. I should be thankful. I shouldn't be complaining so often. I'm such an ungrateful brat.

I really don't deserve to be happy, do I?

We drifted into dreamland for a few hours until Nichole's phone kept buzzing because it was on vibrate. She blindly rejected the calls a few times but the caller was persistent. Annoyed, she picked it up and accidentally pressed loud-speaker on.

I was groaning when we heard a static-like sound burst out from her phone's speakers.

"Guys! We have a problem! Punching! Kicking...swearing! Blood! We - " Emma's panicked voice caught my attention, and made me open my eyes. There was a lot of noise and ruffling sounds, and then another voice took over the phone. It was Sam. And what he said made Nichole and I jump out of bed immediately.

"Brandon and Leo are killing each other. Come here quick!"

Chapter 33

"Where are they?!" Nichole grabbed Sam's collar as soon as she found him. We arrived at school just a few seconds ago. We literally just jumped off the bed and ran back to school regardless of how we looked right now.

Turns out it was a pretty good decision that Nichole and I decided to skip classes after lunch. The teachers didn't hold a discussion and just gave the class time to study. Of course, that meant no attendance, and no class.

But that's not what we came back here for. From afar, it looked like Nichole was threatening Sam for her boyfriend's location. Ironic, because just a few months ago, it was her who was helpless against him over that little misunderstanding.

"Where?!" She repeated impatiently.

"P-Pool!" He stuttered, looking surprised at Nichole's sudden outburst. Or maybe he was surprised to see our shitty appearances. Dude, we didn't even bother fixing our hairs. Or put on a hint of make up to cover up our swollen eyes.

She released him from her clutches and then grabbed my hand. We raced towards the pool, both feeling anxious. Why would Brandon and Leo fight? What happened after we left?

And what would change even if we came here? Both of them were ignoring us for the time being. Everything's just getting better and better huh? Nice, life.

When we got to the pool, a lot of noise echoed throughout the place. The fight was already over, but they were still arguing about something we couldn't understand. It was Leo's voice that was overthrowing everyone else's. He sounded so pissed.

Their team mates were holding Brandon's shoulders from one side, and Leo's on the opposite side. They looked like two bulls getting ready to charge at each other.

Leo's face was flushed in anger, and his eye was getting swollen. It won't be long until he gets a black eye. And Brandon. He got himself a cut on his lower lip and a purple bruise on his cheek.

Nichole and I dived into the crowd of shirtless (and wet) guys. She went straight to Leo, and me to Brandon. When they saw us arrive, they looked like they were shot cold-blood. I don't know. Did we look that shitty for them to react like that?

Emma was outside the crowd, looking frantic and close to tears. Her eyes lit up when she saw us. "I tried to stop them, but they wouldn't listen to me."

"It's okay," I told her, trying to reassure her. It wasn't her fault. None of this is her fault.

"What the hell is wrong with you?" Nichole demanded, slightly pushing Leo's chest. His team mates slowly let go of them and let us handle things from here. "Why are you doing this?"

Leo spared her a quick glance before looking away. He had that pained, guilty expression on his face, the same one Nichole had when she told me about their fight.

"Nothing." He said.

"Nothing?" She repeated incredulously. And then she grabbed his face; he winced from the pain. "This is nothing? You think I'm stupid?"

Leo sighed heavily through his nostrils as he sent Brandon a heated glare. I pushed Brandon back in case he'd do anything stupid, but thankfully he was smart enough to resist the urge to hit his best friend.

I was just keeping him from killing Leo, which I know he was more than capable of, even though it seemed unlikely. Or I think.

I didn't dare look at him. I'm afraid he'll give me a cold stare. Or a glare.

"I wasn't kidding around when I told you. Warned you." Leo said through gritted teeth. He was trying his best not to shout and make the scene they already caused even worse. "I warned you that if you ever hurt her, I'd kill you!"

Who the heck were they talking about? Fighting about? Who did Brandon hurt that'd make Leo lose his cool like this?

"Stop taking everything out on me!" Brandon replied, equally pissed. "I know that's one of the reasons you're mad, but I know you're just blowing up because you screwed up!"

"Shut the fuck up!" Leo replied.

They threw out a series of colorful words at each other, growing more and more pissed at each other. It was pretty stupid. I hope nobody calls the teacher.

Nichole pushed Leo back as I did the same with Brandon. It was unintentional because of his current anger, but Brandon suddenly grabbed my hand that was stopping him from beating Leo up again. He didn't like being restrained.

I winced because of his strength, and because my hand was injured. I forgot my knuckles had bruised since I kept punching the floor and walls to release my frustration earlier.

When he saw this, the anger in his face slowly disappeared. He looked at me slowly, questionably - confused, and hurt. Maybe even guilty. Was it noticeable that I cried earlier? Were my eyes still red?

I bit my lip as I took my hand back and lowered my head to cover my face. He didn't have to see that. He didn't have to look at me like that. He didn't have to pity me.

"That..." I quickly tried to dodge any questions he might ask. I don't think I can talk properly about that right now. "You need to calm down. Alright? Breathe just... just breathe."

I think I was trying to tell myself that more than him. My teeth were clattering and I couldn't speak clearly. I was so nervous and I don't know why. I feel faint.

After a few seconds, he sighed and gave up. He gave Leo a last glance before he went to the benches to where his bag was. I peeked over my shoulder and saw Nichole talking quietly with Leo. The looks on their faces didn't look like they were fixing things between them at all.

I followed Brandon to the benches. The rest of the team backed off, their regular practice was already cancelled due to today's little feud. They were keeping an eye on us though. Lucky their coach wasn't around to witness this. He was always absent at very convenient times.

Brandon began fixing his things and changed into his usual clothes. As he roughly stuffed his towel back in his bag, I cautiously sat beside him, keeping a fair distance.

I can't ask him what happened even if I wanted to. I know he won't tell me anyway. But I needed to know how they were gonna deal with this. They were best friends. I hope they were gonna be okay soon. I hope we were gonna be okay soon.

"Um..." I mumbled. He watched my hands in the corner of his eye but I quickly hid them behind my back. So he can stare at my hands but not my face? "Where are you going?"

He was through fixing his stuff. He was already standing up and getting ready to leave. I stood up as well, anticipating at least one word of reply from him.

"Gonna visit my parents. I can't go back to the apartment for a while."

I was relieved he at least gave me a decent reply, but then I got worried. It was okay if he was going there to clear his head and stuff, but I hope he wasn't going there to avoid this and make matters worse.

Everything just gets worse if you choose to ignore it instead of facing it.

Without waiting for what I have to say, or what I can't say, he left without another word. Emma stopped him near the exit and talked to him, though I couldn't hear what they were talking about since they were so far away.

"You okay?" Sam suddenly appeared beside me. As he asked me that, he was looking at Brandon and Emma. Emma was lightly touching the bruise on Brandon's cheek and he winced. He gently took her hand off his face and smiled at her, as if he was telling her he was fine. I know he wasn't.

I lowered my head. That should've been me over there.

I looked up at Sam and released a forced laugh. "Doesn't matter."

Just as I was still staring at the two, Emma was the first one to make eye-contact with me. She was giving me a worried gaze, and she looked confused. She was sending me a message through her eyes, asking me what happened between me and Brandon. I shook my head slowly, saying it was nothing.

Then Brandon turned to look my way. I held my breath. His eyes fell down to my hands again. I unconsciously closed my fists and slid them inside my pockets. Why did he keep looking at my bruises? His were way worse. And there's no way he'd be worried. I bet he's just curious to what stupid thing I did this time to get these injuries.

After that he left with Emma accompanying him. That's good. Emma should be beside him in case he does anything stupid. She has to tell him to not do anything reckless.

I inhaled a sharp breath. The thing, the dumb thing in my chest is hurting.

I quickly searched for my two other best friends. They were on the opposite side of the pool, still talking. Nichole noticed that I was looking at them. She gave me a small smile and told me to go ahead. I nodded.

Sam held my shoulder and escorted me back to our apartment.

"Nobody saw what really happened," Sam explained as we neared our apartment. I didn't really ask him but he told me anyway, maybe to somehow comfort me. "But one of their team mates said that one minute they were fine just talking like the usual. Then a small argument broke out between them, then Leo suddenly jabbed Brandon. I have no idea why. But I think it was about a girl."

A girl, huh.

"So it's either about me or Nichole." I concluded. I was sure. I mean, who else, right?

"Yeah, maybe," he replied. We were in front of my door now. He gave me a small hug before patting my head. "The four of you will get through this. Years of friendship won't be destroyed by something like that."

I gave him a grateful smile, relieved. He's always saying the words I needed to hear at the right times. I still can't believe I misjudged this guy back then. "Thank you, Sam. You don't know how much you've helped. Thank you."

He nodded and sent me a last smile before leaving. I went inside our apartment.

Well then. Time to mope around.

I woke up the next morning feeling exhausted and dehydrated. I laughed bitterly. I can't believe I cried the whole night. My eyes hurt. I can barely open them.

I mentally calculated my absences in my head. I skipped so many classes these past few months, most of the reasons were because of Brandon.

Ughhh.

Saying his name in my head just made me remember some depressing things again. My chest feels so heavy. My knuckles were sore, and my whole face was swollen. I was in no condition to go to school today.

"We're going to school." Nichole barged into my room, already dressed nicely. Uhm. I just said I wasn't going to school, lady.

She wrinkled her nose and told me to go take a shower because she will 'beautify' me. I don't know what's gotten into her. She was like the usual, yeah, but something seemed off.

I wanted to ask her how it went with Leo yesterday but now didn't seem like a pretty good time. So I just did what she told me and took a nice shower.

I think I needed it.

I didn't notice I was taking my precious time in the bath until she practically destroyed my door with her monstrous knocks. "Stop contemplating your life in there and hurry up!"

Oh was I? Oops.

I went out wrapped in a loose towel. I don't know what expression I was wearing - maybe none, because I was numb. Literally.

She smiled, pleased that I finally took a shower, and made me sit in front of my mirror. She began blow-drying my hair while I lifelessly stared at her reflection.

"I already picked out what you're gonna wear today." She said. "We're gonna show them that we can handle this, Mira. And to do that, we shall not - no - we shall never go to school looking like what we did yesterday. Ever."

I snorted, but I was still having second thoughts. I really don't think I can handle school right now.

Why? Because it has Brandon and Emma in it.

A whole ten minutes of silence passed. She straightened my hair and applied some light make-up on my eyes to conceal how swollen it was. I noticed she did the same to hers. Seems like I wasn't the only one who cried alone all night.

It sucks being a girl. With all the overthinking, the guilt-tripping, the self-blaming, the regretting and the unnecessary excess emotions. It was exhausting.

"We need to talk to the boys." Nichole mused upon staring at my reflection. It took me a good few seconds before I nodded. I'm not as brave as her.

I stood up and changed into the clothes she left on my bed. White blouse, black tights and a pair of gold sandals.

When I was through, Nichole and I gave each other quiet nods and walked to school.

With my arm linked on my best friend's I was feeling the tiniest bit confident as we entered the hallways.

I mean, she had her guy to deal with, and I had mine. Well, not technically my guy, but you know what I mean. Don't make me explain any further, I might just cry in this pretty outfit and ruin the make-up.

Sam was standing beside my locker, waiting for me. When he saw us approach, he quickly left his spot and walked towards us. He looked like he had something important to say.

"Sup?" I said. He sent both me and Nichole a worried gaze.

"You girls okay?"

We smiled at him, touched that he actually cared.

"Of course," Nichole replied. "Who do you think we are?"

Sam sighed with a smile. He looked over his shoulder and leaned a bit closer to us as if he was going to tell us a secret. "I saw Brandon with Leo this morning."

We leaned in even closer, surprised at what he had to say. I replied. "Were they savage?"

He shook his hand. "Actually, they looked pretty civil to me. I think they're alright."

We sighed in relief. This was good news. Great news. But a bit unsettling. How did they patch things up so fast? Dude sometimes I wish I was a dude.

"And..." Sam added, looking a bit distracted. "One of them is coming this way right now. Bye then. See you at class Mira."

He quickly left us before we could even turn around and see which one he meant. Both Nichole and I held our breaths.

We turned around in unison. Nichole sighed in relief when she saw that it was Brandon who was walking towards us, but when she remembered my little issue with him, she patted my shoulder and wished me good luck. She followed after Sam.

"I'm dying." I said out loud. He was already in front of me.

"What?" He asked. He didn't quite hear what I just said.

"What?" I evaded dumbly. A silence of about ten seconds passed before he spoke again. This is awkward.

"Um..." He mumbled, flipping the back of his hair. He always did that when he was nervous or anxious. But was he? Maybe I'm just reading too much into this again. "About yesterday."

Oh. He meant the fight.

"Yeah?" I replied. He wasn't looking at me in the eye the whole time. I hate it.

"We talked." He started. "Leo apologized and I did too. We had our separate problems and we just took it out on each other. It was my fault actually, yet I still lost my cool. We're not really back to normal yet, but we're working on it."

I nodded, understanding the situation perfectly. He said both of them had their separate problems. I know Leo's problem. It was obviously about his complicated relationship status with Nichole. But Brandon.

I really hoped his problem involved me, as weird as that sounds.

"Okay," I said, being cautious with my tone. I don't want him to think I was nervous or awkward talking with him when the truth is I really really am and I am this close to fainting. "So you still staying with your parents?"

He shrugged. "Yeah, just for a couple more days."

I nodded quietly. "I see."

Another round of a ten-second silence passed before he spoke again. I swear he's timing all this.

"Can I see your hands?"

I was surprised to hear him say that, but was quick to hide my hands behind my back. "No."

I didn't bother bandaging it. I mean, it'd attract even more attention right? And it didn't even hurt that much anymore. A bit. Okay, it hurt a lot every time I accidentally hit something but I can manage.

He, on the other hand, looked terrible. The cut on his lip wasn't that deep and the bruise on his cheek wasn't that dark but anyone could tell he got into a fight.

He smiled, looking at his feet. Why do I feel so heartbroken seeing that smile? "You say no a lot these days."

I took a sharp breath before pressing my lips together. Oh no. No. He was referring to that one topic we've been avoiding these last few days. What was the right thing to say? I didn't actually think this through yet. One wrong word and I lose him.

"You don't have to feel bad about it," he said, not giving me the chance to explain. He was finally meeting my eyes. He met my guilt-full ones with his dull ones. And he was smiling.

Stop smiling damn it you damn potato. Stop faking it. "I'm sorry for always making you uncomfortable."

"Brandon - "

I wanted to say something, but the stupid bell just had to ring. It was getting a bit chaotic in the hallways now. I wanted to cry so much. I don't know what to say in situations like this. And even if I did, I always lose things because of my stupid hesitation.

Why does this always happen to me?

"See you around Mira," he said, sliding his bag up his shoulder and walking away. I held back a sob.

He's slipping further and further away from my reach.

Chapter 34

"Until when are you going to look ugly like that? I feel sorry for my eyes." Sam sighed as he sat beside me. It was free period, and I decided to get some fresh air outside, while resting under the shade of a big tree.

"If you're going to complain, then scram."

I wasn't in the mood to be called ugly. I already know I'm ugly - inside and out. Nobody needs to remind me.

He didn't move an inch. "It's okay. You're not that ugly for me to not want to sit next to you."

I made a mental eye-roll. I know he was just kidding around, but I was just the tiniest bit offended. It just added more to my insecurity. Asshole.

I punched his shoulder - not even lightly. "Sorry I'm never gonna be as pretty as Emma."

"What?" He asked, laughing a bit and while rubbing his arm. I didn't hold back on that punch. And then I realized what I just said. I bit my lip. Shit. Didn't mean to say that out loud. "You're jealous of Emma?"

Evade. Evade.

"No. I'm not." I replied defensively.

After staring at me with a wide smirk, I gave in. I technically gave it away already so there was no point in denying it. Plus, I could actually talk to somebody right now. "Okay fine I am. But who wouldn't! She's pretty, she's girly, she doesn't hit guys whenever she likes, she's hot, she's smart, she's funny - "

"Except for the part where you don't hit guys whenever you like, aren't you most of those things you just mentioned?" He interrupted. I gave him a look. I didn't like being interrupted. And I hated getting compliments or empty words of flattery or fake words of comfort.

He sighed heavily. "Again, you don't believe me." He stretched his legs before scooting a bit further from me so he could talk to me face to face. I still wanted to punch him for calling me ugly. "Maybe someone already told you this, but Mira, you're pretty. And not just pretty. You're really pretty. And you're hot, admit it. Why else would I have a crush on you before? Plus, you're smart - "

Smart? Has he heard my thoughts lately? Has he any idea how dysfunctional my brain is? And another thought:

First he tells me I'm ugly, then he tells me I'm pretty? Wow, is my face like, self-renewing it's features every minute?

I snorted at his attempt to comfort me but he continued. "C'mon! You're one of the smartest people I know. You're always in our Math's topnotchers."

I interrupted. "That's because solving stuff with figures is so much easier than memorizing names I can't pronounce much less spell."

He sent me a look. "I know you hate Biology, but putting that weakness aside, you have more A's than B's in all your subjects."

I rolled my eyes as I waved an airy hand. "Stop flattering me Sam. It's not helping. And how do you know all these?"

He grinned sheepishly. "Hello, I liked you before, remember?"

"Stalker." I made the ugliest, most disgusted face I could make before I scoffed. It was his turn to roll his eyes.

"And that, right there, is what made me unlike you. But I still like you of course, in a non-romantic way. You're cool."

I smiled at him. "I know."

"Okay then," he said. "Then let's get to the maint point here. Stop beating yourself up. Grow some balls and just talk to him."

Well, that was abrupt.

Yesterday's conversation with Brandon attacked my mind. Talk to him? Yeah-no. It's a suicide mission for a brain-dead gorilla like me. Yeah, I'm getting more depressed.

I released a frustrated sigh. "I don't know what I should tell him. Even when I think long and hard about what I'm gonna say, even if I already thought about over a hundred conversations with him in my head - it's pointless. You know why? Because as soon as he's here, my brain stops functioning. I can't even look at him in the eyes anymore. I lost my balls, Sam. I never thought I would, but I lost my balls."

"Well get them back." He insisted. "It's not like you had an actual pair to begin with, but theoretically speaking, you can still get your balls back. If you let yourself. And stop blaming your brain."

I suddenly burst out laughing. He looked at me confused for a bit until I explained. "You realize how weird this discussion sounds, right?"

Sam groaned, shaking my shoulders back and forth in the process. "Listen to me! Just stop stalling and stop letting your negative emotions get the best of you. Just tell him you like him and tell him you're sorry. That, my friend, will be the only guaranteed way you'll get your balls back."

I stared at him for a few seconds, thinking. Wow. Simple as that?

He looked disturbed. "What?"

I smiled happily at him. "You're such a girl. At heart." He glared at me, but I just ignored it. I sighed again before letting a quiet ten seconds pass.

He made so much sense.

It's true I wanted to talk to Brandon, but I just lacked a bit of coaching, which was usually Nichole's job, but she was kinda busy with her own dilemma at the moment.

Okay.

So I made up my mind. It sounded simple. Even if it really wasn't, I don't always need a complicated solution to solve a complicated problem right?

I mean, this all started from a simple phone call, and it turned into some complicated shit. I can do vice versa and solve some complicated shit by doing something simple. Right? "Okay. I'll talk to him."

He smiled.

"Great." Sam said, relieved. It was like he had completed his mission (read: to convince me to seriously talk to Brandon) because as soon as I agreed, he crawled to the spot right beside me and laid his back against the tree. Then he closed his eyes and took a nap.

Ah.

Well, whatever. He helped me out again today. I owe this guy a lot. He's a sweet and thoughtful guy in his own way, and it's so easy to talk to him. He moved on so fast and now he's acting like the best friend I never had. I can't believe he used to like me. I can't believe he's okay with all these - he's even helping me go through this shit. He's a great guy.

If I never met Brandon, then maybe...

Nah.

I took a deep breath and closed my eyes as well. It'll be an hour until lunch, which is the only hour I can actually see Brandon.

I released a breath. I'm going to tell him this time. I swear it.

"Hey," I said as Sam and I sat down on our usual table. Nobody but Leo was here. "Where are the others?"

He shrugged his shoulders. "I don't know. I went ahead."

I nodded slowly, not taking my eyes off him. He wasn't looking at me at all.

"And Nichole?"

The mere mention of her name dulled his eyes and formed a small crease on his forehead. I hid a pained smile. "She's... She'll come."

And not a minute later, she did come. She sat in her usual spot beside him, but keeping an obvious distance. She looked so fresh, but I could tell she was stressed. She was just covering it with some make-up and cute clothes.

A heavy silence fell and I couldn't take it. Whenever I encounter this kind of silence, I remember my last phone call with Brandon, and that will just make me want to punch myself.

So, I decided to ease the tension and open up a conversation. Just... just make this heavy silence disappear.

"So Leo," I said, gaining his attention. "Mom asked how you and aunt Maine were doing."

Aunt Maine was his mom. She and my mom worked in the same bank, and she was also the one who offered us to live with them while we looked for a new place to stay back when dad and mom got divorced. We owe her a lot.

He looked a bit surprised, but a quiet smile formed on his face. "Tell her I'm failing Biology. I need her to make me some of her special lasagna to make me pass."

I released a chuckle. Oh yes. My mom's lasagna was the best. She used to make that all the time when we were little. Specifically, when I beat Leo in a fight, verbally and physically. She'd make some lasagna to cheer him up and he'd smile with a missing tooth (courtesy of yours truly) and eat the whole dish in tears.

Ahh, the good ol' days where the only problem was where the tooth fairy put Leo's dollar (again, courtesy of yours truly).

"Sure." I smiled. "Hey, I'm no good at that subject too, but I know a few stuff that'll probably be helpful. Want me to teach you?"

It was a genuine offer. Leo used to help me with my maths before I got really good at it. It's time I returned the favor.

His eyes lit up as he took my hands. "Really? Seriously? You'd do that?"

I laughed. "Of course. You're my best friend, dickwad. I'd at least do something like that."

Plus, I still feel bad for taking the dollar under his pillow when we were kids. I just really wanted to try that new-flavored gum I saw on TV.

He was this close to hugging me, if not for the table blocking his way. He just shook my hands a few times. "Oh man, thank you. Thank you! You're the best gorilla best friend ever!"

I made a pout. Only I was allowed to call myself a gorilla. But I let it slide.

Leo and I were deciding on when and where we were going to study when Sam nudged my shoulder. I knew that gesture. It meant the potato was coming.

I quickly turned around and saw him and Emma casually chatting while walking towards our table. They looked so engrossed in their conversation. They looked good together. They looked so happy.

No. Stop it. Damn it Mira. You already made up your mind to talk to him today. Stop dragging yourself down.

I took a deep breath. I needed a few more encouraging smiles from my friends before I go through this. I need moral support damn it.

When I glanced at Nichole, I was expecting to see a look of good luck, but my anxiousness about Brandon quickly faded away when I saw her smile.

That smile again.

I sent her a look asking what's wrong, but she just smiled wider. It hurt seeing her force a smile for me. "Do your best Mira."

Maybe she meant it, but her voice was shaking.

Sam nudged my shoulder again. "They're almost here! They're almost here!"

I know! I know! But Nichole!

She pressed her lips together before standing up. Leo glanced over his shoulder to see what was happening to her, but he couldn't bring himself to look at her completely. Nichole shook her head, silently telling me not to worry about her.

"I'll be back in a minute. Talk to Brandon, okay?"

No. She can't ask me to do that. Not while she was being like that.

Brandon and Emma were now a few feet away from our table. Nichole quickly took her leave. Sam was looking at me worried, and Leo sent me a quick, guilty look.

I wanted to yell at him to go after her but both of them weren't in the condition to talk about their issues right now. While they were still insisting on their prides, they might jeopardize their relationship.

Which, they're already doing, anyways. Why can't they just calm down and talk about it?

How absolutely hypocrital of me. People must hate me when they read my thoughts.

Brandon and Emma were here, and as they were about to sit down, Brandon sent me a blank look. I can't deal with him right now. I can't leave my best friend. I can't.

I'm sorry, Sam.

I left my bag to Sam and quickly ran after Nichole without another word.

I was panting when I arrived in front of the women's bathroom, not because of running so fast, but because I was scared. Scared because of how Brandon looked at me like he didn't want anything to do with me anymore, scared of that look on Leo's face when I mentioned Nichole's name, scared of what Nichole might be doing to herself right now and scared that I won't be able to do anything about all those things.

Regardless of these thoughts, adrenaline helped me push the door open and step inside the empty bathroom. I was confused to see nobody at first, but then I realized that one cubicle was shut tight.

I gently knocked on that cubicle, certain it was Nichole hiding in there.

"Nichole?" I asked cautiously. I heard the toilet seat squeak and a few sniffles. Yup. She was in there.

"Why are you here?" She asked, a bit annoyed. "Weren't you going to talk to Brandon?"

I knocked again. "My best friend comes first. Open the door Nichole."

It didn't take a lot of effort for her to come out of that cubicle. As soon as I saw her, I quickly pulled her into a hug. I rubbed her back to calm her down.

"It's okay, I'm here."

I felt her shake her head roughly before breaking out a sob. "No." She slowly broke the hug. "No, I don't deserve to be friends with you."

"What? Why?" I asked, a bit panicked. Don't tell me she doesn't want anything to do with me anymore too?

She shook her head slowly as she faced the floor. "I'm a horrible friend Mira. All you've been to me was kind and forgiving - but I... I thought of some really bad things about you, and I feel horrible about it. Mira, punch me. I deserve at least that."

What? What? But why? Why's she being like this? Did I do something wrong again?

"What are you talking about? Tell me in a way I can understand!"

She quietlty sighed as she raised her head, revealing her blood-shot eyes and shiny red nose. I don't know why I feel so guilty. "You were the girl Mira."

She pressed her quivering lips together before she added, "you were Leo's first love."

I felt my pulse stop at that exact moment. I felt like I was shot, stabbed, punched and kicked. And I don't even know how I should feel about this.

I knew Leo liked me when we were in middle-school. He told me himself. But I told him I'd like him better as my best friend. He took it pretty well and now we're here. We're still friends. He can't possibly like me still, right? I mean, he was with Nichole now. It was impossible.

"Nichole, he's like my brother," I insisted. It was the truth. I wanted to apologize, but then again, I had no direct fault here. Why should I apologize? And damn it. I was the reason for all their fights? Me?

It's me who don't deserve their friendship. All I've done is caused them pain.

"I don't think he sees you that way Mira," she wiped away a tear. "I know I sound like a jealous bitchy girlfriend, and I sound stupid, but I just can't help thinking like that, you know? I mean, you two have been together for years. You probably know him better than I do. And Mira, I can't compete with that. I can't compete with tou. I don't want to compete with you. I love you both so much and I hate myself for thinking like this. I'm so sorry Mira. I'm sorry. I'm sorry."

"No, no," I felt my voice shake, tears were pooling my eyes. It wasn't her fault she'd think that way. I think that way when I see Brandon and Emma too. I understand. "Don't apologize. You've done nothing wrong. Nichole - "

She shyed away from my hand and shook her head again. "No. I can't compete with you Mira. I'm so sorry."

"Nichole!" I exclaimed, but she already ran out of the bathroom. I stared at the door for a few seconds, then released a frustrated scream. I watched my hideous reflection in the mirror and buried my face under my hands.

Why? Why doesn't she trust Leo? He loves her. I know he does. And I know his feelings for me died years ago. But how can I convince her? How can I save their relationship? How can I save our friendship?

A sharp pain went through my heart. Why do I feel like I just lost a friend?

I screamed again, but it came out in muffles since I was pressing my palm against my mouth. Screw this life. Why does this have to happen now? How am I going to face her back at the apartment? How am I going to look at Leo in the face now that I know that there might be a chance he still likes me? How am I going to talk to Brandon?

This was all a big, big mess. Just like my life.

I splashed my face with some cold water before texting Sam to meet me under the big tree. I needed to talk to somebody.

He replied with an 'okay' and I stepped out of the bathroom.

I was drained mentally. I want to explode. I want to somehow scream again, or punch something, but I didn't have the will to. Not anymore.

It was almost as if I was already numb.

I blinked back a few tears. I just lost a friend didn't I? And I'm about to lose more. I just know it.

"Mira?" A familiar voice sropped my heart for a second. Fuck. I can't deal with him right now. Not right now. "Are you and Nichole okay? I saw her leave just a few minutes ago."

I stared at floor without saying anything. This wasn't going to last anyway, nothing ever does, so might as well end it before I get in deeper.

Brandon was waiting for my response. I was silent for almost a minute, but he seemed patient. He almost seemed foreign to me now. Everything seemed foreign to me now. I don't know anymore.

"I'm tired." I finally said, breathing heavily after that. He didn't understand. "I'm tired of this game already."

I don't know how he reacted, but that familiar heavy silence made its appearance again. It took me a few more seconds before I gathered enough courage to look him in the face. I held my breath. His expression was blank.

"Brandon," I said, with all the confidence I was able to muster. He waited for what I was about to say. "Do you think you'll ever like me?"

I need to know this thing's going somewhere.

I don't want to keep liking you if you won't even return these feelings.

If you don't like me, then just tell me already, so I can move on with my life.

But still.

I'm holding on this tiny rope of hope.

Please say yes.

It took him several seconds to respond as well. I couldn't even hear him breathe because my heartbeats were so loud.

"Do you think you'll ever like me?" He returned my question.

Why? Why can't he just give me a straight answer? Why couldn't I have just told him on the phone yes? Why did he look so torn? Was it because he knew we were a step away from losing each other? Was it because he was already tired of me, wants to throw me out now that Emma's in the picture?

What did I even mean to him?

The usual silence fell, it was almost comforting to say at the least because of its normal occurence among us friends lately.

Brandon took that answer as a negative, because he said the words I never wanted to hear the most. I was expecting it, but I didn't imagine it'd hurt this bad.

"Game over. No one wins, no one loses."

Just like that?

That only meant one thing: he didn't like me that much after all. It was just me being the idiot, falling for each and every game. It was just me being the loser, falling for him. How naive. How stupid.

I always fail every time I try to love someone. Why do I even bother?

Pathetic.

I couldn't give a reply. I don't think I even moved. Everything bad that's happening is because of my actions. Because of me. Why was I even born if I would just bring trouble to everyone?

I watched Brandon slowly walk away. I think he said something before he left, but I couldn't hear him over my loud thoughts, my loud heartbeats. Maybe he said goodbye. Maybe he said I looked pathetic. Maybe he said he was relieved he was finally free. I don't know.

And I don't care.

I snapped back into the cruel reality and walked outside to meet Sam. I need to burst. And after that I'll go to sleep, after being tortured by my own thoughts.

Nichole will be there. I don't think she wants to see my face. I can't go to Leo, I won't be able to forgive myself if I asked comfort from him. I don't have Brandon anymore. I never did. I can't talk to Emma. I know I'll cry, knowing she's taken my place without even knowing.

I can't take this. Why do problems even exist? Why do I exist?

I felt a tear roll down my cheek as I saw Sam waiting near the tree.

Something weird was piling up in my chest, I just wanted to scream. But I don't want him to see me cry. The last time someone saw me cry, he left. I can't risk losing another on.

I just can't.

Chapter 35

I stayed in my uncle's house for a couple of days. I didn't even go back to our apartment to take some stuff. I was too afraid to face Nichole.

It's either she really hates me, or she really hates herself.

I had the house all to myself because uncle went on a two-week conference somewhere in the world and left me the key to his house. No questions asked.

I went to school as usual, but did my best to avoid Nichole, Leo, Emma and Brandon. I never thought a day would ever come where I would do that.

Sam was my buddy the whole time. Maybe he felt sorry for me so he decided to stick with me like a piece of gum.

"Again," Sam sighed, as we made our way to our favorite spot (read: my favorite spot - he's just stalking me) under the big tree behind school - in the vacant parking lot where I first gave Brandon a taste of my special Mira Kick. "You look ugly again."

I groaned loudly to his utter amusement. A few days ago, I told him about everything that's happened between me and Nichole, me and Brandon, me and Leo, me and Emma.

Me and my dysfunctional brain.

He was sweet that time, hugging me and telling me to just let it all out. But I couldn't cry no matter how much I willed the tears to.

And when I didn't want to cry, tears would flow like the Niagra falls.

Such rebellious tear sacs I have here huh.

And now, he's back to being the usual ass. Well, that was fine, I guess. I don't want everything to be serious and all.

I mentally counted the days I tried to avoid my friends - almost ten days. That long.

I just made a face at Sam. He sent me a comforting smile before patting my head. I'm such a pitiful creature. "Smile, you hag. See you tomorrow."

Smiling. Huh. Sounds exhausting.

On my way back to uncle's house after class, a certain place caught my attention. I combed my hair with my fingers and took a deep breath.

Without much thought, I entered the salon. I've been wanting to cut my hair short for a while now. Better now than never.

I returned to uncle's house after my abrupt visit to the salon. I checked my new look in the mirror and gave myself a quiet smile.

I didn't look half-bad. It almost looks refreshing.

My original hair - waist-length - was now short. Short as in shoulder-length. Not completely short though, I had it layered so it was a couple inches longer in front than behind. It was cool.

I rolled my eyes just thinking what people would say tomorrow at school. I hear that if you cut your hair short, the only explanation must be because you're heartbroken.

That may be true in my case, but that's not the sole reason. Having long hair is really a hassle. I've had long hair for five years. I'm tired of it now.

Will Brandon notice this change and think it's because of him? I'll spit on him then. Because I cut my hair for myself, not for him.

Move on.

I checked the clock and sighed. It was too early. Usually at this hour, my friends and I would be chilling somewhere. Or Brandon and I would be fooling around. Those times felt like ages ago.

Move on.

The house was so quiet. Silent. It clenched my heart. I hate the silence. It makes me think. And I've done a lot of thinking these past ten days.

Not fun.

Damn it, move on.

As I was about to prepare dinner for myself, I heard a knock on the door. Was uncle back already?

Wait. No. He shouldn't be back until next Saturday. Who could it be? Could it be mom checking on me again? I grabbed a fork before treading cautiously towards the door.

Sigh.

I watch too much horror.

I opened the door slowly to check who it was, but when I recognized the face, I opened the door so fast I almost ripped it off the front porch.

Nichole. It was Nichole. Nichole.

Oh. God.

"Mira - " Her wail got cut short when she saw me. Her arms were open, as if she was about to jump and hug me. Her expression was unreadable. I don't know what I'm supposed to feel as well.

Her shocked face mirrored my own. Me because, why was she here? And her, because of my hair probably.

"What..." She mused, carefully touching the ends of my hair. "What have you done?"

I forced a laugh. It came out shakily. "It was hot."

She looked at me sadly for a few seconds before jumping and pulling me into a large hug. That was her original plan, I suppose. "I'm sorry, I'm sorry, I'm sorry, I'm so, so sorry. Please be my best friend again."

I was too relieved to even say yes. I hugged her back tightly. This feels so good. I feel like some weight have been lifted from my shoulders, but of course, there were still some left.

"Why don't you come in?" I said, slowly breaking the hug.

She nodded and I led her to the living room. She sat on the couch as I sat on the one facing her. She wasted no time and explained why she was here.

"I came to apologize." She mused, guilt washing over her entire face. "You didn't go back to the apartment for over a week. And you've been avoiding me. I understand, I was being an ungrateful bitch and it was so much harder on your part and I was just so selfish and I deserve more than just a punch and kick from you. I'm so sorry for jeopardizing our friendship. I can't stand it Mira. You're my best friend and I want us to stay best friends. I understand if you won't forgive me. But please, please come back to the apartment and come back as my best friend?"

Tears were streaming down her cheeks and her voice was shaking the whole time. I knew she didn't like doing this - showing this side of her to anybody. But she was. And that just proves how sincere she was, and that's honestly the only thing I want from the people closest to me.

I was still quiet. Of course I forgave her, but I just didn't know how to say it.

She furiously rubbed her eyes and pressed her lips together, looking so anxious. Maybe my silence meant something else to her. I have to say something before I cause another misunderstanding.

"I was so insecure of you, Mira," she admitted, her head down. "I was from the very start. I mean, you're perfect. And you've been with Leo for as long as you both can remember. We've been having a lot of arguments, and after hearing about his past feelings for you, I guess it just triggered the jealous girlfriend in me. I took it out on you. I didn't listen to him when he said you two already agreed to be friends. I can't help it Mira, I just love him. And I love you too. And I can't forgive myself for what I did."

"No, don't explain." I stopped her, leaving my seat and sliding in the couch right next to her. I gave her a light hug. "I understand. You gotta know I understand how you feel, and I don't blame you for anything at all. Of course I'll be your best friend again, I always have right? I'm sorry too, for avoiding you. I was just scared you'd ignore me and hate me and..."

"Oh God Mira," she interrupted me this time. "How could I ever hate you? How are you so nice?"

Nice. I'm the complete opposite of nice.

I laughed softly, giving her a full hug now. "It's the other way around actually. Thank you, Nichole. For this. For everything."

The happiness bubbling inside me was about to explode. I feel so emotional, and fortunately, all those emotions were positive.

But somehow, something was still wrong with me.

I can't cry.

I rubbed my best friend's back as she did the same. She giggled on my shoulder. "You're too good for me, seriously."

I snorted. We broke the hug and gave each other foolish grins, and then laughed afterwards. Her face was flushed, and I feel guilty for not having the same face. I mean, I feel the same emotions she's feeling, but it's frustrating how I can't let out a single tear.

So frustrating.

"So um," I cleared my throat. There was still something I was curious about. "Are you and Leo..?"

"We're totally fine now," she said, waving her hand happily. "We talked. Yelled. Talked. Cried. Talked. This and that happened. Then clothes were flying - "

"Whoa!" I almost clamped her mouth shut. Nope. Just nope. "Too much detail."

She giggled before squeezing me into another hug. "Now I know how much he loves me, and I understand that he loves you like a sister. I'm sorry again that I misunderstood. I won't do it again, I swear."

I returned the squeeze. "No problem. By the way, how'd you find this place? I told you about uncle's house yeah, but I don't recall giving you the address?" I asked. And then something hit me. I gave her a weird look. "Don't tell me you did some serious stalking in Facebook just to find this place?"

She laughed before slapping my shoulder. Dude. I wasn't kidding. I was asking her seriously. I knew she was a notorious Facebook stalker. "Leo drove me here. He's outside waiting, actually."

"He is?" I said, surprised. "Well let him in. I'll make dinner."

She pinched my cheeks. "You're so wife-material. Brandon's a massive douchebag."

I was smiling until she said that cursed name. I felt like half my energy got drained by that alone, and a flood of memories swallowed my mind like a tsunami. My lips twitched, resisting a frown.

She saw the sad look in my eyes when she mentioned his name, so she held my shoulder. "Actually, Leo wanted to tell you something about that. Wait, I'll call him."

A few moments later, Leo was in the room. He gave me a small smile before his eyes widened in shock, as if he just realized my new look. Which he in fact, did just realize.

"Holy - " He blurted out after a series of incoherent words. "Hair."

I gave my hair a small flip and sent him a sly grin. "I'm still awesome."

He rolled his eyes laughing before ruffling my new do, making a complete mess out of it. I irritatedly swatted his hand away. Nichole whispered something in his ear and then made her way to the kitchen.

"I'll order pizza and some beers. Dinner's on us Mira."

My ears were flying. Oh my God. Happy day!

As soon as Nichole left, Leo stepped forward. That look in his face made me want to make some kind of excuse to go somewhere. Nichole said he had something to say about Brandon. Of course

I was curious, but I wasn't in the condition to listen yet. I wasn't prepared. My mind and heart are still exhausted.

I wasn't ready yet.

"Wait," I said, looking everywhere but Leo. "Just tell me, is it good or bad?"

He sighed. "Well, that's up to you to understand, because honestly, I can't understand him."

I raised a brow. "What do you mean?"

"Well," he explained. "He was at his parents' house for a few days before he went back to the apartment. But even before then, he's been acting weird. He'd just sit there in his room and stare at space. When I try calling him, he won't even spare me a glance. Then hours later, it's like he's high or something, laughing like a robot at the stupidest things. I saw him in his room the other day, taking this weird pair of pyjamas out of a bag. He stared at it, then smirked, then frowned, then groaned, then laughed, then stared at it quietly for the next few hours. I don't know what to do with him Mira. He's just acting weird."

The pyjamas? The potato pyjama-set? He still had it? Why'd he go multi-polar (read: is that a word) over that? Maybe he was just about to throw it out. Maybe he actually -

Leo damn it, you dare get my hopes up again.

"You need to talk to him," he said, almost pleaded. I felt my blood boil for some reason.

"I already did, Leo," I said, a bit harshly. He seemed to understand why and let me continue. "I don't know what sort of weird he's been lately. But listen, all I know is that it has absolutely nothing to do with me. He doesn't like me Leo. I lost the game. He ended it himself."

"Do you honestly think this is still a game?" He asked, surprised.

"Of course not!" I couldn't help raising my voice. I paused for a few seconds, calming myself down. "I don't want this to be a game, Leo. Hell, I wish we never played this damn game. I thought it was gonna be fun, I thought it was gonna be harmless. I almost thought it was real." I paused again. I can't believe the words spilling out of my mouth. "You even warned me about this. But I didn't listen. Because I'm stupid."

"Mira you're not - " He tried to interrupt, but I didn't let him.

"I am." I pressed. "I am so fucking stupid. You know me Leo. You know I've never liked a guy before, you know I don't date because of what happened with my dad. He's the first to make me like this. It scares me. So much. And the thing I don't ever want to feel - my worst fear - it came true."

I wanted to punch something to express what I was feeling right now. I'm just so mad. I'm so mad at myself. And it's so frustrating. I can't cry. I want to cry just let me cry.

"I fell." I said, quietly at first. Leo looked like even he couldn't believe what I was saying. "I fell for him. I am so pathetically in love with a guy I can never have. I love him. I love him. I love him."

I love him.

Leo quietly listened. I heard Nichole break a plate in the kitchen but I didn't mind it at the moment.

I can't believe it. I actually admitted it. I love Brandon?

I took a deep breath to conceal my frustration with my rebellious tear sacs.

"And just like that I lost him." I said in such a low voice it almost sounded like a whisper. "I mean, why am I even surprised? I wasn't even worth it for my father. Why would I be worth it to someone else?"

To someone as good as him?

As soon as my head went down, Leo stepped forward again and pulled me into a hug. He patted my head, the way he did when I cried about my dad. This time though, I just stared at space, wondering why I feel so full of emotions yet I can't let it out.

"I'd be more than willing to beat him up again for you," he offered. I snorted.

"You got socked last time man."

"Yeah well," he shrugged his shoulders. "The second time will be different."

I laughed and then gave him a light squeeze. He's definitely the best brother I never had. "Thank you."

We heard a knock on the door and Nichole rushed out of the kitchen to get it herself. "Pizza baby!"

As soon as she opened the door, she smiled at the delivery guy. "Thank God. Here," then she handed him a couple of bills in exchange for the two large boxes of pizza and a dozen of beers. "And here's a tip. Thanks!"

"Wait," I hid a giggle when I recognized the wallet Nichole was using. "Is that your wallet?"

When I looked at him, he was just closing his eyes, as if shielding himself from the terror of that sight. I pinched his cheek.

Still the same old Leo.

I'm so glad the three of us are back to normal now. At least something went right.

The next day at school, I ate lunch with Sam under the tree behind school. Sure, Nichole, Leo and I were fine now, but Brandon and Emma were with them every lunch. I'm still awkward. I can't just casually return after ten days and sit with them like nothing ever happened.

Sam got called by one of his buddies and he had to leave me for a few hours, which I didn't mind of course. He was getting too fussy.

After relaxing under the shade of the tree for a while, I heard a few muffled voices behind me. I made an annoued huff, thinking that maybe Sam was back, until I heard a female voice.

"...is this okay?" Emma said nervously.

I froze on the spot and made myself as thin as possible so I could camouflage and the tree could hide my whole existence.

Yes, that is possible.

I peeked over the convenient bush beside the tree and felt my heart drop at the sight before me.

Just a few feet away, Brandon was with Emma. They were alone. In this isolated parking lot. Maybe they thought they were alone.

"It's fine," he reassured her. "Please. I need you."

A sharp pain went through my chest. Fuck this. Why am I here? Why am I being made to watch this?

Why is the timing always so convenient?

I heard Emma make a defeated sigh. "Okay."

I didn't hear what Brandon said next. I just saw him smile brightly at her and then he wrapped his arms around her, giving her a huge hug.

Stop.

Stop doing that in front of me.

I didn't want to witness any more stuff that'll just rip my heart to shreds, so I left. I didn't even care if they saw me. I just need to escape.

Damn it Brandon.

"Another one please!" I called out to one of the waiters. I had about four rounds of spicy burgers now. Yes, I went downtown to the place where Brandon and I used to eat spicy burgers.

Don't get me wrong. I didn't come back to this place to reminisce and shit. I just needed something strong in my throat. I wisely decided that drinking alcohol was not an option, and anything and everything spicy was the best solution - so that's why I'm here.

I just stopped eating when I realized how thin my wallet was now. Great. Grudgingly, I left the small restaurant. Better go back to the apartment and mope around now.

I hid a smile. At least I can go back to the apartment without feeling awkward anymore. I wanna tell Nichole everything when I get back.

I was about to call a cab when I remembered my lack of cash. I cursed myself for being so stupid. Ugh. So stupid.

Regardless of being stupid though, my usually illogical brain lit up a thought in my head. I'll call Leo to come get me. Genius.

Upon waiting for him to answer, I started walking back and forth in front of the small see restaurant I just ate at. Something caught my eye at the far distance. It was a guess, but I recognize that face anywhere.

I saw him walking towards me, just a few feet away. He didn't see me yet. I held my breath. Oh fuck no.

It was my father with his new wife around his shoulder. He was holding his little girl's hand, swinging it back and forth like he didn't have a care in the world. And their two other kids were walking ahead of them - chasing each other to be more exact.

They were all smiling and laughing. A big and happy family.

I suppressed my emotions even though I knew can't cry anymore.

That's just unfair.

Why is he happy?

Why can't I be happy?

Why can't I be with someone I love like him?

Why can't I cry?

I ignored the cab right in front of me and just mindlessly walked back to school. Walked.

I should've expected this. Yesterday was a happy day, so of course today would suck. It's just life giving and taking again. I shouldn't be surprised.

It was nearing dark when I came back to school. Most of the students were gone now. I don't know why I didn't just go straight home and call a cab. Oh right. I was broke.

Oh. I need Nichole and Leo right now.

I bumped into someone while I was still trapped in my thoughts. Oh.

"Mira?" Sam said. "Where have you been? I was looking everywhere for you."

I slowly raised my head to look at him. I wanted to cry. I so wanted to cry. Please, God. You made me see enough. I know I deserve it all. I get it now. Okay? Just let me freakin' cry now. Please. Please.

Please make Brandon appear somewhere and make everything alright. This sucks. I hate thinking like this. I hate being so weak and dependent.

Sam looked struck. I don't know. I was probably making an ugly face again, but I don't care. I just really, really wanted to cry.

But I was, actually. I was crying.

Without sound.

Without tears.

My life just sucked. And it kept sucking the more I think about it.

To my surprise, Sam cupped both my cheeks and pressed his lips against mine.

What...

What was happening?

I couldn't move. I don't know what to think. What? What?

But why?

Why was Sam kissing me?

Chapter 36

Brandon

She's not here today again.

Emma and I made our way to the cafeteria to our usual spot. She was trying to cheer me up, saying Mira will be there and everything will be back to normal.

I just tried to keep up an optimistic smile. I know she won't be there. After what I did. No - she'll spit on my face.

I heard from Leo that she cut her hair short. I want to see her. Damn it, I bet she looks amazing with her new look. I know she'd still look amazing even if she were to shave her head bald. But she keeps avoiding me. She keeps hanging out with Sam.

"You are ridiculous," Emma sighed exasperatedly. "Why don't you just go talk to her?"

"I already did," I replied. And then I lowered my head sadly. "She doesn't like me."

Emma stopped walking, causing me to halt in my steps as well. We were just a few feet away from the cafeteria doors now. She raised a brow at me as she folded her arms. "Did she say so?"

Umm.

"Not really but - "

I couldn't finish the sentence because she smacked me hard upside the head. "You fucking idiot!"

I looked at her surprised. Emma... cussed?

It took me a few seconds before I could respond. "But you don't know the whole story yet!"

"I don't need to." She said stubbornly. "But what I do know is that you misunderstood the situation. Maybe you didn't let her finish explaining. Maybe she was too afraid to tell you. Maybe she wanted you to tell her you like her first. God damn it Brandon! She's a girl! We're complicated like that!"

"W-What? What?" I mumbled unsurely, slightly panicking because of her sudden outburst. "But why? How do you know this? Are you sure?"

She sent me a glare. I gulped. Is this really still Emma? Why does she look so annoyed? No, it looks more like she wants to kill me. "In case you haven't noticed, I'm a girl too. God, Brandon! I can't imagine what she must be going through right now. I saw her Brandon. I saw the way she looks at you and me. She's hurt and I don't like being the reason for her being hurt. Maybe she thinks we're together or something."

My eyes widened. What? That's not true. "Gross."

She sent me another glare. "Right back at you. I have a boyfriend, remember? And Tony said he gave my swimsuit to Mira when you guys challenged her to a race. Did she really wear it?"

Tony was my team mate in swimming. He was tanned compared to Emma so it was hard to tell they were siblings. Her boyfriend goes to a different school but of course, he's still the typical overprotective boyfriend. That's why Emma had to give that swimsuit away.

That damned swimsuit.

"She did," I said stiffly, remembering how the guys looked at her when she wore that thing. I think I understand how boyfriends feel now.

Ha. I'm getting way ahead of myself thinking I know how boyfriends feel. I'm not anyone's boyfriend, and I'm certainly not a particular potato's boyfriend. How would I know.

"I see." She replied, knowingly. Then she rolled her eyes at me. She started walking again and this time we made it to our table in the cafeteria. Nichole and Leo were there, and they looked closer than ever. I hid a smile. That's great. I'm happy for them.

And then I looked at the empty seat in front of them.

She's not here today again. As expected.

I lowered my head so they won't see the pathetic frown on my face.

I want to see her.

"Hey Em," Leo sighed heavily just as we sat down. His arm was around Nichole and both wore grim expressions. It wasn't because of their issues this time though. "Do us all a favor and knock some sense into this guy."

Were they talking about me?

She scoffed. "Trust me. I've been trying."

The three of them sent me heated glares and I had to raise both my hands in surrender. "Why is everybody blaming me?"

"Because I hate you at the moment," Nichole said.

"Because you need to grow a pair," Emma second.

I looked at Leo, expecting a reply in the same fashion. "Just talk to her man. And I mean really talk to her. Let her finish explaining, and don't forget to say everything you want to say too. Don't just assume things and beat yourself up. Trust me, been there done that."

I was quiet, letting everything they said sink inside my brain. Can I trust their words? Do I still have a chance?

Nichole was still glaring me.

"I've never seen Mira so messed up since her dad," she said. I was partly sad, partly happy. Was it really me that affected her that much? Can I really believe that? "And I hate seeing her like this. You made her like this and you're not making any effort to fix it. Honestly, I would've kicked your manslut of a face a hundred yards already if it weren't for Leo holding me back."

I had to sink a little lower in my seat. Every word that came out of her mouth was toxic, and I wasn't an idiot. I knew she despised my presence at the moment. And I can't blame her. I hurt their best friend.

"I wanna talk to her, I really do." I said through gritted teeth. I hate myself right now. "But she told me she was uncomfortable with me. If I talk to her now, what if she ignores me? Rejects me? Hates me?"

The table shook and Leo held his girlfriend in place. Seems like Nichole was about to castrate me. She scoffed and groaned before folding her arms impatiently. "Wimp."

I was offended, but that only meant it was true. I am a wimp. But only when it comes to her.

Leo sighed for the nth time before giving me a strict look. Oh. He was in big brother mode again. "This is so annoying. Just talk to her. You won't know until you talk to her right? No ifs. If you really want her, then you have to risk getting hurt. That's what you call love, bro." And then an even more pissed expression grew on his face. "I can't believe you made me say that. As punishment, go to her right this instant and talk to her."

My eyes widened at what he just said. Love? And wait. What? Punishment? "What? But I'm not ready yet!"

I heard Nichole groan before she slammed her hand on the table. I think I want to ask my dad for a restraining order. Just in case, you know, my life depended on it. "Damn it manslut! Shut up, man up and go talk to her!"

Panicking, I turned to Emma, who was leering at me at the moment. Nobody was on my side at all! "Come with me?"

"Hell no." She quickly replied. "If she sees us together again, she'll think we're going out. And if she gets hurt one more time by that misunderstanding, I swear this time, it'll be me kicking your pretty face."

I seriously wanted to cry. Why were they ganging up on me? I'm hurt too. That's not fair!

"Do you know where she is?" Leo asked. I nodded.

"At the tree on the vacant parking lot behind school. She goes there with Sam every lunch time."

I felt my fists clench when I said that. Sam.

When she first mentioned Sam being a great help in their Biology test some time ago, I played it cool. But the truth was, I was so fucking annoyed. Why did she have to insist that he was such a cool guy?

I know I sound like a dick for saying this because Sam did nothing wrong to me, and he's been nothing but nice to all of us, but I don't want her hanging around with that guy. I don't trust him.

He's such a lucky kid, being in all of her classes. He gets to be close to her every day while I only get to see her at lunch and after school. And now, he's with her at those times too. I feel like he stole something from me.

I'm fucking jealous of him.

"And you know that because..?" Nichole asked, raising a brow. I was about to say something in reply when Emma replied for me.

"He stalks her everyday. And he keeps dragging me along because he's too scared to get found out."

My ego is so bruised right now, I don't think I'll even have an ego anymore after these girls are through with me.

Girls are so confusing. And frightening.

"Lord help the poor boy," Nichole mumbled. Then she sent me a pointed look. "Go there. Now."

She didn't have to tell me twice. Just thinking about her and Sam's relationship progressing right this moment is getting on my nerves.

Before I went off, I begged Emma to come with me. If Mira's there with Sam, I'll look like I'm invading their privacy if I go alone. I'll look like a third wheel or something. So I need Emma with me so I can still look cool.

Who am I kidding? Dumb excuses. I'm just scared I'll get rejected by the girl I like.

There was a lot of whining and complaining until we finally arrived in the parking lot. I looked around the place and hid a childish pout. She wasn't here.

"We'll just wait until she arrives," I told Emma. She sighed.

"If she misunderstands again then it's on you." She mumbled. And then she looked at me worriedly. "Are you sure this is okay? I mean, is this okay?"

I nodded unsurely, still looking for where my potato was. Maybe she was hiding under the shade of that tree?

"It's fine." I reassured her. "Please. I need you."

She scoffed silently. "Don't say misleading things like that if she's around okay? You're so dense."

They keep insulting me. Why.

After a while, after seeing my pathetic and hopeless face, she made a defeated sigh. "Okay. Fine. But I'm only going to be with you until here. You talk to her yourself and do all the work. Make it up to her, alright? You'd be the biggest idiot in the world if you let go of someone as amazing as her."

I felt a rush of relief in my system. I agreed with her wholeheartedly. Mira was amazing, and I'm already an idiot for hurting her because I misunderstood a lot of things.

Although, I still don't know which parts I misunderstood. I'm still lost. Guess I'll just have to ask Nichole later.

I want to ask Mira about the last time we talked on the phone too. Maybe I pressured her too much and she ended up saying the opposite of what she actually wanted to say?

Is it okay to hope?

But she said she was uncomfortable with me. What if she was just tolerating me the whole time? Maybe I bother her too much?

I really hope she doesn't hate me. Of all people, I don't want her to hate me. She's too precious to hate someone like me.

Emma tugged my shirt and pointed at something - a figure walking away. I almost gasped in surprise. It was her. Mira. Potato. Where did she come from?

I was only seeing her back this time, but it's been a while since I last saw her. Was it really her? Wow, she really did cut her hair. She still looks stunning from behind. Wow.

"What're you still staring at?" Emma asked me like I was the biggest idiot to ever walk the face of the earth. "Go after her!"

Without another thought, I did. I ran as fast as my legs could take me. My heart thumped loud and hard in my chest. I can't wait to see her. I can't wait to talk to her.

I can do this. Do it for the potatoes.

So...

I transformed into a wimp again and I didn't get to talk to her. Instead, I hid and followed her to where she was going. She rode a cab and so did I. I told the driver to follow the one in front of us.

I was still preparing myself at the moment. I can't go to war without armour. In this analogy, the war is my conversation with her and the armour would be the genius words I'll be saying to get her to come back to me.

As if she was ever mine in the first place.

Minutes later, we were downtown. What was she gonna do here alone?

And why the fuck am I still stalking her? This is beyond creepy. I should seriously get help. I'm losing my mind damn it.

I watched her as she entered a small restaurant. I hid a quiet smile when I realized it was the place where we participated in that burger-eating contest.

I remembered the spicy burgers I ate and I had to resist throwing up.

I entered the restaurant and sat on the table furthest away from her. I ordered a milk shake and watched her eat one burger after another.

How many stomachs can a human girl have?

She looked like she was about to order more until a sad look crossed on her face. I felt my heart squeeze at that expression.

It was adorable. Damn it.

She stood up and left the restaurant, and I followed shortly after.

After walking back and forth outside the restaurant on her phone, (she was probably calling Leo to come pick her up) I hid myself behind a stack of boxes.

Should I go there now? Should I talk to her now?

But that would be weird. She'll think I came out of no where. She'll think I'm stalking her. She'll hate me.

But I am stalking her. What will I say if she accuses me of that and sends me away? There's a lot of people here. I don't want to cause a scene. And this crowded place doesn't look so romantic for a confession.

She stopped pacing back and forth for a moment and stared at something at a distance. I tried looking at the direction where she was currently staring at and I felt all my muscles tense up at once.

It was her dad.

I snapped my eyes back at her and saw how her face had fallen. She hid her phone back inside her pocket and just continued to stare solemnly at her father's new family.

The hurt on her face was obvious. She was getting worse at trying to hide her emotions, and I'm one of the reasons why. I know that's not something to be proud of.

Guilt and hesitance seeped through my pores. I just want to stop hiding already and get her out of this place, away from that bastard she still calls her dad.

But maybe she was still confused at the moment. Maybe I'll just confuse her more if I suddenly appeared now.

But she needs someone right now. I don't want her to go to Sam and show him her tears. I don't want anyone seeing her that vulnerable.

I was so engrossed in my mental debate that I didn't realize she'd already walked away. I saw this as my chance and prepared to chase after her.

Until her dad caught me, that is.

"Hello," I heard him say from behind me. Damn it. Not now. "You're Mira's friend right? What are you doing there behind the boxes?"

I straightened my back and faced him with a polite smile. Even though I know how much of an ass he's been to her, I don't have the right to be rude to him. Might as well be honest with him. "I'm kinda stalking your daughter."

His eyes widened from the surprise. His wife beside him looked confused and his three children didn't seem to understand a thing I was saying.

"Better get back to the job now. Nice seeing you again sir." I smiled brightly at the confused family before I ran off.

Smooth, Brandon. Very smooth.

But oh well. There's no point trying to impress him anyway. It's the principal I should be extra friendly to.

Wait. That sounded wrong.

Shrugging my thoughts aside, I ran after no one in particular. Where was she? I looked left and right and saw no sign of her from the crowd.

Did Leo already pick her up? Did she ride a cab home?

I was about to confirm this with Leo when I saw her on the other side of the street. Thank you, eyes!

I stuffed my phone back inside my pocket and almost got hit by a car for crossing the street like an idiot. I can't help it.

After going through crowds and crowds of people, I was finally this close to her. But suddenly, I lost all confidence again. I hesitated. There she was, but I can't even call out to her.

In the end, I just followed her again. A few hours passed and we were still walking. She looked so lost in her thoughts. I mean, I couldn't see her face because I was only facing her back, but I could tell. I don't know how, but I could.

After following her some more, I realized that we were back at school. This girl. She knows her way from downtown to school but not from the mall to her apartment?

It was getting dark, and most of the students were gone now. Hiding was gonna get trickier without a crowd to camouflage my presence.

What the fuck.

Why am I still even hiding? Why can't I just talk to her? I'm so frustrated with myself. A stupid fucking wimp, that's me.

I waited for about a minute before I entered the school as well. I was trying to figure out what to tell her.

Should I apologize first? Should I just tell her I like her? I like her? That sounds like the biggest understatement in the world.

We were in the hallways now. There she was, just walking ahead mindlessly. Why did she come back here? Did she forget something?

I finaly gathered the guts to go to her when Sam suddenly came out. I jumped and quickly hid behind one of the lockers. I cussed under my breath. Why is the timing always so inconvenient when it comes to us?

I couldn't hear what they were talking about. I wanted to come closer but I'd risk exposing myself. If Emma and Nichole were here right now, they'd bitchslap me senseless for being such a coward.

When I peeked one more time from behind the lockers, I couldn't believe what I saw.

Sam was kissing her.

He was kissing her.

Kissing her.

Touching her lips with his.

Kissing. Her.

And she wasn't pushing him away.

It's safe to say thaf my heart broke into a million pieces. This is what I deserve for being a wimp. For being too late. I wasted so much time. Now he's got her.

Now that I think about it, Sam's not that bad of a guy. He doesn't hurt her. I know he won't hurt her. She deserves someone like him. Someone who won't hurt her the way I did -

What, no!

What the hell am I thinking? I won't hand her over to him. No! But... But what should I do? They're kissing right now and...

They're kissing right now. They're kissing and after that they'll fall in love and get married and have a lot of kids and name them all potato and grow old together and then they'll kiss each other teethless and what the fuck am I making up in my head.

I don't even feel mad anymore. I'm sad. I don't know what to do. How can I get her back?

I'm a fucking idiot. Idiot. I should've just called her out earlier when I had the chance. This is all my fault.

I unconsciously slammed my fist on one of the lockers, causing a loud noise due to the echo. I don't care if they heard me. I can't show my face to her right now.

Fuck my life.

"You bitch!" Nichole screeched so loud I thought my ears were gonna bleed. "Wuss!"

We were back at our apartment now. Leo was even slapping my shoulder nonstop. "What the hell did you think you were doing?!"

I can't even complain or defend my pride anymore. My ego is no more.

I blew it.

But I'm not giving up just yet.

"Brandon," Nichole said, her eyes filled with rage. I noticed how she supressed her anger by closing her eyes and taking a deep breath. "Do you like my best friend or not?"

Was that a trick question? I looked at her for a bit, reading her expression at the same time deciding what I should say. I might get hit again.

"Yeah." I said, color rising from my cheeks.

"Do you really?" She pressed, looking at me suspiciously. I gulped before looking down and analyzing my own feelings.

I don't know why I feel so crushed.

"I like your best friend, Nichole." I said, sincerely. "I like Mira. I like her very much. So much I'm about to lose my freakin' mind!" I almost yelled upon scratching the back of my head vigorously. "Why didn't she push Sam away when he kissed her? Maybe she grew feelings for him. Maybe I'm already too late."

I earned another slap from Leo. "Ouch! Dude!"

"You two think so alike that it's driving me insane!" He mimicked my actions just now and scratched the back of his head furiously. "Why don't I jut tie you up right there while Nichole kidnaps Mira and then we'll push you two together like fucking dolls and force you to talk seriously! Damn it just grow some balls, the two of you!"

I lowered my head for the hundredth time. I don't know what to think anymore, honestly.

She's slipping further and further away from my reach.

Nichole looked like she calmed down now. She sat down beside me and held my shoulder, her face full of sympathy. "Look, sorry for putting so much pressure on you. It's just frustrating to watch you two keep missing each other."

"I'm sorry too," I said. "I'm lost. I really am. I'm sorry for being such a bitter disappointment. It's just - when it comes to her, I can't think straight. And I don't know how to fix things between us while Sam's still in the picture."

"Now you know how she feels when you're with Emma." She deadpanned.

I stared at her. "Does she really think Emma and I are..?"

"Like Leo said," she gestured to her boyfriend. "You two think so alike, it makes me want to slam your heads together."

Some hope and a little bit of excitement lit up in me. "Does that mean she likes me?"

Both of them groaned loudly at the same time. I have no idea what that meant.

"If you wanna know, then ask her! God!" Nichole waved her hands in the air like crazy, showing how much patience she used up in this discussion alone.

I thought for a bit and then slowly nodded my head. "Okay. I'll talk to her. Tomorrow. I swear, I'll do it."

"You better." She threatened. "But if you make her cry again, I swear I'll cut you. And if you can't talk to her because of your wussiness again, I'll cut that useless pair of balls you have right now."

My hand unconsciously guarded my crotch as I looked to Leo for help. He was just shrugging his shoulders, letting his girlfriend say whatever she wants.

But this was sort of a good motivation for me to finally talk to her. If Sam will be with her again tomorrow then be it. I'll take her back. I want her back.

I'm not giving up on her.

Chapter 37

I stood frozen as Sam pressed his lips on mine. When he realized how unresponsive I was, he slowly pulled away, his hands still on my cheeks.

I couldn't look at him. I was confused. What was going on? My head's about to explode.

Just as he was about to open his mouth, we heard a loud noise from somewhere. It sounded like one of the lockers got punched or something. Was someone still here?

"Sorry," he mumbled, ignoring the noise just now. His hands freed my cheeks and found their way inside his pockets. "I couldn't help it."

I was still quiet. There's no right thing to say here. I'm not even mad at him. But I should be. I just don't know what to feel anymore.

"Mira?" He said. I didn't look up. "Remember when I told you that if I do something stupid, it's just purely out of instinct, and you're free to kick me or punch me?" I nodded, recalling him saying that after he confessed to me ages ago. "Yeah, you can do that now."

I can't do that.

He said himself he couldn't help it. And he's been so nice to me these days and I can't keep taking advantage of that kindness. But did he still like me? Why did he kiss me? What do I do? I stood still for another few seconds, contemplating my thoughts. Guess it made him panic.

"I'm so sorry Mira, I won't ever do that again I promise."

He looked so guilty that I had to feel sorry for him.

"It's okay Sam," I finally said. "But, yeah. Just don't ever do that again."

A heard a breath of relief when I told him that. "I still don't feel assured. Can you kick me?"

I snorted as I finally looked at him. "You a masochist now too?"

Everybody wants to get kicked or punched by me these days.

"No," he said a bit childishly, trying to prove his point. "But that's your thing right? You punch or kick the accused, then it's settled?"

I raised my brows to say something in defense but then I realized he was right. I just shrugged my shoulders. "Well, not today. I'm tired."

"I'm sorry," he insisted, looking like a guilty puppy. I rolled my eyes at him.

"I told you it's fine. Now stop apologizing before I really do punch you."

A playful smile appeared on his face as I elbowed him. This was still a bit awkward, but not as much as earlier.

I'm still confused. Did he still like me? Or was that just purely out of instinct?

I grabbed my phone and texted Leo to come get me at school. After that I walked to my locker to get my stuff. Sam followed me as usual.

"Are you okay? What happened?" He asked.

I wanted to tell him. I really did. But the subject regarding my father was too touchy. And personal.

Ha.

Who am I kidding? The truth was, I only wanted Brandon to know about my breakdowns when it came to my dad. This weak side of me was reserved only for him to see, unfortunately.

And the worst thing was, he's the only one who can calm me down. And now he's gone.

Damn all these negativity to hell.

"Just ran into something unpleasant," I said nonchalantly. "Leo's picking me up. Wanna come with? Your house is in the same way right?"

He politely shook his head. "Thanks, but I gotta stop by somewhere first."

"Okay," I smiled, silently thanking the Lord for making things less awkward. Please let Sam lose all his feelings for me. I really want us to stay just friends. "See you tomorrow."

"Yeah," he waved as he spun on his heels to leave. But not before sending me a grin of approval. "Short hair looks great on you by the way. See ya."

I just got out of the bath when I found Nichole waiting near my bed. I was about to ask her what's up until she pulled me into a big hug.

I didn't even have to explain what happened with me today. It seemed like she already knew, though I don't know how. Was I that transparent?

After returning the hug, she shuffled my hair and pinched my cheek. Before leaving, she sent me a quiet smile. "Everything will work out fine. I promise."

I was kinda cheered up after that. Thank God for giving me my best friends. I seriously don't know what to do without them.

Burying myself in my sheet and making myself comfortable in my bed, I sighed contentedly. I'm about to make one of the greatest escapes from my problems - sleep.

In psychological terms, I was already in the second stage of sleep when suddenly, my phone vibrated. It was on my desk so it was loud enough to wake me up.

Annoyed, I blindly reached for it and swore under my breath. I know it's gonna be hard trying to fall asleep again. Damn whoever this is.

I opened my messages and groaned.

| Hey. |

An unknown number. Great. Maybe it was a wrong send?

I put my phone back on the table without bothering with a reply. I just want to sleep. Minutes later, it vibrated again. I ignored it. Then it vibrated again, and again and again...

"God damn it why?!" I yelled as I threw my sheets off of myself and grabbed my phone as if I were to murder it.

I swiped the screen to unlock it furiously and gritted my teeth when I saw that it was from the same number.

| Heyyy |

| Wake up.|

| Reply. |

| Mira. |

| I saw you kiss Sam. |

My heart stopped from those two last messages. This wasn't a wrong send. Oh my God. Who was this?

Okay, I'm awake now. Who could this be?

A chill went down my spine when a thought hit me. Earlier, we heard a loud noise from the lockers. Could this be him? Or her? I'll just use the general term "he" since I don't know the gender of this person. Where did he get my number? Why is he telling me this?

Is this a prank? A threat? Blackmail?

I finally sent my reply.

| Who is this? |

I shakily waited for his reply. It came in about four seconds.

| Your stalker. |

Obviously! Dude!

Could this be Leo pulling a nasty joke on me? But he doesn't know about that kiss. Nichole? No, of course not! Sam? Probably...

Erm... Brandon?

I sighed heavily at myself. Such a joker I am. Of all people, why would he still text me? He wouldn't bother.

But there's still a possibility. I just won't hang on to that possibility.

| What do you want? |

It took him at least a minute or two to reply. He was killing me with the suspense.

| Nothing. I just want to talk to you. |

Okay this was getting creepy.

| Who are you? | I asked again.

| Can't tell you that yet. |

Yet? So he was planning on revealing himself soon?

| Why? |

| Because I know you won't reply if I told you who I am. |

This is getting annoying. I'm sacrificing my precious time of sleep for this?

| Fine. Is there something you want to say to me that you had to go through all this trouble? |

I hope he senses the sarcasm in that text. He must be some special kind of wuss if he can't even talk to me in person.

| Yeah. How are you? |

What the fuck?

| You're sick. |

I checked the clock and groaned. It was already midnight. I calculated the hours of sleep I have left until school. And it just made me more annoyed.

| I know. Forgive me. But this is the only way I can talk to you right now. |

I don't know why my heart jumped at that. Why do I have a feeling this is Brandon? Maybe I'm just tired.

| Just tell me what you want to say so I can go back to sleep.|

| Just wanted to say goodnight. :) |

I can't believe this guy. I didn't bother replying anymore. I placed my phone back on my side table and went back to bed. I'll deal with this in the morning.

"So you don't know who it is?" Nichole asked as I stuffed my books in my locker. She and Leo were walking me to class today. I don't know why though. They looked like they knew something and weren't telling me.

"No." I said. "Do you?"

She shook her head and elbowed Leo. He shrugged his shoulders. "Must be one your admirers. Your wimpy admirers."

"Wuss is the word you're looking for," Nichole nodded her head.

I agreed.

"But I do feel sorry for the guy," Leo added. I raised a brow at him. "He's trying his best."

"Who?" I pressed. I'm starting to think they know who's texting me.

My suspicion that it really is Brandon is increasing.

He shrugged his shoulders again. "Why are you asking me?"

Was that a rhetorical question?

When we got to my classroom, my best friends each gave me a pat on the head before leaving.

What the hell were they hiding?

I went to my seat and found Emma smiling at me like the usual. I smiled back, waving my hand a bit at that.

I saw Sam talking to someone on the other side of the room. Oh God. He left me with her. How can I make this not awkward?

Come back here you damn piece of gum.

"Hi Mira," she said as I sat down.

"Hey."

There was an awkward silence for a few seconds until she spoke again. "I haven't seen you at lunch lately. What have you been up to?"

I stifled a gulp. Sam come back here and save me!

"Um..."

I really didn't know what to say. I can't tell her it's because of Brandon, but I'm guessing she already knows that. She must've noticed how tense I was, because she gave me a small smile, as if telling me to calm down.

"Why are you and Brandon ignoring each other?" She asked. I looked away. Why is she asking all these? He might've told her already. Or maybe she just wanted to hear my side of the story?

I twisted on my seat to face her directly. I'll just tell her the truth then. "Because I said some pretty mean things to him. And he ended the game. So there's no reason for us to - "

"No!" She quickly interrupted. I was surprised with her sudden outburst. Emma was usually calm and collected. What was with her today? She cleared her throat and released a nervous giggle. "I mean, that's no reason for you two to ignore each other right?"

"Are you two going out?" I blurted out. Oh fuck! Why the hell did I ask that? Now I'll look like some desperate idiot and she'll have to feel sorry for me. Ugh! I hate myself.

"Of course not," she replied patiently, but a bit annoyed. Annoyed? "I have a boyfriend, Mira."

My jaw dropped at that revelation. Why do I feel so happy right now?

"I didn't know, sorry," I mumbled. I'm an idiot.

She chuckled at my expression. "Do you still have my swimsuit? My brother gave it to you right?"

I was confused for a few seconds and I started searching my messy memories for what she could've meant.

My eyes widened in realization when I found that specific memory. "That was yours? You're the Tanned One's sister?"

She looked at me confused. "The what one?"

Oh God. I can't believe I said that out loud. Brain! Help me out here!

"I mean yeah, I still have it. Do you want it back?" I said, an attempt to save face. She shook her head.

"No, keep it. I have a jealous boyfriend you see," she giggled a bit. Well that sounded fun. Note the sarcasm. "I asked you because I want to know what Brandon said when you wore it."

My cheeks flamed when I remembered the stupid things I did back at the pool. I showed off my curves because I was trying to piss him off. And then he told me not to wear that thing again unless it was for him. And then he hugged me while I was stark naked under that towel. And we were both wet. And...

Oh, I can't breathe.

Why the hell am I reacting like this to such a simple question?

I noticed Emma's lips twitching up into a very smug grin and I felt the need to bury my face in my hands. Was she teasing me?

"I hope you two work things out. He's trying his best, you should too."

What?

Before I could ask, Sam came back to his seat because the teacher finally entered the room. Damn it, timing!

He was trying his best? At what?

My heart jumped again. My friends were acting so suspicious. Was there a plan I'm not aware of? Do we still have a chance after all?

I hope so.

| You looked pretty earlier. |

I almost threw my phone out the window when I read that text. He always texts late at night. Does he have this scheduled or something?

| Hey stalker. I swear, if you won't tell me who you are right now, I'll report you to the police. |

| Nah, you're too lazy to do that. If you don't like stalker, think of me as an admirer then. |

I rolled my eyes. Heh.

I was kind of sure it was Brandon texting me. I mean, not a hundred percent sure, but based on my friends' actions earlier, I think I got the hint.

I'll test it then. I'll test if it really is the potato who's sending me these messages.

I hate myself for getting excited.

| Can I ask you something? | I pressed send.

| Sure. What is it? | He replied.

| Do you like potatoes? |

His identity will depend on his answer.

Dude. I can't believe I just asked that. Several seconds later, he replied.

| I like potatoes very much. You? |

I snorted. This won't fully confirm it. But anyways, I'll just have my fun at the process.

| Yeah. You're not gonna ask why I asked you that weird question? |

| Nah. I was about to ask you the same thing anyway. |

Huh, really now.

I was thinking on what to say next. I don't know if I'm just bored, but I feel like I want to prolong this conversation. I don't know why I suddenly feel relaxed talking to him.

See this is why the stupid girl gets killed in the movies.

| You probably already know this, but can I ask you something again? | I pressed send. And then he replied quite quickly.

| Sure. |

I hesitated a bit on what I was about to send, but I want to know how he'll react. I mean, I won't know his true reaction since we're just texting, but still.

I mean...

I just want to tell him. I don't know why I suddenly have the urge to tell him everything. I felt like I was really talking to Brandon.

| Why do you think Sam kissed me? |

I don't why I have a strong feeling that this is him. I hope this is really him I'm talking to.

| He likes you, doesn't he? Isn't it natural for someone to kiss the person they like? |

My heart was beating so fast that I had to breathe slowly just to calm myself down.

It was such a safe answer. Now I'm having doubts. Maybe this isn't Brandon I'm talking to after all. I shouldn't have gotten my hopes up.

I was still typing my reply when he sent me another text.

| Potato, if only you were here right now, I would've kissed you long enough to forget about him. |

I dropped my phone like it was hot. I literally dropped it and screamed because one, he called me potato - who else calls me that? Two, because of what he said, and three - I fucking dropped my phone!

Heart still racing, I checked if the screen was broken. I sighed in relief when it wasn't. That mini-heart attack though. Gosh.

Back to my current situation, I wasn't able to send an immediate reply. My hands were shaking and I think I'm hyperventilating oh, God.

I jumped when my phone vibrated again, meaning he sent another message after that.

|I'm kidding, please forget that last text. I'm sorry for that tasteless joke. |

Even though I was kinda panicking, some sort of excitement and happiness bubbled up inside me.

Confirmed: this was Brandon.

I'm pretty sure he knows that I know already, but like what we did when we were still playing that game, we just went along with the flow.

I sent my reply.

| Funny. Do you know who else calls me Potato? |

| Yeah, I'm your stalker I know everything. |

| Tell me who. |

It took him at least a minute to reply. I was trying to scare him. Maybe I did scare him off? Was he busy? Or was he just hesitating?

| Brandon, the biggest douchebag in the world. You don't deserve someone like him. |

I smiled. Yeah. I miss him so much.

| I know. But I did something that hurt him, which is also the reason why we're not talking anymore. I feel horrible. |

| Sorry you had to feel bad by yourself. |

I smiled again. He doesn't realize he's already giving himself away.

| Thank you. But don't apologize for him.|

| No I mean... I'm just apologizing in behalf of the entire male population. |

Nice save. Snorting, I typed in my reply.

| Okay then, male stalker. |

He didn't text back for more than five minutes, so I sent another text.

| Do you think he hates me after what I said? |

I waited for over an hour for a reply, but received none. I was a bit disappointed. Maybe he already fell asleep? Figures. It's already two in the morning.

I set my phone beside my bed and went to the bathroom for a bit. After that, I returned to my room and was about to go to sleep when I saw my phone blinking a blue light, which meant I had an unread message.

I quickly opened my phone and a huge grin broke on my face when I saw how long the text was. So that's why it took him that long. I began reading it aloud.

| He'd be the biggest idiot in the world if he ever hates you just for that. But think about it, maybe he misunderstood the situation because you didn't explain everything. Maybe he thought he was just bothering you. Maybe he thought you were just tolerating him. Maybe he thought you didn't feel comfortable around him. Maybe he thought he doesn't deserve somone like you. Maybe he thought you already liked someone else. We boys are still trying to figure out the female psychology, but try to understand the male psychology too. I'm not saying you should forgive that douche, that's up to you, but try to understand why he did that. I think he's just a big coward and he's really afraid to get rejected. Maybe he was rejected a lot in the past let's say his friends and family, and he's afraid to get rejected by someone as special as you. Ummm. Yeah. So bottom line... I don't think he hates you. I think he'll never ever come to hate someone like you. Ever. Okay, that was pretty long. Does that answer your question? |

Usually, when someone takes some time to text back to me, I'd reply twice as long. But this time, I sent my reply as soon as I finished reading his message.

You could say this was a special case. But I didn't reply in the same length. I was honestly speechless.

| I see. Okay. Thank you. |

After I sent it, I sent another one.

| When are you going to reveal yourself? |

The hidden meaning of thay message was - when are we going to talk and work things out for real?

He replied:

| Tomorrow. :) |

I smiled. Okay. That's good enough for me.

Brandon

I'll tell her tomorrow. This is final.

I know this was pretty low of me, sending messages to her anonymously, though she may already know who I am, but I'm taking every chance I can get.

I'm glad she told me those things. I'm glad I told her what I couldn't say. But it wasn't enough. The most important parts - we'll have to discuss in person.

The texting was just the first step.

"You are hopeless bro," Leo said as he passed by my room. I forgot to close the door.

"Yeah, yeah," I mumbled childishly. I already had an earful from both Nichole and Emma. I don't want to be lectured by him too. I already know what I did wrong. Now I'm just trying to figure out how to make it right.

"Well, at least you have all our support. Good luck."

Well, that was surprising. No slap this time?

I was about to thank him but when I got up, he already left. I chuckled quietly, thankful for all their help. I closed the door with my foot and went back to my bed.

After I sent my reply, she didn't text back anymore. Maybe she already fell asleep? It was already pretty late.

I still wanted to talk to her though.

Seconds before I hit the sack, I received a new message. I jumped right out of bed due to the excitement. Was it her? Was it her?

My face fell when I saw that it wasn't. It was just some random ad from some company I'm not familiar with.

Ughhh.

I climbed up to my bed again and buried myself in the mass of sheets. Before I slept, I had her image in my mind and I smiled all stupidly to myself.

I can't wait to talk to her tomorrow.

Chapter 38

I can't wait to talk to him.

It's today. I couldn't sleep last night because I kept visualizing how he'll look at me, if he'll ever smile at me again, and I kept wondering what he'll say, if he'll confess, if he'll apologize, if he'll forgive me...

I miss him so much.

But I'm too nervous. I hope I don't screw things up again. This is like my last chance.

I took a deep breath. You can do this Mira. Just listen to your guts.

The whole day went by like a millennium. An exaggeration, but that's how I felt. I just couldn't concentrate in any of my classes in anticipation of my long-awaited talk with Brandon.

But I didn't get it though, when he said he'll reveal himself tomorrow - I mean now - what did he mean? Will he meet me? Will he just text me? Did he get my hidden message?

I groaned in my thoughts. My hopes are rising again. I'm setting myself on fire again. But that's okay. I really think things are gonna go well this time.

Just stay positive Mira.

I didn't have class in our last period. The teacher allowed us to go home already because of some family emergency. I think I heard people say his wife was giving birth at the moment. Happy father's day to our dear teacher then.

So, when the rest of my classmates did go home, I didn't. I waited until Brandon's class was finished. I mean, I don't know why I did, he didn't actually say we'd talk at school but...

I don't know.

Nichole and Leo still had class too, so while I'm waiting for that potato, I'll be waiting for them too, since they're my ride home.

I waited near Leo's car in the parking lot. I had no where else to go. I saw Sam with his friends walk out of the school building looking as hyper as usual. Well duh, no class dude. Especially on a Friday. That was something to get hyped about.

He saw me sitting alone in the parking lot so he left his boys for a bit and jogged towards me.

"Waiting for them?" He asked. I nodded with a small smile. Okay, this was still a bit awkward. I mean, he did kiss me. And he still didn't give me a clear reason why he did it.

He looked over his shoulder to see if his friends were still there. They were. And they were looking at us like we were celebrities making a scandal.

As usual, my way of describing things is horrid. Just get the gist of it please.

Sam played with his hands a bit, something he did whenever he was nervous. I stood up from my sitting position. Something tells me this was important.

"Listen," he mumbled, avoiding my eyes. "I'm sorry again for kissing you. Turns out I still liked you after all, and after seeing you like that, I just couldn't help it."

I was about to say something but he kept going, not allowing me to interrupt.

"I know Brandon will have my head for that, that's why I'll apologize to him too. I just don't want to make things awkward between us. And yeah, I know I don't stand a chance so that's why this time for real, I'm stepping down. I won't do anything like that again. You're a great friend and you honestly made me really happy. So can you... like... I mean... Still be my friend? No funny business."

I sighed in relief while giving him a smile. He always makes things easier and he always takes the load off a lot of things. He was too pure this kid. I'm suddenly happy that there are still people like him in the world.

He deserves someone better. I hope he finds the best.

"Of course, you piece of gum," I said. He chuckled at his nickname and I did the same. He was a good piece of gum, always sticking around when I needed him. "Thank you."

He nodded. He was about to leave but then he turned around and gave me a quick hug. I patted his head. I felt a bit guilty that I couldn't return his feelings, but he was so mature about this, and he made everything easier. Well, for me. I hope he made it easier for himself too. "Thanks, Mira."

Sam left after that, giving me a small wave. Now that that's finally settled, I'll just have to deal with Brandon now.

After waiting for half an hour, I panicked.

Okay. Not the best time to panic. But it's almost time! Oh God. I should've fixed myself first. Is my hair a mess? Oh wait, it's easier to manage now since it's short. But I still want to look my best.

I look stupid sitting in the parking lot just waiting for my ride so I stood up and dusted my pants. I also fixed my shirt. I'm getting way too self-conscious for my own good.

Wait. Did my breath stink? I exhaled on my palm and smelled it. Nope. What about my pits? I raised my arms up and sniffed myself. Nope. All good.

I heard a chuckle nearby and saw three guys about to get in their car - not before they watched the awesome show I put on for them to see, of course.

Can I die now.

Luckily, they left after a bit, winking at me as they drove off. Ughh. But whatever. I don't care right now because I'm going to meet Brandon.

I felt my phone vibrate in my bag. I quickly opened it and took my phone out, expecting it to be from a particular potato.

I smiled all giddily to myself when the name flashed on my screen.

Potato Stalker

I opened the message calmly, or some attempt to be calm. I was too excited.

| I can't wait to see you. |

| Very stalker-ish of you. Nice. | I replied.

Smooth Mira, smooth.

| Haha! But really. I mean it. I want to see you. :) |

I winced, feeling my heart do a little flip. Oh, man.

| We're going to meet? | I asked innocently. Heh.

| If that's okay with you. Are you free? |

| Yup. Where? |

| Umm. How about you just stay where you are and I'll go to you after my class is over. Then we'll go somewhere. |

I considered his idea. But something got me curious, so I asked him.

| How do you know where I am? |

| Because I can see you. |

Okay, I admit I was a bit freaked out. But knowing this was Brandon I was talking to, kind of lowered the freakiness-level.

I looked left and right to see if he was somewhere hiding, but I was the only one in the parking lot at the moment. Did he see me over a window perhaps?

| You sound like a real stalker. I'm not even kidding. |

| Hahaha! XD |

His reply made me giggle. I sighed as I sent him another message.

| Okay, so what are you doing right now? |

| Risking my phone's life as I secretly text in Epstein's class. You? |

| Oh, don't do that. Nichole's phone got confiscated by him before. She wasn't even texting, it was just her alarm going off. |

It's true. Mr. Epstein was pretty strict.

| Doesn't matter. You're more important than my phone. :) |

Meh. Cheesy, but it made me smile. Ugh.

I can't believe we're texting so casually now. This was a good start.

As I typed my very sarcastic reply with a foolish grin on my face, I heard an abrupt knock followed by a sting on my arm.

After releasing a hiss, I looked down to see what hit me. A rock.

I glanced up this time, trying to find out where the heck it came from. A nerve popped in my head when I saw a group of guys a few feet away, wearing mischievous grins on their smug faces.

I noticed that they were heading my way, and one guy was kicking the rubble on the road, which explains why I was hit.

I picked up the damn rock and placed it in my palm, showing them the potential murder weapon with an irritated look on my face.

"Did you guys just throw a rock at me?"

The guy in front looked at his companions before they all snickered. I noticed that I didn't recognize them as students from my school. I mean, I know I'm not good with faces and names, but I had a feeling they really weren't from my school.

The one that was kicking the rubble just a few seconds ago approached me with his hands hidden inside his pockets. My self-awareness rose as I analyzed my current situation:

We were the only ones in the parking lot. There were five of them, all guys. I'm the only girl here. They looked like they were looking for trouble.

"Yup. My bad," he said, smirking at me.

The one in front held a hand to his chest, a mock gesture of class. He was tall and I could tell he was muscular under that loose shirt of his "I apologize for my friend here. His ways of getting a girl to notice him is terrible."

I stared intensely at the culprit. He was smiling at me, and not a very friendly one at that. They kept coming closer and closer. Who were they?

"What do you want?" I asked, keeping my voice steady. My knees were shaking a bit, but I kept a strong face. They seemed like none of the guys I faced before.

"Nothing, nothing. Don't let us scare you," he chuckled. As he advanced towards me, I took steps back. That went on until I felt Leo's car against my back. They surrounded me.

What the fuck was happening?

"I'm Nathan by the way, but you can call me Nate." The tall guy, which I assume was their leader, said. "Pleasure to meet you."

"Okay, Nate," I said, feeling a rush of confidence coming back to my system. I took a brave step forward, which caused them to take a step back. This was just a game of who intimidates who first. I know I'm at a disadvantage here but I'm not gonna show any signs of weakness. Never. "Would you please tell your boys to back off? And while you're at it, you might as well do the pleasure of doing the same."

They all chuckled again. I smiled at them menacingly. They thought I was joking? They just stared at me like freakin' psychos. I held my chin up as I folded my arms.

"You want a fight?" I challenged. That was so stupid. I'm gonna get myself killed for real. Again, I'm acting like the stupid girl in the movie.

Another guy stepped forward. He had this vicious grin on his face and I just didn't like the way his eyes raked my whole appearance. "Relax beautiful," he said.

He was about to touch my face or my hair or something but I acted on impulse and grabbed his hand. I twisted his wrist with a flick of my hand and grabbed his elbow, pushing it to the opposite side and then eventually carried his weight and threw him down.

Shit! What have I done?!

His companion was about to fight back when Nate extended his arm to block his way. The rest of them stared at him confused as that guy I just threw down recovered and got back to his feet.

Nate grinned at me before looking over his buddies. "Don't touch her. She's a girl." And then he looked at me again with a distrustful twinkle in his eye. "She's Brandon's girl."

I felt my whole body tense up at the mention of his name. These guys knew Brandon? What? What the - were they part of his enemies back at his potato gangster days?

Not good. Not good.

I panicked again. Did they want revenge or something? But how did they know me? And why does everyone just assume that I'm Brandon's girl'?

My phone kept vibrating in my hand, meaning I kept getting messages one after another. This was no time to text.

And yes, when I threw that guy down just a second ago, I still had my phone on my other hand.

I hid my phone behind my back as I glared at Nate as hard as I could. "What do you want from me?"

"Nothing," he said. Yeah right. "I just wanted to pay our dear old friend a visit. But lucky us, we get to meet his girl instead."

I rolled my eyes at him. "I'm not his girl."

They all howled in unison. Jerks.

"We'll see." He said. I was trying to figure out what he meant by that when one of his buddies snatched my phone behind my back.

I jumped to get it back but then two of them held my waist and arms to prevent me from doing that.

The guy gave my phone to Nate and then he chuckled as he opened my messages. I cursed under my breath, regretting the fact that I took down the passcode in my phone since it was a nuisance whenever I was in a hurry.

A huge grin broke in his face as he read something out loud. "Potato stalker? That's what you call him? Adorable."

I flushed with both anger and embarrassment, still struggling to break free. "You don't even know that's him."

He snorted. "Please. Most of his statuses in Facebook mention potatoes or something. It's so obvious."

I gasped in mock horror. "You stalker!"

"I just happened to come across them in my news feed. That doesn't necessarily mean I stalk his profile," he strongly defended.

YEAH RIGHT.

"Why are you doing this?" I asked, well, stalled. I was planning on what to do to these two knuckleheads keeping me still. Punch them? Knee them? Bite them?

Nate shrugged his shoulders as he continued scrolling down my phone. "Bored. Hey, nice selfie you got here."

I know this wasn't the time, but I was curious which one he meant.

See how fucked up our generation is?

Suddenly, he took his phone out.

"What are you doing?" I asked again.

"Gonna send your pictures to my phone."

"What!" I yelled, 'accidentally' stepping on one of the guys' foot. He grunted. "You're sick!"

Damn it, these guys were strong. And that Nate guy is psycho.

"Don't you have any nudes here?" He said, not taking his eyes off the screens of the phones.

Is he kidding me right now?! And why is he talking so casually? Seriously so annoying!

"Why the hell would I take a picture of myself naked?!"

He looked at me like I was the crazy one. "To send to Brandon. Duh?"

My cheeks flamed inconveniently. What the hell is wrong with this guy?!

"Maybe it's in a private folder? Check her messenger." The guy beside him said.

"I checked. There's none. Maybe it's in Brandon's phone?" He replied.

The guys holding me chuckled. "Maybe she deleted it after she sent it. A girl like her wouldn't be caught dead with nudes in her phone."

My temper was rising. This was harassment and an invasion of privacy! I can sue them for this!

"Well," Nate said, stepping forward, eyeing me maliciously. "We'll just have to make her take new ones. Doesn't that sound fu - "

He didn't finish his sentence when I kicked him right on his jaw. Even I was surprised I could kick that high. I finally perfected the axe kick. The guys were keeping me hostage by holding my arms and waist, but they stupidly forgot that my legs were also very capable of attack and escape.

I took advantage of that moment of shock because I jumped high and hard enough so my head would hit the other guy's jaw above me. Then I kneed the other one so hard I was sure he won't be able to walk straight for days.

The two remaining tried to swing at me but I dodged just in time. I broke the nose of the first guy and gave the second guy a black eye.

This was all adrenaline. This was my first time fighting a group.

This is how you get yourself killed.

The thing about guys is that they're quick to recover in a fight. I was still focused on keeping one guy down that I didn't notice Nate creep behind me. He wrapped his arms around my stomach and pulled me away from one of his buddies.

"Let go of me" I yelled in exasperation upon kicking my legs in thin air. He just tightened his grip, carrying me over his side like I was weightless.

"Stop fucking moving around," he hissed. I did the complete opposite. "Now I see why you're Brandon's - "

"I'm not his girl!" I screamed, knowing what he was about to say. They make me sound like fucking property!

I don't know what he was about to do next. Maybe he was going to take me somewhere. Maybe he was gonna rape me then kill me. With that thought in mind, I struggled my hardest, panicking. I'm being kidnapped!

The next thing I knew, the world spun and my vision turned black. When I quickly regained my composure, I realized that both of us were already on the ground.

I opened my eyes after all that impact and saw Brandon grab Nate's collar, sending him a heated glare. I also heard a multitude of footsteps behind me. And then I saw Leo, Nichole, Emma and a few other students surrounding the guys I just beat up.

I was still on the ground, too surprised to process everything. When did they get here?

"Hi... Hi Brandon," Nate stuttered as he tried to pull Brandon's hand off his collar. It was a futile attempt.

I noticed that his left eye was swelling, so that meant Brandon already gave him a greeting.

"What the fuck do you think you're doing here Nathan?" He asked through gritted teeth.

"Nothing!" He chuckled nervously. And then he gulped. Did he even realize the situation he was in right now? "I mean, we were just... I mean... We just wanted to meet your girlfriend. She's pretty famous in our school and all, and damn she really brings justice to the word badass - "

Before he finished that sentence, he attempted to punch Brandon but he failed because my potato caught it like he had anticipated that attack. Nate gulped again before Brandon gave him a hard left hook.

It was a total knock out.

He left Nate on the ground without a care and then quickly went to my side. This isn't how I expected our first meeting in weeks would be.

He was so focused checking my face for some injuries while I just stared at him the whole time. He looked so worried.

"Are you okay?" He asked as he finally met my eyes. His hands were cupping my cheeks gently.

I shook my head slowly. He's really here. He's really talking to me.

I'm so happy.

Uncle Ray came about a minute later, saying he'll handle those guys himself and call their school. Leo came and gave me back my phone.

"Thank God you didn't get hurt," he told me, squeezing my shoulder.

It wasn't a huge issue, so they didn't involve the police. I knew my uncle was more than capable of handling five delinquents by himself.

"Yeah," I mumbled, secretly glancing at Brandon. He was talking to our principal about something. Maybe he wants to take the blame? Knowing him, he'd probably do that so I won't get in trouble.

"We'll leave you two alone. Okay?" Nichole said, giving me a small smile. I nodded, wondering if Brandon would give me a ride home instead. But... I mean. Was that too much to ask for? Am I getting way ahead of myself again?

When they left, I swallowed hard once again. It's been a while since I've felt like this. Brandon kept glancing at me from time to time as he talked to my uncle, and I could tell he wasn't happy.

Why do I get the feeling I'm gonna get scolded again?

After the guys were taken away, the crowd of students dispersed. Only Brandon and I were left. And I was still sitting on the ground like a duck.

I wanted to say something but what? He wasn't looking at me.

I felt like I was having an anxiety attack. What was going to happen next? Is he disappointed in me again?

When he finally turned around, to my direction, I held back a gasp. I'm too nervous for my own good.

He walked towards me and I tried my best to keep my eyes open. I was fighting back a wince because I was seriously terrified.

While looking at me with those familiar dull eyes, he grabbed my hand and pulled me up without a word.

He wasn't forceful. He was careful the way he led me to his car. He treated me like a baby, carrying my weight up to the front seat, buckling my seat belt and closing the door before he went to the driver's seat.

I was freaking out. He wasn't saying anything.

We arrived at our apartment a couple minutes later. Nichole was out so I guess this was planned or something. Well, part of the plan. I don't think getting harassed by his old enemies was part of the plan.

We were both quiet as we entered my room. My heart was being so loud and I couldn't breathe properly.

I sat on the edge of my bed and braced myself.

"Brandon?" I asked, with all caution in my tone. He just closed the door, but was still not facing me. I took a deep breath. "Please talk to me."

He didn't move for a few seconds. Again, I panicked.

"Please," I whispered. It wasn't on purpose. I lost my voice. I can't breathe. Please, please talk to me please."

At that exact moment, he turned around and finally looked at me. Some unexplainable expression on his face. I bit my lip. No. Tears, don't you dare come back when I don't want you to.

He treaded towards me and I breathed heavily as well as blinking fast so I could stop the tears from pooling my eyes.

When he was right in front of me, I saw a montage of expressions cross his face. Anger, hurt, disappointment, fear, relief, hopelessnes.

Don't cry, Mira you damn weakling. He hasn't even said anything yet.

"What were..." he raised his voice, making me wince. He noticed and repeated what he said, but softening his tone this time. "What were you thinking?"

I looked down. It wasn't supposed to be like this. It wasn't supposed to go this way.

Things were supposed to work out this time.

I didn't say anything.

He looked like he had a lot to say, but he didn't say anything. He walked back and forth in front me, in an impatient manner at that. I just kept lowering my head.

When he finally stopped pacing, he stood still in front of me, waiting for me to look at him. And with all my strength, I did.

The look in his eyes were intense. I was sure he was going to yell at me. But after just looking at each other for a moment, his expression changed. His eyes softened.

"Mira..." He mumbled weakly, slowly sinking to the floor, his hands covering his face. I didn't know what to do. I wanted to cry. Why did he look like he gave up? Did he give up? I don't know. I don't know.

His next words came out in muffles because his face was currently buried in his hands. I just sat there on the bed waiting for what he was about to say. "Stop doing this to me."

Chapter 39

"Stop doing this to me."

I stared blankly at Brandon as he just sat there on the floor like a helpless person. What was I supposed to do? I stressed him out this much.

But what. What the heck was I doing to him anyway? I wouldn't know, because he's not saying anything.

"Are you mad?" I asked, my voice so tiny I can't believe it came from my own mouth.

He peeled his face off his hands and looked up at me, since I was sitting on the bed while he was on the floor. "What do you think?" He said, in a sarcastic way.

Then he stood right up, and started pacing back and forth again. I quietly pulled my legs up and hugged them against my chest. This wasn't happening.

"You really don't think do you?" He started, a look of disbelief in his face. "No, you don't actually get it! You're a girl Mira! Why would you challenge a bunch of guys you don't know into a fight? Do you think you can do anything alone? You're strong, I get it, but you're just too reckless! You don't think at all!"

That outburst popped my nerves. The guilt I was feeling right now turned into anger. I don't know. Maybe I'm getting it mixed up since I've been so tense since earlier.

"What did you expect me to do?" I said, mirroring his tone and expression. "To just stand there and do nothing while they do whatever they want? Say whatever they want?"

"I wanted you to at least call for help!" His voice was raising, and so was his temper. Needless to say, I was about to do the exact same thing. "You could've called somebody as soon as you felt suspicious of them!"

"I was defending myself!" I said. "Why would I call someone for help when I could've handled it by myself?"

Facepalm. That was not what I was supposed to say. I know I'm wrong, but my mouth just kept going on. My bad habit at trying to win every argument is resurfacing at the worst of times.

"Well you did a great job handling it!" He chuckled in mock laughter, waving his hands in the air to emphasize his point. "What could've happened if I didn't come just in time?!"

"Well I'm sorry for that!" I yelled, not sounding sorry at all. "I wasn't in the right state of mind because of you. So I'm sorry okay?!"

Shut up Mira. Shut up shut up shut up.

"So it's my fault now?" He asked, increduously.

"I'm not saying it's your fault you stupid fuck. I'm saying... What I mean to say is..." I started trailing off my words when I realized how harsh I sounded.

My anger melted for a bit. We weren't supposed to be arguing right now. I shouldn't be hanging on my pride just so I can win this argument. I'm gonna lose him.

But bad habits die hard.

I looked at him, my brows creased and my face - I don't know what the hell I looked like. He was staring intensely at me, waiting. "Why should you care? Why are you getting mad at me? Who gave you the right to yell at me? Seriously you're always pissing me off!"

No! No! Stop it! Shut up!

Stop making everything worse!

"It's not that I... You... Argh!" He jumbled in his words, sounding more and more frustrated. He flipped his hair impatiently as he sent me the same hopeless look from earlier, but this time it had a mixture of anger and sadness. "Stop doing this to me Mira!"

"Stop what?!" I flailed my arms as well. "What did I ever do to you?!"

He didn't say anything, but he just kept looking at me. This wasn't about that fight earlier anymore.

I got off the bed and stood up, to show some bit of strength. Even though my knees were trembling. My hands were trembling. My voice was trembling.

My heart was trembling.

"I was living my life just fine." I said, unintentionally giving him an accusing glare. "And then you came along and everything fell apart!"

I could feel a stinging in my eyes. I was about to cry. Damn it. Don't cry. Don't cry. Don't let him see your weak side again. "I knew that game was trouble. But I still went with it. I went with you. I... I let myself be manipulated. I..."

My eyes left his and I found myself staring at the floor, finding the truth in what I was about to say.

"I wish I never met you."

Brandon stepped closer to me and hesitated to hold my arms. He almost took my hands, but he stopped himself.

"That's not fair," he mumbled, sounding helpless, pained. I'm a complete idiot. And then his voice grew stronger. "That's just not fair Mira. You think you're the only one who got hurt? You think you're the only one who's got issues? You think you carry all the problems in the world? Well guess what, you're not! So why do you keep blaming me?"

He was right. I wanted to apologize. I really did. But my responses were automatic, and they got out of my mouth before I could even think about the consequences.

"I'm not!" My tone was stubborn. But he knew I was cornered.

"Yes you are! You may not be saying it directly, but you are. You blame me for everything."

That's what it sounded like, but the truth was, I didn't blame him for anything at all. All of this was my pride. It was my pride talking and ruining everything.

I'm fully aware of it. So why can't I just shut up?

I never knew there was a pain worse than what my father gave me. But this time, it was self-inflicted. I resent myself so much for acting like this, even when I knew the horrible outcome.

I didn't realize the tears strolling down my cheeks as if they were running a race until my vision got blurry.

I furiously wiped them off and looked away so he won't see. I hate this. I hate myself. "This is impossible. Why are you still talking to me? Just leave me alone."

I was slowly walking backwards but he kept coming forward. "No," he said firmly. "I want us to talk. I want to end this."

My heart shattered.

"You already ended things between us, remember?!" I looked at him again, my eyes burning with either tears or fury. I was so mad. I was so mad at myself. "Game over! No one wins, no one loses! That's what you said! Time to move on with our fucking lives! But what did you do? You texted me! I knew it was you who kept texting me. You really think I'm that stupid? What do you really want Brandon? Make up your God damn mind and stop messing my life!"

"No, I won't stop." He said. I walked away a bit just to keep distance. I can't stand him being so near at the moment. But he kept following me wherever I went in my own room. "You're misunderstanding something here. When I said I wanted to end things, I meant I wanted to end the silence, the let's avoiding each other routine. Mira, I just want to talk."

Then what the fuck were we doing right now? Dancing?

"You don't know just how misleading you are, don't you?" I glared at him. His strong expression was breaking, I could tell. It hurt me just as it did him. "Damn it Brandon, just tell me straight to my face that you don't want anything to do with me anymore. Don't attempt to be a gentleman and comfort me with sweet words just so I won't get hurt. I'm already hurt! Just tell me please! Just end this already!"

I said those words, but I wanted him to do the complete opposite. Such a fool I am.

What I meant to say was, please fight for me.

"No!" He said. I was feeling a bit hopeful. Please, fight for me. The way my dad never did. "I'm not gonna end this the way you think. I'm sorry if I misled you in any way, okay? You weren't the only one confused." He was trailing off his words as well. "You weren't the only one afraid to commit because you were afraid of getting hurt."

I suddenly remembered his text last night. Both of us thought the same thing. Dealt with the worst kinds of pain when we were kids, and are now afraid to take a step forward because of it.

"That's the thing," I told him, sitting on my bed again. My legs can't take it anymore. "Both of us are too damaged for each other. Nothing good is ever gonna come out from this because of our shitty lives. We're better off with other people."

I can't explain the flash of pain in his eyes. Now that I think about it, it was true. He doesn't deserve someone like me. I'm the one responsible for all those sad expressions he keeps making and I don't want that. He deserves someone better.

"You mean you're better off with Sam than with me?" He asked, quietly.

I didn't even think about that. But I have to push him away for his own good. I felt my heart squeeze inside my chest. It's the right thing to do. "It's not such a bad idea."

A heavy silence came, and it weighed heavier than before. Am I doing the right thing? I'm doing this for him. For his happiness.

I just hope I'll still be able to love someone again after this is over.

"You're killing me," he finally said, his voice breaking down. He sunk to the floor again. "You're killing me here Mira. Please. Please don't say that."

"Why the hell not? I can go with anyone I want."

"I just can't win!" He stood up again. He stared at my eyes and groaned in frustration. "Don't say you want to go with Sam!"

"Why are you getting mad again?!" I replied in the same volume. I hate it when he yells at me. "Why are you getting jealous?! Wake up Brandon, we're not together. Why would you tell me that?!" He looked like he wanted to hold my shoulders but again, he stopped himself and ruffled his hair furiously instead. "Do you have any idea how much I had to restrain myself when I saw him kiss you? Do you have any idea how much I wanted to punch him lifeless for sticking so close to you everyday?"

My temper rose even higher. Funny.

"You think I don't feel that way when I see you with Emma?"

"This is ridiculous," he said in disbelief. "I don't have that kind of relationship with Emma!"

"Then what are you still doing here? Go after her!" I yelled. "You look perfect for each other."

Stupid. Stupid thing to say when we both know she had a boyfriend. I wish the stupid words would just stop falling from my mouth.

I don't even know what I want anymore. I still want him to fight for me, but I want to set him free. I don't understand myself.

"Stop fucking assuming things!" He yelled.

How long had it been since we started yelling at each other? I'm surprised the neighbors weren't complaning yet.

"Well I can't fucking help it!" I replied. "You put on a damn great show right in front of me everyday, and you expect me not to think like this? You! You... You made my mind a complete mess and I don't know what to think anymore!"

I furiously wiped the tears off my eyes as I stood up and faced him directly. Be strong.

He didn't take a step back when I advanced towards him, so our distance was minimal, but none of us cared at the moment. Both of us were so mad, and exhausted from all the shouting. We were both breathing heavily yet keeping our breaths steady.

"Damn you to hell Brandon!" My voice cracked mid-sentence for screaming too loud. I started punching his chest with all my might, but I doubt my punches had any strength left in them. He grabbed both my hands and squeezed it, before looking at me with the same emotions swirling in his eyes. I struggled to break free but I missed his touch. I missed it so much. "Just go away! Leave! I can't stand your face! Stop messing with my life!"

"Well too bad!" He was slowly walking forward, gripping my hands tighter and tighter until my back hit the wall. "I'm not gonna stop messing with your shitty life because I love you!"

"Well I love you too!" I said, unconsciously.

I was surprised with the words that just came out of our mouths. I couldn't make a clear reaction because as soon as I said those words back, he pushed the back of my head to his face and kissed me.

It was the spur of the moment. I clung to his neck for dear life as he deepened the kiss, at the same time pushing my back against the wall.

We pulled away for air every few seconds only to dive right back in like it sustained life.

I missed this so much. I missed him. But I can't think straight right now. What just happened?

The kiss turned into something gentle, and I couldn't help the tears pooling in my eyes. I can't explain it. Is this a dream?

He pulled away when he felt my tears on his face. We were breathing heavily after that, and we felt each other's hot breaths on our faces.

Gently, he pushed the loose strands of my hair away from my face and tucked them behind my ear. Then he looked at me sincerely before wiping my tears with his thumbs.

"I love you," he said, a hopeless grin forming on his face. "I mean it. I love your shitty life because that made you who you are right now, I love your smile, I love your laugh. I love every little thing you hate about yourself."

And then he kissed my nose as he continued to play with my short hair. "Before I met you, I already liked you. I made that game up because I didn't know how to get close to you without Leo's help. I didn't say it before because I was scared you really thought this was all just part of the game. But then we hung out everyday, that made me extremely happy. I thought I was the luckiest guy in the world. I told you my past, which I never told anyone before, and then you told me about yours. I got to know the real you, and just like that, I fell for you. Fell hard."

I just stared at him. His thumb was brushing my cheek slightly, his hand cupping half my face. It was warm.

"I'm a loser." He chuckled shortly. "I lost the game before it even began. I'm pathetic, right? You win. You won from the very start."

I was honestly speechless. This is all messed up, but I feel incredibly happy.

"You dipshit." I said. He looked surprised. "Manslut. Confusing me again."

"Damn it Mira, I said I love you!" He almost sounded like he was pleading. I smiled widely, adding more to his surprise.

"I meant I love you too."

I felt like all the weight stuck inside my chest had been forcefully lifted and thrown at sea. He finally said it. I finally said it.

He grinned before giving me another sweet kiss. And then we smiled before a pulling each other for a warm embrace.

Leo and Nichole came back a few hours later. After they demanded we tell them everything, they both screamed for joy and pulled us into a group hug.

"Finally!" Leo was groaning, happily. "You two finally grew a pair!"

I rolled my eyes at him as I watched Brandon smiling at me while his face was getting severely pinched my Nichole. "You're finally a man. Guess you can keep yours after all."

He laughed nervously and then looked around. I didn't get it.

Leo threw a paper bag at Brandon and he caught it with his face before his hands. He gave his best friend a pointed look before checking the contents.

And then he looked at me mischievously.

"What?" I asked, genuinely curious. "What's in the bag?"

My best friends gave me a smirk I'll never trust as long as I live. Before I could snatch the bag from Brandon, we heard a knock on the door.

I went to to get it and boy was I surprised to see my mom, uncle and a police officer who looked the slightest bit familiar.

"Hi?" I greeted unsurely. "Am I in trouble?"

Mom quickly entered and pulled me into a hug. Such a great day for hugs. This feels so nice.

"Are you okay?" She asked, checking my face. I was about to ask what until I remembered what happened earlier.

"Yeah," I held her hand. "You didn't have to come all this way though."

"Why not?" She said. "My baby got into a fight and beat up five low-life bastards. This calls for a celebration!"

I laughed at that. Yup. I am my mother's daughter.

"Mira who's at the - " Brandon along with Nichole and Leo came up behind me. "Door. Uh. Hi, dad."

My brows rose at that. I snapped my head back at the officer beside my uncle again. My eyes were like saucers. That was his dad?

The man gave his son a look and then I heard Brandon let out a nervous chuckle. "Mmm yeah I'm in trouble again."

I couldn't help the smile spreading on my face. Mom noticed that and pinched my cheek.

"This is Officer Pierce, an old friend of mine back in the day," my uncle said as he placed a hand on his shoulder. "He'll be in charge of your case Mira."

I gave him a look. "What case?"

Officer Pierce, erm, Brandon's dad looked so strict. He didn't smile once since he got here. Oh no. This is the first time I've met him and I just made a huge bad impression.

He entered our apartment as well, and then my uncle followed. He took my wrists and pulled a pair of handcuffs from his belt behind him.

"Mira Jadsen, you're under arrest for the assault of five boys in school grounds. You have the right to remain silent. Anything you say and do can and will be used against you in a court of law. You have the right to an attorney. If you cannot afford an attorney, one will be appointed to you."

I panicked as he locked one of the handcuff on my wrist. I looked at my mom and uncle for help.

"I'm getting arrested? But that was self-defense!" I reasoned. I don't want to go the prison! Oh no!

Seconds later, the officer burst into a fit of laughter, and then the rest of the adults followed. We kids had no clue what was going on.

Officer Pierce smiled widely at me before pulling me into a hug. Okay, I don't mind getting hugged but why wad he hugging me?

"I'm kidding. Just wanted to make a good first impression on the girl my son's been so crazy about."

I saw Brandon fighting back the red in his cheeks as his father placed a hand on my shoulder. "He'd been moping around the house for a week. I knew it was about a girl, but I never expected it'd be Ray's niece. It's fate."

"Dad." Brandon mumbled. He was embarrassed.

"What do you see in that boy anyway?" He asked me, the smile never wavering from his face. I feel light-headed. "You're too good for him."

Everybody in the room except Brandon laughed. He pinched my cheek like I was the cutest thing in the world. "Just call me Rob, Mira."

I don't know what just happened, but I think I was already accepted in the family.

"Okay. Um, Rob?" I asked, unsurely. He raised his brows in friendly manner. I raised my hand, showing him my handcuffed hand.

"Is scaring the living daylights out of kids by reading them the Miranda rights part of the job?"

The adults chuckled loudly. Rob even slapped Uncle Ray's back. Brandon was grinning and my two best friends were just snickering behind us.

"I like this girl." He said as he gave me another hug. I'm not sure if I should be happy or confused.

He kissed my forehead and ruffled my hair. He then glanced over at Brandon and motioned for him to come closer. His son did as told.

He held Brandon's shoulder with one hand while he held mine with the other. We just looked at each other confused and just went along with his dad's humor.

We didn't understand what was happening because we were too occupied avoiding our parents' eyes until we heard a click.

Rob raised Brandon's hand, causing me to involuntarily raise my hand as well.

Oh my God.

His dad handcuffed us.

"Dad!" He said, laughing. Mom and uncle were laughing as well. "What the heck?"

Rob chortled. "Ain't this a dream come true for you son? You always said you wanted to be tied to the love of your life when you were a kid."

"I didn't mean literally," he chuckled. Then he gave me a joking, apologizing look. "Sorry Mira."

"It's fine," I giggled. "You have a cool dad."

After an exchange of laughs and some chatter (and some unnecessary teasing) Rob uncuffed us. I had to say I was a bit disappointed our fun was cut short.

I'm starting to love Brandon more now that I know his dad. I can't wait to meet his mom.

"Why don't we all go to dinner?" Uncle announced. We all cheered just thinking about all the free food until he gave me and Brandon a pointed look. "We're not finished yet though. But we'll discuss those matters tomorrow. For now, let's celebrate."

My friends and I just looked at each other, smiling. A bit afraid of what's in store for us tomorrow, but we were still smiling.

I couldn't be happier.

After that um, uh, interesting dinner, Brandon drove us back to the apartment. Uncle drove mom and Rob back to their houses as well.

We were silent when we returned, but it was a comfortable silence.

Leo already went ahead. Nichole was washing up in the bathroom. We were alone. At the moment.

I walked him to the door, still quiet. I was feeling a little, I don't know. Shy? His dad exposed his entire humiliating childhood over dinner, and my mom pretty much did the same to me.

Let's not forget how supportive my best friends were as well.

He was outside the apartment now, but was still standing outside the door. He was smiling at me.

"So," he mumbled, smiling all boy-like. It was adorable. "Can we um... have a date tomorrow? Like a real one this time?"

I laughed softly when he said that. Then I nodded my head. "I'd like that. What do you have in mind?"

I honestly didn't want a random date and just wing it. I mean, that's okay and all, but I'd like something he planned himself from time to time. It makes me feel secure.

He gave me playful smirk as he raised the paper Leo threw at him earlier. I raised a brow.

"What's in there?" I asked. He grinned.

"Our outfits for tomorrow's date."

I thought for a bit, and then my eyes widened in realization. I scoffed while folding my arms against my chest. "The potato pyjama set?"

"Yup." He wagged his brows suggestively. "For our sleepover tomorrow. I'm kicking Leo out of the apartment so it's just the two of us. No interruptions."

"Oh yeah?" I said, a smirk tugging up on my lips. "A sleepover, with just the two of us, no interruptions. Hm. I'm not suspicious at all."

He leaned closer, his eyes narrowing. "Remember the deal? This outfit is for our eyes only. Unless of course, you have other ideas - "

I pecked his lips before he could finish. It was just quick, a tease. A foolish grin spread on his face after I pulled away. "Goodnight potato."

Before he could say something witty back, I closed the door.

Yup. The potatoes are back.

Epilogue

| Damn it Mira! He locked me out! How could he do that after everything I've done?! Tell him to open up! |

I snorted as I read Leo's text. Brandon was actually serious when he said he was gonna kick Leo out of the apartment just so we can be alone in our uh, sleepover, as he liked to call it.

| Quit whining. You can sleep in our apartment tonight. I'm going out anyway.|

I didn't even need to say that. I already knew that was his alternative.

| You two planned this, didn't you?! Didn't you?! |

I rolled my eyes. My best friend is hysterical.

He didn't even wait for a reply because he sent another one after that.

| Just thinking about all the things you're gonna do is making me lose my appetite! Promise me Mira, just not the couch, or my room, or the kitchen counter, or the bathroom. |

My eyes were bulging out of their sockets as I furiously sent a reply.

| Wtf Leo! You think we're gonna shoot a porno?! |

| I left a box of protection in the bathroom. You can never be too safe. |

| Leo damn it! We're just gonna watch a movie! |

| But you're gonna sleep over right? And you two are gonna wear those weird pyjamas? |

| Yeah, so? |

| Just do it in his room and we'll pretend this conversation never happened. |

| I hate you. |

I groaned before throwing my phone on my bed. He is ridiculous. Just because I'm gonna sleep over doesn't mean we're gonna do it.

And the couch? His room? The kitchen counter? The bathroom? I mean, what did he think? That we'd screw around the apartment in eighty minutes? What were we, animals?

"What're you so stressed about this time?" I heard Nichole come in. She sat beside me on my bed as she took her phone out.

"Your boyfriend," I scoffed. "He's ridiculous."

"I know." She sighed. Of course she did. "But forget about him. Tonight's your big date right? Be happy!"

A small smile crept on my face, forgetting about Leo's stupid texts for a minute. That's right. Tonight's going to be our first real date.

Unable to express my joy in a completely normal way, I slammed my back on my bed while taking my best friend down with me. I was giggling like a total girl.

Maybe because I am a girl. I forget sometimes.

Kidding.

"Look at you so excited," she struggled to break free from my hug. Not a chance woman. "I'm so happy you're not in denial anymore. Now let go."

"No." I said, tightening the hug. She squealed unhappily.

"Save it for later. My shirt's gonna get all crinkled!"

I paused. I just noticed how nice she looked. Oh.

"You going out?" I asked, releasing her.

"Yeah," she replied, fixing her shirt and glancing at her phone "Leo's picking me up in a bit. We're gonna stay out of your way this time."

I rolled my eyes so hard, I saw my brain. And was surprised to see I actually had one. After all this time.

Kidding again.

God.

I'm losing my sense of humor. Somebody help.

I was about to claw her back into my death grip but she jumped away and escaped just in time. Before leaving the room, she stuck her tongue at me. "Have fun Mira."

I had just finished fixing my hair for the third time when my phone vibrated. It was Brandon.

| I'm here. You ready? |

I sucked a deep breath. Yeah. Sure. Ready.

| Yup. Be down in a bit. |

We decided to eat dinner out tonight. He said it was gonna be in another special place and I was almost sure it was gonna be in his kitchen again.

I was wearing a red, off-shoulder blouse and a pair of black pants. I shrugged, thinking how pointless this was because I was gonna change into that damned potato pyjama set later. But

Brandon was holding on to it at the moment, so I have no idea what he was planning tonight.

When I got down, his car was parked right in front of our building. I was about to open the door to the front seat when I felt someone approach me from behind. A hand barely grazed my shoulder because I quickly caught it.

Are the guys from yesterday back to take revenge?

As a natural reflex, I turned around quickly, about to break the arm of that person until I realized it was just Brandon.

"Oh." I mumbled, nervously. Then I looked around and released his hand. "I thought - "

"It's fine." He chuckled, taking my hand again. He pressed his lips gently behind the palm of my hand and smiled at me.

I feel faint.

I noticed that he was wearing something nice tonight. A blue V-neck shirt, dark pants and his black Toms.

I frowned. "I feel sorry for our clothes."

"Why?" He asked, brushing a thumb over my hand.

"You want us to wear those pyjamas later right? The clothes we're wearing right now are such a waste."

He smiled again before taking my other hand. I just kept looking down because I seriously can't look at him. I still can't believe this is real. He's really here.

"You're beautiful." He said. I finally looked up just to give him a look. Well, some sort of expression to conceal my embarrassment. His smile never left his face. "We're going somewhere tonight. It won't be a waste. Don't worry."

I raised a brow jokingly. "Where exactly? Your definition of special places have given me trust issues."

He chuckled. "Any place with food and with you is special."

"And the sweet words have returned." I announced, feeling the heat rise from my cheeks. I'm just acting tough. This boy, seriously.

He just kept staring at me smiling, and I couldn't help but feel too conscious of my appearance. Maybe I was overdressed again?

"This is gonna sound weird," he mumbled, laughing nervously and looking away for a moment. His ears were red. "But can I hug you?"

"What?" I said, surprised. He looked embarrassed. My self-confidence came back quickly and I grinned at him widely. "Why do you need permission for that?"

He shrugged his shoulders upon sending me a boy-like smile. That was too adorable. "Well. It's been a while."

I laughed before staring at him, slowly killing him with suspense until I nodded my head. He didn't have to ask.

He gave me a big, warm hug as he placed his lips on the crook of my neck. His hands were wrapped fully around my shoulder.

I live for moments like this.

He moved his face away from my neck and kissed my forehead, giving me the sweetest smile ever. God I love his smile so much.

"I missed you, potato babe." He quipped as he played with the loose strands of my hair. "I missed you."

"I missed you too, scaredy potato." I laughed.

I honestly never knew I could say the word potato with so much affection. I'm not even being sarcastic anymore.

I didn't want to break that hug but I forgot we were in public. And the security guard of our apartment building kept staring at us.

Brandon noticed this too and gave me another smile. Then he let go just to open the door for me. Such a gentleman.

I gladly accepted his offer and stepped inside his car.

Please don't let this be a dream.

"Oh God really?" I couldn't control my laughter when I realized where Brandon had pulled over. "Are you sure?"

He grinned at me before he got out of his car and ran to open my door. And then he sent me another grin. I rolled my eyes.

"You don't have to keep opening my door you know," I smiled.

"It's not a problem," he shrugged his shoulders. He took my hand and unbuckled my seat belt. "Opening doors for you makes me feel like a gentleman."

I snorted. "Ah, has the patient wolf returned?"

He smirked. "A wolf's still a wolf."

We both laughed at that short recap before I asked him again, glancing at the small restaurant behind us. "Are we really gonna eat here?"

It was the place where we had that burger-eating contest.

"Yeah," he said. Then he sent me an unsure look, or some kind of guilty expression. "Sorry it's not that romantic, but I wanted to show you something."

"No, not at all. I don't mind," I shook my head and smiled to put him at ease. "What did you want to show me?"

He grinned. Uh-oh. "Let's go inside."

Our orders arrived pretty quickly. We chose a meal we never tried before and were already pleased with the aroma alone.

Sizzling cheese steak, Buffalo wings, french fries and... one spicy burger?

"Is that..?" I pointed at it unsurely until he unwrapped it. I almost gasped in horror. Maybe he didn't notice? "Brandon that's - "

"I know." He simply said, placing it in front of his mouth, ready to take a bite from it. "This is what I'm gonna show you."

I stared at confused and I was literally on the edge of my seat as he took a huge bite from the burger he was supposed to hate with a passion.

I saw a sweat drop from the side of his face and I was half-standing, half-sitting, getting ready to dump a glass of cold water on him.

I mean, that won't necessarily cool his tongue but there's no way I'm offering my neck again. At least not in this situation.

"I'm good." He said weakly while showing me a thumbs up.

"What is this?" I snatched the burger away from him. "Why are you punishing yourself?"

"I'm not punishing myself." He mumbled, trying to get the burger back. "I'm practicing how to eat spicy stuff without half-dying."

I was this close to losing my mind.

"But why?"

He chugged down a whole glass of water before replying with a haggard smile. "I wanna like the same thing you like."

Oh God. Oh no.

"No." I firmly said. "You don't have to force yourself. It's okay, really. What the heck Brandon?"

I was serious. He didn't have to do this, but he looked too damn motivated to stop now.

"And," he added. "I want to get over this ridiculous fear of spices. I want to love it just as much as you and my mom did."

I was in a loss for words. I don't know if I should insist he stop that this instant or be touched. This was crazy.

But after hearing him say it was for his mom too, I kinda gave in. It was his decision after all.

I was still gaping at him when he took another bite, and then another, until he finished the whole thing. His face was flushed and sweaty as he chugged down the whole pitcher of water he ordered beforehand.

At least he was prepared.

"You're crazy," I mumbled as I began slicing the cheese steak. It was a medium-sized steak that was covered in cheese and mushrooms. Yum.

He just laughed, sticking his tongue out a bit to somehow quicken the cooling process. He didn't look so good. "I know."

After dinner, Brandon stopped by a store to rent a few movies while I waited in the car. When he came back, he gave me a nervous smile before driving us to his apartment.

What was that all about?

When we got to his room, he gave me the paper bag containing the pyjama set. Then he sent me a wink when I looked at him.

"You do realize this is ridiculous what we're doing, right?" I rolled my eyes as I took the bag. He snickered in reply.

"It's relationship goals, c'mon."

I don't know why, but I burst out laughing. His grin just got wider and wider. "Said who?"

A faint blush appeared on his cheeks. "Just go with it please, potato."

I laughed again before standing on my toes to peck his pinkish cheek. "Anything for you potato."

"Again," I said as I made myself comfortable on the couch in front of the flat screen. "Are you serious?"

We were already wearing the potato pyjama set and I couldn't help but snort at our silly appearances. Nonetheless, it was cute, and Brandon looked adorable.

"Um. Yeah?" He said unsurely. So this is why he had that weird expression in the car earlier. As for the movies we were gonna watch tonight, he chose three.

Three horror movies.

I smirked at him as he put the first CD in the player. "The Conjuring, Unfriended and Paranormal Activity? Oh goody."

He looked at me with a pout on his face. "Have you seen these movies already?"

"Nope," I shook my head.

Lie. I saw them at least two times each already.

"I don't believe you." He mumbled before grabbing the remote and sitting right next to me in the couch. "Are you ready?"

I smiled my sweetest at him. And then I pinched his cheek. "My potato is so adorable."

He frowned. I giggled.

"Don't worry," I said, my confidence skyrocketing. Best feeling ever. "You can just throw yourself at me if you get scared enough."

My triumphant grin was cut short when he snaked his arms around my waist and pulled me close. He pressed his lips on mine as he poked my ticklish spot, causing me to jump away but he held me firmly in place.

My eyes were as wide as saucers as he made a smug smile with his lips still against mine. "That's the plan."

I couldn't make out a clear expression. Oh my God. Oh my God. My heart.

He was too close.

I liked it.

"Leo said the couch was off-limits," I blurted out before mentally smacking myself. He raised his brows.

"What?"

"The movie's starting." I pointed at the screen. He chuckled before he kissed my lips again and then my cheek before he turned his eyes to the screen. Oh God.

I have no power here.

"Is it over?" He asked, his face buried on my shoulder and his arms around my stomach. "Is it really over?"

I turned my head to look at him. I don't know how and when he got behind me. I was too focused on the movie to notice what he was up to. "Yeah. Congratulations! You managed to finish three horror films without pissing yourself."

He groaned, probably regretting the fact that he chose to watch this movie with me of all people. I was touched though. Maybe he did this for the same reason he ate that burger earlier. Ridiculous, but since it's Brandon, it was fine.

He took the remote and turned the TV off. That's when I finally felt afraid. I don't know. Afraid, nervous, anxious, excited - I can't tell the difference anymore.

He took my hands while he was still behind me, and then he brushed his thumbs across the back of my palms. I could feel his warm breath on my ear. I tried my best to be steady.

He was silent for a bit, just brushing my skin. I felt him sigh. I don't think he realizes how that affected me, since his mouth was so close to my ear and neck.

I was so sensitive to his every move.

I'm pretty sure it's not the body soap I'm using this time.

"They're gone," he said. I still didn't move. His hands felt so warm. "The bruises. They're gone."

I looked down when I remembered how he kept staring at the bruises on my knuckles back when we were still ignoring each other. It wasn't that long ago, but it felt like forever.

Hearing no reply, he continued. "I'm sorry."

This time, I broke away from his embrace so I could look at his face. As I was still adjusting my position, I could see how his eyes dulled, like he was really regretting something.

It was me who felt bad.

"Hey," I said as I crossed my legs. I held his hands and kissed them lightly. "That was my fault. A lot happened and I didn't know how to release my frustration. And didn't you know? I punch walls and floors in a daily basis."

I said that as a joke to lighten the mood, I hope it worked. The corner of his lip tugged up. He intertwined our fingers and stared into my eyes seriously. "I don't want you doing that again. Whenever something like that happens again, we'll talk about it. I promise, I won't take this long again."

I smiled, nodding my head. I trusted him.

After looking at each other for a while, his hand found its way to my face. He caressed my skin as his eyes narrowed to my lips.

I had to refrain myself from swallowing hard and ruin the moment.

"How can I make you forget that Sam kissed you?"

I held my breath before releasing it along with my reply. What was happening to me? "I already forgot about that."

"I haven't." He said, a bitter look flashing in his eyes.

I sighed, feeling bad about myself. I wouldn't know what to do if I saw Brandon kiss some other girl. How should I make him feel better?

I took his hand off my face so I could place my hands on his. I waited until he met my eyes.

I pecked his lips lightly. "I love you." Then I kissed him a bit longer. "I trust you." Then I kissed him again, deeper. "I'm in love with you. You."

After that kiss his eyes were still closed, but a happy grin was on his face the whole time. "Can you do that again?"

I laughed before pinching his nose. "Not a chance."

When he opened his eyes, looking a bit dazed for a moment, he slowly leaned closer and closer until my back was pressed against the couch. "I need to tell you too."

He stared at my lips and out of instinct, I closed my eyes. I felt him kiss the corners of my lips. "I love you too." He kissed me again. "You don't know how much you drive me crazy." And then he deepened the kiss, almost forgetting that he wasn't finished with what he was about to say. I smiled, and I felt his smile against my lips too. "I love you, Mira."

I wrapped my arms around his neck and pressed my lips on his ear. "Leo's not gonna let this one go. Let's go to your room?"

His mouth curled up into a smirk. "Really?"

I nodded. And then I sent him a playful grin. "It's not a sleepover without a bed right?"

His smirk couldn't get any wider. "I'm thinking bed things."

"I'm thinking..." I lowered my voice into something close to seductive as I pressed my hand on his chest, and then moved it lower and lower until I reached his pants. I saw his Adam's apple go up and down quickly. I grinned. When my hand reached my destination, I slid it inside his pocket and took his phone out. When I showed him what I just took from him, he looked at it confused, and then a silly grin formed in his face. I chuckled. "I'm thinking potato pyjama selfies."

He laughed as he peeled himself away from me, and then pulled me up as well. He shook his head smiling, realizing how he got tricked by my little teasing.

"First one to make the best pose wins," he said as we made our way to his room. I sent him a challenging smirk before I took my own phone as well. He's not winning this one.

"You're on."

Five months have passed since Brandon and I officially became a couple. A lot has happened during that time too.

Brandon introduced me to his foster parents. His dad was so happy to see me again that he cooked dinner for all of us. Brandon's mom was a complete sweetheart - she even bought me a few dresses as presents when I came to visit. The nervousness I initially felt before I met them disappeared immediately.

Leo and Nichole were still the same, still going strong. Leo keeps complaining whenever Brandon and I flirt in front of them even when he and Nichole practically did the same since, well, forever. We just brush him off like the usual and did what we wanted to piss him off.

Potato thug life bruh.

Sam met a girl and they've been together ever since. She was his friend's younger sister and I heard she had a crush on him since forever. They were pretty happy together, and thus our circle of friends grew larger.

Emma introduced us to her boyfriend. Yeah, they were still together. He was really nice, and as expected, he was really protective of her. Who wouldn't though?

I met my dad again, but this time it was me who wanted to meet with him. Brandon suggested I do that. I thought that since he did something about his fear, then I can too. I didn't tell my dad what I've felt since he left us, because I know he already knows that. I wasn't even asking for an apology. He introduced me to his new family and I got to meet my half-siblings. They were all nice and welcoming. I'm glad I made that choice and faced him straight on.

Mom and Uncle Ray stayed the best of friends. One time Brandon told uncle that he should hook up with my mom. Uncle just laughed.

Those guys that harassed me - Brandon's old enemies - we met them again. They changed somehow. They were polite towards me, and I sensed that it wasn't just for show. I don't know if my uncle did something or they were just being like that because Brandon was with me.

I was pretty much still the same. Only, my violent habits lessened, which was supposedly a good thing since I was turning eighteen soon. All credits go to my potato.

Life turned out to be pretty nice. I'm thankful everything fell into place. Turns out, all I had to do was face it instead of avoiding it and beating myself up afterwards.

Like I said before. You don't always need a complicated solution for a complicated problem. You can start with something simple, and take baby steps until you reach your goal.

If you think you can do it, and if you do something about it, then you can.

Brandon grabbed my hand as I made my way to the principal's office. No, I wasn't in trouble this time. I just wanted to say hi.

"Wanna go out tonight?" He asked, linking our fingers together. "I saw a pizza-eating contest downtown. I think I might actually beat you this time."

I smiled at him. I can't believe this potato is my boyfriend. I've never been happier in my life.

"Face it, you'll never win against me. But since you asked nicely," I winked at him. "It is so on."

www.ingramcontent.com/pod-product-compliance
Lightning Source LLC
Chambersburg PA
CBHW071951210726
48292CB00020B/136
* 9 7 8 1 9 4 4 2 6 0 2 9 3 *